I0526281

The Hades Project

Books by Lynn Sholes & Joe Moore

Cotten Stone series
The Grail Conspiracy
The Last Secret
The Hades Project
The 731 Legacy
The Cotten Stone Omnibus

Maxine Decker series
The Shield
The Blade
The Tomb

The Seneca Hunt series
The Phoenix Apostles

Novellas
Thor Bunker (A short story)
Bam! Just Like That (A short story)
Brain Trust (A novel)

Books by Lynn Sholes
Woman of the Mists
Touches the Stars
Keeper of Dreams
Walks in Stardust
Spirit of the Turtle Woman
Daughter of the Fifth Moon

Books by Joe Moore
Thorpe's Candle

The Hades Project

Lynn Sholes & Joe Moore

SPEAKING VOLUMES, LLC
NAPLES, FLORIDA
2022

The Hades Project

Copyright © 2007 by Lynn Sholes & Joe Moore

All rights reserved. No part of this book may be reproduced or transmitted in any form or by any means without written permission.

This book is entirely a work of fiction. The names, characters, places, and incidents depicted herein are either products of the author's imagination or are used fictitiously. Any resemblance to actual events or locales or persons, living or dead, is entirely coincidental.

ISBN 978-1-64540-754-6

Acknowledgments

The authors wish to thank the following for their assistance in adding a sense of realism to this work of fiction.

Dr. Seth Lloyd, PhD.
Professor, Department of Mechanical Engineering
Massachusetts Institute of Technology

Cary E. Moore
Special Agent, Office of Special Investigations
United States Air Force

Jimmy Young
Former Officer, United States Secret Service

Jim McCormick
President, CENCORE, Inc.

"The descent to Hades is the same from every place."
—Anaxagoras, Greek philosopher, 500-428 BC

Prologue

IN THE BEGINNING

After losing the great Battle of Heaven, Lucifer, the Son of the Dawn, and his rebel angels were driven from Paradise—cast out for all eternity into a world of darkness. Obsessed with hatred and vengeance, Lucifer, now known as Satan, plotted his first act of revenge against God—the temptation of Adam and Eve.

Seeing that Man was vulnerable and armed with the knowledge that all humans could be tempted, Satan began his battle to prevent souls from entering the Kingdom of Heaven. With each passing Age of Man, he devised ever more elaborate methods to trick the naïve human psyche into repeating Adam's original sin. To do so, Satan's Brotherhood of the Fallen and their offspring, the Nephilim, roamed the earth in search of prey, building their ever-increasing list of souls that were damned forever to the same darkness from which Evil thrived.

There was one who shared their blood, but not their condemnation. She alone stood in the way of Satan's ultimate goal: to claim all the souls on Earth to his Dark Empire. He had the ability to tempt Man, but she had the will to stop him.

She was Cotten Stone, the offspring of the only forgiven Fallen Angel. God formed a covenant with her father, Furmiel, the Angel of the Eleventh Hour. For his repentance, God granted Furmiel mortality, and he was given two daughters—twins. Because Furmiel could never return to Paradise, God took one of the daughters at birth to fill her father's rank in Heaven, but the second daughter was to live on Earth. She was therefore called upon by God to fight in His name.

Cotten Stone had discovered her legacy by coming face-to-face with the Son of the Dawn. She had foiled his plan to bring about an unholy Second Coming, and when she understood that God had given Man free will, the ability to create his own reality, she had thwarted Lucifer's attempt to have Man commit the ultimate sin against God—suicide. Deciphering a message inscribed by the hand of God on an ancient crystal tablet, she led those who would choose to live in goodness to a new world of peace and joy.

Unselfishly, Cotten Stone then returned to the old world to continue to fight against her eternal enemy—a world where good and evil were forever at war.

With each new battle she fought, the End of Days grew closer.

Now two armies were forming: the Ruby, led by the Great Deceiver; and the Indigo, led by the daughter of an angel. Soon, Cotten Stone would again be tested as another battle loomed against the Forces of Evil.

THE HADES PROJECT takes place in 2007

Chapter One

THREAT LEVEL

Rizben Mace stood in the center of the pentagram carved in the stone floor, its five points striking out like the blades of an ancient weapon. Six black-robed children knelt before him, their faces hidden beneath hoods.

Clothed in a ruby-red robe, Mace held a golden cup in one hand and a jewel-encrusted dagger in the other. He said, "I call upon Samael, the Guardian of the Gate."

In unison, the children intoned, "Samael."

Responding to the incantation, a finger of high vapor clouds drifted across the moon that shone down like a pale spotlight.

Candles flickered in the night air, their flames protected by high walls as they cast an orange glow upon the ancient rite. Dark figures, cloaked in black with torches in hand, ringed the courtyard.

"I call upon Azazel, the Guardian of the Flame," Mace said, "the Spark in the Eye of the Great Darkness."

Again, the small voices spoke, "Azazel." At the word, the torches brightened.

"I call upon the Light of the Air, the Son of the Dawn."

"Son of the Dawn," the children repeated.

A hot breath of wind swooped down and furled the robes of the shadowy figures.

Mace held the dagger and the golden cup in outstretched hands. The flames reflected off the polished metal making it appear as if fire burned from within the chalice. He brought the cup to his lips and sipped. The wine warmed him. He had waited with anticipation for the ceremony—

the initiation—the official presentation of these young warriors to Lucifer, the Son of the Dawn. They were the offspring of the Fallen Angels, the latest Nephilim soldiers in the ranks of the Ruby Army amassing in preparation for the Final Conflict. A wave of pride rippled through his veins as he held up the cup for all to see.

"In the name of your mighty sword and the flowing lifeblood that gives you the power to conquer, enter into the minds, hearts, and souls of these young warriors, and fill them with your terrible and crushing strength."

Mace raised his arms high, and the children rose from their knees and merged into a single line. Each, in turn, kissed the blade of the dagger and took a sip from the chalice. When all had done so, they returned to their places and pulled back their hoods revealing their young faces.

Mace opened his arms in a sweeping gesture. "Oh, great Son of the Dawn, behold the newest soldiers of your vanquishing Ruby Army."

***

Mace walked out of the building and down the three levels of narrow steps onto the sidewalk. It was always such a jarring transition, he thought, going from the medieval open sky courtyard hidden deep in the heart of the building out into the harsh glare of the Washington, D.C. streetlights, and from his ceremonial robe back into a suit.

He reached in his pocket and took his cell phone off vibrate. The text message during the ceremony had forced him to rush through the ancient ritual. He wouldn't want to have to explain to anyone what kept him.

Once he waited on the sidewalk, Rizben Mace glanced to his right at the sphinx-like granite lion that stood guard at the entrance. It had a woman's head with a cobra entwined around her neck. To Mace's left, the matching sentinel also defended the entry. His limousine waited at curbside. An FBI agent opened the door for him.

A black Suburban with a forest of rooftop antennae sat poised like a timber wolf in front of the limo. Two police cruisers, one at the front of the small caravan, the other at the rear, were at the ready. Their blue and red strobes cast a hypnotic glow on the tall bronze temple entrance behind him.

Mace slipped into the back of the limo, and the armored door shut with a bank-vault thud. Immediately, the caravan pulled away. The air filled with the shrill of sirens and the rumble of engines. The swift acceleration pushed him deep into the leather seat as he checked his watch. A few minutes past 11:00 p.m.

"What do we have?" Mace asked his advisor, who sat opposite him.

"About an hour ago, we received word of a significant increase in cyber intrusions on a global scale. The Internet is down in parts of Asia and Africa, and it's spreading across Europe. Three-quarters of our worldwide monitoring stations are experiencing simultaneous attacks, and over four hundred thousand servers have been infected and shut down."

"Is it just the Internet?" Mace asked.

"So far."

"What are the source addresses?"

"Mostly from China—a few in Malaysia."

"Random targets or a focused assault?"

The advisor forced out a long breath. "It looks random. But it's huge."

"Has anyone notified POTUS?"

"Not yet."

Mace tapped his lips with his index finger during a short pause. "Make the call." He could still smell the smoke from the torches and taste the faint sweetness of the wine on his lips. "I'm going to recommend the threat level be raised to orange for specific infrastructures. No reason to get the public in an uproar."

"I agree, sir." The advisor picked up one of several phones from the communications console and pushed a speed-dial number labeled POTUS. In a moment he said, "The Secretary of Homeland Security is calling for the President."

Chapter Two

THE TOMB

Cotten Stone stared at the massive columns inside Assumption Cathedral and marveled at the sacred murals encircling each one. The church was one of the oldest structures within the walls of the Kremlin.

"Nothing is by chance in a Russian cathedral, Ms. Stone," said the president of the Russian Federation in stilted English. "The columns support the ceiling, and the saints support the church. That is why the saints are painted on the columns." He motioned toward the lofty recesses overhead.

"Breathtaking, Mr. President," Cotten said and shifted her gaze upward to the splendor of the centuries-old artwork.

A small camera and sound crew from Satellite News Network and a handful of Russian Presidential Security Service agents accompanied Cotten and the president. Bathed in the glare of the camera floodlight, the two strolled through the building—each footfall and word echoed before they faded among the hallowed shadows. It was after hours, and Assumption Cathedral was empty of tourists.

They paused in front of the iconostasis, a collection of sixty-nine painted icons that stretched from floor to ceiling.

"The history of the Bible from the Old Testament to the Last Judgment is illustrated here." The president extended his right arm then swept it across the view. "So, now I believe we have seen all there is."

"Mr. President, I can't thank you enough for sharing the amazing magnificence of these wondrous churches with our SNN viewers."

"This is the heritage of Mother Russia. We are proud to share it."

"And you should be." Cotten reached to shake his hand just as a boom rocked the inside of the cathedral and knocked her to the floor. The chandeliers went out and threw the interior into darkness. Only a spatter of emergency lights flickered inside the perimeter of the church.

Cotten raised her head, dazed. She saw the SNN cameraman on the floor—his mounted floodlight shattered. Small bursts of light sparked from several locations in the church—muzzle flashes. The weapons must have been silenced, for she only heard the sickening thuds as their bullets found the soft flesh of those around her. Her cameraman cried out, but the darkness kept Cotten from knowing how badly he was wounded.

"Are you okay?" she called.

There was no reply.

The Protective Security Specialists agents shouted orders, drew their guns, and returned fire. Another concussion grenade a few yards away made the cathedral shudder—so violent, Cotten expected the ceiling to collapse and the sacred columns to crumble.

The president's strong hand gripped her arm and pulled her to her feet. "This way! Keep low!"

"What the hell's going on? Who's shooting at us?"

"Could be Chechen rebels. Assassins."

Bullets impacted the marble, spewing up shards of stone that bit her legs as he shoved her behind one of the enormous columns. Beside him were two PSS agents, guns blazing.

She looked over her shoulder in time to see her soundman get up off the floor to follow her, only to be struck down by a barrage of bullets. He lay motionless in a crumpled heap. Nearby were the still bodies of three Russian security officers.

One of the other two PSS agents turned to his commander-in-chief and spoke—his Russian sounded like a recording played at double speed. The second agent fired a volley of shots toward their attackers.

"Keep your head down!" the president shouted as the four broke into a run across the open space to the next column.

They crouched behind the thick pillar as a hail of bullets flaked away the five-hundred-year-old masterpiece above their heads.

Another concussion grenade exploded—a supernova in the darkness, the shockwave reverberated in Cotten's bones.

The lead agent tried his radio. No answer.

The president turned to Cotten. "We've lost communication, and they've blocked our exits."

"How do we get out?" A torrent of bullets slammed into the column and rained down more slivers of ancient artwork.

"We will pray with the tsar," he said, then instructed the agents.

Before Cotten could ask for an explanation, he pulled her toward a far corner of the cathedral. Two agents covered their backs.

Bathed in the strange shadow-world produced by the minimal emergency lighting, Cotten saw a small structure, perhaps twenty feet high, surrounded by a metal railing. The base of the structure was about ten feet square. With its pointed spires, it reminded her of a miniature pagoda-like cathedral—its decorative white surface intricately carved.

As they dashed toward it, the president shouted orders, "Ivan the Terrible's praying seat."

The two agents began cover fire while Cotten and the president scrambled over the metal railing.

"This way." He guided her to the narrow space behind the Tsar's Praying Seat and the wall. There, he opened a gate and led her into the miniature cathedral. She saw the single chair where the tsar had once presided during high mass. The president shoved the chair aside to reveal a trapdoor in the floor.

One agent who accompanied them slumped, even though he held his hand over his neck wound, blood gushed between his fingers. A second later, bullets hit the other agent and threw him against the railing. The back of his head was now a mass of blood and tissue. With a thump, his gun bounced on the floor beside the praying seat.

Cotten shuddered at the sight. *Am I going to die? Like that with my brain oozing out my shattered skull? All of us?*

The president lifted the trapdoor then let it fall backward. As it slammed against the wooden floor, a bullet struck his arm. He sank to his knees. "Get the pistol," he said and nodded to Cotten.

The bullets chipped away at the ornate structure, and the wood splintered around her. She grabbed the dead agent's gun. When she turned back, the president was already in the hole.

"Hurry!" he yelled.

Cotten sat on the edge of the opening and felt with her foot for the first step of the stairs. The air buzzed with bullets and debris. A blast of wood and stone grit peppered her back. *Who are they? Bound to kill us— why?*

Her toes found the first rung, and she began her frantic descent. Her hands so sweaty it was hard to get a confident grip. Another earthshaking blast. The ladder quavered. Cotten squeezed her eyes closed and bit down on her lip. Her knees and hands shook so she feared she'd lose her balance. *Come on, Cotten. Do it. Do it.*

After a dozen steps down, she came to a platform. Like a landing. She stood silently, gulping air, her palms icy hot.

The president leaned against the wall. He moaned and said, "Turn on the light."

Cotten ran her hand along the cold stone and located a small switch mounted on the wall. She flipped it, and a bulb below the platform flickered a moment, then dimly glowed. Her eyes searched the small area. *More stairs. To where? How far down are we going?*

The president sagged and reached out to her.

More shots. Flashes in the darkness. The smell of gunpowder, the roar and crack in her ears. *Gotta keep going. Get out of here.* Her breath now sputtered. Erratic heart rhythm, skipped beats then a series of rapid ones.

Pounding.

Pounding.

"We've got to move. Hang on to me," Cotten said. She tucked the agent's pistol inside her waistband. When his hand took hers, she moved down the steps. "Easy, one step at a time. We've got to move fast but safe."

At the bottom, another narrow tunnel. She found the next light switch to the string of bulbs that ran along the center of the ceiling. *Light.*

"Go!" he said.

She looked back at the president and saw that the arm of his jacket was dark red soaked in *his* blood. Cotten got a good look at his pale face. His face contorted, eyes squinted. The president's lips had lost color. All telltale signs of pain and increasing weakness. "Don't die on me." She jostled his shoulder.

Bullets, fired from the trapdoor opening, battered the platform. Chewed-up-wood confetti whirled in the air. "Come on. Let's go."

Cotten coached the president through some deep breathing for less than a minute. It did appear to give him more energy. *We've got no more time. Get moving.*

"Let's go," he said with a stronger voice that surprised her.

The body's attempt at a last rally? Doesn't matter if it gets him moving. Cotten led the president through the tunnel until it widened and split into two passages.

"Which way?" She ducked and drew him low as bullets battered the wall near them. Whatever energy his breathing had helped, now vanished. The president's eyes were half-closed, the lids bluish. *Stay alive until you can get us out and safe.* Cotten took his face in her hands and patted his cheeks until his eyes fluttered. "Which way?"

The president's words were weak, almost whispered. "Stay left."

With more room to maneuver, she draped his arm over her shoulder, ran hers around his waist, and headed into the tunnel.

Footsteps echoed from behind.

Ahead, the tunnel opened into a series of large drainage pipes and more passages.

"Mr. President, which one?"

He raised his head. "Always stay left."

The footfalls grew louder. Maybe they didn't know she had a gun. She could buy a few seconds, perhaps a minute, if she fired several shots. She propped the president against the wall, then drew the pistol from her waistband and prayed that when she pulled the trigger, bullets would come out. The Russian agent could have emptied the gun before going down.

Cotten peered around the corner. Like alien creatures, figures in black combat gear tread single file down the narrow tunnel. They wore helmets, thick body armor, and each face was covered by a strange apparatus—night vision devices, she assumed.

She pointed the pistol at the lead rebel and pulled the trigger.

The sound was deafening in the hard-rock walls. The recoil jolted her. She readied to fire again. This time she steadied the gun with both hands and braced for the kick.

Again and again, she fired. *Aim for center mass. If close enough, go for the head shot.* A tip she had learned from her report on military combat.

The restrictive tunnel gave Cotten an advantage. She didn't have to be a perfect shot. *What's the saying about shooting fish in a barrel?*

The first rebel fell—whether she had killed him or not, she didn't know, but she had hit him. A second and then a third rebel dropped. The crack of more gunfire came from farther back and sent sharp-edged rock fragments and wooden splinters flying.

Cotten evaluated the president's condition by the look on his face. She couldn't leave him behind. "Can you keep going?"

He nodded. The assassins would not stop, she knew, but maybe not come as fast now that they knew she was armed. If they didn't know when she would fire at them again in the tight confines of the passage, they would be more cautious, and that would give her a slight advantage.

As she and the Russian president rounded a corner, a set of stone steps angled up the wall.

"Up." he said. "Go up."

Cotten assisted him as they climbed to a stone platform. A large door, black and old, maybe iron, loomed before them.

The president outstretched his arms then pushed, but the door didn't budge. She knew he was too weak.

"I can do this," she said. *Please, Lord. Give me the strength.*

"One, two, three." Cotten rammed her shoulder into the door. With a loud metal shriek, it gave.

They stumbled into what appeared to be a storeroom. It only took a moment to locate the dangling light cord then pull it. By the looks of the room, Cotten figured the space had not been used in a long time, perhaps decades. But someone had made certain all the electricity was maintained. *An escape route for just such an occasion?*

"Bar the door," he said so weakly she could barely understand what he said.

Cotten forced the heavy latch into the locked position. "Now what?"

He gestured to the door on the opposite wall.

She turned its handle, and the door swung forward and led to yet another hallway. But his one was different. Black marble—floor, ceiling, walls—all dark and shiny. The lighting was indirect, soft, and modern. As she closed the door behind them, she heard pounding on the tunnel entrance door. The rebels were blocked. But for how long? *Where the hell are we?*

The president pointed to the end of the short hall.

A few steps later they entered a spacious room. It, too, was raven black and softly lit. A thick red carpet covered the floor. A long glass-enclosed display was positioned in the center. Small at the bottom, the display flared out at the top. Metal framework supported the glass walls. Eerily, it seemed to glow.

It took Cotten only seconds to realize what she gazed upon. A sarcophagus.

There before her, lying in repose, was the body of a man. His face waxen, his head rested on a white pillow. He was dressed in a black suit, a white shirt with a collar, and a tie—his right hand clenched.

"Is that—?" Cotten asked.

"Yes," the president said. He motioned for her to follow the path around the display bier. On the opposite side, a wide hallway led to the formal entrance.

"Are we locked in?" she asked.

"The doors open from the inside in case of an emergency." He leaned against the wall, coughing and swaying. He nodded his head toward a large red button mounted beside the doors.

"Got it." She hit the button. With a great rush of air and a loud whoosh, the doors opened. Immediately, alarms and klaxons screamed as red strobes flashed overhead.

Exhaustion and weakness worked through her body. As they passed into the chill of the Moscow night, Cotten stared upon a surreal scene—a sea of police and military vehicles raced across Red Square. They headed toward the Savior Tower entrance to the Kremlin in response to the rebel attack. But attracted by the sirens and strobes from the mausoleum, many slowed and changed direction.

"Over here!" Cotten shouted and waved. "Help us!"

The president's legs folded, and he collapsed. Cotten wilted beside him on the cold cobblestones outside Lenin's Tomb.

Chapter Three

AFTERMATH

"The Russians call you a national hero," said Ted Casselman, SNN news director.

"So I've heard," Cotten replied into her cell phone. She stared at the Moscow River from her tenth-floor room at the Rossiya Hotel, twenty hours after the Chechen rebel attack. As she watched a tour boat glide along the river, she pictured Ted Casselman—her boss, friend, and mentor. The forty-eight-year-old black man had been like a father to her since she started at the Satellite News Network over seven years ago. Serious health problems had slowed down Ted, but he still ran the news department with the force of a general and the heart of a teddy bear. Ted was always the one to pick her up each time she fell. her to ever greater heights when she hesitated. Without Ted's guidance and support, her career as a successful network correspondent would never have gotten off the ground.

"The image of you standing next to the president of Russia in his hospital room has shown up on the front page of every newspaper in the world."

Cotten watched the tour boat disappear around a bend. "My heart aches for the crew, especially those killed. I met those guys only a few minutes before the video shoot. Hardly had time to learn their names."

"Our Moscow bureau says the cameraman will survive. He's pretty bad off, but thank God, he'll pull through. The soundman was from Minsk. They're flying his body home tomorrow. We're taking care of all the arrangements."

Cotten shook her head. "I still can't forget the sounds—the screams, bodies hitting the floor, bullets striking flesh and stone." She pressed both hands on her temples as the scene spun through her mind. "Every sound seemed to echo forever."

There was a long pause. Then Ted said, "I've seen all the reports and interviews, including yours. The government is keeping tight-lipped about everything. Do they really know how the rebels got in?"

"I heard they've already arrested six top officers in the Russian military—sympathizers who helped the assassins get fake IDs, everything. It's a mess. Everyone in the Kremlin is looking over their shoulders."

"If this had happened back in the bad old days, those traitors would have been dragged out and shot."

"That's still a good possibility."

"The rebels picked a perfect time for an assassination attempt. The ideal situation—small crew, little security, empty church."

"This was all well planned, Ted. Ironically, the president told me that nothing happens by chance in a Russian church. Boy, was he right."

"What's the damage to the building?"

Cotten shook her head in sadness. "A disaster. The curator estimates it will take years before they can think about reopening. But even when they do, almost nothing in the cathedral is replaceable. Treasures accumulated over centuries are destroyed."

"How are your injuries?"

Cotten glanced down at the bandages on her legs and arm. "What does it say about combat pay in my contract?"

"I don't think you have a contract."

"Then I guess I'll live."

"The conspirators must not be too pleased with you. Do you feel safe?"

"The government emptied this floor of the hotel and stationed two large, serious-looking Russian men outside my door."

"I'm impressed."

"Hey, when you save the president's life, you get to hang out with guys carrying machine guns."

Ted gave an uneasy laugh. Then he said, "John called."

"I missed his call. He rang my cell, but I was live on the air with the BBC." In her mind, she formed an image of John Tyler—his smile, his eyes—the bluest she had ever seen. Probably the only man she had ever truly loved. *You always want what you can never have, Cotten Stone.*

Cardinal John Tyler was director of the Venatori, the ultra-covert intelligence agency of the Vatican—and the most important person in her life.

They had met years ago when she was a rookie reporter, and he was a priest on leave-of-absence from his duties—but not his vows. Together, they uncovered and stopped an attempt to clone Christ. The plot became known in the media as the Grail Conspiracy.

"I plan to call him as soon as I can get a moment's peace and gather my thoughts."

"I assured him you were fine, but a bit banged up. He said he's been following all the reports. Anyway, I'm sure the Russians have already fully briefed the Vatican. He's worried about you, Cotten."

"I know. Ted, I'm completely spent. I've got to get some sleep before my flight tomorrow."

"I won't keep you a minute longer, kiddo. Take it easy and get back to us safe."

"Deal."

"Oh, by the way, someone else called for you—I mean besides the mountain of media requests for interviews."

"Who?"

"Said she was an old friend from your hometown. Saw you on the news and needed to get in touch right away. It had to do with her daughter."

"Did you get her name?"

Cotten heard a rustle of paper through the phone.

"Here it is. Jordan, Lindsay Jordan. I told her where you were staying. Hope you don't mind. She sounded legit."

"No, that's fine. I haven't heard from Lindsay in ages. Wow, I wonder what it's all about."

"That's everything I've got from my end. We can't wait to get you home."

"Same here. Thanks, Ted."

Cotten pushed the button to end the call. She would wait to contact John when she could think clearly. Right now, all she wanted was a good night's rest.

She watched the last rays of the sunset fade and the blanket of city lights come alive across the capital of Russia.

Lindsay Jordan? Her closest friend from childhood through high school. Why would she be calling after so many years?

Chapter Four

TERA

The sound of the crickets reminded Lindsay Jordan that she'd left the window open. It was careless. Too careless. She closed it and tested the brass lock.

Earlier, just before nightfall, Tera, her eight-year-old daughter had stared out that window. Lindsay had opened it for her. "What are you thinking about so hard, Tera?" Her daughter's response rocked Lindsay. It caught her so off balance she had forgotten about the open window until now.

Lindsay checked the dead bolt on the front door then paced in her living room. She glared at her cell phone and tried to decide whether or not to make the call. How was she going to explain without sounding crazy?

"Damn you," she said and lifted a framed picture of her husband from the end table beside the sofa. Then she clutched the photo to her chest. Sometimes she not only grieved for him, but she was angry with him for dying and leaving her and their daughter alone.

Lindsay put the picture back on the table before she followed the glow of the nightlight down the hall. Quietly, she opened the door to her daughter's room and peeked in.

Tera slept curled under a pink coverlet printed with ballerinas striking elegant poses. Tendrils of Tera's hair spread out on the pink pillowcase. Her favorite stuffed animal rested just below her chin.

How precious Tera is, Lindsay thought.

She stared at her only child for several more minutes until the fear inside her built to such a staggering panic that she was afraid she would cry out and wake Tera. Lindsay closed the door and returned to the living room.

Again, she looked at her phone.

***

Cotten Stone fumbled in the dark hotel room for the telephone that rang on the nightstand.

"Hello," she said, her voice whispery and gravelly with sleep. She squinted at the red numbers on the clock radio. 5:19 a.m. The faint sound of a siren drifted up from the Russian streets below.

"Cotten, I don't know who else to turn to. You've got to help me. Please. I'm desperate."

"Who is this?" Cotten said.

"It's Lindsay." When there was no response, she said, "Lindsay Jordan, from back home."

Remembering Ted's comment about her calling, Cotten suddenly recognized the voice. "Lindsay? It's five in the morning. What's wrong?"

"I'm sorry to call like this. I phoned SNN earlier and they put me through to your boss. He told me where you were staying. Sorry I woke you. I wasn't sure what time it was there, Cotten, but . . . Oh, God, I don't know how to explain."

Cotten sat up and switched on the lamp. "Slow down. It's okay you called. Are you all right?"

"It's Tera."

"Oh, my God, has something happened to her?"

"Not yet." A moment of dead time passed before Lindsay said, "Tera is…different, Cotten. I've known it since she was just a baby. Special. I know that's what every mother says, but Tera really is. I can't explain it

21

all to you on the phone. I need you to come here and see Tera. Then you'll understand."

"Lindsay, what's going on? What's this all about?" Puzzled, Cotten pushed up against the headboard to sit.

"You have to trust me." Lindsay heaved out a sigh. "You won't believe me if I tell you. You've got to see for yourself."

They used to remember each other's birthday, but over time, even the exchange of Christmas cards faded. So, for Lindsay to make this frantic call now meant something had to be terribly wrong.

"Lindsay, I'm flying home tomorrow." She looked at the clock. "I mean today. After I get this Moscow story squared away, I'll call you. I've wanted to come to Kentucky to do a piece on thoroughbred racing, anyway. I could come by to see you and Tera in a couple of weeks—"

"No." Lindsay's voice was sharp. "You can't wait that long. I'm going to lose her, Cotten. I'm certain of it. She's had these dreams—nightmares. I say they're nightmares, even though they don't frighten her. But when she tells me about them, it scares the hell out of me." Lindsay's voice cracked. "I wish I could explain better."

"Dreams are only that, Lindsay," Cotten said to calm her friend.

"There's much more. It's not only the dreams."

Cotten raked back her hair. She had heard that Lindsay's husband died—a fall from the barn roof he was repairing. Someone, she couldn't remember who, sent her the local newspaper clipping and obituary. Maybe Lindsay hadn't yet recovered, and her world was crashing in.

"Lindsay? Are you there?"

"I'm here. Cotten, I don't want you to think I'm nuts or that Tera is a freak—but she sees things, knows things. I don't understand, but I believe Tera does. And I think you will. That's why I'm calling. Please, you've got to help us."

"Lindsay, if you don't have any clue what Tera's dreams mean, why would you think—"

"Because of who you are, Cotten. The stories in the news over the years—all the religious stuff you've covered and been involved with. You're the only one who will understand. Just believe me, please."

"I do, Lindsay. I do. Tell you what. Let me give you my cell number. That way if anything changes, you can call me no matter where I am."

"Hang on, let me get something to write on," Lindsay said.

"Okay. Go ahead," Lindsay said.

Cotten gave her the number. "Leave a message on my voice mail if I don't answer. I'll get back to you as soon as I can."

"I promise I won't pester you." Lindsay's voice cracked and there was a moment of silence as if she had to stop herself from crying before she could speak again. "Cotten, today Tera was staring out the window, and when I asked her what she was thinking about, she looked right in my eyes and said, 'Momma, they're coming for me.' "

Chapter Five

PROBE

A Secret Service agent ushered Rizben Mace into the Oval Office. The outer-office staff had gone for the night. "Good evening, Mr. President," Mace said with a respectful nod as the door closed behind him.

"Rizben, come in and make yourself comfortable." The president motioned to an empty wingback chair. He wore a jogging outfit—and his brown hair was tousled and lacked the expert grooming normally seen when he made public appearances. "Your call gave me a good excuse to take a break from the nightly treadmill."

Philip Miller, National Security Advisor, occupied a second chair. Dressed in a tuxedo, he smiled—a kind of smile that made Mace believe it was forced because Miller was probably annoyed he'd been pulled away from some other Washington function.

Small gathering, Mace thought as he glanced at the two empty couches facing each other in the middle of the room. The couches were separated enough to display most of the Great Seal of the Presidency embroidered in the carpet.

Mace acknowledged Miller with a cordial handshake. "Phil, how are the kids?"

"Hopefully sound asleep by now," Miller said. The Harvard Law School graduate had been the only opposing voice in the cabinet when the president nominated Mace to direct Homeland Security. Mace knew Miller still held a grudge from years ago when he'd backed Miller's opponent in the Arkansas governor's race. It would be more than a grudge if Miller knew the real reason he had done so.

The president sat behind the historic Resolute Desk, built from the timbers of the HMS Resolute. It had been a gift from Queen Victoria to Rutherford B. Hayes in 1880. "Gentlemen, thanks for coming at such a late hour." He turned to Mace with a slight lift of his hand. "Rizben, bring us up to date."

"Mr. President, as previously reported, significant portions of the Internet were brought down this evening by attacks from primarily Chinese and Malaysian sources. Since the first call to you tonight, we have confirmed that over a million servers across Asia, Africa, Europe, and India have crashed. The word got out quickly, so the damage is subsiding as everyone still online takes preventative action, but from a commercial standpoint, the attack has already caused considerable damage."

The president removed his glasses. "How much?"

"Too soon to tell, Mr. President," Mace said, "but preliminary estimates are approaching the multibillion-dollar mark."

"Is there any evidence that specific organizations were targeted?"

"No, sir," said Mace. "It looks like some type of flood attack meant to disrupt service. So far, we have received no reports of loss of data."

"Maybe we're getting all revved up over nothing," Miller said. "Could it have just been malicious hackers?"

"Crackers," Mace corrected. "Criminal hackers."

"Sorry, Crackers?" Miller asked.

"Again, it's too soon to tell." Mace spoke with a deliberateness he knew Miller wouldn't miss.

"And you're recommending raising the threat level?" the president said.

"Yes, sir, but only for selective infrastructures."

"Isn't this an overreaction?" asked Miller. "I mean, just because a bunch of Europeans can't log on to their favorite porn sites for a few hours—does that warrant scaring the hell out of the nation?"

"I wish it was that simple, Phil," Mace said. "The fact is we still have to consider the possibility that events like this could be the first wave of a cyber-terrorism attack. It's a whole different threat than being hacked. This could easily have been a probe to see our reaction and gauge vulnerabilities."

"But the damage to our infrastructure was minimal, correct?" the president asked.

"So far," Mace said.

"This is the same argument we keep going over, time and again," Miller said to Mace. "I just can't believe that terrorism will come from the Internet. Terrorists don't want to see some guy denied access to his AOL account. They want the shock factor of jet airliners crashing into buildings, subways filled with toxic gas, big trucks running over crowds of people and dead bodies scattered in the streets. Hell, how about trying to assassinate the president of Russia inside the fucking Kremlin, for God's sake. That's terrorism." He turned to the president. "Their objective is to terrorize, not piss off. We'll be justifiably accused of crying wolf over this. Corporations and agencies in this country are doing a hell of a good job hardening access to their assets. We need to reserve adjusting the national threat level to real threats, not what happened tonight. Leave the level at orange."

"You're right, Phil," Mace said. "Striking at the heart of America with physical attacks does create the most impact, but that doesn't mean we have to ignore more subtle probes into our virtual heartland. The true damage can take place without shedding one drop of blood or blowing up a plane."

Silence settled over the Oval Office, broken a moment later by a slight squeak of the president's chair as he leaned back. "I tend to agree with Phil," he said. "Rizben, send out an official alert bulletin to all private and public organizations that would be vulnerable to this sort of intrusion. Advise them what happened and suggest they review all security procedures involving cyber-attacks." He gave Mace a patronizing smile. "Let's keep a sharp eye on this one, but not get our knickers in a knot." He stood. "Thanks again, gentlemen. Keep me informed of any new developments."

The three men shook hands. Miller led the way out of the Oval Office, Mace behind. Beyond earshot of the president, Miller turned. "Sorry, Rizben, but we can't be trigger-happy, can we?"

"No, we can't," Mace said with a nod. He stopped the conversation and pulled his cell phone from his pocket. He glanced at the caller ID and said, "Got to take this, Phil." Miller waved over his shoulder as he rounded a corner.

Rizben checked to make sure he was alone before he pushed the talk button. "Pastor Albrecht, do you have the girl?"

"No. She and her mother disappeared."

"But she definitely identified you?"

"Yes."

"Then we have a problem."

"Actually, there's an even bigger problem."

Rizben switched ears. He had been riding high on the predictable response from the president and Miller and wanted nothing to spoil it. Now, this. "And what would that be?"

"Cotten Stone just showed up."

Chapter Six

LORETTO

Cotten's drive from the Louisville airport to Loretto, Kentucky, brought with it a flood of memories. The ribbon of road threaded through the countryside, embraced by the rolling land of expansive horse farms and the more modest hay, soybean, and tobacco farms. Cotten's roots were buried deep in this soil, even though she had created another life very different in New York with SNN—a galaxy that glittered and spun in all directions, so unlike the universe of her childhood she had put behind her. With much effort she had even discarded the southern accent so it only put in an appearance when she got excited.

Cotten turned off Highway 49 onto a series of back roads until finally steering into Lindsay Jordan's long dirt driveway. The house sat in the middle of what had once been 520 lucrative acres of tobacco fields, a crop that had supported the Jordan family for generations. But Lindsay's farm hadn't grown tobacco in twenty years, yielding to soybeans.

Closer, Cotten noticed that the house seemed in disrepair. Weeds spiked through the grass to knee height. A slat in the porch rail hung loose and jutted out at an angle. She glimpsed the barn from which Neil Jordan fell on a stormy, summer afternoon.

Neil Jordan. Wow. She and Lindsay had both had crushes on him. He was definitely the catch of their high school class—good looking, smart, first string on the varsity football team, voted *Most Likely to Succeed*. Lindsay had wound up with him. Pregnant. They got married a week after graduation, and Neil went to work with Lindsay's family on the farm—his *Most Likely to Succeed* plowed under with the next crop. Two months later, Lindsay miscarried. It was another nine years before

Tera was born. Strange how life takes everyone on a different path, Cotten thought as she parked the car in front of the house.

At the front door, Cotten heard a mewing sound. She looked down between the cracks of the wooden porch. A mother cat with a litter of kittens stared up.

"Hey, kitty, kitty," Cotten said softly before returning her attention to the door. She rapped on it. "Lindsay?"

She waited a moment before knocking again, this time louder.

"Lindsay, it's me, Cotten. Hello."

Still no answer. She made her way around to the rear of the house and climbed the wood steps to the back porch. The screen door twanged shut behind her. "Hello."

To her right was a metal storage cabinet and stacked beside it were five cases of canning jars. To her left were cans of spray paint, a hand trowel, and a jug of Roundup sitting atop an old maple dresser.

Cotten knocked on the back door, its white paint peeling away. "Lindsay? Anybody home?"

She turned the tarnished brass knob, but the door was locked. Cotten pressed her forehead onto the window and held her hand against the glass, but the window was draped from the inside. She tried to get a glimpse by looking sideways at the edge of the window, thinking maybe there was a gap between the drape and the glass. No luck.

Cotten glanced around. The place looked like no one had cared for it in months—it appeared deserted. And there was no car. Unless it was in the barn.

Something brushed her leg, and she flailed backward into the storage cabinet. The metal doors rattled and clanged, flapping open in unison with a high-pitched screech.

The cat sprang off the porch, hair on end. A pair of pruning shears latently clattered onto the floor.

29

The damn cat, she thought then laughed at herself. Poor thing was looking for affection, and she had scared the living daylights out of it.

Cotten picked up the shears and cleared a space for them on a shelf inside the storage cabinet. As she did, she saw a faded blue and red box of Diamond kitchen matches. When she and Lindsay were young, the spare key had been kept in that box. She wondered if. . .

She slid open the box and wriggled her forefinger through the thin layer of matches. Bingo. She plucked the key from the box and tried it in the lock. The door opened.

Before going inside, Cotten closed the matchbox and put it back inside the cabinet, but she slipped the key into her jeans pocket.

She entered the kitchen. It was uncomfortably warm and musty, as if fresh air had not circulated in a long time, and there was an awful smell that made her gag. She breathed through her mouth to help. *Through your mouth, Cotten.*

A piece of an old quilt was nailed over the window and sealed on the edges with duct tape. Lindsay obviously didn't want anyone to see in or out. Cotten turned on the lights. Fluorescent bulbs strobed before emitting a steady light.

The deep porcelain sink held a couple of food-crusted dishes. Cotten turned on the faucet. It choked and sputtered but finally rusty, cloudy water streamed out. Once it cleared, she filled the sink to let the dishes soak.

"Lindsay, are you here?" She pushed the swinging door that led from the kitchen to the dining room and moved through the house turning on the lights. With each empty room she became more nervous. It was so dark with the sun blocked out.

The smell grew worse, and she heard the buzzing of insects. *Flies.*

As Cotten moved into the living room, she saw that all the windows were covered, like the one in the kitchen. Quilts, bedspreads, and sheets had been nailed and taped over every opening.

And the damn stench was horrid. What the hell had gone on here? She imagined finding a body—Lindsay's body. Perhaps there had been an accident. Or worse. And where was Tera?

Cotten crept down the hall and came to a halt in front of the utility closet. When she cracked the door open, the rank air seemed to congeal and overwhelm her. No mouth breathing could stop the gag reflex.

Chapter Seven

PAINTINGS

Cotten reeled backward as swollen black trash bags tumbled from the utility closet. A rupture in one bag allowed its guts to spew out—a dark red sauce coating wormy threads of old spaghetti, the decomposing remains of a zucchini, chicken bones, banana peel, and other more unrecognizable contents. A putrid gelatinous puddle formed on the gray linoleum.

"Jesus," Cotten said, getting a full complement of the dreadful stench. Why had Lindsay been storing her garbage in the closet?

Cotten shoved the bags back with her foot enough to allow passage down the hall. The door to the first room stood open. Tera's bedroom, she thought, seeing the ballerina-print coverlet as she turned on the overhead light. Instantly, her eyes were drawn to the walls. Paintings, beautiful paintings, covered the walls. Unframed canvases of portraits and landscapes, surreal visions of light and shadow, haunting depths of color, stunning and amazing works of art.

Cotten stood in front of a portrait that was probably five feet high by four feet wide—a breathtaking, angelic child, her blonde hair tumbling to her shoulders. A halo of soft, deep blue light surrounded the child. Clear blue eyes seemed to transcend the canvas and look right into the viewer's soul. Was this Tera? Cotten turned in a slow circle, taking in the dozens of paintings covering the walls.

Dazed by the magnificent artwork, she sat on the bed and noticed a journal on the nightstand. Even though she felt as if she were violating Tera's privacy, she couldn't resist seeing what it contained. Cotten opened the cover and read the first page.

The Glaze
Burns the stains from the water
The soul of the swan finds solace
Transcending the perfect hour
To swirl in the glory
Of the mysteries

Wow. This was not normal reading for an eight-year-old girl and certainly not the writing of one. If Lindsay had written it for her daughter, what was she thinking?

Cotten turned the page and leaned against the headboard as she read.

I asked you,
Come with me
The weeping Selene draped me in ebony
And cast my tears onto a cloth of obsidian
I asked you,
Come with me

On page 3, she read more.

The stillness stole the rhythm
Silence crashed on the shore
But above the mighty river
Soar, soar, soar
Can you feel the light as it touches your mind?
Hear the roar of the whisper
Across the twinkling edge
Soar, soar, soar

She fanned the pages with her thumb. Incredible. Page after page of poetry written in a beautiful, flowing hand. Mature and controlled, not the handwriting of a child.

She set the journal on the nightstand before continuing her search of the house. In what must be Lindsay's room, Cotten turned on the ceiling light along with the lamp on the dresser and another on the nightstand.

Unlike Tera's bed, Lindsay's was unmade. The quilt lay rumpled on the floor at the foot of the bed, the pillows askew. But like Tera's and every other room, the windows were covered and sealed.

There were paintings here, too, gracing every wall—some fanciful and others astonishingly realistic. Cotten moved close to one and ran her finger over the face of a brown-skinned child whose large dark eyes peered up at a star-filled sky. A soft, cerulean halo surrounded the child. She touched a painting of a white horse with its mane blowing in the wind as it stood atop a hillcrest against a brilliant blue sky.

Cotten wondered when Lindsay had started to paint. Maybe after Neil's passing, she thought. Perhaps it had become her therapy. None of the paintings were signed. Instead, each bore a simple blue slash at the bottom—a mark that reminded Cotten of a thunderbolt.

Lindsay could certainly sell her work, and Cotten wondered if her friend had tried. If Lindsay hadn't made the connections she needed out here in the middle of the Kentucky farmland, Cotten would get her in touch with someone in New York. She had little knowledge of the art world, but she knew these paintings were incredible, moving, and probably valuable. Maybe she'd ask the SNN art critic to have a chat with Lindsay.

She moved in front of the dresser and lifted a photograph—Neil with his arm around Lindsay, who was holding a baby. Tera, she assumed.

Where were Lindsay and Tera, and what was that desperate call all about? Cotten explored the rest of the house and found nothing unusual other than the covered windows. The other rooms had a painting or two hanging on the walls, but nothing like the collection in the mother's and daughter's rooms.

A stack of mail sat on the coffee table in front of the couch in the living room. Cotten plunked herself down and picked up the envelopes. Junk mail, gas bill, the typical pre-approved credit card offers, a magazine, MasterCard statement.

She tossed the mail back on the table. That's when she caught sight of the blinking light on the phone. She leaned over to the end table and pressed the button on the phone to play back the message.

Hello, Lindsay. This is Pastor Albrecht. I wanted to say there's no harm done. I understand your daughter is still under a great deal of stress with the death of her father and all. Sometimes things get the best of young girls that make them go a little . . . Lindsay, no one feels worse than me about the outburst at church. I came by to visit but you and Tera were not home. I'll try again.

The date—four days ago.

Outburst? Cotten glanced around the dark room at the covered window. What the hell was going on here?

Chapter Eight

CONNECTION

Cotten sat on Lindsay's couch. The message on the answer machine distressed her. What kind of outburst was this guy, Pastor Albrecht, talking about? And why were Lindsay and Tera living like this, sealed up in a house full of clutter and garbage? In her call to Cotten, Lindsay feared for her daughter.

Cotten wondered if she should call the authorities. But what would she tell them? That Lindsay was a messy housekeeper? That she left bags of rotting garbage around and had a compulsive fear of direct sunshine and fresh air? Her daughter had an outburst at Sunday service?

Cotten reconsidered. It had been a week since Lindsay's middle-of-the-night plea. What if something had happened to them, and she was too late?

No reason to take chances. A local phonebook on the counter had all emergency numbers, plus the number for police when not an emergency. *Perfect.* She dialed the non-emergency number.

"Sheriff's office." The female voice sounded young and bored. Cotten thought she heard the smack of chewing gum.

"I'd like to report a missing person—two missing persons," Cotten said.

"Your name?"

"Cotten Stone."

"What is your location?"

She gave the address for the Jordan farm. "Hold please," the girl said.

A few moments later, a man came on the line. "I don't suppose this is *the* Cotten Stone? Furmiel and Martha Stone's daughter? World-famous news correspondent?"

"I'm not so sure about the famous part," Cotten said.

"Ms. Stone, this is Sheriff Maddox. I can't tell you how proud we are of you around here. Not only do my wife and I watch you on SNN all the time, but when we saw what happened over there in Russia, well, we're just so proud. And, if I might add, you sure have grown up to be a mighty pretty young lady."

"Thank you, Sheriff." She remembered Maddox. He had investigated her father's death—Furmiel Stone's suicide.

"Now, what's this about missing persons?"

"I'm at Lindsay Jordan's place. She and her daughter appear to be missing."

Maddox gave a loud, heavy sigh.

"What's the matter?" Cotten asked.

"Well, how should I put this? She tends to get a bee in her bonnet now and then, takes Tera and leaves for a few days. Just picks up and goes on the spur of the moment. I think she simply needs to get away from Loretto sometimes, even if it's only a day or two. Lindsay once told me she felt like she was living underwater in the deep end of a swimming pool. I believe taking these little mini vacations is the way she comes up for air."

"I'm not sure she's gone on vacation this time. I got a phone call from her. That's why I'm here. She sounded upset and scared. She begged me to come."

"I'm sure she's overreacting to what happened at church the other Sunday."

"What did happen?"

"It was embarrassing for Lindsay, Cotten—may I call you Cotten?"

"Yes, please."

"I wasn't there, mind you, but apparently a couple of Sundays ago was the first time Lindsay had taken Tera to church in a long time. The girl didn't like being there because that was where she last saw her father after he died. Tragic accident, you know. That's the church where they had the funeral. We have a new pastor there—Reverend Albrecht. It was the first time Tera had met him. Well, as soon as she laid eyes on the pastor, she went berserk and called him evil and the devil and such. I heard it was awful. She was screaming and crying. Poor thing had to be sedated by the doc. Lindsay took her home, and they haven't been heard from since."

Cotten realized the sheriff had placed his hand over the receiver for a moment to give an order to what she figured was a deputy.

"Sorry, Cotten," he said, "we've got a minor fender-bender out on five-twenty-seven. Where was I? Anyway, I think Lindsay has been battling emotional demons since Neil passed. And what's worse, I think it has taken a toll on Tera. She's a sweet little girl, but not like any other eight-year-old kid I know."

"What do you mean?"

"Always claiming to see things—ghosts, spirits, visions. I believe she wants attention. Can't blame her, I suppose."

As Cotten listened, she tried to push away the haunting question of why Lindsay had contacted her in the first place. Now, she was confident that her friend not only needed to be found, but it sounded like she could use professional help—for her and Tera.

"I'm sorry to hear all this," she said. "When Lindsay called me a week ago, she did say that Tera was having unusual dreams. But Lindsay seemed so scared—frightened that she was going to lose her daughter. She sounded desperate."

"When you get right down to it, Lindsay is in a pitiful state. Though a lot of folks have offered to help, she refuses. I'm sure she'll be back in a couple of days. If she doesn't show up soon, I'll look into it. Meanwhile, I'll call around and see if I can find out anything else."

"Thanks, Sheriff Maddox. I hope you're right, and that I have reason to be sorry I bothered you. I would appreciate it if you'd get back to me with any information. Anything at all." She gave him her cell phone.

"You bet," he said, then chuckled. "I still don't believe it. A real celebrity right here in Loretto. Stop by and say hello. Everybody would really get a kick out of meeting you."

"I will, Sheriff."

Cotten ended the call. She felt empty. And gloomy. Her friend was obviously suffering and there seemed to be nothing she could do about it.

Something still bothered her, though. Maybe she was being overly cautious—the news reporter coming out. *Question everything*. That was what got her the senior news correspondent position at SNN.

She wasn't ready to call it quits, yet. Instead, she would dig a little deeper.

Cotten started with a thorough search of the house, hoping to come up with something that would convince her to either go home or stick around and investigate further.

She headed down the hall then entered Tera's room again. It was a typical girl's bedroom, except for all of her mother's paintings. There was a large collection of books on the shelves along one wall. Cotten scanned the titles: *Evidence of God*; *Experiencing Prayer*; *Peace on Earth*; Billy Graham's *The Journey*; *The Power of Intention*, by Dr. Wayne W. Dyer; *The Isaiah Effect*, by Gregg Braden. Not the usual reading for a kid Tera's age.

On another shelf were Tera's schoolbooks. Cotten brushed them with her fingertips recalling Lindsay's phone call. *Because of who you are, Cotten. The stories in the news over the years—all the religious stuff you've covered and been involved with. You're the only one who will understand.*

Cotten took a deep breath.

She continued through the house, exploring cubbies and nooks, drawers and cabinets. In the kitchen, beneath the dinette, she found a stack of teacher's manuals that matched Tera's texts. There were also folders with tabs marked math, reading, and spelling. Lindsay was home- schooling her daughter. Why had she chosen that route rather than sending her to public school?

Cotten fanned herself with an empty folder. Even though it was early fall and the weather cooling off, the today was unusually warm.

With the windows closed and covered, the air inside smothered her. Not to mention the stench of spoiled garbage.

Cotten sensed the walls closing in and likened it to what a claustro- phobic must feel in a crowded elevator. She made her way back to the living room, snatched the blanket off the front window and slid up the bottom pane. Then she unlatched the front door and helped it coast back until it hit the stop on the wall. A breeze blew through. The screen door whined behind her as Cotten stepped onto the porch. The sun washed away the cloying darkness of the house, and she let the pureness of the day stream over her.

After she cleared her head, Cotten strode to Lindsay's bedroom where she rifled through drawers and the closet—all of which were in disarray. It struck her that the rooms looked like they might have been searched before she arrived. Maybe somebody else was eager to uncover clues to where Lindsay and Tera had gone.

On top of the dresser was a framed photograph that caught Cotten's attention. As she lifted it, a wave of familiarity swept through her—a sensation akin to déjà vu.

She touched her finger to the face in the picture—a little girl whose wispy blonde hair tumbled around her shoulders. Her blue eyes, like her mother's, were clear and wide as she smiled at the camera. She held a calico kitten to her cheek, seeming to relish the softness of the fur. The girl looked to be seven or eight. It had to be a recent photo of Tera.

Cotten felt herself well up with emotion. Not because she was concerned for the child, of course she was, but because of an unexplained connection—like she knew more about Tera than she realized. Almost as if a distant memory was on the verge of recall.

Perplexed, Cotten set the picture on the dresser and backed away. She parked herself on the side of the bed and tried to rationalize an explanation for what happened. Never had she experienced anything so unexpectedly stirring. Lindsay was right, there was something unique about Tera, and Cotten was determined to find out what had happened to her friend and the girl.

At the foot of the bed sat an antique trunk. She lifted the lid, and the unmistakable sharp scent of cedar permeated the room. Cotten removed a crocheted throw blanket, and beneath it discovered pencil drawings— amazing detailed drawings. She sorted through them, overcome with wonder at Lindsay's talent. There were also small paintings with the same dramatic detail as those on the walls. Each bore the tiny blue thunderbolt signature.

Reams of poetry filled a cardboard box the size of a toaster oven. Cotten read several writings before she replaced the lid. Next, she found a scrapbook. Fastened in corner mounts on every page were black and white photographs. It had to be Lindsay's mother's album. Near the back were some faded color photos as if bathed in yellow light. One was of

Cotten and Lindsay in high school. There was a folded piece of paper shoved under the picture—a corner sticking out. Out of curiosity, Cotten removed it and gasped. Her name was written on it.

She unfolded the note then read.

> *Dear Cotten. If you are reading this, then it is too late. We have gone into hiding. Tera told me that a guardian angel would come to protect us. I know that must be you. She said they are hunting us, and they will stop at nothing to keep you from finding her first. They are pure evil, Cotten. Please pray for us. Lindsay and Tera.*

Despite the warm, stale air, Cotten felt a chill. Desperation flowed from Lindsay's words. Cotten felt like someone was watching her, coming so close she could feel hot breath. She turned and glanced around the room. No one. Cotten folded the note and placed it in her pocket.

It was time to make the call.

Chapter Nine

DEVIN

"Does Dolphin Stadium have a Code Adam?" Alan Olsen asked.

"No, sir," the Miami-Dade police officer said. The cop led the way into the men's room. As he entered, he keyed his shoulder mic. "Unit forty. Possible missing child. Stand by."

"How can you not have an emergency alert?" Alan's face burned with frustration. "You know how many kids come to these games? How could you not . . .?"

"Unit forty, possible missing child. Ten-four," replied the thin, metallic voice from the police radio.

"I've already checked in here," Alan said. "Devin came in, but I never saw him come out."

"Start Me Up" by the Rolling Stones blared from the giant stadium speakers. The Dolphins and Jets were ready for the second-half kickoff.

The officer moved along the line of stalls. After confirming there were no children in any, he said, "Let me see your tickets."

Alan reached into his pocket, then handed the officer the stubs. "Have you gone back to see if your son is at your seats?"

"Yes. I did that, too." Heat built inside Alan, and the pressure in his head thudded. "I've done all that. Can't you alert stadium security?"

"Let's have a look just to make sure. Kids do this all the time. Wander off then wind up back in their seats wondering where their parents are. First, let's see if he's there."

"But if something is wrong, we're wasting…" There was no sense finishing the sentence. Alan could tell he was being ignored. Maybe the police dealt with this all the time, but he didn't, and he wanted to see some sense of urgency in the cop's attitude. Besides, the policeman didn't understand about Devin.

"Listen," Alan said. "We're wasting precious time. If we find him, then no harm done, but if he's in trouble . . ."

The officer headed up the tunnel ramp with Alan a pace behind. Turning onto the steep steps leading upward, Alan's gaze focused on their empty seats.

No Devin. His gut tensed, forcing air out of his lungs in an unexpected rush. He was close to panicking—something he never did. It wasn't part of his nature.

The deafening roar heralded the kickoff. Alan and the officer climbed the steps until they stood beside the two empty seats.

"Take a good look around and see if you spot him," the officer shouted to Alan. "He might be in the wrong seat."

Damn the cheap seats, Alan thought. He could easily afford a corporate skybox, but he wanted Devin to experience the game like most other kids his age. Please don't let it prove to be a mistake, he prayed.

He scanned the nearby crowd while the officer spoke into the shoulder mic, but the cheering fans made it too noisy for Alan to hear what he was saying. He hoped it was the call to alert the security staff.

He followed the officer down the steps and back through the tunnel. A few minutes later, they entered the Miami-Dade Metro Police Substation on the ground floor of the stadium. The space was compact with a small waiting room and a few chairs. The officer showed Alan into a second room where another officer sat behind a desk. "This is Sergeant Carillo. He'll take it from here. Show him your ID, then give him a full description of your son."

"Can we make this fast?" Alan said. "Devin is missing and nobody's looking for him."

"Don't worry, Mr. Olsen," Carillo said. "Parents get separated from their children here all the time. We'll find your son."

Alan removed his driver's license from his wallet and handed it to the sergeant.

"This your correct address?" the sergeant asked, making a few notes on a pad.

Alan nodded and clapped his hands together to still the shaking and contain the anger. The delay was becoming unbearable.

Carillo returned the license, took a brief look at Alan and said, "Have a seat. Can you give me a description of your son?"

Alan felt his jaw clench as he pulled the chair out. The wood legs scraped the floor. "His name is Devin. He's eight, about four-six, four-seven. Sixty pounds. Blond hair, blue eyes. He is wearing jeans, a yellow T-shirt, and a Dolphins jacket. Oh, and a Dolphins cap."

Carillo scribbled on a pad of paper not even looking up when he asked the next question. "When did you see him last?"

"During halftime, we went to get a snack. Devin said he had to use the bathroom, but the lines were a mile long." Alan wiped the sweat from his face with his hand. "He has a bladder control problem and has to urinate often—at least once an hour."

"You want something to drink?"

"No!" Alan took a deep breath. "Sorry. No, I don't need anything to drink."

"Okay, what else?"

"We went to the front of the line and I asked this guy if Devin could please cut in line ahead of him. The poor kid was standing there with his legs twisted like a pretzel and a look of agony on his face." Alan wiped his brow again. "The guy took pity on Devin and let him by."

"What did you do?"

45

"The concourse was packed. I walked over to the outside stadium wall and waited."

"How long?"

"Eight, maybe ten minutes."

"That's a long time for a kid to take a piss." Carillo locked his eyes on Alan's.

"I realize that. That's why I'm so upset."

The cop made a few more notes. "Did you hang around there or did you wander around, maybe leave and come back?"

"I never moved."

"Did you talk to anyone?"

"No. Well, yes. Some guy struck up a conversation with me about football statistics. I found him a bit overbearing and boring. I'm not that big of a football fan."

"Then why did you come to the game?"

"Devin loves the Dolphins. This was his first NFL game."

The officer tore the page from the pad and stood. "Anything else you can tell me before I call this in?"

Alan hesitated. There was more, a lot more. But probably the guy wouldn't understand or believe him. "No, nothing else," Alan said.

Chapter Ten

THE BARN

Cotten retrieved her purse from the rental and pulled her cell phone out of its side pocket. She checked her watch—12:30 p.m. in Kentucky, 6:30 p.m. in Rome. She leaned against the car and scrolled through her phone list to the private Vatican number for Cardinal John Tyler. After getting his voice mail, she dialed his cell.

"*Ciao*," came the response after a half-dozen rings.

"John. You're working late."

"Actually, I'm in Washington for a security conference. We're winding everything up this afternoon. Hang on a second."

Cotten heard the mumble of background voices diminish as John must have found a quieter location.

"I was just thinking about you."

"Really?" she said. "We must have ESP." She shifted her weight to her other foot. His words flooded her with warm memories and a deep yearning. *I've always wanted what I could never have.* "It's great to hear your voice."

"How are your wounds healing?"

"Not everybody can brag about being shot at by Chechen rebels."

"That's not funny. Ted told me you're investigating a story in Kentucky? How's it going?"

"What is it they say, fair to middling?"

"I don't hear that colloquialism around the Vatican very often. But I believe it means less than terrific. What's going on?"

Cotten started with Lindsay's call, a description of the farmhouse, Lindsay's paintings and poetry, Sheriff Maddox's comments, the outburst at church, what happened to her when Cotten saw and touched Tera's picture and ending with the note in the scrapbook. "Pretty suspicious, isn't it?"

"It's all suspicious. What part in particular?"

"All the above, but mostly what happened when I touched her photo."

"Knowing you like I do, nothing would surprise me. Your connection with Tera tells me there's something else going on there, something deeper than the sheriff's explanation."

"It was as if I felt whole—complete—like she was an extension of me."

"Any idea why?"

"Not yet."

"What are you going to do?"

Cotten scanned the area around the farmhouse. There was a barn nearby. "I've got a few more things here to check out. Then I'll head back to town and ask around to see if anyone knows anything. If it turns out they really are in danger, I'll find a way to get them some protection."

"I had planned on flying back to Rome in the morning. What if I delay that a few days and come to Kentucky?"

"You sure you can take the time? I mean, I'd love to see you, but I don't have much to go on here."

"Your comment about the connection to the girl concerns me."

"How so?"

"Things have been unusually quiet for a long time. Too, quiet. This could be the start of another round with our old friends."

"That occurred to me, too." Cotten closed her eyes, thankful that John would be by her side if their concerns proved true. Even if there was nothing to worry about, she'd be happy to be near him again. She touched the mouthpiece of the phone as if it might magically bring him closer. "How about I pick you up in Louisville? It's a nice drive between there and Loretto."

"I'll call you back with my flight info."

Before she stopped them, the next words tumbled out. "I miss you."

There was a pause. "Same here." She heard him take a deep breath. "I'll call you in an hour or two."

She wandered down the hard-packed clay path toward the barn. Lindsay's cat sat off to the side at a respectable distance.

Like the house, the outside of the barn needed repair and a fresh coat of paint. Farm tools lay scattered in thin, overgrown grass. Weeds grew between the logs in a stack of firewood. Bees buzzed about a patch of purple wildflowers near the corner of the old structure. An ancient oak provided shade.

How could Lindsay be so talented and yet live in such shambles? Perhaps the paintings and poetry were her distractions from a crumbling life. Maybe they had become obsessions to help get through the days . . . and nights.

Cotten stood in front of the barn doors. She would take a quick look inside before heading back to town. The heavy latch scraped and groaned as both twelve-foot-high doors swung open lazily. The aroma of turpentine and oil paint flowed out.

When Cotten's eyes adjusted to the dim interior, she marveled at what she saw.

Overhead, suspended from rafters, hung dozens of paintings in many sizes. They weren't just beautiful works of art, there was something spiritual and mystical about them. Paintings and drawings also covered the barn walls. And scattered about were racks of blank canvases along with boxes of oils, acrylics, charcoal, brushes, and palettes. The entire barn had been converted to an art studio. The smells of linseed oil and gesso replaced the aromas of hay and earth.

An unfinished painting drew Cotten to the rear of the barn. It was a portrait of a man. Unlike the other beautiful images, his face was twisted, warped. His eyes filled with hate and rage. Outlining his body was a pale, red glow.

Cotten wandered through the barn, perusing all the stunning art. She stopped in front of another painting, this one of a child sitting on a cliff at sunset, a brilliant ball of light cupped in her palms. She stared at it. The girl in the painting looked somewhat like Lindsay when she was a child. *Lindsay painting herself as a child? Memories? Imagination?* And like the girl in the painting in Tera's room, she was haloed by a soft, deep violet-blue surrounding. It took Cotten's breath.

But it wasn't only the painting that had caused the reaction—it was the easel—the small easel. A child's.

Chapter Eleven

WINDBREAKER

"Mr. Olsen," Sergeant Carillo said, "we now have over sixty security officers looking for your son. If you'll have a seat in the waiting area, I'll call you the instant he's located."

"Thanks," Alan said and stood. He had started to tell the officer about Devin's . . . *talents*. But he decided they didn't need to know that in order to find the boy. If need be, he would go into detail with the police later. Chances were it wouldn't ever come to that.

Alan sat in the small police substation lobby and watched the officer behind the glass enclosure talk to someone who had lost his wallet. The constant muffled roar of the stadium crowd rumbled in the background.

Devin was his only child. He'd lost his wife six years ago when a drunk driver ran a stop sign as she on her way to pick up their son from daycare. From that moment, the boy became Alan's entire world. If something happened to Devin today, he would never forgive himself.

The door opened, and an officer led a teenager past Alan into the next room. There was blood on the young man's shirt. A fight, Alan thought.

With sixty officers looking for Devin, they would have to find him soon. Even though Dolphin Stadium was huge, it was a contained area with controlled exits. He couldn't stay lost for long.

And then there was the other possibility—one that Alan kept pushing back in the shadows of his thoughts.

What if someone had kidnapped Devin?

"Mr. Olsen?"

Alan looked up as a man in a dark green golf shirt and Dockers slacks stood in the doorway. A gold badge was attached to his belt as was a small automatic in a black holster.

Alan stood. "Have you found Devin?"

"I'm Lieutenant Martinez. Metro-Dade."

Alan shook his hand. "My son?"

"Sir, please come with me."

Alan's stomach tightened as he followed the detective out onto the concourse. Twenty paces later, they stepped into an elevator. As the elevator dropped, the knot in his gut pulled even tighter. When the doors opened, they were in the underbelly of the stadium.

Martinez led Alan along a well-lit corridor to a door labeled *No Admittance*. The detective slid a card through a security lock mechanism, and the door unlocked. He opened the first door in the hallway then motioned Alan into a dark room.

Alan saw they were in the video surveillance center. Dozens of video monitors covered the far wall. All showed live color feeds from cameras throughout the stadium.

Three officers sat at a long table in front of the monitor wall. Martinez guided Alan to a position behind one of the seated officers. "Mr. Olsen, take a look at monitor thirty-three, please," Martinez said. He tapped the shoulder of one of the tech officers at the table. "Rewind that recording for me, again."

A moment later, Alan stared in amazement as the monitor showed him leaning against the wall while he watched the mass of fans flow by. He saw himself turn and speak to a bearded man who had wandered over and stood beside him—the man wore a red windbreaker.

At one point, the guy took hold of Alan's arm. He remembered the guy spouting off a bunch of boring statistics on the history of the Miami

Dolphins. As he thought about it, the man seemed like he was trying awfully hard to keep Alan's attention.

At that moment, the seated officer froze the picture, and a set of numbers on the bottom of the image designated the individual video frame.

"Now take a look at monitor thirty-four, Mr. Olsen," Martinez said. "Watch the left side of the image."

As Alan watched, he saw the exit to the men's room. "There's my son! That's Devin." He pointed to the screen.

Devin Olsen emerged from the exit and turned to his left. The officer froze the picture. The numbers on the bottom of the image matched the frozen image on thirty-three.

"Now, play both in sync," Martinez said to the officer.

As the two images played, Devin walked away from the men's room exit and blended into the crowd. Two boys, who appeared to be slightly older than Devin, followed right behind until they were out of frame. At almost the same instant, the guy beside Alan in the adjacent monitor turned and wandered away, also disappearing into the river of fans.

"I don't understand," Alan said to Martinez. "Where is my son? Where did he go?"

"Mr. Olsen, I'm sorry, but we believe he left the stadium with two other boys."

Alan took a step back. "That's impossible. He would never . . ."

"Mr. Olsen," Martinez said, "please look at monitor fourteen."

Alan followed the detective's gesture. He moved forward and glared at the video monitor labeled 14. It showed the parking lot somewhere outside the stadium.

Alan swallowed hard, unable to believe what the video showed. A wave of nausea swept over him when he clearly saw his son playing a handheld video game while walking with the two boys who had followed Devin from the men's room. A few paces behind was the bearded man in the red windbreaker.

Chapter Twelve

TRUCK STOP

Tera thrashed in her sleep, her breathing rapid as she trembled in her mother's arms.

Lindsay curled behind her daughter and snuggled her. "Shh, baby. It's okay. It's okay," she whispered and stroked Tera's hair.

Soon, the girl settled into slow, rhythmic breaths as she drifted back to sleep. But Lindsay's eyes stayed wide open. She stared out the rear window of the Dodge conversion van. The fold-down seat seemed comfortable at first, but after several hours in the cold, cramped space, she ached. Her limbs were stiff and sore.

Lindsay had spread an old sleeping bag on top of the makeshift bed and used a wedding ring-pattern quilt for warmth. It was a wonder the child could sleep at all with the glare of the lights from the truck stop signs and the never-ending growl of the big diesels as they came and went in the night. But it was cheaper than staying in a motel. Once the cash she had withdrawn from her checking and meager savings accounts ran out, there would be nothing left.

How could it have all wound up like this?

The cause of their flight started two weeks prior, when Tera and Lindsay were grocery shopping. Suddenly, her daughter dropped a bag of fruit and gasped.

"One of them is here, Momma," Tera cried looking up at her mother. "He's here to take me." Her little eyes welled up and spilled over. The tears left shiny streaks down her cheeks. "I don't want to go."

Lindsay held Tera. "You're not going anywhere, baby. No one can ever take you from me. Not ever." She rocked back and forth, holding her daughter so close she felt both their heartbeats.

As she consoled Tera, Lindsay caught sight of a man at the end of the aisle. He was tall, gaunt, with a shock of snow-white hair. He appeared to be watching them. When he saw Lindsay's stare, he turned and walked away.

Lindsay had learned long ago that Tera saw and intuited things. In Tera's earliest years, Lindsay and her husband found it amusing, almost entertaining. Sometimes Tera would tell her mother that the kitties were at the door waiting to be fed. The door would be closed, but when Lindsay went to look, sure enough, Bogey and Bacall would be waiting for their dinner. Or, Tera would take Lindsay or Neil's cellphone to them seconds before it would ring. She did the same thing with the landline. She'd stand beside it with her hand on the receiver. And from the time Tera could compose sentences, she talked about Heaven and how she had one day looked down on Earth and chosen Lindsay and Neil as her parents.

If not for Tera, they would never have joined the local church. Before Tera showed signs of her talents, Neil and Lindsay had no interest in religion. God was never a part of their lives.

But as Tera grew, she seemed to communicate directly with God. It wasn't that Tera told them to join a church. She hadn't. It was rather that Neil and Lindsay sought answers about their remarkable daughter and hoped to find them there.

Tera's talents grew more thought provoking as she got older, and as others noticed, she became regarded as strange, peculiar—an oddity.

About three weeks after Tera started kindergarten, Lindsay got called in for a conference.

"Tera is a lovely little girl," the teacher said. "She is certainly bright. Even gifted. And her artwork is amazing. But Mrs. Jordan, we are having a little problem with her. Sometimes Tera frightens the other children."

"Frightens?"

"Well, she, um, says inappropriate things to them or tells them things that upset them."

Lindsay sat numbly. "What do you mean? What kind of things?

"Like today. She asked a classmate why his father had drowned all their puppies. The boy argued that the puppies got sick and died. But Tera insisted until he ended up terribly upset and crying. His mother came in, and as you can imagine she was disturbed. She told me that their family is financially struggling right now and couldn't afford to feed a litter of pups. Her husband had done what he had to do. But they didn't want their son to know. He is too young to grasp what had happened." The teacher shook her head. "I don't understand how Tera—"

"I'm so sorry," Lindsay said. She wasn't sure what else to say or how she could explain. All she wanted to do was run home and enfold her daughter in her arms.

"And there have been a few other instances," the teacher continued. "But not quite as upsetting as the latest incident. I thought you would want to know so you can talk to Tera."

"Yes, I will. I'll do that. Thank you."

"Most everyone around here knows you and Tera, but you have to realize the boy and his family moved here recently. His mother wanted to know who Tera was. She asked for your address and phone number. But it's against policy to give out that information."

"I appreciate that." Lindsay hoped she would not have to confront the mother. The woman would never understand about Tera.

Afterward, Lindsay did talk to Tera, but it was hard for her daughter to comprehend there was a problem with something that seemed to come so naturally to her.

A year later, there was a similar conference with another teacher, but that wasn't what drove Lindsay to withdraw her daughter from public school and start home schooling. She made that decision on Tera's seventh birthday. She had sent out a birthday party invitation to every child in Tera's class.

No one came.

Lindsay's heart broke for her baby girl. She promised to shield her from the rest of the world—a world unready and unwilling to deal with a child like Tera.

Besides becoming aware that Tera was special and had incredible gifts, Lindsay also learned to trust her daughter's insights. If Tera said someone was in that grocery store to take her away, Lindsay suspected she was telling the truth.

Lindsay thought back. After seeing the tall, gaunt man at the end of the grocery store aisle, she had grabbed Tera's hand and left, abandoning the half-filled cart. As they were about to pass through the doors, Tera hesitated and turned to stare into the store.

Lindsay looked back in response. He was there, standing to the side of the checkout counter, watching.

"Hurry," Lindsay said and tugged her daughter's hand to lead her to their van.

As Lindsay had driven along the main highway that day to go home, she had checked her rearview mirror. A silver car followed. It was never close enough for her to see the driver. Her instinct told her not to go home. She turned along a road that headed in the opposite direction from her farm.

The car followed.

Lindsay made another turn toward the local Wal-Mart.

Again, the car followed. Then it dropped back. The driver must have sensed Lindsay's suspicion. The silver car turned off onto a side road. Slowly, as it headed away, the car finally disappeared.

For days after the grocery store incident, Lindsay kept a vigil at the window, anticipating the silver car to ramble down the dirt driveway. Then, one night Lindsay awoke from a frightening dream. In the dream, she had walked to the end of the drive to take the garbage out for roadside for pick up the next day. It was near twilight, in that nether realm, right before daylight surrenders to the night. A sound made her look down the road. The silver car raced toward her, then turned onto Lindsay's drive, passed her, leaving Lindsay behind in terror. She ran, but as often happens in dreams, Lindsay's legs didn't respond, and she fought for every sluggish step. Before she could reach the house, two men in black suits carried Tera to the car. One man threw the girl in the rear seat, her arms tied behind her back. He climbed in with her, and the other took the driver's seat.

"Momma," Tera screamed before her next cry was muffled then silenced. The car sped off and passed Lindsay again but in the opposite direction, spraying grit and dust in her eyes. The dream came to an abrupt halt, and Lindsay sat up in bed, her mouth and throat dry, as if she had breathed in the cloud of dust.

Lindsay shot to her feet and scrambled to Tera's room, relieved to find her daughter safe and sleeping. She crawled in next to Tera and held her.

Not long after that night, Tera had stared out the window and told her that someone was coming for her. That's when Lindsay called Cotten.

She covered every window after locking them all. Neither Lindsay nor Tera left the house, living on the food stored in the pantry and freezer. She had not even taken the garbage to the roadside.

Out of supplies and terrified that at any moment someone would come and rip Tera from her, Lindsay decided she could no longer wait on Cotten.

Lindsay and Tera slipped out of the house in the middle of the night with only a few hastily packed items and headed south. She drove straight through the night and stopped only for short breaks to stretch and fill up with gas. In the late afternoon, Lindsay pulled into a truck stop in Brunswick, Georgia.

Now, as she lay with Tera in the back of the van, the midnight cold seeped into her and reminded Lindsay of the chill of being followed that day not so long ago. Since the incident in the supermarket, she had tried countless times to figure out who would want to take Tera. And why? If she knew, then maybe she would know how to fight for her daughter. Until then, they would stay on the run. Hopefully, Cotten would find her note and come searching for them.

The monotonous on-off cycle of the red neon truck stop sign reminded her of what happened when she and Tera had arrived home the day they were followed from the grocery store.

"You okay, baby?" Lindsay had asked.

"He was ruby," Tera said, so low that Lindsay wasn't sure she heard right. Tera's gaze had left the window to find her mother's eyes. "That man in the store. He was ruby red. Like Pastor Albrecht."

Chapter Thirteen

ARRIVAL

"This is it." Cotten pulled the rental into the dirt drive of Lindsay Jordan's farm.

John Tyler sat beside her. "You're right," he said. "Doesn't look like anyone's taken care of the place in quite a while."

Cotten had gone to Louisville to pick up John after spending the previous afternoon searching the barn and farmhouse again for additional clues to Lindsay and Tera's whereabouts. Once she realized an eight-year-old girl created the artwork and poetry, their lifestyle and sudden disappearance became even more of a mystery.

On the drive from the city to the farm community of Loretto, Cotten and John discussed every detail of what she had discovered. She showed him the note from Lindsay that said they could wait no longer for Cotten and had already fled.

It took many miles before Cotten had calmed her nerves at seeing John for the first time in almost a year.

She had waited like a schoolgirl with butterflies of anticipation until she saw him emerge from the crowd of arriving passengers. When he took off his sunglasses, she stared into those deep ocean-blue eyes.

"You look wonderful," John said.

She tilted her head, taking in all of him and smiling. "Not too bad, yourself." The urge to cry with happiness swelled, and she pushed it back into the secret place, deep inside, where it lived. Her words felt forced as she struggled to make light conversation. "I thought you'd be decked out in your official cardinal's robes and a gold cross around your neck. Instead, you show up in jeans and a polo shirt. What must the ranks of Heaven think of you?"

John smiled warmly. "They're all preoccupied with much more important matters." He took her hands in his. "So, Cotten Stone, how are you?"

"I'm wonderful now that you're here. But I feel guilty pulling you away from real work and making you come to this out-of-the-way place. After all, this may turn out to be nothing but a wasted trip."

"I'm here because you're here," he said. He wrapped his arms around her. "I wanted to see you, mystery or not."

She hugged him back then put her palm to his cheek. "Thank you." For a moment she felt frozen, her eyes locked on his as if she couldn't look away—didn't want to look away—deliciously drowning in the sea of blue.

When she met John seven years ago, he was teaching biblical archaeology at a small college in upstate New York. She sought his expertise in identifying an ancient relic that was thought to be the Cup used to collect the blood of Christ at the Crucifixion. Working together they delivered it to the Vatican after stopping a plot to use the human DNA from residue found in the Cup to clone Christ. The Grail Conspiracy thrust John and Cotten into the harsh limelight of notoriety.

John was called to Rome and appointed by the Holy Father as prelate of the Pontifical Commission for Sacred Archeology. He was soon consecrated a bishop.

Cotten became senior investigative correspondent for the Satellite News Network specializing in religious antiquities. Over the years, she and John embarked on a number of adventures, including uncovering a new cache of ancient scrolls in caves near the Dead Sea, and in Jerusalem they oversaw the discovery of the thirty pieces of silver that Judas Iscariot was paid to betray Christ.

The two worked together to locate a five-thousand-year-old crystal tablet some believed was inscribed by the hand of God and contained a secret to entering the Kingdom of Heaven. During that adventure, John revealed to Cotten that he had been given the role of director of the Venatori, the intelligence-gathering arm of the Vatican, and arguably the oldest spy organization on Earth. In taking on the duty as head of the Venatori, he was again elevated by the pope, this time being named a cardinal.

Cotten had fallen in love with John, probably from the moment they met, and although he could not act upon it, he had professed his love for her as well.

With every stolen glance at John on their ride to Loretto, she knew in her heart more than ever how much he meant to her.

Cotten shut off the engine, and the sound of the tires crunching on dirt and gravel stopped. "Why don't we start with the barn? You're going to be amazed."

John nodded, and they got out. She led the way down the hard-packed dirt path. Once inside, they went from painting to painting, pausing before each. "Can you believe an eight-year-old child did this?" Cotten took John to the special painting in the back of the barn, the portrait of the man with the evil eyes and red glow. "What do you make of it?"

"Scary," John said. "I can't imagine what could have been going on in a child's mind to create something so sinister and evil."

When they finished exploring the barn, they went inside the farmhouse. Cotten showed him how the windows had been draped and sealed with heavy tape. She had already removed most. The smelly garbage was gone, and she had done light cleaning and dishwashing. She pointed to the closet where the garbage had been stored. A slight odor lingered like something long dead.

"This is fascinating," he said as he stood in Tera's bedroom. "Such ambiguity and contrast." He motioned to the ballerina bedspread and other evidence that a little girl lived here, yet she was surrounded by so much magnificent artwork. "Tera is an extraordinary child. There's no doubt that something unusual has happened here. And that they are in some sort of danger. The question is why and from whom."

"Follow me." She led him into the living room. Once they sat on the couch, she pushed the play button on Lindsay's old answering machine, and the message from Pastor Albrecht blared from the small speaker.

"Outburst at church?" John said once the recording ended. "Wonder what caused that?"

"Good question." Cotten watched him pick up the pile of mail from the coffee table. "There's not much to go on."

"I don't know. Maybe." He opened the MasterCard statement and looked at the charges. Then he pulled his cell phone from the leather belt holster and pressed a speed dial number. A moment later, he said, "This is John. Please, do me a favor and run a trace on a credit card. Charges in the last seven days." He gave the card number then waited for a moment. "Okay, call me back." He looked at Cotten. "Tracing Lindsay's purchases might help us establish her trail and find out where she is." He folded the statement and put it in his pocket.

"So, mister secret agent man, where would you like to begin?"

"That's easy," John said. He stood. "We'll go have a chat with the good Pastor Albrecht."

Chapter Fourteen

A SHADOW IN THE FOREST

Benjamin Ray stood on the bank of Cold Springs Lake at sunrise. Purple coneflowers and late-blooming white aster covered the ground under the thick maples and basswood. A morning mist lay across the water like a gossamer quilt—not a breath of air moved a leaf or caused a ripple.

A faint snap came from Ben's right. His pulse jumped as he halted. He turned his head and looked into the eyes of a doe standing only ten feet away. For a few seconds, he wondered who the real deer in the headlights was. Even after three months of hiding in the Ozark Mountains, his nerves were still raw. He had hoped that once he started venturing out from the remote cabin on his early morning walks, he would be able to stop looking over his shoulder. But then, why would anyone come hunting for him?

Seeming to sense no danger from the bald, heavyset man, the deer turned and walked back into the thick brush, her coat blending with the forest as she disappeared.

A shadow in the forest. Like me, Ben thought.

He had secretly arranged for the purchase of the cabin and surrounding eighty acres a few months before the federal indictment was filed. Always pays to plan ahead. It was just about the time everything started falling apart. His partner referred to it as the wheels coming off the wagon—the collapse of Presidium Health Care, their chain of ninety-seven for-profit hospitals and extended-care facilities across the country. After filing for bankruptcy, investigators discovered that Ray and his partner had inflated profits and concealed more than a billion dollars of debt. Thousands of their employees lost their jobs, and many thousands more lost their life savings. His partner was sentenced to forty years for multiple counts of fraud and conspiracy, the same sentence Ben faced before "dying" of advanced coronary artery disease. The truth is, he did have heart disease and was getting his medication mailed to him under the name Ben Jackson from a pharmacy in Tijuana. Same name that was on his driver's license, the title to his Jeep, and the deed to the cabin. It was amazing what money could buy—a death certificate, not too hard to come by in your own medical facility by a doctor on your payroll, and of course followed by a speedy cremation. He often wondered what was really inside his funeral urn. *Every man has his price.* Ben remembered his father swore by that adage. It was the understatement of a lifetime.

After the first month of total isolation, Ben started taking morning walks. All the family vacations in Aspen and St. Moritz had given him a great love of the mountains and forest. He and his wife of thirty years enjoyed hiking and camping. She would like it here if she knew he was alive. He regretted her not knowing, but this way, if he was ever caught, she could not be held as an accomplice.

Ben's cabin was roomy and comfortable. At great expense, he had arranged for electricity, running water and satellite TV. There was a new Wrangler in the carport and a great deal of cash hidden in a basement water heater. Actually, there were two heaters—one brand new and environmentally efficient—the other old and rusty, pushed like an afterthought into a nearby corner. Ben told the plumber he didn't need it hauled off, saying he planned to convert it into a planter. Now, it contained more than two million dollars in mixed denominations.

He had spent that much just on living-room furniture in his Ocean Drive, Palm Beach, winter home, Ben thought with a chuckle as he turned away from the tranquil Cold Springs Lake to head back. The woods were thick as he made his way along an embankment down into a rocky ravine. He remembered taking this path once before. A few hundred yards beyond the other side of the ravine, the forest opened to a serene meadow filled with the last of the blooming wildflowers and tall autumn-gold grass. At the far edge of the meadow, an old dirt logging road led past the rear of his property. From there he was only a short walk to his morning reward: fresh coffee and scrambled eggs.

For now, he was a shadow in the forest.

As he crested the opposite side of the ravine, he heard an approaching vehicle. A rare event this deep in the woods.

A white panel van came into view along the logging road. It ground to a halt. The driver's door flew open, and a bearded man in a red windbreaker jumped to the ground.

"I've had just about enough out of you," he yelled as he slid open the side door.

Ben hid behind the trunk of a thick maple tree and watched as the man grabbed what appeared to be a young boy from the floor of the van. He pulled him out and dropped the boy onto the side of the dirt road. The kid was blindfolded, and his hands were bound behind his back.

"Stand the hell up," the man ordered. He yanked the boy to his feet.

Ben's impulse was to approach the man and ask him what was going on. *I might be guilty of a white-collar crime, but that doesn't mean I have no conscience.* Still, he didn't dare risk his anonymity by getting involved. At this point all he could do was watch. Damn, he thought. What kind of man have I become?

The driver untied the boy's hands and pushed him around to the back of the panel van. "Hurry up and pee—you've already made us late." The blindfold remained on.

Ben felt a cheap sense of relief. The guy was annoyed but wasn't going to hurt the kid. At least not right now.

The boy fumbled with his zipper and relieved himself. As soon as he finished and zipped up his jeans, the man forced the boy's arms behind his back and re-secured them. He guided the boy to the side of the van and shoved him in, then slammed the sliding door shut. Back in the cab, the man closed the driver's door, put the van in gear, and continued on down the logging road.

Ben stepped from behind the tree and moved across the meadow to where the van had stopped—the sound of the engine already faded on the wind through the autumn leaves.

The road was rarely used—the tire marks left by the van were the only noticeable tracks. Ben glanced down at the dark spot in the dirt where the boy had urinated. What was that all about? *Why in hell did I have to witness a kidnapped kid being bullied and mistreated by an asshole?* The earnest sense of shame clutched up in his chest. *Ben Ray, I don't even know you anymore.*

Ben put the fingertips of his right hand over his carotid and felt his stuttering pulse. He couldn't think about what just happened. He had to get back to the safety of his cabin.

Taking several deep breaths, he concentrated on relaxing. After a few moments, he calmed down and was ready to head home. The last thing he needed was to come in contact with anyone.

When he had first moved into the cabin, he had shaved his head, mustache, and goatee. He started wearing thick-rimmed glasses. He'd even called up a hint of his mother's Virginian southern accent. It was important to blend. But it wouldn't take a Columbo and a few probing questions about his background to raise suspicion. He had fabricated his history and rehearsed it often, but if pressed and stretched, he was certain it would tear. As far as the locals knew, he was a retired banking executive from Atlanta. The simple fact was that he couldn't afford any amount of time with the authorities or anyone else who might scrutinize him if he wanted to keep from spending the rest of his life in prison.

Reporting what he had just seen on the old logging road was out of the question.

Ben massaged the back of his neck before he looked around. He wondered where the road led. He had never followed it. No matter.

The van and the boy were gone.

He took a last look around then crossed the road and entered the woods.

Like a shadow in the forest.

Chapter Fifteen

VIGILANCE

"Welcome, Sister Stone." Pastor Albrecht extended his hand. "The Almighty is so pleased to have such a notable daughter of Loretto come and visit His holy house."

"Thank you, pastor." Cotten shook his hand as they stood in the old brick Church of the Risen Savior. "I'd like you to meet John Tyler, a friend of mine."

"Brother Tyler, so nice to see you," Albrecht said. "I must say you look somewhat familiar."

"I have one of those faces, Reverend Albrecht. It's my curse in life."

"Well, I can sure think of worse crosses to bear." Albrecht motioned to the front row of pews. "Please, be seated and tell me how I can be of assistance."

Cotten savored the smells of the old church—the heaviness of the dark cherry paneling, the sweetness of half-spent candles, and the fragrance of fresh-cut flowers around the sanctuary. A soft rainbow prism streamed from the stained glass windows and radiated across the pews. The old wood creaked when she and John sat. Although she had never been inside this church, she remembered watching it bathed in early morning mist as she glanced at it through the window of the county school bus.

"I'd like to talk to you about Lindsay and Tera Jordan," Cotten said. "I received—"

"How are those two sisters of God?" Albrecht remained standing, as if he were about to give his next sermon.

"Well, that's just it. I received a call from Lindsay recently in which she expressed concern for the safety of her daughter. She asked me to come to Loretto and help her ease those concerns. Once I—"

"Actually," Albrecht said, "there was an unfortunate incident not too long ago that might have upset Lindsay. I sincerely hope it didn't. But you know, it occurred right here where you're sitting."

"Why don't you tell us what happened?" Cotten said.

"By all means, Sister Stone." Albrecht opened his arms in a grand gesture Cotten knew he had rehearsed in front of a mirror a thousand times. "As you may have heard, I am new to this congregation. It was only my second Sunday service when Lindsay and her beautiful daughter entered the church and took their seats right there." He pointed to Cotten and John. "I was in the sacristy making my final preparations for our ten-thirty service. As our small, but dedicated, choir began their opening hymn, I walked out to the middle of the sanctuary to lead the congregation in song. I recall looking down at the faces of those in the front row, and it was at that point that the young lady met my welcoming gaze. Suddenly, she emitted the most blood-curdling scream I have ever had the misfortune of hearing. I must tell you, it seemed to come from the very depths of Hades."

"What was Lindsay's reaction?" Cotten became increasingly uncomfortable in the presence of Albrecht. The term *snake oil salesman* came to mind.

"Her mother tried unsuccessfully to calm the girl, but the child had become hysterical. There was no soothing her. The poor creature had to be removed from the church by two of our larger male parishioners. It was a most unsettling and embarrassing experience for all concerned."

"Why do you think it happened?" Cotten asked.

"I have absolutely no idea, Sister Stone. Even as I recall it now, I tremble."

"Were there any other instances of an outburst like this? From Tera or anyone else?"

"No. None whatsoever. It was a one-time occurrence, I can assure you. We are all at a loss as to what could have provoked the incident."

"You've been helpful, Reverend Albrecht." Cotten stood, John following her lead. "We appreciate your time."

"I really don't know what I've done to help except to describe an awkward event for that poor child. I have tried to contact Lindsay and ask if I could minister to her and her child. I've left messages, but she has not returned my call."

"Apparently, they've left the area," Cotten said. "Can you think of any reason why they would feel that leaving town was necessary?"

Albrecht shook his head. "I'm afraid not unless it's the embarrassment. Unfortunately, Tera's outburst was the talk of the town. But I do hope that wherever they are, Lindsay can get help for that pitiful child."

She shook Albrecht's hand and turned to walk down the aisle.

As John followed, Albrecht said, "You're a mighty quiet man, Brother Tyler. But I believe there is a storm of thoughts going on in your mind. May I ask you a personal question?"

John turned and faced the minister. "Of course."

"Do you believe in the devil?"

Cotten watched as John's face hardened, his eyes darkened, and his body tensed.

"Yes, I do."

"Good. Remember that Peter said, 'Be ever vigilant.'"

"Thank you for that advice, Pastor Albrecht."

As they walked down the steps to the Church of the Risen Savior and headed for the car, John said, "He just couldn't resist playing his cards."

Chapter Sixteen

CYBERSYS

Alan Olsen stood in his downtown Miami office and stared out the window at Biscayne Bay in the distance. Twenty stories below, members of his staff and others from surrounding businesses wandered across Biscayne Boulevard and over the lush carpet of grass to spend a relaxing lunch break near the water. His hands balled into fists as he realized all of them were going about their normal day while Devin was still missing. Gone for four days. Disappeared in the parking lot of Dolphin Stadium as seventy-five thousand fans cheered inside.

He propped one hand on the glass and leaned on it. Even his work was no distraction.

"Alan, are you sure there is nothing I can get you?" Kai Chiang stood behind him and massaged his shoulders.

Alan didn't turn to face her but saw her reflection in the glass. Porcelain skin, black almond eyes rimmed with long lashes, and long, straight black hair that shone like onyx under light. She had joined CyberSys six months ago as his personal assistant, but their relationship quickly became physical, with all the passion and recklessness of teens in the back seat of a car. She was his first love affair since the death of his wife. Kai made no demands on Alan and was not a clinger. She was there when he needed her, no questions, and he found he needed her more and more, especially since Devin's disappearance. To her, Alan confided his deepest thoughts, not only about business but also about his personal life.

Kai pressed her body against his back and wrapped her arms around him. She kissed his shoulder and neck. "I wish I could do something."

"You are."

"You still have the two o'clock meeting. They called a few minutes ago and wanted to know if you were up to it. They would understand if you wanted to cancel. I said I would check and get right back to them."

A long spiraling breath came from Alan. "No, I'll be fine. Maybe it will get my mind off Devin."

Kai reached beneath Alan's suit jacket and scratched his back with her long red nails, then pulled away. "I'll tell them the meeting is on."

When Alan heard the click of the door closing, he wandered to his desk and sat down. Inlaid in the desktop was the blue thunderbolt logo behind the CyberSys name. He remembered choosing the color shortly after learning of Devin's condition. If only news of Devin's whereabouts would come as fast as the idea for the design of Alan's famous corporate symbol. This waiting—the not knowing—was ripping him apart. Miami-Dade police negotiation specialists and detectives were encamped in his private conference room. If Devin had been kidnapped, they were prepared for the ransom call. Alan was rich. Extremely rich. And he had received his share of threats and crank calls.

As founder and president of CyberSys, Alan had amassed a personal fortune in the hundreds of millions directing the development of high-speed encryption technology for government security systems. His programs, produced by CyberSys engineers, were used by U.S. government agencies worldwide, and his team's research into the latest quantum computing hardware was getting closer each day to building the first working model of the elusive supercomputer.

As yet, there had been no calls or demands, and the police had no leads, no information, nothing. Nothing but the blurry parking lot surveillance recording of a white panel truck leaving with Devin inside.

They had issued a statewide Amber Alert, but he'd had to force them to do so by calling on friends in the government. A Florida State representative happened to be his neighbor and helped put the pressure on law enforcement to issue the alert. The reason they had hesitated was their insistence that Devin had appeared to leave the stadium voluntarily. There was no physical evidence of abduction or threat on the video. Devin was playing a hand-held video game and seemed to go with the two older boys without a sign of an argument or resistance.

That was bullshit!

Yes, Devin was…different. His diagnosis was a specialized form of autism—specifically a rare type that produced prodigious skills. Devin could recite or write and solve complex mathematical equations—some that covered hundreds of pages. He could list every city in every telephone area code and Zip code.

It was no challenge for him to identify most classical music compositions after listening to only a few bars and tell the date the music was written and the composer's birth date and place of birth and death. By the time he was seven, he had read more than four thousand books and could recite the contents of any page from memory. His doctors called him an autistic savant. Alan simply called his son's talents a great gift.

Devin lived with extraordinary ability and disability. He was resistant to change, had difficulty expressing his needs, and had no real fear of danger. One of the most prominent symptoms of his autism was poor social interaction. Even as a baby, he had stiffened when someone held him. Devin would have never voluntarily left the stadium with a stranger. That would be out of character for him. A thought snapped into Alan's mind. *Unless he was lured. Like by giving him a chance to play a video game…*

Alan glanced across his penthouse office through a door to an adjoining room, a playroom for Devin with a small desk in the far corner—one he had set up for Devin where his son would come and spend the afternoon after school. Devin loved to play video games, so Alan had his favorites installed on the CyberSys central server and placed a work-station on the boy's desk. Even now, he could picture his son sitting at the desk for countless hours, engrossed in war games, his favorites. Devin even had his father show him how to access and view the code engines that made the games work. To the amazement of the CyberSys senior engineers, he could recite any portion of the code back to Alan.

Devin was special, loved . . . and missing. Yes, lured by a video game made sense. But that meant what Alan feared the most—kidnapping.

Once again, he went to the window. A cruise ship navigated Government Cut leading from the Atlantic into the Port of Miami. Traffic along the MacArthur Causeway shimmered in the South Florida sun. The high-rises along Miami Beach formed a jagged spine along the horizon.

Life went on.

Alan was imploding. All he ever wanted was for Devin to live a normal life. He despised the label of autistic savant and everyone's quick association with the character in *Rain Man*.

There was one other label attached to his son, one that he chose not to mention to the police. The one that had inspired the color of the corporate thunderbolt logo.

Indigo.

Chapter Seventeen

MAGIC KINGDOM

Daylight seeped through the blind's slats and formed a ladder of light on the van window. Lindsay squinted then rubbed her eyes. Sleep had been nearly impossible. The grumbling engines of eighteen-wheelers pulling in and out of the truck stop had gone on all night, but at dawn the number rose substantially as the big rigs got on their way.

Lindsay sat up and rolled her head to stretch the tight muscles in her neck. When they left Loretto, she hadn't been certain where they were going, only that they needed to leave and not come back. During their all-night journey, she decided on what might be the safest place for Tera. She had heard an old saying that to keep something from being found, hide it in plain sight. So, she would take Tera to a place where she was surrounded by thousands of kids.

"Wake up, sleepyhead," Lindsay said. At least her baby girl had been able to sleep. She swept Tera's hair from her face. "We've got to get this show on the road. I have a surprise for you."

"What?" Tera's voice was soft with sleep.

"You'll see."

"My throat hurts."

Lindsay pressed her palm to Tera's forehead. Warm. She grabbed her purse and fumbled through it until she found a bottle of Tylenol. She dumped one tablet into her palm then retrieved a half-consumed bottle of water from the drink holder.

"Okay, lazybones, swallow this, then we'll go take a shower. You'll feel better."

Later, inside the truck stop travel center, Lindsay bought toiletry essentials she had forgotten to pack in the frenzy of leaving their farmhouse. She paid $2.00 for a shower and a towel.

"Can I have one towel more for my daughter?" Lindsay asked the clerk. "You only paid for one shower."

"Please," Lindsay said.

The clerk stared at her for a minute, then acquiesced.

"Thanks."

The multi-showers were self-contained, each with a small dry area to dress.

"All right, Ladybug," Lindsay said. "Off with your jammies."

Lindsay adjusted the temperature of the shower then stepped in the stall. Tera followed.

"Like camping, isn't it?" Lindsay said and lathered shampoo in her hair. Over the rush of the cascading water, she heard a sound like the door rattled. She rinsed the shampoo from her hair and face so she could see her surroundings.

"Tera?" She reached out to touch her daughter with one hand while she wiped the water from her eyes with the other. Her daughter was safe, blowing soap bubbles from the ring she made with her thumb and forefinger.

Paranoia runs deep, Lindsay thought.

***

"Feeling better?" Lindsay asked through the van window as she finished filling the tank with gas.

Tera nodded. "Where are we going?"

Lindsay climbed in and turned on the ignition. "If you could go anywhere, where would that be?"

"Heaven," Tera said.

Lindsay's heart stammered, and she felt the blood drain from her face. "No, baby," she said. Her voice lacked the exhilaration it had a moment before. "I mean if we could go on a vacation, a really wonderful place, where would you want to go?"

Tera's face beamed. "Disney World."

Lindsay pulled out onto the Interstate. "Then Disney World it is."

Tera clapped her hands. "Yay, Disney World!"

The sight of Tera's excitement sent a flurry of emotions through her mother. Lindsay didn't get too many glimpses of her daughter being simply a happy little girl, and so she cherished this fleeting moment.

By afternoon, they reached Orlando. It seemed like the whole area was a theme park, lit from corner to corner with neon, strobe, and animation. Every store, every gas station, motel, and restaurant along International Drive competed for tourists.

Lindsay pulled into the parking lot of a bungee jumping site. She felt Tera's forehead. It was warmer than it should be, but not too hot. Maybe only the onset of a cold, Lindsay hoped. "How's your throat feel?"

"A little sore."

No more truck stops for now, Lindsay decided. If Tera was getting sick, she needed a good night's sleep and the comfort of a real bed. "Well, here's the deal, Ladybug. We're going to find a nice motel, take a nap, and chill out this afternoon. Then we'll go pick out a Mickey Mouse shirt and hat and get a bite to eat at a totally cool restaurant. And tomorrow, when you feel better, we'll tackle the Magic Kingdom. How does that sound?"

Tera stretched to look out the windows. "I want to go now," she said.

"Me, too. But I think we'd better give your throat a chance to get better. You won't enjoy it as much if you aren't feeling good."

***

Inside the $39.99-a-night room of the Tropical Breeze Motel, the cheapest she could find, Lindsay sat on the end of the bed.

Tera hopped up and started jumping.

"Guess you are feeling better."

Tera bounced higher.

"Hey, you're going to bust your noggin." She grabbed Tera's legs and brought her down. Lindsay tickled her daughter's sides. She loved the sound of Tera's uncontrolled belly laugh.

"Who loves you, Ladybug?"

"You do!"

"That's right." She hugged Tera and kissed the top of her head. A moment of silence passed. Nobody would ever take Tera from her. Nobody.

"After a little nap, we'll find that Mickey shirt and hat." Lindsay pulled down the covers, and they snuggled beneath.

***

Lindsay was awakened by a tap on her shoulder.

"Mom. Momma."

It was Tera's soft voice, nearly a whisper.

Lindsay turned onto her back to see her daughter staring down at her. "Can we go now? My throat hardly hurts at all."

It was 4:48 p.m. on the nightstand clock. "Wow, we must have been tired. I was sleeping hard." Lindsay yawned as she sat up. "Are you ready to go shopping?"

Tera's face lit up.

"Let me make one phone call first." Lindsay reached for her cell phone on the nightstand. She took the paper from her pocket that had Cotten's cell number written on it. She made the call and heard the ring at the other end but was disappointed when she reached Cotten's voice mail.

"Hi Cotten, it's Lindsay. I'm sorry I couldn't wait any longer for you. Tera and I had to leave. Hope you found my note. We're in Orlando. I brought Tera to Disney World where she'll blend in with all the other kids. I'm going to try to stay inside the park, but don't know how much it's going to cost or how long I can afford it. I'll call you back with specifics. Please come. I'll find a way to repay your expenses." She paused a moment and wondered if there was something else she should say. She glanced at Tera then said, "Thanks, Cotten."

Lindsay ended the call. "Okay, let's get going." As Lindsay rounded the bed, she noticed a motel notepad and a pencil were on the floor. Several sheets were torn off and scattered about. Tera's sketches. "So, you've been awake for a while."

"Yep."

Lindsay stooped to pick up the papers. "What have we got here?" But before she could collect them, Tera burst from behind her and scooped them all up.

"One of them is a surprise for you," she said.

"What is it?" Lindsay asked. Her lips turned up in a smile.

"There are really two surprises." Tera sorted through her papers "This one." She held out one. "And this one." Tera held a second paper to her heart.

"Oh, Tera," Lindsay said when she finished reading a lovely poem her daughter had written about a mother's love. "Every word is true. I do love you exactly that way. And more."

Tera held out the other piece of paper. Lindsay took it, stared at it, and then her gaze shifted back her daughter. She shook her head, confused and astounded. "Oh, my goodness, Tera? How did you . . .?" She was so astonished by the drawing that she didn't know what to say.

Lindsay set both papers on the dresser and knelt to be at eye-level with her daughter. She held Tera's face in her palms. "You are incredible, Tera Jordan. You always amaze me. And I love your double surprise." Lindsay touched the sketch. "But how do you know what she looks like?"

Tera broke into a wide grin, and her eyes sparkled like the stars in the heavens.

"Because she's my sister. My twin sister."

Chapter Eighteen

THE STORM

Ben Ray leaned against the railing on the front porch of his mountain-side cabin and stared out over the thick forest. Bathed in the vibrant morning sun, the fall leaves turned the valley beyond into myriad tones of orange, red, and yellow. The weather had cooled from the previous day. The chilly autumn temperature made him shiver. From the deck, he watched the wind brush across the valley treetops like a hand through fur.

Ben had tossed and turned for hours during the night. When he closed his eyes, he saw the blindfolded boy, hands tied, being jerked from the van like discarded trash. When he stared into the darkness of his bedroom, he heard the edgy voice of the bearded man in the red windbreaker. The scene played out over and over through the night.

Ben's reaction to the boy made no sense. He was labeled as "the iceman" in the press—the CEO who had stood by and knowingly let the life savings of thousands of hardworking employees turn to vapor while he bled his company dry. He watched the falsely inflated value of the corporation's stock rise like a Roman candle, only to explode and die a quick death. And through it all, he slept soundly every night. But there was something different about what happened in the woods the previous day. Maybe it was because the boy seemed so helpless, blindfolded and standing on shaky legs beside the meadow.

Ben was not proud of what he and his partner did to their company. Happy he was rich and not going to prison, but not proud. Possibly, it was because he never saw the faces of those who went down with the corporate ship. He never saw the face of the boy in the woods, either. But he knew the kid was real. Alone. Helpless.

If he went out and looked for the boy, chances were he would find nothing, anyway. The Ozark National Forest was a big place—more than a million acres.

The road might go on for miles. Maybe the van was only passing through, taking a shortcut.

But what if the boy was in real danger? Would it be worth the risk to try to find him? So far, Ben had stayed hidden from the outside world. He limited his trips into town for supplies and gas to once a month, usually around midmorning on a Monday when everyone was at work. No one seemed to waste time looking at a short, pudgy man minding his own business.

If he searched for the kid that would be outside Ben's game plan. It would take him into the unknown and remove his ability to control his environment. That was not part of his nature. He had to be in control, or control those who were.

A casual drive along the logging road was all Ben would do. Nothing more. It was a big forest, and he was still a shadow in its midst. He turned away from the autumn view.

Dressed in jeans, hiking boots, and long-sleeve T-shirt, he slipped on a jacket before he headed down the stairs. He backed the Wrangler out of the carport then steered up the dirt drive. A half-mile later, he emerged on a two-lane blacktop country road that ran along the border between his property and the National Forest.

He turned east and drove at a leisurely pace, scanning the tree line for the entrance to the logging road. He saw one other vehicle—a green Forestry Service pickup coming from the other direction. The ranger gave him a friendly wave, and he returned the greeting. Ben watched the truck fade in his rearview mirror.

Soon, he caught sight of the turnoff to the logging road. Rarely used, it resembled two parallel ruts with a high grass backbone that disappeared into the dark woods. Ben put the Jeep in four-wheel-drive then left the blacktop.

As he entered the forest, the sun fought to penetrate the trees and created ever-changing patches of light and dark. The woods still retained its brilliant foliage even though most of October had slipped away.

The road threaded through a valley bounded on each side by bluffs and dense underbrush. After ten minutes, Ben found the meadow where he had first seen the white van. He stopped long enough to open his thermos and take a sip of steaming coffee while he listened to the wind and the distant call of a crow. He wondered about the deer he met yesterday along the banks of Cold Springs Lake. It was hunting season.

He closed the thermos and set it in the cup holder before cranking the Jeep and driving on.

The road followed along the floor of the valley. Ben caught glimpses through the trees of the steep mountain slopes that bordered the road. He became aware of rushing water and soon came upon a small, swift stream that flowed parallel to the road. The water swept over rocks and deadfall in the same direction he traveled, telling him he was headed in a gradual downward grade.

After a mile, the road made a sharp turn away from the stream. The sound of cascading water faded into the sudden rush of wind overhead. It was then that Ben realized the sky had darkened. Out the window, he spied charcoal gray clouds through a break in the trees. A fast-moving mountain storm threatened.

Ben debated whether to continue on or head back. If the weather got nasty, he didn't want to get caught so far from home.

Soon, a light rain fell. He'd driven about five miles, he figured, since he left the blacktop. Through the steady drizzle, the mountains grew darker. He was about to turn around when he spotted a tall, chain-link fence ahead on the left. The logging road ran along the perimeter of the fence. When he got near, he saw the fence was old and falling apart. The concertina security wire that had once spiraled along the top had snapped in many places and sagged or fallen to the ground. Corroded and barely readable, a metal sign attached to the fence bore the warning: *No Trespassing. U.S. Government Property.*

Ben drove on through the light rain until he noticed a clearing on the other side of the fence, and he came to a gate. The logging road continued past the gate and disappeared into the woods beyond.

At the gate, he looked for any evidence that the van had passed through or continued on. If there were tracks from a vehicle, the rain washed them away.

On the other side of the gate, a one-man guardhouse stood like a ghost from a bygone era—its wooden frame in disrepair. A snarl of vines had taken over the small structure and seemed to be the only thing that held it together.

A padlock secured the gate. The rain slackened to a light mist, so Ben shut off the engine and got out for a closer look. The padlock held together the ends of a chain that coiled through the gate frame. Although the chain was old and rusted, the lock appeared fairly new.

He noticed that several of the clamps that fastened a section of the chain link to the metal frame had long ago fallen away. With a lot of effort, he pushed on the mesh and produced a space big enough to slip through. He would just have a quick look around and then move on.

Past the old guardhouse, he followed the dirt road for a hundred yards until a large block-shaped structure loomed out of the drizzle. It stood in the middle of a collection of smaller buildings—perhaps five or six in all. As the details of the buildings became clearer, he saw that all were in as poor a condition as the guardhouse and fence. Most were single-story, wood-frame structures with broken windows and dark, hollow openings for doorways.

The largest of the structures was a windowless concrete building that appeared to be about one hundred feet wide and towered over him. At least three stories high. Paint peeled, gutters and drains slumped, and the entire area was thick with overgrowth.

What had once been a paved road was now dirt, with only small chunks of asphalt remaining. It ran off into the distant forest seeming to indicate there was another entrance. For the most part, weeds and brush had reclaimed it. Perhaps he had entered through a back gate.

Atop the main structure was a radar dish frozen at an odd angle in a paralysis of rust. The building's main entrance was boarded up with plywood. Heavy bolts held the panels in place. The wood bore the dark stains from long-term exposure.

Ben took a few more moments to explore. He wandered around the side of the building and came upon a door with a sign that read *Authorized Personnel Only*. When he tried the knob and it didn't give, Ben moved on to the back of the building where he found another door, this one labeled *Danger. High Voltage*.

The skies opened, and the rain came down in sheets. The wind picked up and roared across the open area. The raindrops turned into pinpoints of pain. Thunder shook the ground as a bolt of lightning struck nearby. He pulled on the door, and it gave way with a resistant groan. Ben stepped inside and shook the rain from his hair and clothes.

He left the door ajar for what little light came in from the dark sky. Thunder cracked again and shook the walls of the huge building. He had entered some kind of utility room. The only entrance was the single door. Mounted on the rear wall was an electrical connection box. It had to be four feet wide and six feet tall. Six thick metal conduits, each about the diameter of a baseball bat, ran from the top of the box and disappeared through the ceiling. He was no electrician, but it was obvious that the building once required a tremendous amount of power.

Like the gate, a padlock also protected the electrical box. He examined it. A Sargent & Greenleaf high-security U.S. government padlock. Heavy duty, indestructible, and as shiny as the day it was made.

Why protect the electric service of an abandoned building with such an expensive lock? Curious, Ben glanced around. Other than the electrical box, the room appeared empty.

Then he saw it.

Mounted high over the door, barely noticeable in the murky light, the tiny red LED on the motion detector stared down at him like the cold eye of a predator.

Chapter Nineteen

HARVEST MOON

Cotten steered the rental out of the church parking lot and back on to Burks Spring Road. "Was the good ole preacher boy's remark about keeping vigilant what I think it was? A warning?" It was getting dark fast, and shadows hung heavy over the rolling Kentucky hills as she switched on the headlights.

John looked over his shoulder at the fading image of the church and said, "That's the way I read it. First, he asks if I believe in the devil to get my mind on that track, and then he makes the vigilant comment. I think that was his way of informing us who we are up against as if that wasn't already becoming clear. He was warning us to back off."

"Puts the nail in the coffin, then. Tera must have somehow recognized Albrecht as being evil. Whatever she saw scared her pretty bad."

"If Albrecht is a member of the Nephilim, or worse, one of the original Fallen, and Tera is able to identify them, then they definitely want her to vanish. And that means she is in grave danger. We can assume that they're already hunting her down. We've got to find her before they do."

Cotten's hands tightened on the wheel. "And they know we're onto them, and that we'll be searching for Lindsay and Tera, too. They'll be hell-bent on stopping us."

She looked over at John who seemed puzzled and distant in thought. "What is it?" Cotten asked. "What are you thinking?"

John laced his fingers and tapped his thumbs together. "There's something else, something more to it, I just can't put my finger on it.

Tera is a unique child, and she may be able to ID the Nephilim and the Fallen, but it doesn't seem like that's enough."

"What do you mean?"

"She's a little girl growing up in the middle of nowhere, so it's not like she'd come across a huge number of *them* out here in the sticks. Her encounter with Albrecht could have been a coincidence. She freaks out when she sees the pastor, so what? The whole town thinks the kid is off kilter. Why would Tera be such a threat to them?"

Cotten smacked her lips in agreement. "You may be right. Maybe that's exactly why Albrecht is way out here in Loretto in the first place."

"Hopefully, when the Venatori office in Washington gets back to me with the credit card info, we'll have an idea where to start."

"I'll give Ted a call and ask for additional time to investigate this."

"Cotten, I can follow up from here if you need to get back to New York."

"I know, but Ted is aware that this is a personal matter. Let me call him first and clear it." She reached to the center console then hesitated. "Check to see if you're sitting on my phone. Or maybe it fell on the floor."

John leaned forward and felt beneath him, then looked down between the seat and the console, then the seat and the door side pocket. "I don't see it."

Cotten ran her hand behind her and on both sides of her seat, then dug in her purse. "I could have sworn I left it in the cup holder on the console to remind me to recharge it while we drive."

John checked around again, including the glove box.

"Must be under your seat or mine," she said. "I'll check when we stop."

"I'm serious about taking it from here," John said. "You don't have to ask for time off."

"No, no, no. Lindsay called me for help. And besides, you know as well as I do that this is what I'm supposed to do with my life—it's my birthright, so to speak. Granted, it's taken long enough for me to come to terms, but I can't deny it any longer."

"Yes, it has taken a long time," John said. "A difficult road for you."

Her eyes stung at the onset of tears. "You were right—it's been quiet way too long. I knew something like this would eventually happen, I just didn't know when. I tried to make myself believe it was over, that I could live a normal life. No more supernatural bullshit." She turned to John. "This is never going to end, is it?"

John brushed a loose strand of Cotten's hair behind her ear. "Let's try to take it one step at a time. So far, we are only speculating. Good speculating, mind you, but no real proof, yet. So whether it's our old adversary we're dealing with here or only the active imagination of a depressed widow and her talented but high-strung daughter, our first goal is to find Lindsay and Tera. Agreed?"

Cotten nodded. She held back the tears. She wiped her eyes, and that was the end of it. The urge to cry wasn't out of self-pity, it was for Lindsay, Tera, and all the friends and acquaintances she had lost along the way.

The introspection was broken when John said, "I hate to change the subject, but my stomach is growling. Hungry?"

Cotten reached for John's hand, and he took it. "Thanks for giving me a few minutes to re-collect and rant. This never gets any easier for me."

"It's not an easy task you've been given. No one expects you to think otherwise, especially me."

She squeezed his hand. "You're hungry. We can go back to Lindsay's and scrounge around for something to eat. But there's not much left in her pantry. There's a diner about a mile from here. Want to try good old country cooking?"

"Sounds perfect." John stared out the window. "What's the claim to fame in your hometown?"

"We're just about to pass it." Cotten motioned up ahead on the right. "They're closed for the evening now, but that's the entrance to Maker's Mark Distillery. They've been making Kentucky straight bourbon there for a long time. Growing up, I used to like the smell of the fermentation when I would ride my bike into town. A poor man's aromatherapy."

"Hmm." He patted her thigh. "You had the potential to become a bourbon aromaholic from an early age?"

"Very funny. I would love an Absolut over ice right now. Not something we'll find at the diner."

"Did you enjoy growing up here?"

"There were great times, many with friends like Lindsay. But once my father died, my mom and I didn't do so well. She suffered from depression after we lost the farm. We moved to Lexington, and she went to work in a textile mill there. After I graduated from the University of Kentucky, I left and never looked back."

Cotten turned into the parking lot of the Goldenrod Grill. "It's not much on ambiance, but the food is good."

Before going in, she searched the car again for her cell phone.

"Maybe you left it at Lindsay's," John said.

"No. Before we went into the church, I checked it to see if I had any messages or missed calls. I'm sure I set it in the drink holder in the front console." She sighed. "Well great." Cotten closed the car door, and they headed for the diner.

Inside, they seated themselves in a booth. The vinyl seats were a mustard-yellow, and the tables were wood, covered with what looked like a half-inch layer of polyurethane. The menu was embedded under the polyurethane.

"Guess the menu never changes," John said.

The waitress brought tall, amber-colored plastic glasses of ice water and straws. "Let me know when you're ready to order," she said in her southern drawl. "Give me a wave." She turned to leave, but then wheeled around and cocked her head. "Well, I'll be dipped. That *is* you, Cotten Stone." She walked closer to the table. "It's me, Caroline. Caroline Duckett. Andy's sister. You dated my brother in eleventh grade."

"Oh, my heavens," Cotten said, realizing the waitress was the younger sister of a high school boyfriend. "Caroline." Cotten got to her feet and hugged the waitress. "I haven't seen you in forever. How is Andy?"

"He's great. Every time he sees you on TV he tells his wife about how you two dated. He thinks it makes her jealous, but I think it just pisses her off."

They all laughed and Cotten scooted back in the booth. "Caroline, this is John Tyler, a friend of mine."

"Pleased to meet you, John."

"Hey, do you remember Lindsay Jordan?" Cotten asked.

"Sure. What a tragedy, Neil dying and all."

Cotten nodded. "Very sad."

"I don't think the child ever recovered from losing her father. Tera is real peculiar. Beautiful little thing, but an odd girl. She didn't fit well in school either, so Lindsay started teaching her at home. I think she's been under a lot of stress trying to do it all."

"I'm sure," Cotten said. "Have you spent much time around Tera?"

"Not really. I hear she's quite an artist. Her mother said that was because Tera was…what did she call her?" Caroline tapped the pencil eraser on her chin. "I remember. An Indigo child, whatever that means.

That's what I've heard." She shook her head. "Small towns don't have much going on, so gossip spreads like wildfire. Believe me, if you strike a match, everybody in Loretto knows it before you can blow it out. Like the fit Tera threw at church a few Sundays ago. Phones were ringing off the hook. That's all you heard folks talk about in here for days. Nobody's seen Lindsay or Tera much since."

"I came to visit Lindsay. But it looks as if she and Tera have left town. In a hurry."

"Wouldn't surprise me. I know they've gone away before. Always came back though. Maybe this time, they'll get a fresh start somewhere, not in a small town."

"Let's hope," Cotten said.

***

When they left the diner, their hunger satisfied with generous portions of country-fried steak, collards, mashed potatoes, and sweet tea, John motioned toward the sky. "The moon looks so much bigger out here in the country."

"That's a harvest moon." Cotten took his arm. "I ordered it up special for you."

"I need to find a place to stay tonight. I saw a sign for the Hill House Bed and Breakfast."

"You'll do no such thing. There's plenty of room at Lindsay's. Discussion closed."

"Well then, I guess I'm staying at the Jordan farm tonight," he said as they got in the rental.

Cotten pulled onto the highway, still annoyed that she had lost her phone. She took her mind off it and peered upward through the windshield. "You're right, that is an amazing moon." The huge orange ball

94

brought back memories of parking on lover's lane many years ago. "Looks like there's a glow on the horizon under the moon."

"Is there a factory or mill out that way?"

Cotten watched the glow in the distant night sky. As they traveled toward it, it grew brighter. Suddenly, she caught the flashing of red lights in her rearview mirror followed by the drone of a siren. She eased the car onto the shoulder as a fire truck roared past, its emergency lights casting a scarlet blanket over the nearby fields. Before Cotten could pull back onto the highway, a second emergency vehicle shot by in the wake of the fire truck.

As they rounded a bend in the highway, Cotten noticed a collection of red and blue emergency lights up ahead. A half dozen fire and police vehicles had converged on the site. Flames bit at the black sky as the huge harvest moon hung above the scene. It seemed to grow brighter, fed by the heat of the fire.

Then it became obvious. Fire engulfed Lindsay's farm.

Chapter Twenty

DEVIL OR ANGEL

Alan sat on the bathroom floor, the image of his son's face burned inside his head. For the past hour he had huddled over the toilet until he thought he would retch up his very insides. Even with nothing left to purge, his body didn't want to relent. The nausea came and went with his thoughts of Devin, like giant sickening waves that rolled over him. Today it had gotten the best of him.

There was a knock on the bathroom door. "Alan?"

"Kai, not now."

She opened the door and came to him. "Sweetheart, I'm only here because I care." She pulled Alan to his feet, undressed him, and helped him into the shower.

He heard the click of the door as she left him alone.

Alan stood under the hot flowing water for a long time, trying to wash away the fear and sorrow as much as the stench from throwing up. He soaped up then rinsed, but stayed under the shower's spray until he thought he was done with vomiting.

Through a heavy fog of steam, he got out, dried off, and slipped on a bathrobe. Then he wandered into the dark bedroom and lay on the bed, exhausted.

He felt Kai join him and pull away his robe. He realized she was naked as she straddled his thighs. She trickled warming massage oil onto his back, then closed the bottle and tossed it next to her. The air became rich with the scent of almond.

"Relax and let me work out some of the tension," she said, spreading the oil. Her thumbs pressed along either side of his spine as she slid them up his back, stretching out long lines of muscle and tendons. "This will make you feel better, I promise. We'll order something for dinner later. For now, let me help you unwind."

"That feels great." Alan sensed the stress and tension abate beneath her hands. He had worried about Devin to the point of numbness, and his mind couldn't think any more. He gave in to this moment of reprieve.

The tingle and warmth and the firm pressure of Kai's hands were a mixed sensation. Alan wasn't sure which he wanted to respond to, the relaxing of his muscles or the mounting sexual arousal. Whichever, it was total respite from the nightmare of the kidnapping.

Kai's magical fingers kneaded his shoulders, then down his upper arms, returning to his neck, then across his shoulder blades. Then she massaged his lower back and flattened out every knot and kink.

When she finished with his back, she dragged her fingers through his hair at his temples, working in circles across his scalp. Alan hadn't noticed how taut his facial muscles had been until he felt them start to relax.

"Are you an angel?" he whispered.

"I am whatever you want me to be."

God, she was good, Alan thought as she slipped down his legs until she sat on his ankles, her perfect ass on his heels. She dribbled a little more of the oil down each of his thighs and calves. Alan not only felt the oil warming at her touch, but he detected her heat resting on his ankles.

After massaging his legs, she feathered her fingertips up and down, from calf to upper back, a fine delicate, pleasing tickle on his skin. She lightly nipped his buttock before urging him to turn over.

"Mm, Mr. Olsen," she said.

***

Alan woke to movement on the bed. He opened one eye and saw Kai climbing in beside him. She was still naked, her hair mussed. He perceived the light scent of soap.

"I was a little on the greasy side. But, don't think I'm complaining." She snuggled next to him. "I'm afraid we've ruined the sheets. I don't think the oil stains will come out."

"Screw the sheets," Alan said.

Kai laughed. "We kind of did."

Alan put his arm around her and drew her closer so her head rested on his shoulder.

"Next time, I give you a massage, we'll spread a beach towel."

He kissed her forehead. "I needed that. Maybe now I can focus."

"I know you can't stop thinking about Devin. For your sanity, it is good for you to take a minute or two to shut out the world." She stroked the soft tuft of hair on his belly.

"I don't get it. No ransom, nothing. I would rather have received some type of demand. At least I'd know what they want, and then I could give it to them. This is more like a pedophile or sicko who hurts kids."

"Don't think like that, Alan."

"I try not to, but it is a possibility."

Kai nuzzled in the crook of his neck. She whispered close to his ear, "I've grown to love him, too, and his father." Alan shifted and so did she, both seeking a more comfortable position. "So far, the kidnappers don't want money, she said. "Thatmight eliminate one motive. It could, God forbid, be a pedophile. What else is there?"

Alan turned and kissed her again. "I haven't told anyone this, but there is one other possibility that scares the hell out of me. It could put Devin in more harm's way than he already is."

"Maybe you shouldn't tell me, either."

"No, I need to talk to somebody who cares about him, who loves him."

Kai caressed his jaw.

"Let me start in the beginning so you can see the whole picture. You already know about Devin's . . . talents. They used to call people like him idiot savants. But there's nothing idiotic about him. Since he was diagnosed, I've spent years studying autism. Most recent theories indicate that in autistic savants who are extreme, like Devin, there is no communication between the left hemisphere of the brain and the right. When normal people, like us, attempt to learn things, our brains are being bombarded with other information, and it searches for connections to past experiences or ways to make generalizations, that kind of thing. There is a lot of interference. But Devin's brain doesn't work like that. He experiences pure learning with no interference. That's why he has a photographic memory.

"Amazing the research you've done."

"There is an abundance of data out there. But what I was getting at is that Devin literally remembers everything he sees, hears, and reads."

"Interesting." Kai lifted her head and looked at Alan. "But what has that got to do with what's scaring you?"

"You know how Devin memorizes books the first time he reads them?"

"Yes."

"And you know he's got a thing for numbers."

"Right. And dates."

"Devin has seen the programming code to the operating system for Destiny, the quantum computer we're working on. And because he's seen it, I know he's memorized it, like he memorizes all the names and numbers in a hundred telephone books."

Kai was silent for a moment. "And?"

99

"What if someone wanted to steal that information? You know we have the tightest security possible at CyberSys. No one is ever allowed to bring in or remove any object from the building not even a paper clip or tissue. You can't wear a watch or wedding ring past the detectors."

He stared up at the ceiling. "But every time Devin comes to see me, he walks out of the building with our most valuable data right in his head. Kai, trust me, when I say that there are people who would do anything to get the Destiny OS code."

"OS?"

"Operating system. You see if we have as much success with Destiny as it appears, it will make all current encryption methods instantly archaic."

"You're talking over my head, darling."

"Sorry. Encryptions are based on mathematics. The more computational difficulty involved, the more difficult to decrypt. It's not that they are impossible to break, it's that they are impossible to break in a reasonable period of time. It would take hundreds, even thousands of years for current computers to decrypt most of the military's most securely encrypted information. Codes that deal with launching nuclear weapons, for instance. Most of the world's security networks, from financial institutions to global positioning satellites, depend on encryptions devised in this manner. The CyberSys computer itself is just hardware—a collection of lasers, ion traps, mirrors, lenses, and photodetectors, all made from metal, silicone, and plastic. You need an operating program to control the hardware and interpret the computing results, like a home PC needs Windows to make the hard drive talk to the modem or the DVD player to communicate with the sound card. If someone knows that Devin has memorized the code to the operating system, after they get what they need from him, there's no reason to keep him alive." Alan stared at her. "Kai, they'll kill my son."

"But you're the only one who knows he has memorized the code."

"I pray that's the case because if not, Devin is as good as dead."

They held each other for a while in uneasy silence. After several minutes, Kai scooted out of bed. "Want to order pizza?" She moved around to his side of the bed and looked down on him with a coquettish arch of her brow. "Drink a little wine, watch a movie? Maybe get tipsy, skinny dip, and fuck like rabbits in the hot tub?"

***

Alan pushed the pizza box off the nightstand so he could see his cell phone and check the caller ID. It was Max Wolf, CyberSys' director of engineering. Alan answered. "What's wrong?"

"Everything, starting with the interaction noise levels."

Alan heard the click of a cigarette lighter. "You're not supposed to be smoking in the lab."

"You want this shit to work or not?"

Alan sat up. "I want you to live long enough to see it work and not blow up my building. Now, what happened?"

"Your idea of using the nitrogen vacancies in the diamond almost worked," Wolf said. "Right up until the whole thing crapped out."

Alan visualized Max with his bushy, walnut-brown hair and wearing one of his hundred Hawaiian shirts, cutoffs, flip-flops, and a perpetual cigarette hanging from his mouth. Alan often found it hard to be in the same room with Max—he was a brilliant scientist, but he reeked of cigarette smoke. Wolf had joined CyberSys right out of MIT. Within six years, he was heading up Alan's quantum computer project, code-named Destiny.

"Suggestions?" Alan asked.

"It's the same old shit. Right now our qubits are turning to junk when we probe with the laser. It all boils down to bad spectral-hole-burning material. Your suggestion of diamonds with impurities was the closest we've come. But no cigar."

"Max, go home. Get some sleep. We'll all meet tomorrow and debrief. I firmly believe we'll find the right material. It's got to be out there somewhere."

"Maybe you're right, Alan. I've had it for tonight."

"Go home, or you're fired."

"You'd just rehire me tomorrow."

Alan ended the call and placed the phone back on the nightstand. He turned to see Kai standing naked by the doorway holding a bottle of wine and two glasses.

She winked and gave him a seductive smile. "I'm feeling more like a devil than an angel."

Chapter Twenty-One

CRASH

"Shit!" Ben stared up at the motion detector. The LED glowed indicating it had sensed his presence. Storm or no storm, it was time to go.

He opened the door enough to slip through. The storm had turned the forest into a combat zone with almost constant strobes of lightning and booming thunder. Ben ran along the side of the building and around the corner toward the road leading to the gate.

"Hey you!" came a yell.

Ben looked over his shoulder to see the white panel van in front of one of the older wooden buildings. The guy in the red windbreaker had gotten out and was yelling for Ben to stop. The man jumped back in the van and put it into gear.

Ben's heart slammed against his chest as he ran along the asphalt road. He could see the guardhouse and gate in the distance—sheets of rain rolled across his vision. Over the sound of the storm, he heard the van approach, its engine racing.

At the gate, Ben pushed through the small opening. A coil of the old concertina wire hung down from the top and cut his bald head like a scalpel. The pain was intense as his foot caught in the fence, and he fell into the mud. He scrambled to his feet, jerked open the door to the Jeep, and hopped in. His hand twisted the key, and the engine cranked. As he turned the Wrangler around, he caught sight of his face in the rearview. Blood ran in rivulets, his head covered in red.

Ben heard the van slide to a halt behind the gate and its bumper slam into the chain link and metal frame.

The forest boomed with thunder, and the wind whipped the trees into a swirl of madness. Ben raced the Jeep along the logging road. He wiped his face on the sleeve of his jacket and saw it come away bright red.

"Damn it!" he screamed and pounded the steering wheel. "I knew it, I knew it." The pressure built in his chest. The deep cut on his head hurt like hell. "This was a God damn mistake!"

The Jeep swished along the muddy road through the torrents of rain. Ben wiped the blood from his face and gritted his teeth. The pain in his chest worsened. Limbs and branches whipped at the Jeep, the wipers barely able to keep up with the downpour.

He passed the stream, now to his left. It rushed by, swollen with the runoff from mountainsides.

Lightheaded, Ben found it hard to steer. The road seemed to split up ahead. He didn't remember there being two roads. Which way? He would follow the one. . .

The airbag blasted Ben back into the seat as the Jeep slid off the road and crashed into the trunk of a huge oak. A second later it deflated. He tried to breathe. His chest burned from the impact of the airbag and the stress on his heart. Through blurry eyes, he saw movement in the rear-view mirror. A white van. A red windbreaker.

Chapter Twenty-Two

BLAZE

The Jordan farm burned. Flames shot skyward before jumping to the surrounding trees and fields. The ancient oak that had provided a century of shade had become a ball of fire, a freak sun that blazed in the night sky. The paintings, the poetry, all traces of Lindsay and Tera Jordan were being erased.

Cotten knew her age-old enemy had just declared war. She slowed down as they approached the entrance to the farm. "What should we do?"

"Keep driving," John said.

"Do you still have doubts about who we're dealing with?"

"None." He had turned in his seat to watch out the rear window. "Let's go a little farther, then double back and make another pass."

"Someone wants all the evidence gone. Especially the painting of Albrecht. Not very flattering with the wicked red glow around his body."

A state police car came from the opposite direction and passed them, lights flashing, siren blasting.

"What do you make of your friend Caroline's comment back at the diner? That Tera was an Indigo child?"

"I've heard the term," Cotten said. "SNN ran a special on gifted children about six months ago. Some of the kids were referred to as Indigos. It has to do with their auras. There are psychics who claim they can see indigo auras surrounding those kids. And it shows up using special photography."

"Kirlian photography—I think they call it."

"Right, that's it."

"If Tera has an indigo aura, then Albrecht must have a red one, John said. "That's what she was painting, Albrecht and his aura. That might be how Tera identifies them. A red aura, how appropriate."

John's cell rang. "Yes," he answered. "No, that's quite all right. What have you got?" He listened intently for a few moments. "Can you make flight arrangements for Ms. Cotten Stone and me? Yes, out of Louisville. As soon as possible. We can be at the airport in a couple of hours." Another pause, then, "Thank you."

"What did they find out?"

"Lindsay purchased gas in Brunswick, Georgia, four days ago. She used her card again at a motel in Orlando the next day."

Cotten thought for a minute. "Nothing after that?"

"No."

"Maybe she has headed to Disney. Think about it, John. What a perfect place to hide Tera. There are millions of kids there. She'd be hard to pick out in a crowd like that. Pretty smart, if that's the case."

"It's going to make it hard for us to find her, too."

Another state trooper flew past. Cotten pulled onto the shoulder of the road. "Ready to go back and take one more look?"

John glanced at the dashboard clock. "I think we got the message. Let's get on to the Louisville airport. Was your luggage at Lindsay's?"

"I didn't even think about that," she said as she drove back onto the roadway.

"We'll pick up whatever you need at the airport or in Orlando."

"Oh, shit," Cotten said.

"It's just material things, Cotten."

She looked at John. "I was thinking about the mother cat and her kittens. I hope they got away."

"I'm sure they did. Animals have an instinct when it comes to fire. They don't hang around."

John's cell rang again. He stared at the caller ID. Then he gave Cotten an expression of bewilderment.

"What's wrong? Who's calling you?" she asked.

"You are."

Chapter Twenty-Three

HADES WORM

"The onion routers are in place," Tor said. "They went online right after the initial flood attack last night."

Tor's face, narrow glasses, short hair, goatee, and pompous smile, filled the video screen as Rizben Mace watched from a windowless, dark-paneled office in the basement of his McLean, Virginia, home. He remembered the first time he met Tor, twenty years ago. Mace was conducting the induction ritual into the Ruby Army of a dozen of the Nephilim, the offspring of Fallen Angels and mortal humans. Tor had been one of the eight-year-olds who received the honor. Mace had chatted with the boy after the ceremony and realized that Tor stood out as brilliant and technically gifted. He had predicted the boy would prove himself a valuable asset in the future.

When Mace was tasked with recruiting special Rubies for the newly conceived Hades Project, Tor was the first candidate who came to mind. He found Tor at a science and technology convention in New York. Now, twenty-eight and a respected scientist, Tor chaired the consortium of two hundred universities in conceptualizing Internet2 and was giving a presentation on the development of optical transmission service beyond one hundred gigabits per second using photonic crystal fiber. When Mace offered him the position as project director, Tor agreed.

As Mace sipped black coffee from a DHS mug and stared at Tor's face in the video monitor, he said, "How long before the e-mails go out?"

"Within the next twenty-four hours, ten million will be sent in the first wave. We've developed about a thousand different packages covering everything from PayPal, eBay, major banks, credit card providers, and discounts from national retailers, even Omaha Steaks and Linens 'n Things. Some are set up as customer satisfaction surveys and credit bureau alerts. Multiple languages are utilized for international targets. Each package is indiscernible from the real thing. We've had them designed to fool even the security experts at the companies we're faking. All the components such as graphics and text are pulled in real-time right from the authentic site. It's the links that are ours. They set the hook."

"The first phase of Hades is the most critical," Mace said. "I have high expectations, Tor." He could see the rows of floor-to-ceiling server banks over Tor's shoulder in the video feed. Like seeing a reflection of a mirror in a mirror, they seemed to go on forever into the stark recesses of the master Hades control center. Tor had once told Mace they could generate more computing power than NASA ever needed to launch the space shuttle—a thousand times more.

"Just don't be clicking on any links in any e-mails for the next few days," Tor said with a grin. "We wouldn't want your home PC infected with the Hades worm."

Mace nodded. "The onion routers will give you total secrecy?"

"Absolute. We are behind three layers of anonymity with 256-blowfish encryption between the layers."

"And you feel confident with the rootkit approach?" Mace asked.

"Completely. The minute the target clicks on any link, including unsubscribe, the rootkit embeds the worm in their system. And we can use cross-site scripting to get them to one of our fake sites. Doesn't matter whether it's Linux, Solaris, Unix, or Windows—even Macs. It can't be detected."

"Have you finalized the launch mechanism?"

"You'll be proud of its amazing simplicity. Like my original proposal stated, all computers go out each day to sync their clocks with government clocks. The Worm's payload remains dormant until we shift the Atomic Clock giving Hades the launch command. All the harvested information from the targets will be placed on floating P2P servers for later retrieval. And like I said, we are completely invisible. Because we're using a distributed, anonymous network, there's no way to trace IP addresses or, for that matter, anything in the header of the messages. Traffic analysis is also impossible. With the multiple layers of the onion routers, it would take a quantum computer to crack us."

"How far are we away from completing our own quantum computer?"

"Sooner than you think. The CyberSys guy's kid is just about finished giving us the code. But he's unpredictable. One minute he's typing away, and the next he's staring at the ceiling and spouting off the names of every professional football player since the dawn of the sport. Depending on his mental state, I believe we're only a few days, maybe a week from starting phase two. I call it information exfiltration and networking entrenching."

"Clever. What about our retired banker friend from the cabin in the woods?"

"What a stroke of luck we had finding him. While he was unconscious, we ran his fingerprints. You'll never guess who he is."

"I give up?"

"Ben Jackson is actually Benjamin Ray."

"I thought he died of a heart attack days before the federal sentencing."

"Faked his own death. Been hiding out in the woods ever since. He's even got a bundle of cash stashed in an old water heater—did have, that is."

"You can't trust anybody these days," Mace said with a smile. "He'll play the part of the desperate kidnapper?"

"Yep. Once we get the final chunk of code from the kid, we take them both back to the cabin. Jackson will compose a ransom note referring to Devin Olsen who happens to be tied up in the basement. An anonymous call will lead the authorities to the cabin where they'll find kidnapper and victim dead of an unfortunate gas leak. Identification confirms that Jackson is the previously departed Benjamin Ray—a man used to living like a king and who became desperate for money. That's why he snatched the kid of a multimillionaire, and it'll explain why a ransom note was never received—Jackson died before he could send it. A sad story with a sad ending."

"You're a genius, Tor."

"I know."

"Are we on track to meet all deadlines?"

"By the time we get to phase five, we will control the global GPS satellite system, time will stand still, communications worldwide will cease, airplanes will fall from the sky, and ICBMs will fuel up."

"And the Hades Project will live up to its name," Mace said. "Good work. Keep me informed." With a farewell nod, he switched off the video feed.

"He is such an excellent choice, Pursan." The voice came from behind him, but Mace knew who spoke. He was rarely called by his Fallen name, and hearing it reminded him of when he once belonged to the Order of Thrones, the highest tier in the celestial hierarchy. Such a loss fanned the flame of bitterness to this day, even though it was ancient history. The Hades Project would give him and all the Fallen sweet revenge.

Mace swiveled around in his chair to greet his visitor. From the far shadowy corner of the room, the Old Man stepped forward. Mace watched him move to a red velvet chair in front of the desk. He ambled as if his joints were rigid. His hair was the color of ash, and his face barely wrinkled and worn—amazing, considering his age. His clothes were black, and there was a general darkness about him, except for his eyes, which glinted like smoldering embers.

When the Old Man sat, Mace said, "You're right, young Tor is perfect. You might remember, I predicted his talents many years ago at his initiation ceremony."

"You've always had good instincts. The girl is still lost?"

"No." Mace held back a smile. "We stole Cotten Stone's cell phone from her car while she and the priest were meeting with Albrecht. We used it to intercept a message from the girl's mother. They are in Orlando. We left her credit card alone so we can track her. She has little liquid resources and only one card, so hopefully she'll keep using it. To punctuate Albrecht's warning, we called the priest's cell from Stone's phone and gave him a warning to back off before things got deadly."

The Old Man's face brightened. "Nice touch." But then his expression darkened. "I am intrigued by this child, this Tera Jordan." He rubbed his nose, sniffing. "It's so chilly in here, Pursan. Can't someone as important as you afford heating?"

Ignoring his visitor's sarcasm, Mace said, "Her abilities also impressed me. Let's hope she's nothing more than a freak and is the only one who can identify us."

"The thought of there being others like her is unsettling," the Old Man said and sniffed louder. "But I think the chances of that are slim."

"Really?" Mace said. "Explain." When the Old Man did not respond, Mace said, "Phase two of your Hades Project will soon begin. Would you like to know the technical details of what happens then?"

"Do I look like I want to know?"

Rizben chuckled. "I don't blame you." He rocked back in his chair. The Old Man was being particularly difficult today. "Can I ask you a question, since you brought up the girl?"

"Do I not always answer your inquiries?"

Mace stood and walked around his desk. "Would you like a drink?" He strolled to the glass bar.

"Nothing for me. You need something to fortify your backbone before you ask your question?"

Mace didn't answer, instead he lifted a bottle of Pasion Azteca tequila from the shelf under the bar and filled two shot glasses. The Old Man was right. He needed a drink to give him the balls to question his superior. Mace cowboyed one shot, foregoing the lime and salt. "You have ordered a lot of attention to this child from the beginning, sending Albrecht to Loretto, the constant surveillance, and now the chase. The level of attention to her has risen to what I think is unjustified, unless she is more of a threat than you are telling me. And the most puzzling element is your hands-off policy. Why have we spent all this energy tracking, stalking, watching her? If she is such a threat because she identified Albrecht, and may identify all of us including our Ruby children, why haven't we taken her out? Be done with it. There have been plenty of opportunities. Event to make it appear accidental. The child and her mother could have perished in the fire. We could have torched their farm weeks ago. Or set up a tragic car accident. I can think of a dozen ways." Mace knocked back the last tequila shot and set the glass down. "I don't understand."

The Old Man nodded, his eyebrows pinched. "I can see why you are perplexed. Down through the eons, I have learned the hard way not to rush things and risk a mistake. Every decision and move I command must be thought out—like you have done by taking my idea and turning it into the Hades Project. And how we handle the girl must also be well planned and executed, no knee-jerk reactions." His piercing eyes locked on Mace.

The Secretary of Homeland Security felt the heat of the tequila in his belly and the chill in the air. He broke the burning stare. "I understand, and I'm not questioning your judgment. All I want to know is what have you not told me about the child?"

The Old Man stood and went to the door. He reached for the door-knob then turned to Mace. His features hardened, frozen stone-like in anger. In a reverberating voice that seemed to come from somewhere other than his physical body, he said, "I think God has played a trick on us."

Chapter Twenty-Four

SOUVENIR

After cleaning up and Tera taking another dose of Tylenol, Lindsay and her daughter drove to a nearby strip mall and walked down the sidewalk lined with Disney souvenir shops. Lindsay was deep in thought. What had Tera meant about the person in the sketch being her twin? Tera was an only child. But Lindsay recognized the face. What kind of confusion was going on in her daughter's mind?

They entered a busy store called Heigh-Ho, Heigh-Ho. It was crammed with rows of Disney character toys and costumes, along with the excited cries of exuberant kids. The soundtrack from Snow White and the Seven Dwarfs played in the background. Once inside, Lindsay and Tera were immersed in a Disney fantasy world.

Lindsay placed the traditional Mickey Mouse ears hat on Tera's head, and they agreed on a Minnie Mouse shirt. Lindsay added a Cinderella nightgown for Tera.

As Lindsay handed over her credit card to the clerk, Tera tugged on her arm. Lindsay looked away from the clerk and fixed her eyes on her daughter.

Tera's face was all scrunched up. "What's wrong?" Lindsay asked.

"The ruby people."

"What ruby people? What do you mean?"

"The ruby people are here." Tera's eyes brimmed with tears, and her bottom lip quivered.

"It's okay, baby." Lindsay glanced around. Tourists packed every aisle—no one stood out to her. "Stay calm. Okay?"

Tera nodded, but her expression showed increasing concern. Her little eyes squeezed shut, and her hands fluttered at her sides.

The clerk handed Lindsay the receipt to sign.

As she did, Lindsay asked the clerk in a low voice, "Do you have a restroom?"

"In the back on the right."

"Thanks." She took Tera's hand and led her away. "Pretend you're looking at more things to buy," Lindsay whispered. "Don't look at anything but the stuff on the shelves."

Tera did as her mother told her and trained her eyes on the souvenirs.

Lindsay and Tera maneuvered through the aisles. Lindsay tried hard to appear casual as if they were still shopping. "How many?"

"Four."

"Where?"

"Two by the front door. One in the next aisle over and one at the counter."

"Okay. Keep smiling and looking at the toys. Don't let them know we see them."

Lindsay spotted a hallway in the back of the store. A sign read *Restrooms*.

The bathrooms were at the end along with a third door labeled *Employees Only*.

She held Tera's hand as they walked. Instead of entering a restroom, Lindsay opened the third door. It was a stockroom chock full of stacked boxes and overflowing shelves. As they moved between the metal shelving, Lindsay discovered a back window. She unlatched it and raised the lower sash. One hard shove on the screen and it tore away.

"Okay, princess, up you go." She helped Tera stand on a crate so she could climb through the opening. Then Lindsay wriggled her way through the window. A moment later, she was clear. They were in a service alley and appeared to be alone.

Lindsay stooped down. "Okay, baby, we're going to run as fast as we can to the end of this alley, then get back to the parking lot and find the van. Are you ready?"

"Yep."

Hand in hand, they raced down the alley and soon were back on the strip mall sidewalk.

"This way," Lindsay said. They darted into the parking lot and raced through rows of parked cars. "I see the van."

At the instant they reached the van, Tera froze. "Momma, they're coming," she screamed.

Lindsay had already pushed the remote to unlock the doors. She grabbed the passenger door handle and yanked it open. "Get in, get in!"

But Tera remained rooted to the spot. "Red, red, ruby red!" she cried. Lindsay slammed the passenger door then pulled on the side sliding door. She pushed Tera inside, stumbled in behind her, and with a push of a button, the door began its track to close. Lindsay scrambled to over the console and into the driver's seat. She jammed her key in the ignition switch. The engine turned over, and she backed out without looking for other traffic. She jerked the gearshift into drive and floored the accelerator. With a screech of rubber and a cloud of gray smoke, the van shot out of the parking lot.

Lindsay looked into the rearview mirror but saw no one following as they sped down the street and merged into the traffic. Who were these ruby people? How had they found Tera and her so quickly?

Then a pang of doubt shot through her. What if there were no ruby people? What if no one was chasing them and it was just Tera's overactive imagination—just her daughter's mixed-up emotions? What if all Tera was doing was reaching out in some strange manner for attention, unable to cope with the death of her father? What if they were running from nothing but phantoms and ghosts? What if…?

Chapter Twenty-Five

INFECTION

The woman stared at the computer screen. Her e-mail inbox had thirty-five messages. She could tell by the subject lines that most were spam. There seemed to be no end to the junk mail—Amazon deals of the day, wrinkle creams, software specials, hot penny stocks. As convenient as e-mail was, she sometimes wanted to toss the PC and go back to snail mail letters and phone calls. But it was a fast way to keep in touch with her daughter at college and her mother out on the West Coast.

Delete, delete, delete. She tapped the key again and again after a quick preview of each message. Wait. Firewall update. That sounded important. How often had she been told to keep her antivirus and firewall programs up-to-date with the latest versions and security patches?

The choices read: *click here to download and update or click here to be reminded later*.

Dinner had to be started—her husband would be home soon. She would download the update tonight after she wrote a note to her mom. Occasionally, the files took a long time to download, and afterward, the PC always required rebooting. Too much trouble for now. It would have to wait.

The woman clicked the button in the message to remind her later. Then she got up and headed for the kitchen. Her stomach was already growling, and she wanted to open that new bottle of Yellow Tail Shiraz and sip on it while she cooked. As she left the room, she didn't notice the LED on the front of her computer glow for a second indicating a quick burst of hard drive activity.

***

"Of course, I heard about it. It's all over CERT-dot-org." The kid was a third-year information technology major working nights as a maintenance engineer at WebCorps, an Internet service provider hosting sixty-five thousand websites. The company was located in a two-level basement in downtown Cincinnati. "I'd have to be living on another planet not to have heard about it."

"Just asking." His friend, a communications major, stood behind the engineer as he used a cordless Makita to back the mounting screws out of the rack holding the Dell PowerEdge server. "It must have been quite an event to take down so many ISPs around the world."

"Happens all the time," the engineer said. "Assholes in China like to blow up our mainframes with denial-of-service assaults. Nothing better to do, I guess." He slid the server out of the rack and placed it on a roll-around cart.

"What do you have to do with that?" the friend asked.

"New hard drive. This one crashed a few hours ago." As he pushed the cart down the long line of computer racks, a message popped onto the service video monitor beside him. "Another patch? Jesus Christ, is that all Microsoft has time to do, issue service patches?"

"What's it for?"

The engineer read the reference code. "Yet another buffer overrun issue. Not my decision to install the hotfix."

"What are you gonna do?"

"Leave it for the geniuses who work the dayshift." The engineer took the mouse on the pullout keyboard rack shelf and clicked the cursor on download; do not install. "There, now it's someone else's problem." He pushed the cart toward the maintenance shop. "Let's get a snack."

***

The supervisor for the Air Traffic Control Emergency Notification Grid in the Seattle FAA center listened to air traffic controller chatter from the speaker on his desk. A large widescreen display on the wall showed a live feed from Seattle-Tacoma International Airport tower's Terminal Radar Approach Control (TRACON) system. As he listened, he read the flash bulletin on his PC monitor. The Joint Interoperability Test Command at the Department of Defense had scheduled a security systems test for tonight. It requested compliance and was signed by the commander of JITC, Fort Huachuca, Arizona.

"They did the same test a week ago," he mumbled to no one, since he was alone in his office. "Some pencil-pushing desk jockey with too much time on his hands."

The problem was that the DoD tests ate up bandwidth and always seemed to occur during peak traffic. Right now there was a freak autumn blizzard moving down from Canada that had already created a thirty-minute delay across the board. This time, he would make them wait. He guided his cursor to the choice to reschedule the test which caused the small message window to display a momentary hourglass before closing. Good riddance, he thought and went back to watching the TRACON display.

Chapter Twenty-Six

THE SKETCH

"Lindsay would have called my cell by now," Cotten said.

John glanced out the window of the plane to see wispy cheesecloth clouds gliding past. Illuminated by the brilliance of the moon, they had an almost supernatural quality that harnessed his thoughts. He imagined standing in their midst, the coolness breezing past. It seemed that would be the epitome of simplicity and peace, a sanctuary from this troubled place.

He looked at Cotten, her face drawn, and her eyes glassy. "Why don't you rest before we land in Orlando?"

"I don't think I can. John, they've got my phone. If Lindsay calls, they won't answer, they'll let her leave a message." Cotten pushed back in the seat. "They're going to get to her first."

"There's nothing you can do right now. If you don't rest, you won't be thinking clearly later."

"I know, I know, but I can't stop trying to unravel this mess. And like you said, why call out the big guns to go after a little girl? Just because she painted a red aura around some country preacher?"

"That gnaws at me, too," John said.

"The damn phone. It's my fault. I should have locked the car. But we were in a church parking lot—in Loretto, Kentucky. It's not like a back alley in Detroit or something."

"Quit beating yourself up. That won't change anything. You can dwell on it forever, but the facts will remain the same. Direct all that energy toward a solution—something positive."

Cotten sighed. "You are so good for me."

Even through all the rough peaks and deep valleys she'd wandered over the last several years, she still had innocence about her, John thought. Part of her charm. "Come on," he said, cradling her head with his palm. "Lean on my shoulder. Let a little peace settle over you."

Cotten yielded and leaned against him. He took her hand in his. In a few minutes he felt her relax and heard her breathing slow down and even out. They were scheduled to land in forty-five minutes. He was glad she slept, not only because she needed it, but because it gave him time to think about the call from her cell.

The voice sent a clear warning that if John cared for Cotten, he would convince her to back off. The man on the phone conceded that they could not kill her—she was of their bloodline, and they did not kill their own. But they could hurt her, maim her, disfigure her, cause her immense pain and suffering. And they would, without hesitation. All John had to do to save Cotten from such consequences was make her stop looking for the mother and child. It was as simple as that. They were leaving it up to him.

John stroked the top of her hand with his thumb. She depended on him, thought he could work miracles. But he was only a man, not a miracle worker. He hadn't told her exactly what the message said—only that it was a warning to retreat.

John's ears popped as the plane began its descent. What should he do? Convince Cotten to call off the search for Lindsay and Tera? He already knew what her answer would be, but continuing the hunt would put Cotten at grave risk. He wouldn't be able to live with himself if something happened to her. He knew that by the time the wheels touched the tarmac he would have to decide.

*＊＊

"I'm sorry, but I don't have a reservation," Lindsay said to the clerk at the front desk of the Contemporary Hotel in Disney World. She had followed the signs as they approached the theme park and arbitrarily chose the Contemporary. Inside the Disney property, with its strict security and protection, she felt they would be safe, and harder to find.

"Well, you're in luck," the clerk said. "We were totally booked, but a European tour group got stranded in severe weather up north. Their rooms have opened up for one night."

When asked for a credit card, Lindsay had a revelation. That's how they had tracked her, found her so fast—her credit card. "Oh, no," she stammered. "My husband would kill me if I put anything else on plastic. I've kind of run up the cards. I'll pay cash. How much?"

The clerk grimaced. "I'm sorry, but we require a card on file. Policy. But we don't charge anything to your account until you check out. Then you can pay the tab in cash when you leave if you like."

A sick feeling grew inside Lindsay. One night would be all she could afford, and that was stretching it. With reluctance, Lindsay handed over her MasterCard.

***

The next morning Lindsay checked out, paying in cash for the room and day passes to the Magic Kingdom. She inquired again if anything had been put on her card. Relieved there were no charges, she arranged for the hotel to hold her bags for her to pick up later.

On the fourth-floor concourse of the Contemporary, she and Tera caught the Monorail and headed into the park.

Tera wanted to see Cinderella's castle first, and that is what they did. Tera stood enchanted and wide-eyed in the middle of Main Street USA, craning her neck to look up at the blue and white castle, its spires pricking the blue sky, truly what fairy tales were made of. They wandered through the castle and learned that the top floors were originally an apartment where Walt Disney stayed during his visits. Tera was disappointed that it wasn't a castle inside even though she appeared captivated by the beautiful mosaics on the walls depicting Cinderella's story.

Lindsay checked the dwindling cash in her wallet. "How about we have lunch, here in the castle? Wouldn't that be fun?" It was expensive, but that would be the last splurge. They would only be here for one day. She wanted it to be memorable as well as safe, and a diversion for Tera. But to Lindsay's surprise, Tera shook her head.

"It's not really Cinderella's castle, Momma."

When Tera seemed satisfied that she had seen all there was to the castle, she and Lindsay sat on a bench and studied the park map. They decided on their first stop—It's a Small World.

It wasn't a long walk, and the sun felt good in the 72-degree temperature. The line snaked back and forth, winding through the maze-like path, but it moved much faster than Lindsay anticipated. Their wait was less than five minutes.

"Okay, Ladybug, hop in the boat," Lindsay said. It wasn't a real boat, just a theme park car with rows of seats that traveled a rail in a couple of inches of water. The boat chugged off into the dark mouth of the tunnel, and in an instant they were surrounded by a rush of cool air and the repetitious chorus of "It's a Small World" theme music.

Mesmerized, Tera looked in every direction at the animated characters and magical scenes all around her. Her eyes sparkled with delight.

The boat glided along a meandering water path, bringing new sights into view every few minutes. Dolls that donned the dress of countries around the world sang and danced, swung on glittering pink crescent moons, swayed beneath windmills, rode in gondolas, and walked beside the Taj Mahal. Room after cavernous room, hundreds and hundreds of animated dolls sang the infectious theme song. Sometimes there was a brief and subtle native influence, like the ukulele in the background as they passed the hula dancers, and the Spanish guitar in the scenes from Mexico. But always clear and foremost were the words reminding everyone what a small world it was. No wonder they called this the Magic Kingdom, Lindsay thought. It really was—a hiatus from the real world.

Lindsay watched her daughter and was glad they had come. She hadn't been able to bring herself to tell Tera that they wouldn't be able to stay another day—it was too much money. She knew she had already overdone it, but it was worth every cent to see her daughter so happy.

Tera squealed with amusement as the boat rounded the next turn, coming into a room revealing new characters and giant long-necked giraffes in a jungle setting.

Lindsay put her arm around her little girl and pulled her close. "Are you having a good time?"

Tera's face beamed. "This is the best ever."

Lindsay thought back to their harrowing race from the strip mall the previous day. She had driven around the area for over an hour checking the rearview mirror repeatedly for signs that anyone followed. There had been none.

But even as she sat next to Tera in a place filled with joy and happiness, she couldn't shake the dull fear that resided deep inside. Her heart beat heavy, and she felt jittery and apprehensive.

Lindsay touched the back of her hand to Tera's forehead. A tad warm, or maybe not? Tera sneezed and coughed several times in the night, so Lindsay suspected Tera was simply catching a cold. She was thankful it was nothing more serious.

She turned and glanced at the rows of people in the boat behind her. As they passed through a dark tunnel, their faces were momentarily hidden. Were they tourists like her? Just there to enjoy the ride? If any of them were the ruby red people, Tera would have said something long before they got on the boat.

Panic gripped Lindsay. The reality was they were surrounded by thousands of strangers and in the dark. If something happened, there was no place to hide, nowhere to run. Her pulse quickened as she faced forward and checked for an escape route.

Cold sweat washed over her—a sour taste rose into her mouth.

The ride lost all entertainment for Lindsay, and vulnerability crept its way into every corner of her body. She held Tera tighter and glanced behind once again.

Then brightly painted daisies and pansies, flowers of all varieties and sizes surrounded them, announcing the end of the ride with goodbye inscribed on their giant heads in multiple languages.

Adios. Ciao.

The automated recording grew louder and louder. "Please remain seated until your boat comes to a complete stop at the dock and you are asked to disembark."

Lindsay made out daylight ahead and her panic waned. They had to get out of the boat. No more rides. No more dark tunnels. This had been a bad idea.

She stepped out of the boat and helped Tera onto the platform.

"Momma, are you all right? Didn't you like the ride?"

"Yes, sweetheart. I got kind of claustrophobic in there. Let's get outside in the sun."

Lindsay felt the world crashing down on her. There was little cash left. No more credit card charges. Where were they going to spend the night? In the back of the van? Where was Cotten? Why hadn't she returned her call? As soon as they were outside, she would call again and beg her to come find them. If Cotten was not coming, then there was no one left.

***

John rented a car at the Orlando airport, and after a thirty-minute ride they arrived in the parking lot of the Tropical Breeze motel where Lindsay had last used her MasterCard.

"I'll pretend Lindsay is my sister and I was supposed to meet her here," Cotten said. "Then we'll play it by ear."

"I don't have a better plan." He parked the car, and they went inside to the front desk.

"Welcome to Tropical Breeze," the clerk greeted. "How can I help you?"

"I'm looking for my sister. She's staying here. Lindsay Jordan."

The clerk scrolled down the guest list. "Jordan? No, I'm sorry, she checked out."

"Darn it," Cotten said, then looked at John and rolled her eyes as if exasperated. "She's such a ditz." She looked back at the clerk. "Do you have any idea where she might have decided to go?"

He shook his head.

"By any chance, did she leave a message for me?"

"Your name?"

"Cotten . . ."

The clerk searched a box under the counter. "No, sorry." He smiled. "I do remember she checked out the same day she checked in. I took the call, actually. She said they had left the motel, to please check them out and charge the room to her credit card on file."

Cotten frowned. "Are you sure there's no message for me? Please, would you check again?"

The clerk scanned the mailboxes behind him, then returned to the counter and fumbled through what sounded like papers. "Nope. Oh, wait a minute." His head bobbed up. "I see a note here that we have some of her belongings in lost and found—stuff she left in the room."

"Well, isn't that just like her? We tease her all the time that she must really be a blonde," Cotten said and laughed. "I'll be glad to take it to her."

"You'll have to sign for it," the clerk said.

"Sure. It's going to give us something to rib her about."

The clerk disappeared into a backroom for a moment before he reappeared with a small suitcase and a plastic bag. He ripped off a slip of paper that was taped to the bag and stapled it to another one he had removed from the suitcase. Then he pushed them across the counter to Cotten along with a pen.

Cotten signed...*Cotten Tyler*. She stared at it a moment. "Thanks," she said and forced her eyes off the signature.

"I've got this." John took the items from the clerk. Outside, he opened the car door for her. "You okay?"

"Yes," she said as she slipped in the front seat. Cotten took the plastic bag from him and set it in her lap. She heard the trunk pop and the suitcase thump inside. As John went around to the driver's side, she peered inside the plastic bag. A lipstick. Two toothbrushes. Toothpaste. A hotel message pad and loose drawings. She pulled out the drawings.

John got behind the wheel. "What have you got?"

"Miscellaneous." She flipped through the papers.

"Any ideas where we go from here?"

Cotten's examination of the bag halted. Stunned, she studied one of Tera's drawings, ran her finger across it then handed it to John. "Look at this." She watched John's expression turn somber before he shot a glance back at her.

"Am I right?" she asked, knowing John would understand her question. He nodded and peered again at the sketch. "It's definitely you."

Chapter Twenty-Seven

TOR

Ben opened his eyes. His lids felt as if bricks held them down. He turned his head from side to side. Pain. His neck and chest hurt. The airbag had slammed into him hard. His face stung—probably caused by the hot gases from the deflating airbag. He still had his clothes on but his jacket was gone. He touched the top of his head. A bandage. Someone had treated his cut.

Ben tried to sit up but did not have the energy to overcome the pain. Everything hurt. He managed to prop himself on an elbow.

He was in what looked like a small dormitory. Eight single beds—four lined each side of the room—and a metal locker beside each. Overhead fluorescent fixtures lit the room but only one was on.

As he took in his surroundings, he realized he was not alone. Someone sat on a bed at the other end of the room—a small boy wrapped in a blanket up to his neck, his back to Ben.

Ben summoned the strength to swing his legs over the edge of the bed. Dizziness. He leaned forward and placed his face in his hands. This was going to be tough, he thought. But he had to find out where he was and then try to get out before anyone recognized him.

"Twenty-eight thousand, eight hundred forty-six."

Ben looked up. The voice had come from the boy. Soft, almost whispered. "What?" Ben said. "Did you say something?"

"Twenty-eight thousand, eight hundred forty-six." The boy repeated a little louder.

"I don't understand." Ben leaned forward to hear better. "What do you mean?"

The boy turned around. "How long you were asleep," he said. "Twenty-eight thousand, eight hundred forty-six seconds."

Ben shook his head. "And how do you know this? Do you have a stopwatch or something?"

"I just know."

"You mean you counted every second I was asleep?" As he spoke, Ben looked around the room. The walls were painted gray, and the floor was a dull, cream-colored linoleum. Each bed had a blanket and pillow. Plain and basic, like temporary sleeping quarters for a fire station or a military bunkhouse. He remembered seeing pictures in a magazine of the bunks for airmen who manned underground missile silos. Then he recalled the stark concrete building with the old radar dish on top. Was that where he was? But there were no ICBM silos in Northern Arkansas.

"I just know," the boy said again.

Ben studied the boy. Could this be the same kid he saw blindfolded and pulled from the van beside the meadow?

"That's amazing," Ben said, humoring the kid. "What's the deal? What are you doing here?"

"Play games." The boy scratched his ear.

"Games?" Ben tried to get up. "What kind of games?"

"Show them how to play games."

"Who?" He stood on shaky legs holding his arms out for balance. "They want me to show them how to play games."

"Okay," Ben mumbled to himself, "we've established that." He walked to the end of the bed where the boy sat. A door led from the room, and Ben tried the handle. Locked.

He stared down at the kid. He was probably eight or nine. Short blond hair, round face. "What's your name?"

The boy looked up at the ceiling. "Olsen."

"Well, hello, Olsen."

"No, Olsen is my last name." He grinned. "I'm Devin Olsen."

"Okay, Devin Olsen. Nice to meet you. My name is Ben." He sat on the end of Devin's bed. "Do you know where we are?"

In a matter-of-fact tone, he answered, "We are in Arkansas, the twenty-fifth state. It entered the Union on June fifteenth, eighteen thirty-six. The state motto is *regnat populus*, which is Latin and means 'the people rule.' The population is—"

"Hang on, hang on," Ben said. "Where is this place?" He pointed to the floor. "This building."

Devin shrugged, looked away and rocked. "Arkansas."

"You're a pretty smart kid. How do you know we are in Arkansas?"

Devin stopped rocking, but still didn't make eye contact. "The last stations on the radio were all Arkansas stations."

"The radio stations you listened to in the white van with the guy with the red jacket?"

"Uh-huh."

Clever kid, Ben thought. The door opened.

"Mr. Jackson?"

Ben looked up to see a short, slim man in the doorway. He looked to be in his late twenties or early thirties, and was dressed in black track shoes, jeans, and a T-shirt that read, *Qubits or Cubits, they all add up.* He had a narrow face with a dark goatee, wore wire-rimmed glasses, and his brown hair was cut short. The man extended his hand as the door closed behind him.

"How's the head?"

Ben stood, but didn't shake hands. Before the door closed behind the guy, he caught a glimpse of a large, low-lit room filled with racks of electronic gear—he heard the hum of computer cooling fans. "Who are you?"

"Call me Tor." He motioned for Ben to sit back on the bed.

Ben remained on his feet. "What are you doing with this kid?"

Devin remained sitting crossed-legged on the mattress. The boy shed the blanket, and Ben saw he wore a yellow T-shirt and jeans. A Miami Dolphins jacket and a pair of sneakers rested on the floor.

Tor smiled. "Devin is here to help us with some computer issues. Once he's done, he'll be going home."

Ben turned to the boy. "Devin, where is your home?"

"Miami." He stared up at the ceiling, again. "Incorporated on July twenty-eighth, eighteen ninety-six. Population at the time was four hundred and forty-four—"

"Thank you, Devin," Tor said.

The boy gave Tor a brief stony glare, looked away, and crossed his arms.

"What's going on here? Did you kidnap this kid?" If that was so, Ben figured he was caught in a huge bucket of shit.

"Mr. Jackson." Tor held up Ben's driver's license. "Like Devin, you are now our guest here. If you behave yourself, you will eventually be allowed to go back to your cozy little mountain cabin and continue doing whatever it is you do there. For now, I suggest you make yourself at home. You and Devin will be well cared for as long as you do as you're told." He nodded toward the boy. "I would hate to have anything happen to him because you decided to become heroic and try something stupid like attempt to escape."

Ben felt his pulse speed up. This asshole was telling him what to do. Giving him orders. In that instant, he realized that he must remain calm. As far at this prick was concerned, he was Ben Jackson, retired banker, who loved the solitude of the Ozark woods. Nothing more.

"Do you understand, Mr. Jackson?" Tor said.

Ben nodded and sat back down on the bed.

"Good decision." Tor smiled. "Now it's time to play our games, Devin." He waited while Devin put on his shoes.

As Tor opened the door, Ben said, "Where is this place?"

Tor glanced around the small dormitory as if it were a museum and its walls covered with great works of art. A slow, malevolent grin stole across his lips that sent a chill through Ben. "This, Mr. Jackson, is Hades."

Chapter Twenty-Eight

SILVER TEARS

"This is so fucked," said Scar, the teenage boy with the long, dyed black hair. The bottom of his dark trench coat snagged the grass as he walked in six-inch platform leather boots along the dirt road near the Potomac River. He carried a flashlight to light the way in the dark Maryland woods.

"Shut up," said Crow, a bit taller than Scar, and dressed equally gothic in an all-black outfit—alchemy shirt, crossroads bandana, triple hex belt buckle, wool trench coat, and raised boots. His shaved head was hidden under his hood. The light of the lantern he carried reflected off the silver studs and hoops of his facial piercings.

"How did you ever figure out where to find it?" Scar asked and looked over his shoulder at the moon burning orange through the trees.

"Legends, my man," Crow said. "Urban-legends-dot-com."

"Everyone says the stories are bullshit."

"Well, we're going to find out if the legend is crap or the freakin' truth tonight," Crow said. "You can only witness it on Halloween. Guess what, dickhead, it's Halloween. And we're gonna find it tonight. Now shut the fuck up."

"Who's supposed to be buried there?" Scar asked.

"What part of shut-the-fuck-up don't you understand?"

Scar stopped and turned around to face his friend. "Hey, fuck you, man. I'm out here in the cold when I could be back at the party screwing that blonde bitch from second period, who by the way said she'd suck my dick anytime I wanted. So fuck you."

Crow looked at Scar and weakened slightly. "You're such a prick. First, you can bang her any time. Second, tonight is Halloween. The only night in three hundred and sixty-something days a year that you can see it. Either you want to go with me and find it or you don't."

Scar flashed the light in his friend's face. "Asshole." They started walking again.

"You ever wonder if we're playing with shit we don't need to be messing with?" Scar asked. "I mean with all the frigging spells and incantations and Satan shit?"

Crow yanked back his hood. "I give up. What is it with you? All I want is fucking quiet time so I can get into the mood of this whole thing and you won't shut up."

"That's it, asshole." Scar turned and headed back along the dirt road. "You go find it by yourself. Fuck you."

Crow watched Scar until he was out of sight in the darkness. *If he wants to miss out on the greatest event in his life, screw him!*

As the moon crested over the trees, Crow continued on, deep in thought as to what he would find hidden in the heart of the Maryland woods.

The wind ran through the forest, carrying with it the call of the great horned owl. Crow pulled the hood over his head, wanting to become part of the night and the wind. He envisioned himself a vapor, a specter, a spirit of the underworld. Forgetting Scar, he slipped on through the shadows.

He had heard the legend many times—the story of the haunted fire ring, the one that could only be seen on Halloween. The story went that, in the early 1700s, a group of young village girls claimed to see and communicate with the devil. They were branded witches and burned alive in the town square. In a common unmarked grave deep within the Maryland woods, the village elders buried the children's bodies—the location marked by a ring of rocks. But the legend tells that each Halloween the girls rise up and roam the woods, crying out in torment as they search for the devil among the thick forest. Those who claim to have witnessed the apparitions say the girls' bodies are engulfed in flames.

Crow came upon a small stone marker in the weeds beside the dirt road. It was a mile marker placed there hundreds of years ago when colonists heavily traveled the road. Standing beside the stone marker, he recalled the instructions from the website. Six hundred sixty-six paces due north of the marker lay the resting place of the Potomac Witches beneath the haunted fire ring.

He took in a deep breath and stepped forward, eager to become a master in the netherworld of the occult, Satan worship, and the black arts.

***

Mace pulled his BMW into the grove of witch hazel and black walnut trees. Other cars were already there—he was the last to arrive. As he got out, he looked at the moon shadows on the ground—silver and shimmering. What a wonderful night. A perfect Halloween.

The air chilled him as he slipped into his ceremonial scarlet robe and moved down a sloping path along a hillside to the circle of rocks. He smelled smoke—pungent but sweet. It drifted through the forest like wispy tentacles that beckoned him to the heart of its heat.

"Good evening, Pursan," said a tall man in a flowing black robe standing beside the path. He bowed slightly.

"Urakabarameel," Mace said. "We've missed you the last few gatherings."

"I've been spending a lot of time in the Middle East. War is hell."

Mace chuckled. "That it is." He placed his hand on the other's shoulder as they walked down the hillside. "So all that's your doing over on that side of the world?"

"I can't take complete credit. Ezekeel and Dagon have had a hand in it as well."

"Give them my regards," Mace said as they approached the circle of fire—a ring of stones about thirty feet in diameter. In the center, a cone-shaped pile of logs blazed, sending sparks into the heavens. A dozen children held hands around the fire, their faces hidden by the hoods of their black robes. Behind the children, a circle of black-robed adults formed an outer ring.

"A good gathering," Urakabarameel said.

"Yes," Mace said. "Our new Ruby Army grows so quickly."

"How is your Hades Project coming along?"

"It's a challenge. I'll tell you more after the initiation."

Urakabarameel took his place among the adults.

Mace was handed a golden chalice of wine and a jewel-encrusted dagger before he stepped through a gap in the circle of children. "It is time." He glanced around at everyone. "Let us begin by calling upon Samael, the Guardian of the Gate."

In unison, the children intoned, "Samael."

A rush of wind stirred through the forest causing the branches to bow beneath the star-filled sky.

"I call upon Azazel, the Guardian of the Flame," Mace said, "the Spark in the Eye of the Great Darkness."

Again, the small voices echoed, "Azazel."

A tongue of flame swirled up and crackled as it fed on itself. "I call upon the Light of the Air, the Son of the Dawn."

"Son of the Dawn," the children repeated.

The Old Man came to stand next to Mace, his face aglow in the heat of the flames. "The time grows close," the Old Man said to the gathering. "You are our newest warriors." He spread his arms in a sweeping gesture as if gathering the children in an embrace. "The great Ruby Army will soon unite, and you will be our future vanguard. Stand proud in your purpose, for this world will belong to us. Soon we will take back from Him all that He stole from us. Now, come forward and dedicate your souls to me and the future of our new world."

Mace sipped from the chalice then said, "In the name of your mighty sword and the flowing lifeblood that gives you the power to conquer, enter into the minds, hearts, and souls of these young soldiers, and fill them with your terrible and crushing strength."

Mace lifted his arms high as the children formed a single line. Each came and kissed the blade of the dagger, then took a sip from the chalice. Once done, they returned to their place in the fire circle and drew back their hoods.

"Oh, great Son of the Dawn, behold, the newest soldiers of your vanquishing army."

The Old Man surveyed his youthful warriors. "So be it."

Each child turned to be congratulated by his or her father—a Fallen Angel. The ceremony finished, the children and adults dispersed.

Mace waited for the area to clear and then returned the dagger and cup to a nearby Fallen brother. As he did, he moved close to the Fallen's face and whispered, "We have a visitor—a young man enchanted by the lure of legends and darkness."

"I am aware of him. He lurks in the distant shadows."

Mace smiled. "See that he finds what he seeks."

"Of course."

Mace nodded a thank-you before he turned and walked up the slope where Urakabarameel waited. "Oh, yes," he said. "I intended to tell you more of the Hades Project." Side by side, they strolled along as Mace talked. "What we're going to do will amount to the biggest trick since the Son of the Dawn tempted Eve to eat from the Tree of Knowledge. And, as they say, a little bit of knowledge . . . That's the clincher to this whole idea. Men will make decisions according to what they think they see, what they believe is happening, based on their knowledge, when indeed there is nothing really there to see and nothing is really happening. Only an illusion we create. And based upon those illusions, they will eventually turn against one another and commit the gravest of sins against God."

"I don't understand. What do you mean?" Urakabarameel said.

"It is probably premature for me to go into such detail, but let me give you an example. Let's say we alter GPS satellite diagnostic and control systems by displaying a problem or error. Upon seeing that, the human operator will make appropriate corrections. However, since the problem is contrived, when the operator makes his corrections, his response will actually create a problem. In other words, we skew a few numbers and the operator compensates and skews all GPS coordinates."

"Interesting."

"It gets better." Mace relished his position in the Fallen hierarchy and could not resist the opportunity to flaunt that he was one of the Son of the Dawn's chosen insiders. He would not miss this opportunity. "Maybe I shouldn't divulge so much, but the grandeur of the plan is magnificent, and I must share with you. Let us say that the authorities receive word that a hundred inbound airliners have been hijacked and they rush to land all planes."

Urakabarameel smiled. "Because the GPS coordinates are wrong, planes descend over the wrong areas."

"Yes. Air traffic controllers panic and instruct pilots to take drastic measures to land, resulting in numerous crashes while other planes run out of fuel and fall from the skies."

"That's quite original, Pursan, but I assume there's more to it than airplanes crashing?"

"Oh, yes. We will affect global systems such as banking, defense, communications, utilities, and finally the power grids in an equally chaotic manner. The end result will be a complete, worldwide shutdown of all resources. On the evening of the last day of Man, each individual will be at war with his neighbor. Many will take the lives of others before their own, and we will welcome their souls with open arms."

"I like it already," Urakabarameel said. "And you'll be guiding everything from within?"

"I've already started."

"Keep me informed."

"Are you heading back to the desert?" Mace asked.

Urakabarameel nodded. "Dealing with terrorists is like communicating with mongrels, but I enjoy the challenge."

As Mace arrived at his car, he waved to the departing Urakabarameel. He removed his robe and glanced toward the dark woods nearby, aware that the young visitor was still there. He smelled the boy's fear.

Mace got behind the wheel and started the long drive out of the forest back to the Virginia suburbs. The Ruby initiation ceremonies always invigorated him, and he smiled with the excitement of knowing the Hades Project was about to become a reality.

***

Crow watched from behind the cover of the forest as the BMW left. Soon, all the cars had gone, and the night was quiet, the wind calm, and the moon spread a pewter haze over the Maryland woods.

But Crow was not calm and quiet. He had already shed the heavy trench coat as sweat soaked his body. "What the fuck?" he whispered.

He stood and stumbled down the hillside toward the fire ring. He had to either confirm what he had seen or find reason to laugh at his misunderstanding. Crow prayed for the latter. Either way, he had to know.

Smoke hung heavy in the air, almost like a cloudy sentry standing guard. He approached the rock circle with caution. The fire had died, only embers glowed from the black mass of spent logs.

He still couldn't grasp in his mind what he had witnessed. And yet he knew it went way beyond the role-playing he and Scar did with their make-believe spells and incantations. Scar was never going to believe this. No one would believe it.

He looked at the stones and touched one with his foot. The heat burned through his shoe. The acrid smell of smoke stung in his nostrils, and he had no doubt that he had trespassed into an evil place. The air, laden with the odor of sulfur, had moments ago been inside the bodies of those vile creatures. Now it was in his lungs. That thought convinced him he had experienced enough.

Suddenly, the embers sprang to life with the brilliance of an exploding sun. A flame shot over Crow's head, bringing with it a blast of heat. He backed away, fearing his feet would melt into the ground.

Then he saw them. The Potomac Witches.

They appeared before him just outside the stone ring, only a few feet away, their naked bodies consumed in fire.

He turned to run, to get as far from this place as possible. But when he did, the witches materialized in front of him and blocked his way. They forced him back to the fire that now raged. He felt the intense heat bite his neck. His shirt and pants burst into flames. The air filled with howls as the witches rushed forward. Their wails were matched only by his shrieks of terror. As he fell into their embrace, the metal objects piercing his skin melted and ran down his face like silver tears.

Chapter Twenty-Nine

THE CODE

Ben awoke to the sound of someone whistling the national anthem. Lying on his side facing away from the other beds in the small dormitory, he turned to see who was there.

"You are supposed to stand." It was the boy, sitting on his bed at the other end of the room. He whistled another bar, then sat Indian style.

"What?" Ben nudged his legs over the side. He rubbed the sleep from his eyes.

"Supposed to stand at attention when you hear 'The Star Spangled Banner.'"

"You're right." Ben glanced at his watch. It had been about five hours since Tor had taken Devin from the room. He must have been asleep when the boy returned. "But I see that you're not standing."

"It's over. You don't have to stand when it's over." Devin held his arms outstretched as if to emphasize the obvious lack of any whistling.

Ben glanced at the plastic tray holding a Styrofoam plate on the floor by his bed. There was a partially eaten ham and cheese sandwich and a can of ginger ale. Tor had brought Ben lunch a few moments after taking Devin away. Ben asked where he had taken the boy, but the guy had said nothing other than to enjoy the food.

Ben was glad to see that Devin had returned and was okay. He walked toward him and pulled up a folding chair next to the boy. "Are you all right?"

The kid didn't look him in the eye. Instead, his focus was off to the left, not much, but noticeable. And the boy's face showed little expression.

Devin scratched his scalp beneath the mass of unkempt blond hair. He continued staring off in space, shaking his hands near his head as if his fingers had gone numb and he was trying to bring the circulation back. Ben had seen him do that several times, like a nervous tic. The kid seemed brilliant in some areas and yet there appeared to be this odd, gaping deficit.

"Devin?" Ben waited for the boy to stop shaking his hands and pay attention. "Where did Tor take you?"

"Games." He had stilled his hands but didn't alter his focus. "Can you look at me?"

The boy's eyes wandered before landing on Ben's. "What kind of games?" Ben asked. "Video games?"

"They let me play Minecraft, Warlords, Prey, and Ghost Recon." He scratched his head again. "Tom Clancy's game. Heard of Tom Clancy?"

"Sure, I've heard of him." He got the feeling that the kid was, in a strange way, talking down to him. "Is that it? They let you play video games?" There had to be more to it than just entertaining the kid, he thought. What was going on?

"Then I type." Devin held his hands out and mimicked typing on an air keyboard.

"Type what?"

"Code."

"You mean like Morse Code?"

Devin gave Ben a look as if the question was stupid. "Destiny code."

"Okay, I give up. What is Destiny code?"

"Software code. My dad's computer. He calls it Destiny."

Ben leaned forward. He was on the verge of getting some answers. "Who is your dad?"

"Alan Olsen."

"What does he do?"

Devin looked confused.

Ben rephrased. "What is his job?"

Devin answered, still with a slack face. "Boss of CyberSys."

Now it was starting to make sense. Ben had watched the news reports covering the kidnapping of the Olsen kid. Dolphin Stadium—home of the Miami Dolphins. Autistic child. No ransom demands. No trace or clues. CyberSys was the quantum computer outfit. Ben even owned stock in the company a few years back. Made an 18 percent return if he remembered correctly. Not too bad by his standards. Now they had everyone looking for this kid who was sitting right in front of him. This was not good. Worse than he had thought. If the FBI located Devin, they would also find Ben Jackson, the retired banker from Atlanta, and they would ask questions. Next thing you know, Ben Jackson becomes Ben Ray, the new federal prison inmate in cellblock . . . Fuck.

Ben stood. Maybe the kid wasn't telling the truth about who he was or what he did when they took him away to play games. "How do you know the software code, Devin?"

"Memorized it when I played games in Dad's office."

Ben shook his head. From the little he knew about computer codes, there was no way a kid, or anybody, could do such a thing. Ben grinned. "You're pulling my leg, aren't you?"

Devin glanced at Ben's legs. "Why would I do that?"

This was another discovery about Devin Olsen. He took everything literally.

"I mean wouldn't that be a lot to memorize?"

"Not really. Hundred thousand lines of Destiny code, ten thousand of classic PC code."

"Are you telling me you memorized a hundred and ten thousand lines of software code? That's impossible."

"No, it's easy. Like memorizing books."

"How many books have you memorized?" Ben wondered if the kid was just playing with his head.

Devin shrugged. "Six thousand, four hundred, twenty-eight. Last one I read was *The Language of God.*"

Ben had never heard of the book. "Okay, if you're telling me the truth, what's the first line on page . . . thirty-three?"

Without hesitation, Devin answered. "If you started this book as a skeptic . . ."

Ben stared at the kid as if he had just revealed where Ben had hidden his Playboy magazines when he was a teen. He had no way of confirming that those were the first words on page 33 of the book, but Devin's amazing confidence convinced Ben that the answer was probably correct.

"Let's say I believe you have memorized the code to your father's Destiny computer. Wouldn't it take a long, long time to type it all out? I mean, how fast can you type?"

"I don't know. World's record is held by Barbara Blackburn in the town of Salem, the state capital of Oregon. Population three million, four hundred twenty-one thousand. Barbara Blackburn can maintain one hundred and fifty words per minute. That's thirty-seven thousand, five hundred keystrokes. Her top speed was two hundred and twelve on a modified keyboard. It's in the Guinness Book of World Records."

Ben's head reeled. They had kidnapped this eight-year-old to steal memorized computer code. He was obviously a genius—a true prodigy.

The big question was what they intended to do with him once they had what they needed.

Devin shook his hands again.

"Devin, do you have any idea why Tor needs the code?"

"Don't know."

Ben was an impatient man, but for some reason he sympathized with the kid. What must it be like to be in Devin's head? What was locked inside this eight-year-old? And these assholes had no conscience. He cringed at the thought of what they would do once they got all they needed from Devin. But still, it would take a while for him to type a hundred and ten thousand lines of code, even at Guinness speed. The lengthy process of typing the code would give Ben time to figure out how to escape and take the kid with him.

There was the question of what they intended to do with Ben Jackson. He didn't have anything to offer like Devin—no value.

Ben's future seemed bleak. It would help if he knew the timeline. How much code was left? And what if they only needed a portion?

"Devin, do you have a lot of code left to type for Tor?"

"Lots."

"How much is lots? How long will it take you?"

Devin shrugged.

Ben felt his gut tighten. "A couple of days?"

Again, Devin shrugged.

"Maybe less?"

Devin stared blankly.

Ben let out a long sigh. Once they had the Destiny code, they would most likely have no further need for Devin. And, Ben thought, there was no reason to delay his own demise. That could come at any minute. He was amazed they hadn't done away with him already. Why were they keeping him alive? "Then I'd better think of something fast to save us both—the handwriting is on the wall."

Devin's head jerked up and his gaze spun from one wall to another.

"No, no, there is no real writing on any wall. It's just an expression."

Ben paced. "Devin, while I figure out how we can escape, we have to keep our plans a secret from those cutthroats. Understand?"

"Yep," Devin said, dragging his finger across his neck like a pirate slicing a captive's throat.

Chapter Thirty

ARTIFACT

"Secretary Mace, you have such a magnificent collection," the woman said. In her elegant evening gown, she moved with grace from one display case to the next in the grand study of Rizben Mace's home. The low, indirect lighting contrasted with the soft glow of the displays and made them appear like jeweled islands in a sea of dark mahogany and Persian rugs. She stopped at a case containing Egyptian artifacts. Whispering to her husband standing beside her, she pointed to a bracelet arranged on scarlet velvet.

"That one is a favorite of mine," Mace said. As other dinner guests joined him, he took a sip of champagne from his crystal flute and continued. "The ancient Egyptians adopted the scarab, the dung beetle, as a symbol of the sun god because they were used to seeing the insect rolling a ball of dung on the ground. The action suggested to them the invisible force that rolled the sun across the dome of the sky."

"It's stunning," the woman said. "Darling, buy it for me." She elbowed her husband who pretended to go for his wallet.

The group chuckled as Mace beamed, proud of the collection that had taken him so many years to amass. "The gold, by the way, is encrusted with lapis lazuli."

"And this one, Secretary Mace?" another female guest asked about a different case. "Tell us about it."

"Aztec." The group followed him and gathered around the multicolored vase, radiant in the delicate wash of strategically aimed spotlights. "The face on the front is the god Tlaloc. Those are coiled serpents around his eyes. The vase symbolized the water that brought forth the bounty of their crops."

The woman bent for a closer inspection. "It looks frightening."

"They were a brutal people, and their art reflects it." Mace smiled with the knowledge that many of the Brotherhood of the Nephilim were once Aztec priests and warriors.

"Secretary Mace?" A man in a tuxedo gestured to an elaborate crystal box about the size of a toaster oven in its own display case. "Your collection has so many amazing pieces, yet the most breathtaking display contains what looks like a mundane black object. What's so special about this one?"

Inside the crystal box, atop white satin, was an object the size of an eyebrow pencil. It was so black that there seemed to be no detail to it, nor did light reflect off its surface.

"That is my prized possession," Mace said.

"It's so plain?" the first woman said. "Worth more than your five-thousand-year-old beetle bracelet?"

Her remark brought a grin from Mace and laughs from his dinner guests. "I never thought of the Egyptians as Beatles fans. From now on, I'll refer to that piece as Ringo's bracelet." This brought a bigger laugh.

"I think it's wood." a male guest said.

"You're close. It started out as wood. What you see is actually crystallized sap. But the wood it originated from is what makes it so unique."

"You're keeping us in suspense, Mr. Secretary," a guest said. "Please tell everyone what it is."

Mace set his flute down on a side table and stood over the display. He withdrew a set of keys from his pocket and unlocked the case. "The story is a captivating mixture of biblical history and legend. Let me ask you all, would everyone be impressed if I told you I owned a unicorn?"

There were collective nods.

"What you're looking at is just as rare as the mythical unicorn." He opened the display case and touched the top of the crystal box with his fingertips, almost like he was caressing the skin of a lover. "For those familiar with the book of Genesis in the Bible, God instructed Noah to build a vessel in preparation for the coming Great Flood. Noah was to construct the vessel out of resin-wood and pitch. Down through the centuries, many men have searched for the final resting place of the Ark. A number of years ago, a group of explorers located what they believed was the remains of the Ark on the snow-covered slopes of Mount Ararat in Eastern Turkey. A few remnants of the crystallized sap from those resin-wood planks detailed in Genesis were found preserved. What you see is a small piece of Noah's Ark that survived the Great Flood over five thousand years ago."

Mace loved to watch the predictable expressions of surprise on his guests' faces each time he revealed the identity of the tiny black object.

"You're serious?" the man said, staring at Mace. "The real Noah's Ark?"

"Yes." Mace moved around to the opposite side of the display so he could face his friends. "This particular piece, along with a handful of others, once rested in the Baghdad Museum, brought there by the expedition that discovered the Ark. The Baghdad Museum was a remarkable depository of antiquity. You might recall that in April of two thousand and three, right after the collapse of Saddam Hussein's regime, the museum was ransacked. It was a despicable act of looting comparable in scale to the sack of Constantinople and the burning of the library at Alexandria. Those like me who treasure the antiquity of mankind were devastated. It was only shortly before the start of the Iraq War that I came into possession of this artifact."

"If it was part of the museum's collection, how did you get it?" another guest asked.

Mace had practiced this little spiel he was about to give in front of his bathroom mirror, testing the sincerity of his expressions that would make his lie convincing. As rehearsed, his appearance became melancholic.

"Despite the immense fortunes amassed by Saddam Hussein," he said, "little of his money went to the preservation of the region's heritage—not even his own country's archaeological treasures. Most went to his personal palaces and extravagant lifestyle. To raise funds for the museum, from time to time the curator would hold an auction. Actually it was more like a raffle. It would cost each patron a million dollars to buy a lottery ticket." It was at this point he allowed his face to brighten. "This was the prize, and I won."

Mace evaluated his audience. Not a single questioning raised eyebrow. He forced back a smile.

"Were the other stolen pieces of the Ark recovered?" a male guest asked.

"No. The thieves may not have even realized what those pieces were. They could have easily been overlooked among the thousands of other more notable artwork, sculpture, and such that were taken. The ransacking was chaotic beyond belief. Sadly, this may be the only remaining piece from Noah's Ark in existence."

"Amazing," a male guest said. "You're lucky that you got it before that terrible event."

"Mr. Secretary, you have an urgent call."

The group turned as a young man in a black suit stood nearby. He held a cell phone in his outstretched hand.

"If you all will excuse me for a moment." Mace closed the display case and locked the crystal box and artifact inside before he took the phone. Not until he was in the privacy of an adjacent hallway did he hold the phone to his ear. "Mace, here."

"It's Tor."
"Is this going to upset me?"
"Yes."

Chapter Thirty-One

MOTNEES

John stared at the sketch. "How could an eight-year-old girl that you've never met draw a detailed portrait of you?"

"There's got to be a logical explanation," Cotten said. She watched the dribble of traffic come and go in the Tropical Breeze motel parking lot as she and John sat in the rental car.

"I'm sure you're right. We're on edge right now and tend to read too much into everything." He scratched his day-old stubble. "Tera must have seen a picture of you."

"That's it. In her scrapbook I found a picture of Lindsay and me back in high school. It was with the note she left saying they were on the run."

"But that was an old picture. The sketch isn't of a high school girl. It's the way you look now. Unless, of course, you haven't changed a bit."

"I'd like to make that claim, but it was seventeen years ago." Cotten gave him a challenging glance, daring him to comment on her age.

He seemed to pick up on her body language and held up a hand in defense. "I can't imagine you being more beautiful than you are today."

A grin flickered across her face. "Right answer." She took his hand in hers. The playfulness drained from her eyes. "You're right, the portrait isn't based on my high school picture. But Tera could have seen me on TV. After the Russian incident, I was all over the press."

She turned to look out the window as a thought bubbled up inside. "But there's something way too coincidental going on. I think she left the sketch behind on purpose in case we came along. I think she meant for me to find it. Like a kind of message."

"Which is?"

"No idea. But we won't find out sitting here."

"Well, that's another problem we need to discuss."

"What problem?"

"The call. The one that came from your cell phone back in Kentucky."

"You said it was a warning to back off. So, what else is new? How many times have the Nephilim used that old, worn-out line?" She shrugged. "We've heard it before. You and I know that they won't kill me. It's against their covenant that protects the offspring of the Fallen. John, my father was Furmiel, Angel of the Eleventh Hour. If he hadn't repented and become mortal, I would not have been born. I am Nephilim. They won't kill me."

"But they can hurt you. That was the warning. Back off or they will hurt you. Badly." He held her hand with both of his. "Maim, disfigure, take you to the edge of death—a place filled with constant pain. Is finding a kid who had a run-in with a backwoods preacher worth the risk?"

"You know it's bigger than that." She leaned her head back on the headrest and stared through the windshield. "Something happened when I touched Tera's picture. Something so odd, so intense. It was special, like I connected with my mortality, my soul. My perfect reflection." She rolled her head to the side and looked into his eyes. "This goes way beyond sketches, paintings, poems, and red auras around Pastor Albrecht. I'm compelled to find her." She stopped short of revealing who she thought Tera was. John would think she'd finally lost it.

He took the sketch and studied it for a moment before setting it on the dash. "You said 'my reflection.' Are you talking about Motnees, your twin?"

Cotten nodded. God, John knows me so well, she thought. There was not another person in the world who knew so much about her—knew everything about her, the good, and the not so good. "Her name sounds so silly, now. But that's what I called her. Her angel name. Even though she died at birth, her spirit still came to me when I was a child. I've told you how she would appear in my room and comfort me when I was sick—speak to me in our made-up twin-talk. When I touched Tera's picture at the farm, it was exactly the same memories that flooded back, the strong bond, the incredible connection. I could almost hear her calling me."

"In Enochian, the language of angels—your twin-talk?"

Cotten felt tears well up. "Yes." It took a moment to gather her composure. "If Tera is the incarnation of Motnees, it scares the hell out of me."

"Why would you be afraid of her? I don't understand."

"No, not her. I'm afraid of what it means. Why would she come back after so many years? We may not yet know the reason, but her presence means something terrible is about to happen. She must be a profound threat to the Fallen. That's why they're pursuing with such ferocity. She can identify them just by seeing them. Tera has a key role in confronting them, and they suspect or are certain of it. They'll never give up until they have hunted her down."

"I don't want anything to happen to you."

"I know." She leaned against him and felt the security that his closeness always brought.

He stroked her hair. "But, I can see I'm not going to get anywhere trying to talk you out of this. If the connection is that strong, then there must be something to it. We won't know until we find Tera. Albrecht isn't running this show. We need to find out who it is and bring him or them out into the open. Who has the Force of All Evil tapped this time to carry out his bidding?"

Cotten sat up in her seat and looked at John, her eyes wide with surprise. "My God, we're so stupid."

"I don't understand."

"We want to know who they are. John, they've got my cell phone." Cotten smiled. "We'll call and ask."

Chapter Thirty-Two

DEGRADE

"What do you mean it's not working?" Mace said. He had left his dinner guests to take the call from Tor. With the phone to his ear, he walked out onto the river stone patio of his home that overlooked the Virginia countryside.

"It's what I suspected all along," Tor said. "The thodium has degraded from thousands of years of exposure in the freezing Turkish mountains."

"You're telling me that it's not going to work?"

"I didn't say that. Only that it's not one hundred percent reliable. I'll need more time to isolate a workable sample from what you gave me."

"How much time?"

"Too soon to estimate."

"What about using the artifact I've got here?"

"It's all from the same place. I can try it, but no guarantees that it will work any better."

"What's the alternative?"

"Unless you can find me a *pure* source of thodium, we're back to the drawing board."

"We're going to proceed with the artifact I'm going to send you. I'm not going to accept delays. Is that clear?"

"You're the boss, but—"

"Just do it." Mace pinched the bridge of his nose. "How's it going with the kid?"

"Slow. He's unpredictable."

"And our banker friend?"

"He and the kid are getting chummy. But Jackson, aka Benjamin Ray, doesn't have much luck with the kid either. Sometimes I think we should have hacked into the CyberSys mainframe rather than dragging the code out of an eight-year-old—especially this one."

"It would have been the chicken and the egg routine if you had. You need a quantum computer to hack in and you need to hack in to steal the OS to run the quantum computer. The kid has got to be the easier of the two."

"Then you come up here in Hicksville and try your luck."

"I don't have the patience for such matters. Keep at it. In the meantime, I'll have a courier bring you the other thodium artifact. They'll fly to Little Rock and drive it out to you."

"That's fine, but like I said, no guarantees it will work any better than what you already gave me."

"I don't need guarantees, only results."

"Have whoever's delivering the artifact call my cell when they get into town. This place is a bitch to find, so I'd rather go meet him. And for that matter, he's not staying. The place is already getting too crowded with the Olsen boy and the banker. I designed this system and I can run it myself."

"Fine. Keep working and get the rest of the code from the kid."

Mace pushed the end button on the phone. He hadn't counted on the thodium being degraded. That could present a big problem in his timetable. Where would he find other sources? The answer was buried in the story of the Great Flood, of that he felt certain. If he could locate a better sample, all the better. But Tor was going to have to pull this off with or without.

Mace paced the patio, trying to recall the many facts of the Flood kept hidden or lost down through the ages. There were details of the event not documented in the Scriptures, thanks to the Fallen's influence over the arrogance and egos of the men who approved and assembled the Bible. Many ancient writings, scrolls, and books were left out because they didn't conform to the teachings of the Church or because the Son of the Dawn chose to have them eliminated. Selective inspiration, he called it.

One fact dealt with the construction of the Ark. Mace knew that in Genesis, the wood used to construct the Ark was called gopher wood or resin wood—an obscure, prediluvian material that by design was not well defined—and did not exist anywhere in the world today. In reality, the wood used to construct the Ark was lumber originally cut from the Tree of Life east of the Garden of Eden. After the flood, the Ark was disassembled, and Noah's descendants carried pieces of the wood to faraway lands as they repopulated the world. The fragments of the sacred evidence of God's reward for being faithful would be used to rebuild houses, furniture, livestock troughs, and tools. But it was the sap the wood excreted that held the key. Once it crystallized, it transformed into a material of unusual powers and properties—fitting for a material that originated in the Garden. The crystallized resin of the Tree is what Tor called thodium, the power behind the Hades computer.

The Tree was now gone forever. It gave up its last limb and branch to the Ark five thousand years ago. But the fact that the wood was dispersed to Noah's descendants meant that *other* objects may have been made from it and might still exist.

The small remains of the Ark on Mount Ararat had been so easy for Mace to obtain—the ransacking of the Baghdad Museum a convenient diversion for stealing them. The task ahead to find other objects from the Ark would not be so unproblematic. He'd have to consult with the Son of the Dawn and delve into his leader's eons of wisdom and in-depth knowledge of the Bible and other ancient documents. Somewhere, a pure source of thodium waited. Now it was a matter of finding it before the

Hades Project was discovered and the future of the Ruby Army was compromised.

With a sense of renewed determination, Mace walked back into the grand study where his guests awaited and said, "Ladies and gentlemen, let's have dessert."

Chapter Thirty-Three

THODIUM

Max Wolf looked into the camera as the Satellite News Network reporter said, "Dr. Wolf, please let Mr. Olsen know all our prayers are with him for the swift return of his son, Devin."

"Thank you," Max said. "I'll pass that on to him." Max Wolf and the reporter, along with the SNN remote location crew, gathered in the shade of palm trees across Biscayne Boulevard from CyberSys headquarters in downtown Miami. A weather front had moved through South Florida the previous night. Now the air was cool and crisp under a pristine blue sky as the late fall breeze rattled the palm fronds and mixed with the hum of afternoon traffic.

The reporter had wanted to hold the interview inside the company's labs but corporate security regulations forbade cameras being brought into the restricted research areas. They settled on the lush tropical park nearby with the CyberSys building and its dynamic cobalt blue thunderbolt logo in the background.

"Without getting too technical, can you explain for our viewers exactly what Project Destiny is?" the reporter asked.

"Destiny is the codename for what we hope will be the world's first fully functional quantum computer."

"And what is a quantum computer?"

"Perhaps a way to visualize it is to compare it to the classical PC that we're all used to seeing. Imagine the PC as the space shuttle and a quantum computer as the fictional Starship Enterprise. One travels at tens of thousands of miles per hour, the other travels at close to the speed of light—in the movies at least. One of the biggest differences in the two computers is the speed of performing computations."

"That's quite a strong comparison, Dr. Wolf, and a huge leap in technology."

"Speed is everything in quantum computing. For example, some modern simulations that are currently taking China's Sunway Tai-huLight supercomputer years to do would only take a quantum computer a matter of seconds."

"Impressive," the editor said. "Now, many in our audience are familiar with CyberSys and the fact that you are a leader in both the development of high-speed encryption technology and quantum computing research. Tell us, what is the main obstacle standing in your way to creating a working Destiny system?"

"You've asked a question that requires a technical answer. I know you wanted to keep this simple, but the answer isn't simple. I'll start with one word," Max said. "Decoherence. In a quantum computer, all data is stored in what's called a qubit—basically one bit of information per atom. In the process of computing, we need the qubits to interact with each other, but not interact with their surroundings, which can induce noise and other undesirable results. We must keep the computer in a coherent state—the slightest interaction with the external world causes the system to decohere, thus creating our biggest enemy, decoherence and the corruption of our computations."

"How close are you to finding a solution?"

"We still have a way to go. The problem is storing the qubits. We've tried using just about everything. Gone through virtually all known atoms—even something as exotic as nitrogen vacancies in diamonds—to find the perfect storage material. Nothing works well enough to avoid some level of decoherence."

"If you've tried every material there is, then can we conclude that it is impossible to build a real quantum computer?"

"Well," Max said and smiled, "what I meant was every *known* substance that we can get our hands on. Most of us were taught in school that only ninety-two elements exist in nature, but scientists have discovered additional ones from time to time under specialized testing conditions. A recent discovery that we think would produce positive results is an element called thodium, a previously unknown atom high up the periodic table."

"How do you know it would work?"

"So far, it's a theory based on quantities of one or two atoms created in particle accelerator tests."

"Not enough for your needs?"

"No. We can't produce enough to confirm its compatibility, and unfortunately, we are unaware of any natural source. At this point, the natural existence of the element is hypothetical."

"I must admit I'm not familiar with thodium."

Max chuckled. "There aren't many who are. Thodium, like a handful of other elements that are either theoretical or extremely rare, is usually confined to the footnotes of science journals."

The reporter nodded. "I remember a couple from back in college. Never knew why we bothered studying something so scarce that the total amount in existence would fit into a thimble."

"You're probably thinking of astatine or francium. It's estimated that there is only one ounce of astatine in the entire world, and scientists tell us that there are about five hundred grams of francium in all of nature."

"Can you describe thodium?"

"Technically, it's a specific form of crystallized resin. Our simulations show that it exhibits all the characteristics needed to avoid decoherence in the storage of qubits. If the theories are correct, thodium would be a perfect spectral hole-burning material. With it, we could address individual thodium atoms using our lasers and read out their states with no problem. We theorize that thodium atoms interact strongly with each other, allowing us to perform fast quantum logic gates. And we believe that it possesses an atomic transition of two hyperfine energy levels that are so wonderfully insulated from the surrounding environment that a qubit could live there effectively forever, undisturbed by noise or decoherence."

The reporter gave a light shake of his head then scratched his temple. "That's a lot to take in. You were right when you said the answer wouldn't be simple. Let me see if I've got this straight and can whittle it down to translate in plain terms for our audience. In essence, all you have to do is round up a batch of thodium and you can build the first fully functional Destiny system?"

"Theoretically, yes."

The cameraman signaled that the segment time was almost up.

"This has been fascinating, Dr. Wolf. I know our viewers can't wait for news from CyberSys that you've solved the problem of decoherence and built the first working Destiny quantum computer. When you do, we hope you'll invite us back to cover the story."

"Absolutely," Max said.

"One more question, Dr. Wolf."

Max nodded.

"If someone could build such a powerful computer as your Project Destiny, how would it affect us all?"

"It would render useless all cryptographic systems in use today." As an afterthought, Max added, "And strike fear into the hearts of every security agency in the world."

Chapter Thirty-Four

GAME ROOM

The door opened and Tor walked into the small dormitory. Sitting on the edge of his bed, Devin immediately started shaking his hands as if he were trying to air dry them. Ben leaned against the wall at the other end of the room and watched.

"Devin, it's time to go play your games," Tor said.

"Play, play, play, play." Devin repeated the words at machine gun speed.

"You know how much you like playing." Tor stood beside the boy. "We just installed the latest version of Call of Duty. You love that one, remember?"

"I don't want to go. Nope. Nope. I want Ben to go. Ben go."

"You're making things difficult, Devin."

"I think he wants me to tag along." Ben was thankful that the kid was following their plan. He hoped Devin would remember everything.

"Mr. Jackson doesn't play video games, Devin," Tor said.

Devin put his hands in his lap and rocked—his focus just barely to the left of Tor.

"What harm could it do? Maybe he'll be more cooperative."

Tor turned and looked at Ben. "Maybe." He hesitated a moment then said, "Did you hear that? Your new buddy is going to join us and watch you play. Now, will you come, Devin?"

Devin stopped rocking and stood.

"Things are getting better already." Tor walked to the door and opened it. "Right this way, gentlemen."

Ben fell in behind Devin as the three left the dormitory. They entered the much larger room Ben had only glimpsed earlier. The first thing he noticed was the frigid air—cold enough to see his breath. He assumed this was to keep the rows of computer equipment from overheating. He and Devin followed Tor past twenty-five rows of six-foot metal racks as they made their way to the other end of the room. Ben estimated each row ran for more than fifty feet. He found the overwhelming hum from the electronics to be unsettling. Thousands of tiny, multicolored LEDs blinked back from the dark rows of equipment like alien eyes. Ben noticed no one else as they walked along, but felt that Tor could not be the only one here. And he had seen the man in the red windbreaker in the woods and just before his crash. This was much too big an operation for just one person.

He stole a couple of glances at the ceiling to confirm the placement of the jet nozzles—exactly like the ones in the data storage vaults of his hospitals many years ago before the banning of CFCs. But the regulations did exempt certain critical users such as the military. If that was the case here, and the Halon tanks were still armed, then his plan might work.

At the other end of the room, Tor led Ben and Devin up a flight of metal stairs to a second level of what Ben guessed were once offices—each with a large window that overlooked the electronics room.

In the short time that they had walked from the dormitory, Ben's teeth had begun to chatter. "Do you have to keep it so cold?"

"Those mainframes would melt down in a matter of minutes if we didn't. Besides, you get used to it."

"Maybe *you* do," Ben said.

Tor motioned the two into the first office and flipped on the overhead fluorescent lights. It was significantly warmer in the office, for which Ben was grateful. Casually, he glanced at the light fixture. Right beside it was a Halon nozzle.

Inside the room was a desk and chair set up against one wall with a PC, keyboard, monitor, and joystick. A couple of other folding chairs were against the opposite wall.

"There you go, Devin. The latest version of Call to Duty. Have a seat. You've got the usual thirty minutes to blow up the bad guys. Then I'll be back to get you started from where we left off yesterday." He patted the back of the chair and Devin sat.

Within a moment, the sound of combat filled the room.

Tor motioned to a handful of metal chairs along the wall. "Sit, Mr. Jackson. I'll be back soon." As he started to leave, his cell phone rang. "Yes." Tor listened for a moment. "Okay, you're only about twenty minutes from here. Stay on the county road that runs along the edge of the Ozark National Forest. The main entrance to the old military base will be on your right. It looks all closed up. Don't worry. Just wait for me at the gate and I'll meet you there." He listened again for a moment. "Any problems getting the thodium through security?" A final pause. "Good. See you then."

Tor tapped something into his phone and rested it on the desk. As he flipped through papers on a clipboard, a male voice answered on speaker. "Yeah?"

"Come up to the game room and watch the kid and Mr. Jackson. I've got to go meet the courier." He placed the clipboard in a rack on the wall.

"Right," the voice replied.

Tor picked up his phone, tapped it, and stuck it in his pocket.

Ben heard the clank of footfalls on the metal stairs. The bearded man in the red windbreaker appeared. Tor spoke to him in a hushed voice then headed down the stairs. The man grabbed one of the chairs from the game room and placed it just outside the office, its back to the observation window.

"Can't stand the sound of those games," he said as he closed the door behind him.

Ben heard a clunk and knew the door had automatically locked. He stared at the back of the man's head until he was sure the guy had mentally drifted away.

"Devin," he said softly. "Don't turn around. Keep playing your game. We need to change our plan."

The boy continued to manipulate the joystick and keyboard. Ben wondered if he had heard him.

"Devin, did you hear me?"

Devin stopped for a second and shook his hands. Then he went back to blowing things up.

Ben walked over behind the boy and placed his hands on Devin's shoulders. "Okay, here's what I want you to do."

Chapter Thirty-Five

FIND MY PHONE

"That's correct," John said into his cell phone. He gave Cotten's phone number to the Venatori IT specialist at the Vatican Embassy in Washington, D.C. "It's an iPhone." While he spoke, he nodded to Cotten. Then he handed her his phone. "This is Jenny, our Internet super spy. Give her your Apple username and password."

They sat on a bench under a massive mossy oak along the banks of Lake Eola in downtown Orlando. A huge circular fountain that reminded Cotten of a UFO dominated the center of the lake, spraying plumes of mist into the warm, Central Florida sun. Mothers with strollers, inline skaters, and tourists moved along the park paths surrounding the twenty-three-acre lake.

Cotten gave the info then returned the phone to John. "We're ready to make the call," he said to Jenny. "Get back to me as soon as you have a location. Thanks." John ended the call. "We're all set."

"I'm nervous," she said, shifting her gaze back to the fountain in the center of the lake. "I'm not sure what to say."

"Just what we discussed. They know who you are and understand you are someone they have to deal with. See if they'll agree to meet with us."

"It sounds so easy now." She wrung her hands. "But when I get on the line, I know I'm going to be nervous."

An elderly couple walked by conversing in Spanish. Once they were out of earshot, John said, "Okay, let's do it."

Reluctantly, Cotten took his phone and stared at the screen. Who would answer? Man or woman? They would see the caller ID and know it was from John. She had to show confidence in her voice. No hesitation. No stammering. John had told her to be in command and control.

She gripped the phone and pressed her picture in his favorites list. With the phone on speaker, she looked into John's eyes, thankful that he was with her.

One ring. Two rings. Three rings.

Hi, this is Cotten. I can't answer your call right now but leave a message and I'll get back to you real soon.

Beep.

She held the phone close to her mouth and said. "This is Cotten Stone. Leave Tera and her mother alone. You need to meet with me. It will be easier if you agree, or I will hunt you down, and it won't end well for you or your kind. It never has before, and it won't this time, either. Call this number."

She pressed the *end* button and looked at John. "Bad?"

"No. You left a strong message. We knew they wouldn't answer, anyway. No surprise there. Now, relax and let's see what happens." He stood. "Time for lunch."

Would they return her call? She gave it as good a chance as meeting the aliens from the UFO fountain in the middle of Lake Eola.

***

"They're going to let us stay for free, Ladybug," Lindsay said as she and Tera stood at the door to room 14 of the Dos Palmas Motel, a few miles south of Key Largo. "Isn't that the best news?"

Tera shrugged. "I guess."

Lindsay stuck the key in the lock and opened the door. They stepped inside and she flipped on a light switch. A lamp glowed on a bedside table. The room was small and worn—way overdue for new paint, furniture, and carpet. The refrigerator was compact, half the size of the one at home, and the oven and stove combo was also a midget version. It would do. The guy at the front office said they were in the process of renovation, but Lindsay saw no evidence of tools or workmen anywhere on the grounds of the out-of-the-way, old motel in the Florida Keys.

The deal she made with the manager was a free efficiency in return for housekeeping, running the laundry, and a bit of bookkeeping in the front office. The job was seven days a week, but the motel had only twenty units. The manager assured her she would be done by mid-afternoon each day. Probably a lie, she thought as she put away their meager belongings into the dresser drawers. She supposed a lot of people came down here to disappear just like she had.

Tera plopped onto the bed and used the remote to turn on the TV. The image was washed out. "What's wrong with the picture?" she asked.

"It's an old TV, sweetie," Lindsay said. "Try to make do."

She never expected to live this way, but she and Tera were safe. They didn't have to register or use her credit card. She had given fake names, and she hadn't been asked for any ID. She'd be paid a small, off-the-books cash compensation—considerably less than minimum wage—enough for food at least. They would get by.

While Tera searched for a kids' channel, Lindsay stood by a window and looked west over shallow Florida Bay. Across the shuffleboard courts, through the palm trees, she could see the gentle lapping waves. Suddenly, she felt empty and spent. Her life had come down to a tiny, grimy room in a 1950s motel. She was no different from the burnouts, the dead-enders, the baby- boomers still stuck in the sixties who found refuge in this part of the Sunshine State. She had a gifted daughter who might be going crazy, and there was no word from Cotten.

Lindsay felt alone, abandoned, helpless. She covered her mouth to mask her sobs from her daughter.

***

Cotten and John had just finished their sandwiches at the Terrace Restaurant beside Lake Eola when his cell phone rang.

"Here we go," he said. "This is Tyler."

Cotten watched a few of the swan-shaped paddle boats cruise around the edge of the lake as she sipped her tea. She listened to John's conversation and tensed in anticipation of what Jenny had found.

"Really?" John's eyebrows rose. "You're absolutely certain? All right, I appreciate the extra effort confirming it."

"Well?" Cotten said.

John shook his head. He stared out over the lake for a moment then turned to her. "You're not going to believe this one."

"Try me."

"They had no problem tracing the location of your phone. But the result was so unusual that they repeated it three more times." He leaned forward to keep his words quiet and private from anyone in the restaurant. "Your cell phone is in Washington."

"Where?"

"In the White House."

Chapter Thirty-Six

HALON

Ben pressed on Devin's shoulders to get his attention as the boy continued using a joystick to wreak havoc across the virtual battlefield.

"Remember how we were going to get into the security system and make the fire alarms go off tonight?"

"Fire, fire, fire," Devin said, never losing a beat with the game.

"No, no, shh. Don't talk. Just listen." He leaned over Devin like he was closely watching the action of the game. "We have to change our plan. I want you to make the alarms go off in three minutes—in 180 seconds."

Ben looked back to check on their guard. The man had moved his chair and now faced them. His eyes fastened on Ben.

Ben waved at the guy in a friendly manner and returned to his position over Devin's shoulders. He hoped he could get the kid to understand without giving away his hand. They needed to take advantage of Tor's absence. "Okay, Devin," he said softly and patted the boy's back as if he was congratulating him for a win in the game. "Make the alarms go off in one hundred eighty seconds. Then set off the Halon five seconds later. But—and this is very important. Make the gas go off only in this room. Can you do that?"

Devin nodded. He paused the game and opened the control panel to change the game's settings. He also opened another window that displayed the facility's internal security configuration settings.

As he did, Ben checked his watch and positioned himself to make certain he blocked Red Windbreaker's view of the computer screen. Ben wasn't a computer whiz and couldn't tell what adjustments Devin made. He could only hope.

"Devin," Ben said in a whisper, "as soon as you hear the alarms, be ready to run to the door. That guy will come in to get us. When he does, the Halon gas will go off. I'll take care of him while you run out of the room. You've got to get out fast or you won't be able to breathe. The gas replaces all the oxygen in the air. Understood?"

The boy had already gone back to the game. He nodded as he blew up an enemy position.

Ben prayed the kid understood and would do as he asked. But Devin was unpredictable and other than the kid nodding, Ben didn't see any convincing indications that Devin comprehended. He couldn't force an eyeball-to-eyeball conversation with Devin while under the guard's scrutiny. All he had to go on was the kid's nod. Ben clapped as if in reference to a move Devin had made in the game. Then he whispered, "Once you're out of the room, run down the steps and find a door to the outside of the building. The system should unlock all the doors automatically. Get out and head for the woods. Don't stop. Don't wait for me. Just keep running. Do you understand?"

Devin nodded again.

Ben stood behind Devin until there were eighteen seconds left. "Okay. I'm going to go sit down. Remember, when the alarms go off, get ready to run." Ben walked back to his chair. He nodded and smiled at Red Windbreaker. *I hope you like a chair in the face, asshole.*

Casually glancing at his watch, Ben took a seat in the folding chair and stretched his arm across the back of the one next to him.

Five seconds.

His pulse raced. Sweat poured from under his arms. This was it. The boldest move he would ever make. Much more so than standing in the courtroom and denying with a blank expression that he did anything wrong when he hid billions of dollars in debt and wiped out thousands of employees' retirement funds. Much more so than faking his own death. This would be the most important moment of his life—saving an eight-year-old boy from certain death. The closest thing to redemption he—

The alarms screamed and strobe lights flashed around the computer mainframe room below while revolving red emergency lights swept the walls with a scarlet wash.

Devin froze in his seat. He whimpered and waved his hands near his ears, shaking his head.

"Devin, get up!" Ben yelled, then jumped up and yanked the boy to his feet.

Devin blinked repetitively and rested his hands at his sides.

"When the door opens, run," Ben said. "Ready?" He grabbed the metal chair by its back and held it up, prepared to swing at Red Wind-breaker.

As the man opened the door, the Halon discharged from the nozzle overhead, its ear-splitting hiss resembled the launch of a rocket. The Halon formed a white cloud as the sudden release of pressure cooled the gas when it came in contact with the moisture in the air.

Ben swung the chair full force. It struck the man in the face and chest and sent him flying against the window.

Devin was still rooted in place.

"Run! Devin, run!" Ben screamed. As he pulled the chair back for a second swing, he felt the first stab of the heart attack. Its sledgehammer force hit him so hard that he doubled over. Straining to stand, he saw Windbreaker stagger forward through the Halon fog. Blood flowed down the man's face and his arms flailed at the air.

Ben shoved Devin toward the door. "Run, damn it!"

As the man took a step toward him, Ben swung the chair again and slammed it into his assailant with all his strength. He heard the unmistakable sound of bones cracking. A grunt from Red Windbreaker told Ben he had struck a devastating blow.

The pain in Ben's chest exploded. He sank to his knees. He too had been dealt a fatal blow. The sound of the screaming alarms faded. As the lack of oxygen blurred his vision, he remembered standing on the bank of Cold Springs Lake at sunrise. A morning mist lay across the slate-flat water. Beside him stood the doe, her eyes calm and tranquil. In them, he caught a glimpse of his redemption as he vanished like a shadow in the forest.

Chapter Thirty-Seven

THE CARLYLE

The president looked across the table at the head of Central Command. "General, I appreciate the frankness in your report on the war on terrorism. Your detailed analysis was both enlightening and thought provoking."

The president, his cabinet, and visiting military officers, sat in the Cabinet Room of the White House as the forty-five-minute meeting came to an end.

"And Madam Secretary," he said turning to the Secretary of State, "I trust you will deliver my message to the prime minister in no uncertain terms?"

She nodded affirmatively.

The president leaned forward and looked down his side of the table at Mace. "Secretary Mace, thank you for the in-depth follow-up report on the recent Internet global cyberattack. I think I can speak for everyone that we are relieved at the news that there was little damage to this country's networks and virtual infrastructure."

"You're welcome, sir," Mace said, knowing most of his report had been carefully fabricated to diminish the recent flood attack and hide the widespread propagation of the Hades Worm. If the president and his advisors had seen Tor's latest progress report, they would have called for an emergency meeting of the National Security Council and Homeland Security.

Everyone in the Cabinet Room stood as the president rose and strode out. While most of the attendees remained to chat, Mace went into the corridor and pulled the cell phone from his suit jacket pocket. It had started vibrating ten minutes before the end of the meeting.

While the press secretary remained in the Cabinet Room, Mace walked down the hall and ducked inside the press secretary's empty office.

"Yes?" Mace said, just above a whisper.

"Do you still have Stone's cell phone?" It was his key advisor inside the Department of Homeland Security.

"Yes," Mace said again while he watched the hall in case the press secretary headed his way.

"Dump it! The surveillance division of the Venatori knows it's in the White House."

Mace pushed the end call button with enough force to send it in for warranty service. He stepped into the hallway and walked toward the corridor leading to the cloakroom on the first floor, West Wing lobby. Inside the large walk-in closet, he pulled his heavy overcoat from the hanger and slipped it on. He knew he had to get rid of Stone's phone, but doing so would mean losing all contact with Lindsay Jordan and her daughter in the event they left any more messages. Without their voicemail messages, there would be little he could do to track their whereabouts. He had no choice. The phone was a direct link to him.

"Rizben, can you grab mine while you're at it?" It was his single adversary in the cabinet, National Security Advisor Philip Miller.

Mace turned to Miller. In an instant he knew he had found his dumping ground. "Sure, Phil. Which one is it?"

"The navy one, two down from where yours was hanging."

Mace turned his back to Miller. As he pulled the presidential advisor's coat from the rack, he reached inside his own and grabbed Cotten's cell. In one swift motion, he dropped it into the deep side pocket of Miller's heavy woolen coat.

"Here you go." Mace handed the overcoat to his colleague. "Stay warm out there."

***

Cotten called her boss on John's phone. "Ted, I want to see Tera Jordan's face all over SNN. Give her so much air time that whoever is hunting her and Lindsay will see it and start pissing blood."

"Jesus, Cotten," Ted said. "Calm down."

Cotten and John were speeding down the Bee Line Expressway on their way to the Orlando International Airport.

"I don't want to calm down," she said.

"Okay, okay. I'll see what I can do. I've got a good bit of sway around here, but I don't know how much I can do outside of the normal channels."

"Ted, I don't ask for much." She heard John give a nervous cough. "But whoever stole my phone—whoever threatened my life—whoever burned down Lindsay's farm—is in Washington. The Venatori trace placed my cell in the White House, for Christ's sake. How much more newsworthy do you want?"

Cotten glanced at John who was trying to maneuver through the heavy traffic. She whispered to him. "How much longer?"

He pointed to the airport off ramp sign. "Just got to drop the car at the rental lot. We'll make our flight with a few minutes to spare."

"Ted, we'll be landing in Washington at 3:47. Get a crew and remote truck ready to meet me curbside."

"We can't go live with this, you know that," Ted said.

"Not asking you to. We'll tape it, and I'll send you a final edit as soon as we get back to the local affiliate."

"A White House connection could be big, or it could burn your ass to dust."

"Just have the crew ready. Once John has the Venatori run the trace on the phone again and we know the exact location, I'm going to find out who's at the bottom of this."

***

The constant hum of Interstate 395 a block away drifted along Campbell Avenue in Arlington as National Security Advisor Philip Miller emerged from the Carlyle Restaurant. Beside him was his wife. Two FBI agents had waited outside for the couple. The Millers were heading home after dining on jambalaya pasta and Hong Kong-style sea bass. The temperature had fallen below freezing, and Miller was wrapped tightly in his heavy overcoat.

As his Lincoln Town Car pulled up, the bright floodlights mounted atop a Sony XDCAM came to life, bathing the sidewalk in white light.

"Dr. Miller."

The National Security Advisor turned toward the camera light.

Cotten approached Miller with a mic in her extended hand. "Do you have a moment to answer some questions this evening?"

An agent stepped between them, but Miller held up his hand to indicate there was no threat. "Hello, Ms. Stone," Miller said. "It's good to see you back safe and sound from your Russian adventure. If your question concerns what I think of the excellent cuisine here at Carlyle, I can assure you that Mrs. Miller and I enjoyed every bite, especially the vanilla bean crème brûlée." He started to turn toward his car to signal the end of the impromptu interview.

"Actually, I was wondering why you are trying to harm an eight-year-old child."

Miller motioned his wife toward the car then turned to Cotten. "Excuse me?"

"Tera Jordan? And her mother, Lindsay? Do their names sound familiar?"

Miller stared at Cotten. "I have no idea what you're talking about."

"So you're denying responsibility for burning down their farm in Kentucky?"

He shook his head. "I can honestly say I've never been to the great state of Kentucky. What's this all about?" He stiffened and crossed his arms. "And can we please turn off the camera?"

"So, you did not have my cell phone that was stolen from my car in Loretto, Kentucky, then used it to call Cardinal John Tyler, a Vatican diplomat, and convey to him that I was to back off in my search for Tera and Lindsay Jordan or else?" Despite the rage building to a boiling point inside her, Cotten worked at remaining calm and steady. "What exactly did you mean by 'or else' when you threatened me, Dr. Miller?"

"Ms. Stone." His words had the subtleness of a leaking steam pipe. "I have never threatened you. I don't even know you except by reputation. I had nothing to do with any fires on any Kentucky farms. I don't know anybody named Tera Lindsay."

"Tera Jordan," she said.

"Whatever." He flipped his hand in a patronizing manner. "And I absolutely did not steal your cell phone. This is ridiculous. Now, if you will excuse me . . ."

Cotten nodded to her female producer who stood a few feet away. The woman tapped the screen on a phone she held.

"Dr. Miller," Cotten said. "She is calling my number right now."

Five seconds passed as the stood on the freezing sidewalk outside the Carlyle Restaurant. Only the hum of the traffic could be heard.

Miller shrugged. "What does that mean?"

Cotten listened for the ring of her cell, but only silence followed. She lowered the mic away from Miller. They'd screwed up somehow. But they had traced the phone here to the Carlyle, and Miller was the obvious White House connection. How could they have been wrong?

Chapter Thirty-Eight

ESCAPE

Devin stood in the doorway. He choked on a violent, deep cough and rocked from side to side—his hands covered his ears to block out the horrific sound of the alarms. Reacting to the strobes, he blinked repeatedly. His overloaded senses induced a state of panic and he panted. His nose and throat became dried out and they hurt.

With a heavy thud, he saw Ben kick the door shut. Devin heard the familiar clunk of the lock. He was alone on the second-floor open hallway. He stood motionless with his hands still clamped over his ears. Finally, he spun around and raced to the head of the metal stairs. The blare of the siren and the pulse of the lights herded his focus to a single compulsive need to flee.

He scrambled down the stairs, each footstep clanged and echoed in the icy-cold mainframe room. He ran from wall to wall, searching for a way out, an escape from the terrible shriek and flashing lights.

The door at the end of the last row of electronics racks was ajar, automatically unlocked to allow an emergency escape from the building. Devin heaved it wide open and burst into the sunshine. The sirens dampened without the echo inside the building.

He didn't stop to look back, but followed Ben's last orders and ran as hard as he could. He avoided the dirt road and headed across a wide expanse of fields toward the far-off timberline.

Within the shadows of the forest, Devin took his hands from his ears—the sound of his blood that drummed in his head was louder than the alarms he left behind. His heartbeat thudded in his chest, his neck, his temples, his calves—and his lungs stung with each frenzied gulp of air. A muscle cramp in his side made him stagger. Exhausted and confused, he plunged deeper into the cover of the woods. Soon, he could go no farther, and he collapsed.

Devin sprawled face down, and his nose filled with the dank odor of humid soil and decomposing vegetation hidden beneath the brittle crust of fallen leaves. He sputtered and spit a scrap of debris from his lips.

Once his breathing calmed, he crawled up beside a tree and propped himself against the rough-barked trunk. For over an hour, he sat and counted the autumn leaves—something he never saw in South Florida. He stacked them in heaps of one hundred each. Small mounds, vibrant with the blends of gold, and red, and orange encircled him.

He stood and turned in a circle to search for a landmark or clue which way to go. But there were no landmarks, nothing familiar, only endless shadowy woods. He chose a direction opposite from the one he had come and started walking.

Hours passed, and the forest grew denser, thickening with coarse underbrush, brambles, and spent berry bushes with needle-like thorns that pricked and snared his jeans.

As the sun went down, Devin succumbed to his weariness. He chose a place between the sturdy trunks of two trees and cleared a spot on the ground. A thorn caught his thumb and slit a thin line in his flesh. It stung. Devin let out a hollow-sounding yowl, then put the tip of his thumb in his mouth and sucked away the tiny beads of blood.

He curled on his side, frantically shaking his left hand next to his ear. Devin's belly grumbled with hunger, and gooseflesh broke out on his skin as the temperature dropped. He drew into a tight ball, stilled his left hand, and tucked it under his chin. He turned his head so he could see a small swatch of sky above. When the heavens darkened, he found some solace counting the stars until he drifted into sleep.

***

Devin woke with the first stab of light through the trees. He became so cold during the night that several times he had gathered the leaves around him and brushed as many over him as he could. He needed to pee, but it was too cold and too dark to get up. Still, he couldn't control his bladder. He'd been off the bathroom routine for days now. Devin felt the warmth of his urine on his legs as it seeped beneath him. There was comfort in the warmth at first but it transformed to cold moisture that permeated his body to the bone.

He sat up, the leaves cascading off him like molting feathers. The earth was steeped in fog so thick he could see the fine droplets of water in the air. It was still so cold, and he was still so hungry. Devin huddled, his hands rubbing his upper arms. He had to pee again, but held it, thinking of the cold. Finally, he could wait no longer.

He got up and walked several yards from his makeshift forest bed. As he reached for his fly, he heard a loud pop. A sudden stab of pain struck beneath his right collarbone and seared all the way through to his back. Stunned, Devin saw a perfectly round hole, about the diameter of a pencil, in his shirt at his upper right chest. A small red stain rimmed it that started to soak the front right side of his shirt.

He heard voices nearby and looked up for a moment. He cupped his hand over the hole in the fabric and stared at the rim of his palm that was spidering with streaks of blood. Perplexed, he gawked at the sight for a moment before his knees buckled.

***

Alan burst through the glass lobby doors on Cold Springs Medical Center. Kai trailed a few feet behind. The room's tile floor, a glossy gray, seemed to stretch for acres between him and the information desk.

"Devin Olsen," he told the lady at the desk in the pink volunteer uniform.

Kai came beside and entwined her arm with his. She held his hand, and they laced fingers.

"Room four-o-six," the woman said after looking at her computer. "Pediatrics."

Alan turned away from the volunteer and scanned the lobby to find the elevators.

Kai picked up the slack in his manners. "Thank you," she said, then matched Alan's stride.

He repeatedly punched the up button until the elevator door slid open.

The ride to the fourth floor was silent. Kai leaned her head on Alan's shoulder and stroked his arm. He stared at their reflection in the stainless steel. He was lucky in so many ways. Thank God his son was going to be all right. The bullet had passed straight through his shoulder, miraculously missing all vital organs and bone. Alan had plenty of questions for the police, but first, he wanted to see his son.

The doors opened. Rooms 400 through 418 were to the right. Alan glanced down the corridor and immediately knew which door belonged to Devin's room. A uniformed police officer sat in a chair beside it.

"I'm Alan Olsen," he said as he approached.

The man stood. "ID?"

Alan took his driver's license from his wallet and handed it over. He nodded toward Kai. "She's my personal assistant. She's no threat."

The officer looked over Alan's license then gave it back. "Detective Zimmer is inside."

Alan nodded a thank-you and entered Devin's room. Kai fell in be-hind, their arms stretched apart, but hands still linked.

At Alan's arrival, the man who sat in the corner of the room rose.

"Alan Olsen," Alan said and raised his hand to whom he assumed was Detective Zimmer.

"Can I speak to you outside?" Zimmer asked.

Alan's eyes fired at the man. What was the cop thinking? This was the first time Alan would see his son since the kidnapping.

Kai extended her arm across Alan's chest and placed her hand over his heart, a silent signal of support as well as a reminder of keeping in control. Her simple gesture soothed him, and instead of responding to the detective, Alan moved to Devin's bedside. Asleep, he appeared so pale and small in the whiteness of the sheets and grayscale-colored, sterile hospital room. He brushed the hair from his son's face.

"Hey, sport. Dad's here."

Devin opened his eyes. He blinked twice and each time his face pinched.

Alan leaned close. "It's okay, Devin. It's me." He scooted a metal frame chair under him so he could sit beside his son. That's when he noticed the restraints. He touched Devin's hand. Jesus, why had they done this?

Devin's eyes closed, and he slipped back into sleep.

Alan stood and looked at Kai. "Stay with him. I'll be back in a mi-nute."

"Mr. Olsen," Zimmer said. "We need to talk."

"Give me one fucking minute, will you?" Alan whispered. He stalked out of the room and headed to the nurses' station.

"I want the restraints off my son," he said to the nurse at the desk. "You can't do that to him. You don't understand."

"I'm sorry sir, you are . . .?"

"My son is in 406, and his hands are tied down. I want the restraints off."

"Devin is sedated, Mr. Olsen, because sometimes he thrashes and rips out the IV lines." She looked at Alan. "You are Devin's father, right?"

"Yes, I am, and I want the restraints removed. If Devin is sedated, then why the hell do you need the restraints?" Alan shoved his fingers through his hair.

"It's for his own safety, sir."

"No." Alan said. "Devin is autistic. Didn't anybody tell you that?" She shook her head.

"Who is the idiot who gave the orders?" As soon as he asked, he knew it didn't matter at this point. "Look, Devin has little quirky things he does . . . has to do . . . like shaking his hands beside his head. Preventing him from doing that will cause an unbearable amount of frustration. What if you had an excruciating itch and somebody bound your hands so you couldn't scratch? What would that do to you after hours of being tied down? It's the same thing. You need to talk to the charge nurse or the doctor right now because I'm going back in there and cut off the restraints. You do whatever you have to do to keep the IV lines in, but tying him down is not an option. Have I made my point?"

"I'll see what I can do," the nurse said.

"Good." Alan marched back to Devin's room, already fishing his pocketknife out of his pocket. If he had flown on a commercial airliner rather than the CyberSys corporate jet, the knife would be in his luggage.

Detective Zimmer waited outside Devin's room. "I didn't mean to rush you."

Alan passed him without acknowledging the comment and went inside. Kai nodded and smiled. Devin slept even as Alan cut the restraints.

"There you go, sport," he whispered. Turning to Kai, he said, "If he wakes, come get me. I'll just be in the hall."

Kai took Alan's hand, brought it to her lips and kissed it. "Don't worry." Alan backed out of the room and pulled the door part way closed. "Okay," he said to Zimmer. "Talk."

"Mr. Olsen, we've found Devin's kidnapper."

Chapter Thirty-Nine

MILLER

Stunned, Cotten reeled back. She had been so sure they would nail Miller on camera. But there was no ringing cell phone.

As embarrassment rushed through her, she was ready to apologize and grovel on her knees if she had to. Then Miller's expression changed from belligerence to puzzlement, and his right hand dropped to the side of his overcoat.

"What's in your pocket, Mr. Miller?" she asked, barely able to get the words out of her dry mouth.

Shock rolled over his face. The National Security Advisor looked down at his overcoat. Hesitantly, he reached into the pocket and removed a vibrating cell phone. With a look of confusion, he held it out as if it were a snake about to strike.

"Aren't you going to answer," Cotten said.

"I have no idea how this got in my overcoat." Miller stared at the phone in his hand.

"Either you do and you're lying," said Cotten, "or someone in the White House found out we ran a GPS location trace on it and planted it in your coat to distract us.

"Mr. Miller, we didn't do this blindly. We obtained a list of everyone in the White House at the time of the trace. The second trace identified the Carlyle as the phone's current location. Next, we had our crew check out every patron. That little birthday celebration going on inside was staged by SNN so we could take photos of everyone in the restaurant without arousing suspicion. We uploaded them to our research department and guess what? Your face is the only one that matches up with the people on the White House list. What other conclusion should I draw?"

Miller looked around the sidewalk as if to gauge the reaction of the others there.

"Before we broadcast this as a feature story, would you like to discuss it in private with me?"

He glanced at his watch. Then he motioned to the restaurant's entrance.

"I certainly would, Ms. Stone."

Moments later, Cotten and Miller were alone in the manager's office of the restaurant. The SNN crew waited outside in the remote truck while the two FBI agents and Miller's wife occupied a booth in the hastily closed restaurant.

"First, I'm impressed with your attention to detail to narrow it down to me," Miller said. "The fact is I'm not lying. Why would I have taken the phone out of my pocket? It didn't ring. If I was guilty, I'd have ignored the vibrating phone." He leaned forward in the chair. "But I don't care whether you believe me or not. What I *do* care about is why the phone was in my coat in the first place. Someone put it there." He stared at Cotten who stood on the opposite side of the desk. "We're talking about a group of people with the highest security clearances in the country, starting with the president on down." He scored his bottom lip. "The entire cabinet, along with two members of the Joint Chiefs and the head of Central Command were present at the same meeting I attended. Not to mention the vice president and the White House senior support staff. Then there's all the other staff wandering about, right down to the cook."

"Anyone there for the first time or out of the ordinary?" Cotten asked.

"I wouldn't know other than those present at the meeting." Miller stared off into space as he seemed to picture who was in attendance. Then he said, "At least not in the cabinet meeting. Even the generals have all been there several times."

"You mentioned the support staff? Anyone new to the White House? Someone you never saw before?"

"I didn't notice any unfamiliar faces. Aside from the Oval Office, the Cabinet Room where we were is the inner sanctum of executive power. Nobody gets in there that doesn't belong. It's impossible. I can't speak for those not in the Cabinet Room who might have found access to the cloakroom. But I suspect that type of opportunity is unrealistic."

Cotten dropped into a chair in front of the desk, not wanting to believe someone high up the political food chain could be connected to the Brotherhood of the Nephilim, or worse, one of the Fallen Angels. Trying to think of an alternative, Cotten asked, "Could someone have put the phone in your coat pocket before you arrived for the meeting?"

Miller shrugged. "I went in late today, driving directly from my home to the White House. I have two people that work for me—a housekeeper and a secretary. The housekeeper was sick, and it was my secretary's day off. That leaves my wife and my dog. Both are loyal beyond reproach." He smiled.

"I believe you," Cotten said, returning the smile, "about their loyalty, that is." She removed her small notepad from her pocket and scribbled on it. "That doesn't change the fact that you had my phone—the one stolen from me in Kentucky while I was investigating the disappearance of a mother and her daughter. The same phone used to threaten my life." Cotten tapped the end of the pen on the pad. "It looks like we're at a stalemate here."

Miller folded his arms on the desk. In a hushed voice, he said, "What the hell is this all about?"

***

Thirty minutes later, Cotten and Miller, along with his wife and the agents, emerged from the Carlyle. Cotten stood on the sidewalk and watched the National Security Advisor assist his wife into the back of the Lincoln Town Car. As he followed his wife into the car, Miller turned and gave Cotten a reassuring nod. A moment later, the car sped off into the Virginia night.

Walking the half block to the waiting SNN remote truck, Cotten realized that if what Miller had told her turned out to be true, it would rock the nation to its core.

Chapter Forty

RACKY-SACKY

The corridor of the hospital was cold and colorless. Only gray, white, and a rare blotch of muted green stretched in all directions. A person could get sick in here just from the chill and the boring decor, Alan thought.

"Your son is a lucky boy," Detective Zimmer said.

"Seems so," Alan responded. "Obviously, I haven't seen the doctor yet, but I talked to him on the phone. Devin's going to be fine." Alan glanced at the officer who still sat outside the room, then back at Zimmer. "I think I need a little more explanation of what happened. You say you've caught the bastard? I hope he burns in hell."

"Your wish might be happening as we speak. The guy is dead," Zimmer said. "We found him this morning."

Alan stared at Zimmer. "Who? Why did he do it? Please tell me it wasn't some sicko, some child molester. Since there was no ransom demand, all I've been able to think about was . . . I know the doctor said Devin showed no signs of sexual abuse. But shit, you can't tell what the guy might have done to my son."

"Mr. Olsen, you can relax," Zimmer said. "It wasn't anything like that. Why don't we go have a seat in the waiting room?"

"No, I want to be here if Devin wakes."

"I understand. Then let me start with a question and we'll go from there. Do you recall the recent financial scandal surrounding Presidium Health Care, the for-profit health care conglomerate?"

"Sure," Alan said. "What's that got to do with anything?"

"And remember one of PHC's big guns under investigation was Benjamin Ray?"

"Right," Alan said, nodding in frustration. "His partner is already in prison. I read where Ray died before he could be sentenced."

"That's the way it seemed. Mr. Ray had enough money to have his death falsified—from death certificate to cremation. Ray didn't die. He was hiding out in a remote cabin near the Ozark National Forest using the name, Ben Jackson. He was running short of cash. The government struck a deal with the foreign banks to seize his funds so they could return the money to the stockholders. Ray was caught in a desperate situation and decided to try his hand at kidnapping for ransom. He fingered you as a rich guy with an only child. I don't think he had any plans of hurting your son—he's a white-collar criminal, not a murderer—but he counted on getting enough money from this one shot at you to live on for the rest of his life."

"But there were no demands. I didn't get any calls or a ransom note."

"He simply hadn't sent it yet. Who knows why the holdup. Maybe he was waiting for the heat to die down. He was holding Devin in his cabin. That's where we found Ray—collapsed on the floor of his basement beside a few of your son's belongings. Ironically, it looks like he died from a heart attack—the same thing he faked just before his sentencing date in court. A real quirk of fate, wouldn't you agree?" Zimmer paused when Alan didn't laugh, then went on. "There was a ransom note addressed to you demanding two-and-a-half million dollars. From the prelims, it looks like Ray croaked before he could send the note."

"Christ," Alan said, drawing his hand down his face. "I'd have paid that and more, no questions asked."

"I'm sure you would have, Mr. Olsen. But before he could pull it off, he dropped dead and Devin wandered off into the woods. Kind of ended in a sweet payback."

"Except that Devin was shot."

"No, of course I didn't mean that. But still, how lucky it happened the way it did. The hunters who shot Devin could have panicked and left him, but they didn't. It was foggy out there, and we believe it was an accident. The fog was a blessing in a way. If Devin had been two hundred yards away instead of thirty, the bullet from that 30.30 would have ripped his shoulder apart. He would have probably bled to death before they got him out of the woods. But being so close, it passed straight through. I'll tell you those guys were pretty shaken when they got here. They called 9-1-1 on the way in and told dispatch they were on their way to the medical center. It's up to the county prosecutor, but at this point, I don't see any charges being filed. Can't speak for the FBI, but they'll likely see it the same way."

"Sure, right," Alan said. "I understand it was an accident."

"Alan?" Kai's voice came from Devin's room.

"Excuse me." Alan left Zimmer in the hall.

"Somebody is awake," Kai said in a sing-song voice. She stroked Devin's head. "Your dad is here, sweetheart."

Alan kissed his son's forehead. "How are you feeling, big guy?"

Devin blinked several times and looked off to the side.

"He hasn't said anything to anyone," Zimmer said, coming in behind Alan. "Non-communicative. Does he talk?"

"Of course he talks," Kai said. "He's autistic, not mute."

Zimmer shrugged and held up his hands. "I don't know much about that autism thing. No intention to offend."

"It's okay." Alan motioned to Zimmer and moved to the open door. He kept his voice below the level of the hum of the monitors hooked to Devin. "Even the experts don't understand it. Devin does talk. He's extremely bright in specific areas. His language is delayed, but not his . . . It's difficult to explain. His brain is wired differently."

"Maybe you can get him to talk to us," Zimmer said. "We need to ask him some questions."

"Well, that's uncertain," Alan said. "Social skills, reactions to strangers, relationships, are all unpredictable—other than the fact that they are poorly developed most of the time."

"We could use his help to wrap this thing up."

"We can try," Alan said, "But there's no guarantee he can tell you anything useful. Right now I'm exhausted and I just want to spend a little quality time with my son. Mind if we give it a go tomorrow?"

"No problem," Zimmer said. "But the Feds will have questions, too. They should be here soon. I know they were on their way in. A word of warning—I don't think they are as sensitive as us locals." Zimmer arched his brows. "Just my humble opinion. Anyway, I'll be dismissing the officer outside now that you're here. But I'll be back in the morning."

"Fine." Alan shook Zimmer's hand then returned to the bedside and gazed down at Devin. "So, sport, you've been on quite an adventure. Feel like talking about it?"

Devin shook his head. His eyes darted to the door, then around the room as if taking attendance. He looked back at his dad. "Juice," he said.

"You want some apple juice?" Kai asked. Devin shook his head.

"Orange?" Kai asked.

Again Devin gestured a negative response. "100 percent vegetable juice. Ingredients, from concentrate, tomato concentrate, reconstituted vegetable juice blend, water and concentrated juices of carrots, celery, beets, parsley, lettuce, watercress, spinach, salt, vitamin C—ascorbic acid, flavoring, citric acid—"

"V-8 juice," Alan said, recognizing the ingredients his son spouted. He'd heard it a million times. Devin memorized everything he ever read, even down to the labels on food products. Kid wonder, Alan thought. He wished he could understand his son's mind. "I don't think they have V-8. We might have to settle for plain tomato juice." Devin frowned but nodded.

A rap at the door drew their attention to a dark silhouette in the doorway.

"Mr. Olsen? I'm Agent Roselli, FBI."

"I'll speak to you outside if you don't mind," Alan said. "In the waiting room."

The agent backed out of the doorway.

"Looks like more visitors for your dad," Kai said to Devin. "But we'll be just fine, won't we Dev?"

Alan gave Kai a peck on the cheek, tousled his son's hair then joined Agent Roselli.

"Boom-a-racky-sacky," Devin said to Kai after his father left.

"Oh, no," Kai said. "You know I'm no good at that."

***

"Boom-a-racky-sacky," Devin said, breaking into a full-fledged smile. This was a game he often liked to play. Alan had taught him the game, which was a revised version of a college drinking game. Kai knew Devin enjoyed playing with her because it was such an easy win for him. One of them would start counting, beginning with the number one, and they would alternate each number. Beginning with three and every multiple of three thereafter or any number with a three in it, instead of saying the number, they would say boom-a-racky. For the number seven and its multiples and numbers with a seven in it, they would say boom-a-sacky. For multiples of both three and seven or with any three and seven combination, they would say boom-a-racky-sacky. Because of frequent playing, Kai was okay until about 252, but after that she fell off. Alan usually got out a calculator after about 1225.

Devin allowed it so he could keep playing. When he played with Kai, he appeared simply to like the win.

"All right," Kai said. "One."

"Two," Devin said.

"Boom-a-racky," Kai said.

"Four."

"Five."

"Boom-a-racky."

"Boom-a-sacky," Kai said. She sighed. "Were you scared out there in the woods alone? It must have been awful."

"Eight," Devin said.

"Boom-a-racky." She brushed back Devin's hair from his forehead. "I'm glad you're home again. Knowing how you can't sit still, you must have been terribly bored."

"Ten. I played games. Games. Games. Games." Devin jolted his hands in the air.

Kai grabbed his arms and pulled them down. "Whoa, Devin, you're going to pull out your IVs."

"Boom-a-racky-sacky. Boom-a-racky-sacky. Boom-a-racky-sacky."

"Okay, Devin, okay. Take it easy," Kai said. "Eleven. Were the games fun? What kind of games? Were you good at them?"

"Boom-a-racky. Call of Duty. Code. Call of Duty."

"Boom-a-racky. Were you good at the game, Devin?"

"Boom-a-sacky." Devin simulated the sound effects and began moving phantom video game controls.

"Boom-a-racky," Kai said. "And what about the code? Were you good at that, too? Tell me more about that, Devin."

"Sixteen. Devin is smart."

"How is Devin smart? Did you finish the code game?"

"Play, Kai. Play."

"I'll play after you tell me more about the code. Was it the Destiny code game?"

"Say boom-a-sacky. Devin is smart. Say it, Kai. Play the game."

"Boom-a-sacky," Kai said. "Tell me how smart you are."

Devin's voice rose as if agitated. "Racky sacky, racky sacky, boom, boom, boom."

Kai heaved out a frustrated gush of air. "I am playing, Devin. Eighteen. I mean boom-a-racky."

"Nineteen. Racky sacky, boom, sacky, racky, boom."

"Stop it, Devin. Just tell me about the code."

"Boom, boom, boom, racky. Play the game."

"Twenty," Kai huffed. "Fucking twenty, okay. Now explain to me how you are so smart. Did you finish the code game?"

Devin tossed his head from side to side in rhythm to his chanting of the name of the game. "Boom-a-racky-sacky. Boom-a-racky-sacky. Boom-a-racky-sacky. That's the name of the game, not racky sacky, boom, boom. That's how Devin is smart." He shook his hands near his ears and Kai ignored it.

Her face suddenly paled. Kai grabbed Devin's wrists to still them. "You mean you mixed it up? Scrambled the code?"

Devin's face bloomed with a big smile. "Devin is smart."

Kai dropped his wrists. She picked up her purse from the floor and dug through it until she found her cell, then moved to the window. She kept her back to Devin and made a call.

Chapter Forty-One

BOOK OF EMZARA

Mace stood back and waited until the group of Asian tourists moved away from the front of James Smithson's memorial inside the Castle of the Smithsonian Institute. The guard had told him they were the last group to come through and Mace would have about ten minutes of privacy until closing. Intrigued by the substantial collection at the Institute, he came often to meditate among the relics of the ages. As he stood in reverence to the founder of the Smithsonian, he heard a voice.

"He was the illegitimate son of the Duke of Northumberland and Elizabeth Hungerford."

Mace turned to see the Old Man standing behind him.

"Some of the best men in history were bastards," Mace said. "This one died in Genoa, but Alexander Graham Bell brought his body here." Mace looked into the eyes of his mentor, hoping to soften the blow of the bad news he had delivered earlier when he requested the meeting. News that the boy escaped before giving Tor the complete operating system code of the Destiny computer and that the kid may have scrambled parts of it. Then there was the fact that the banker and Tor's assistant were both dead. Finally, the second thodium artifact sent to Tor was only slightly more reliable than the degraded original. "It's a shame Smithson didn't bother to add objects made from thodium to his vast collection here."

"That would have made it too easy, Pursan." The Old Man came to stand beside Mace. "Has Tor located the child?"

"He spent the day searching the woods but no sign of the boy. I had him take Jackson's body to the banker's cabin along with some of the boy's belongings."

"Tor must make sure there is no trace of either one of them at the Hades facility. If the authorities do come around, they must find nothing more than a collection of rundown buildings on an abandoned military installation."

"We have all the paperwork in place that shows one building is being used by an Internet data storage company operating out of the Midwest. They have a long-term lease on file with the Department of the Interior to rent the property. All the documentation is in order in case Tor must prove he has a permit to be there." Mace watched the stoic expression on the aged face of the Old Man. "These problems can all be handled. The bigger issue is where we will get a non-degraded source of thodium. All we have had to work with were small raw pieces of planks left of the Ark. Even extracting the crystallized sap from the wood has been a task."

The Old Man smiled—the all-knowing expression that often annoyed Mace. "Then we must find out if there were other objects made from the Tree."

"But if there were, wouldn't they have vanished in the Great Flood?"

"Maybe there was something taken aboard Noah's barge. Certainly if there was an object made from the Tree of Life, it would have extraordinary sacrosanct value to Noah. Such an article would not have been left behind. And then there is the obvious—the lumber of the Ark was distributed and used in the new world to build houses and furniture and produce tools. It could be worth the effort to track the family lineage. Who knows what may have been passed on from generation to generation?"

"Mr. Secretary," a young FBI agent said as he approached Mace. "We need to leave in five minutes."

Mace gave him a be-right-there wave and waited until the man walked back to the entrance to the shrine of the Smithsonian's founder. "How can we find out what might have survived?"

"There are several ancient writings dealing with Noah and his clan—documents that were ultimately rejected by the Church at the First Council of Nicaea. The reason given was that some would have been contradictory to Church teachings at the time and possibly taken the faith in a different direction. Instead, they were destroyed or hidden away from the eyes of the world."

"Which should we be seeking?" asked Mace.

"One comes to mind—the Book of Emzara."

"Which is?"

"Pursan," the Old Man said in a condescending tone. "I would have thought you to be more versed in these matters."

"Ancient scriptures are not a topic that interests me."

"In order for the Hades Project to succeed, ancient writings like the Book of Emzara will be the key." He looked harshly at Mace. "Emzara was Noah's wife. She is not named in Genesis, but the Book of Jubilees identifies her. In Jewish tradition she is called Naamah, but I prefer the latter. Emzara was the designated scribe of their ordeal, and she kept good records of the event, including a manifest of the Ark's inventory. Maybe she chronicled the family history after the Flood. The Book of Emzara may lead us to your alternative thodium source."

"Mr. Secretary," the agent said, walking toward Mace.

"Coming." He waited until the man retreated. "Where is this Book of Emzara?"

"Among a collection of other sought-after remnants of religious antiquity." In an instant, Mace realized he knew the location.

As they turned to leave, the Old Man said, "There is one other thread that needs tying up—the matter of your fellow cabinet member."

Mace smiled. "It's being taken care of even as we speak."

Chapter Forty-Two

THE NEWS

Lindsay fluffed the pillows to make them look a little more attractive in their yellowed cases. This was the third room she'd cleaned this morning, and it was only 8:00 AM. The majority of the guests were either fishermen who got up before dawn or were long-haul truckers who left the do-not-disturb signs on their doors most of the time.

She smoothed the wrinkles from the bedspread and stepped back. It was the best she could do. The material was faded, like the walls and carpet in every room of the Dos Palmas Motel. She knew the linens were clean because she had laundered them all herself. The management didn't provide bleach, just a generic brand of detergent. She'd been told that bleach would shorten the life of the linens gradually eating them up. Maybe putting some of the sheets and towels out of their misery would be a good thing, she thought. She bought bleach at the Winn-Dixie supermarket nearby, kept it in her room but took it with her when she did the motel laundry as well as her own.

While she worked, Tera sat on the floor with a baggie of Cheerios and leaned back against the foot of the bed.

"Get up," Lindsay said. Her face grimaced at the thought of what lay hidden in the depths of the carpet. She grabbed a clean but threadbare towel off the cleaning cart parked outside the room. "Sit on this." She tossed it to Tera.

Tera spread the towel and plopped down, Cheerios in one hand and the TV remote in the other.

Lindsay moved on to clean the bathroom. She heard Tera change the channel on the television. "I hope you're watching something educational, young lady. If we were home, this would be school time."

Lindsay scrubbed the tub, but the glossy finish on the porcelain was long gone, and no matter how clean she got it, it still appeared dull and drab. A lock of her hair fell in her face and she used the back of her forearm to sweep it away. When was this ever going to end? She wanted normalcy in her life. Lindsay sat back on her heels with her rubber-gloved hands in her lap. She couldn't recall the last time her life had been normal. It had to have been before Tera was born. It was hard to remember what that had been like.

She leaned over the tub again and sprinkled more cleanser as if it might make a difference.

And where was Cotten? She hadn't even responded to the message Lindsay had left. After getting no return call the first time, Lindsay didn't bother to call back. She assumed she would become a nuisance to her old friend. After all, they hadn't seen each other in years. What had she thought, that Cotten Stone, famous television journalist, would drop everything and come running? "Stupid, Lindsay. Just plain stupid. You and Tera are in this by yourselves."

"Momma," Tera called.

Lindsay had a hard time finding her voice. It wanted to crack with the threat of tears, and she didn't want Tera to hear that. "What, Ladybug?" She scrubbed the dull porcelain in circles with more and more pressure as if that helped her fight back the urge to cry. In a moment, when her daughter hadn't responded, she stopped and listened. "Tera?"

No answer. Lindsay chucked the sponge in the tub and got to her feet. "Tera?" She bolted out of the bathroom. Her fear dissipated as soon as she saw Tera was safe.

Her daughter stood in front of the television, her gaze fastened on the screen, the bag of Cheerios open, a small sea of oat circles on the floor.

"What is it?" Lindsay snapped off the gloves and dropped them on the dresser.

Tera touched the television screen with her index finger.

Lindsay's attention moved from her daughter to the story on the morning news, only catching the tail end. "And so what could have been a tragedy ends on a happy note," the reporter said. A video of a man embracing a boy filled the screen. "Devin Olsen is safe and home again." There was a pause. "In other news—"

"We have to go see him," Tera said.

Lindsay had seen several reports in the newspapers and on television about the boy's disappearance and was happy to hear he was found safe. She felt for his dad and understood how helpless the man must have been. And the boy was autistic on top of it all. Most stories of missing children with disabilities didn't have happy endings. Why did Tera have such an interest? "Why do we have to go see him, Tera?"

"I know him."

"No, you don't sweetie. He's from Miami, not Loretto."

"No, I mean from before."

"Before what?" Lindsay took both her daughter's hands in hers. "We've never met that little boy."

"Not you, Momma. Me."

Lindsay pulled Tera near the bed and had her sit on the end. She cradled her daughter's face in her palms. "That's impossible."

Tera smiled with knowledge that seemed to go beyond her years. "You weren't with me then."

"Where, Ladybug? Where did you go without me? Where did you meet him?"

"Before I was born. In Heaven."

Chapter Forty-Three

EXFILTRATION

Tor looked at his watch. Five minutes to go. Mace would call for an update, and he wanted to be ready.

"It's freezing in here," he said to himself and rubbed the end of his nose to warm it. He had lowered the temperature to fifty degrees earlier in the day. Icing down the building was necessary to prepare for the enormous flood of information that would pour into the system over the next twenty-four hours as the Hades Worm—hiding dormant deep inside millions of computers around the world—was triggered as each system went out and synchronized to the international atomic clock.

Although the data from infected systems would trickle out information about the users, the computers, and the affected business enterprise networks, the overall amount of data would be enormous. The mainframes in the Hades facility would be working at maximum capacity, and overheated processors were the last thing he needed.

It seemed like everything got on his nerves as the pressure of the phase-two deadline loomed. First off, he was now alone at the old military base in the middle of the Arkansas backwoods since his assistant was killed when the kid escaped. Burying the body in the rocky terrain had taken half a day away from his work, which hadn't been going that well in the first place. The frigging quantum computer still wasn't as stable as he would like. Even if every phase of the Hades Project went flawlessly, if the computer didn't maintain stability using the degraded thodium sample, he would never be able to crack the government encryption codes. And to add to the aggravation, Mace was calling two, three, sometimes four times a day. He insisted on proceeding even though Tor had told him about the stability issue.

Tor much preferred to talk to Kai—in many ways. It amazed him that Mace was vain enough to believe that the Chinese beauty was attracted to him—and dedicated to his cause. Mace didn't understand that Kai Chiang always fucked the highest bidder. Years ago, Tor had once been the guy with the biggest payoff. How the hell did Mace think Kai found her way into Mace's life, anyway? Tor had been a stepping-stone—he'd known it and really hadn't given a rat's ass. She'd been a wild ride for a short time—no investments, no commitments. Suited him just fine. Tor knew the bitch would sell out anybody—just like she was doing to Alan Olsen. One day she'd hock Rizben Mace for the next stone to step on.

As if on cue, the phone rang.

"Are we on schedule?" Mace asked.

Tor looked at his watch again. "Thirty seconds to midnight GMT."

Starting at 12:00 a.m. GMT and each hour following, as the next time zone clicked over to midnight, the Hades Worm would come alive and identify servers on each affected network. Once the servers were identified, an attempt would be made to log in using null password authentication—searching for any usernames with blank passwords. If the worm resided on a computer where the user had administrative privileges, it would hijack the user's credentials and complete the login.

Once the Worm accessed the system with borrowed administrative privileges, it would act as the authorized user and instruct the compromised computer to look for other hosts across the network. Utilizing basic ping requests, which would appear as benign traffic, it would try to connect to specific domain names followed by their respective .com, .net, .org, .edu, .gov, and .mil extensions. Each of these specific hosts held pieces of the virus. As each ping hit the host, the reply to the compromised computer would include more and more pieces of the virus.

Tor knew that the great part of using these common ping packets was their ability to hold hidden data in unused sections of the packet header. Virus hunters would never think to look at the headers to reveal the pieces of the Hades Project code. Like a cyber scavenger hunt, the compromised computer would eventually bring all the pieces together to assemble and execute a rootkit program, with the sole mission of giving the Hades Project complete control and backdoor access to the compromised computer.

A novice hacker would have had the worm connect to the host computer via IP addresses instead of host domain names. In that scenario, once the authorities took down that IP address, the game would be over. But Tor had designed the worm to look for host computers via domain names. The domain name address could point to as many IP addresses as there were that hosted mirrored versions of the virus. Even better, Interpol and the FBI chase IP addresses all day while new IP addresses were assigned to the sole domain name. Since Tor had already hacked into and hidden the virus on host servers all over the world, the authorities should give up the hunt after dealing with the headaches from hosting providers in multiple countries. By the time they got to the end of the trail, phase two of the Hades Project would be old news.

"Are we poised to begin phase three?" Mace asked.

I've told the bastard a thousand times already, Tor thought. That's the way he would like to answer Mace, but he knew better. It didn't matter that Tor was Nephilim, the offspring of a Fallen Angel and human—which made him a Ruby—Mace would have him out on his ear or worse if he showed insubordination. "Yes, we're on schedule. Remember, Rizben, we're creating millions of zombie computers out there.

It'll take time to distribute the rootkits. As soon as we do, phase three will begin."

Tor liked to call phase three "ID Recon"—the identification of specific, main targets to manipulate their systems. The final success would depend on a predictable human reaction causing a domino effect of catastrophic proportions.

Mace said, "We're only going to get one shot at this. The reaction we're predicting must be correct."

"I just do the geek stuff. You're the one who calculates how people will think. I take no ownership in that part."

Tor reviewed the main targets in his head. The GPS Satellite diagnostic and control systems; Air Traffic Control Emergency Notification Grid; SWIFT Global Banking network; Defense Information Systems Agency Network and its Global Information Grid; the U.S. Power Grid Network and corresponding foreign networks; the maintenance channel for Safety Parameters Display System that monitor and control nuclear power plants; eighty supervisory control and data acquisition networks that included electricity, natural gas, water, sewage, railroads, and telecommunications; and the mother of all targets—the AT&T Global Satellite Communications monitoring station.

He glanced at the monitor that displayed the operating system interface to the Hades quantum computer. The little shit thought he was so smart, Tor thought, picturing Devin Olsen typing away in the game room, trying to trick him by mixing things up. But Devin wasn't the one with doctorates in theoretical physics and mechanical engineering. Tor was. After the call from Kai warning him that the kid had tried to be clever, it only took Tor a few hours to straighten out and complete the code. Who's the clever boy now?

One last time, Tor looked at his watch. A few seconds to go.

The screen was blank. He could feel the heavy beat of his heart in his chest. Despite the chill, he started sweating. His grip on the phone tightened. He heard Mace's breathing on the other end.

Midnight.

Tor held his breath. This was it. No second chance.

The Hades Project's master control monitor blinked. A line of text appeared on the bottom of the monitor.

XOCSSOV.MOLDAVID.echo.YORK.0022039

He leaned forward. A second line appeared under the first, moving the original line up.

XOCSSOV.LANCAST.echo.ABBY.0022048

Before the second line could finish, a third appeared at the bottom and then a fourth. As each appeared, the previous lines moved up the screen. Then, like a floodgate opening, the lines came rushing in by the dozens, hundreds, and then thousands. The progress of a line appearing and pushing the previous text up became a blur.

Tor smiled. "Rizben?"

"Yes."

"We have liftoff."

Chapter Forty-Four

BLUES

Lindsay tossed their belongings in the back of the van and took a last look at the Dos Palmas Motel before climbing in the driver's seat.

"Are we coming back?" Tera asked, buckling up.

"I don't know yet." Lindsay started the engine and twisted around to check as she backed out of the parking space.

"Then why are we taking all of our stuff?"

"Because we might not come back."

Tera pointed at the jangling key ring. "But you have the key."

Lindsay looked in both directions, then pulled out and headed north on U.S. 1, the Overseas Highway.

"You need to buckle up, too, Momma. Are we spending the night in Miami?"

"Maybe."

"Won't they miss you at work tomorrow, if we do? You'll get into trouble."

Lindsay sighed with exasperation. "Yes, Tera, you're right. Listen, here's the deal. You said you wanted to go see this Devin Olsen boy, so that's where we're going. I don't know what will happen after that. Maybe you know the answer but I don't." She stared at her daughter. "You always seem to know more about everything than you tell me, anyway." She immediately regretted her words.

Tera turned away and stared out the side window.

They rode in silence for miles. Lindsay knew she was tense and had snapped at Tera without real reason more than once that day. Tera was just being a kid, wondering what was going on. Lately, both of their lives had been so unpredictable. Tera simply wanted to find out what she could count on—what to anticipate in her immediate future. Who else would she ask but her mother? Children felt safe with routine and structure, two elements sorely missing from their lives.

Lindsay massaged the back of her neck. Tera deserved better than her less-than-stellar parenting skills of late. She latched her seatbelt then reached across the center console for Tera's hand. "I'm sorry, Ladybug. I love you."

"I love you, too."

"Want to stop at Shell World? You can pick out a pretty shell." Tera's small face brightened.

***

At Shell World, Tera spent half an hour searching for just the right shell, finally choosing a conch. She said it was so beautiful, admiring its shiny gloss surface on the inside. The man at the register told her how conchs had been used long ago in the islands to announce weddings and had been used by sailors for centuries. He took one from under the counter and blew through the man-made hole in the top, creating a most exotic bellowing horn sound. Tera told her mother she loved it and wanted to carry the conch out in her hands—no bag.

Once they got back on the highway, Tera drew several sketches of her conch shell, but complained that she wasn't happy with them because of the unsteadiness of the pencil in the moving van.

Almost two hours later, Highway U.S. 1 merged with Biscayne Boulevard in downtown Miami. Lindsay turned up the radio volume until it blared, and she and Tera sang the chorus of "You're the One That I Want" along with Olivia Newton John and John Travolta. They were in the middle of belting out "Ooo, ooo, ooo," when the CyberSys building

217

appeared ahead on the left. Lindsay's voice dropped off and questions rolled around in her head. What on earth was she going to say when they walked into the building? How would she explain why they had come?

The song ended with Tera gazing at her mother, her enthusiasm for singing also lost.

Lindsay parked the car in a nearby lot. "You know, they might not let us in. Devin's father doesn't know us. Nobody does." She brushed Tera's hair back with her fingers. "I'm sure Devin's daddy loves him as much as I love you. And he just got Devin back from a bad experience. He'll be cautious and protective of Devin, and want to keep him safe, like I want to protect you. He probably won't understand why we're here." *I don't understand why we're here.* Lindsay leaned close to Tera. "And I'm not sure, either, Ladybug."

"Don't worry. I'll tell his daddy that Devin is like me."

"What do you mean, sweetheart?"

"He's blue."

It took a moment for the word blue to register with Lindsay. "You mean Indigo? You believe Devin is an Indigo child? You think he has special gifts like you?"

"Yes, yes." Her eyes twinkled. "Devin is very special. Like me."

"Devin is special, sweetie, but not in the same way you are. He has something called autism. It makes him think different and feel things different."

"Like me," Tera said.

"No, not like you."

"He doesn't draw," Tera said. "But he does other things."

Lindsay wondered what an autistic kid could do that Tera would think of as a special gift.

"Devin knows things like I do. He will remember when I picked you and when he picked his mom and dad."

"What?"

"We all got to pick."

Lindsay shook her head in confusion.

"We looked down and picked our moms and dads. I picked you and daddy. Devin picked his dad and his mom. All the Indigos get to choose."

"Tera, we talked once when you asked about babies—where they come from. Remember that? I told you how—"

"I don't remember being a baby inside you. I don't remember being one year old."

"Of course you don't. Nobody remembers when they were babies."

"But I remember before I was a baby. I remember Devin and all the others and my sister—my twin—she was already here."

Lindsay pressed her spine against the seat and leaned back. She stared up at the sagging headliner. "You can't go around talking like that. People will think you're—"

"Devin won't. He was there. There are a lot of us. He'll remember."

"Us?"

"Blues. You know, Indigos."

Lindsay sat quietly. How in the hell was she going to walk up to Alan Olsen and tell him her daughter wants to talk to his son, recent kidnap victim, because they were some place together before they were born? What the shit had she been thinking? *Who's the crazy one, Lindsay Jordan? Who drove all the way to Miami with such a bizarre notion?*

"You'll see, Momma. I promise. Please believe me. I know why they took Devin."

"What do you mean?"

"They needed the numbers in Devin's head."

"Okay, look. If Mr. Olsen agrees to see us, it's probably better we don't talk about the kidnapping or you knowing Devin before you were born and all that stuff. It might scare him away." She swept a wisp of Tera's hair from her face. "Follow along with whatever I say. Do you understand?"

"Okay."

Lindsay unbuckled their seatbelts then drew Tera into her arms and held her close. She swayed back and forth like she had done years ago while holding her daughter as an infant. Lindsay breathed in the sweet bouquet of Tera's hair and felt the softness of her daughter's skin against hers. She wished she could absorb Tera, enfold her precious child and protect her from the world forever.

"I love you, baby." She released Tera and looked deep into her eyes. "Let's go meet Devin's dad."

Chapter Forty-Five

SECRETS

"Zilch," Ted Casselman said. "You got *nada*."

"That's not exactly true." Cotten sat alone in one of the sales department's office cubicles at the Washington SNN studios. Ted had made her promise to call him at home in New York as soon as she finished the interview with Miller. It was 12:30 a.m.

"Then let me recap. You arrange this elaborate confrontation with the National Security Advisor of the United States, bring in a dozen of my Washington staff to stage a fake birthday party—with me paying them overtime, I might add—utilize one of our remote trucks, call in a producer, tie up enough video gear to shoot Steven Spielberg's next movie, and you come up with nothing but egg on your face." He paused. "What part of that is not exactly true?"

"You're exaggerating the facts. And I did come away with something. Miller told me he thinks he knows who planted the phone in his coat."

"Of course he told you that, Cotten. It was getting late, and he wanted to go home. He would have said he suspected the Easter Bunny if you'd have pressed him hard enough."

"He said it was someone in the White House. In the Cabinet."

Ted let out a breath. "Look, I trust you explicitly. I've come to know that your instincts are like a razor. And I know your secrets—secrets that go beyond . . ."

She heard the faint scratching sound from the stubble as he rubbed his face, and pictured him sitting on the side of his bed in the dark, trying not to awaken his wife. Cotten hated so much to disappoint him.

"But this time," he said, "you're pissing in the tall grass with the big dogs. The friggin' presidential cabinet, for Christ's sake. Do you have any idea what kind of position you could be putting the network in if this thing goes south?"

"I understand there's a lot at stake."

"A lot at stake? Cotten, forget losing your job. Hell, how about me losing mine? What about the credibility of the network?" He paused again. "You tend to forget that there are a whole bunch of folks I have to answer to, and they have a whole bunch over them called the board of directors. And the board answers to the stockholders. And none of them give a flying fuck about your instincts or your . . . secrets. Remember that a reporter is only as good as her last story. Don't you understand that?"

Ted stopped. There was silence for a full minute. Then he said, "Miller gave you a name, didn't he? Who does he suspect planted the phone?"

"I promised I wouldn't reveal the name until he has concrete proof."

"How can I give you any support if I don't know what I'm dealing with? Is it the White House cook or the president? And why in God's name would someone in the White House want to steal your cell phone, burn down a farm in Kentucky, and threaten your life? It doesn't make any sense."

"From what I've learned about Lindsay and her daughter, Tera, I think this goes way beyond the theft of a cell phone."

"Fine, so rather than Watergate, now we got Lorettogate. Come on, Cotten. How stupid does that sound?"

"I asked you to trust me with the Grail Conspiracy, and I was right, wasn't I?"

She heard him grunt.

"I asked you to trust me when you agreed to the live London broadcast just before we opened the time capsule and found the crystal tablet. Remember how many lives that saved? I was right that time, too, wasn't I?"

Another grunt followed by a heavy sigh.

"You said my instincts were second to none, right?"

Silence.

"That you know my secrets, my—"

"All right, already. Enough. There's no winning an argument with you. I never have, and I never will." He paused as if in reflection. "And thinking back, I thank God that I didn't win all our arguments. But this time, I need something to go on—a direction—something that will help me justify the expenses and time. Who does Miller suspect?"

Cotten listened to the sound fragments coming from throughout the building—the SNN graveyard shift. She heard a faint ring of a phone, a distant conversation, a radio playing soft jazz, a chuckle. But beyond the solace and calm, somewhere out in the night, the Fallen and the Nephilim were amassing their forces. All the signs pointed to another attempt to strike at the one thing God treasured most—his prized creation—man. They had tried it with the attempt to clone Christ and create the Antichrist. They had caused a global suicide epidemic that resulted in the deaths of thousands, perhaps millions. And now, they were raising their evil heads again. She knew it because one fact overshadowed all others. God had sent her a message—he had given her back her sister who died at birth, Motnees—Tera. There could be only one reason—it would take them both to stop the Forces of Darkness. She had to find Tera before they did. As with any battle, there could be only one winner.

"Cotten? Are you there? What's the name?"

"It's the Secretary of Homeland Security, Rizben Mace."

Chapter Forty-Six

THE SHELL

Lindsay gripped Tera's hand—her daughter's palm was warm, but hers was clammy. They walked through the double plate-glass doors into the lobby of the twenty-story CyberSys building. Inlaid in the marble floor was the corporate logo with its blue thunderbolt.

Tera pointed to the symbol. "Look. Just like mine."

Lindsay stared at the logo, then at her daughter with a feeling that things were spiraling out of control.

They stopped in front of the security desk and spoke to a man in a starched khaki uniform. She glanced at the badge—a gold G4S Security Solutions badge. "We'd like to see Mr. Olsen," Lindsay said.

"Do you have an appointment?"

"No. But it's very important. It's about his son."

The guard's countenance told Lindsay that he thought she was one of the many kooks who loitered about downtown Miami. "What's your name?"

"Lindsay Jordan." She nodded toward Tera. "This is my daughter, Tera." Without taking his eyes off Lindsay, he picked up the phone and made a call and spoke quietly into the receiver. Almost as soon as he hung up, several security officers, clad in the same G4S uniforms, appeared and marched toward her.

Lindsay held up her hand. "Wait, we mean no harm. I think we have information Mr. Olsen would want to know. Please, give us a minute to speak to him."

"Excuse me," a man in a navy blue suit said following behind the guards. He made his way to Lindsay.

She assumed he was not part of the security team, but rather a personal assistant or spokesperson for CyberSys.

"Mr. Olsen wishes everyone to know he appreciates the outpouring of sympathy to his recent situation and is thankful for their support. But he is not seeing anyone at this time. I'm sure you can understand and respect his privacy."

Lindsay squeezed Tera's hand. This venture was doomed from the start—the meeting with Alan Olsen was not going to happen. "I understand," she said. "It's just that I believe Mr. Olsen will want to know what we have to tell him. It's about the kidnapping of his son. If I can just speak to Mr. Olsen for a moment and explain."

"I'm certain you mean well, but if you have any pertinent information, you should contact the FBI." The man reached in his pocket and thumbed through his wallet. "Here." He handed her a card. "Call this number and ask for—"

Tera spoke up. "I have something for Devin. It's a present." She held out the conch shell.

"That's very nice." The man reached to take the shell. "I'll be happy to see—"

But before he could take it, a commotion came from the direction of the elevators—stiff leather-soled shoes on the marble floor echoed throughout the lobby. A man holding the hand of a boy emerged from the elevator surrounded by a handful of uniformed guards. They marched across the lobby toward the front entrance.

Lindsay knew it had to be Alan Olsen and his son. One of the guards she had been speaking with took her arm and pulled her aside.

"Step this way, please," he said.

Suddenly, Tera bolted toward the group and darted up to the boy before anyone could stop her.

Upon seeing the girl charge toward them, two of the guards attempted to block her, but Tera had already scooted her way between them to Devin.

The group halted as Tera held out the conch shell to the boy. Everyone stood in silence as the Devin broke into a broad smile.

Tera lifted the shell to Devin's ear.

Lindsay pulled away from the guards and ran to her daughter's side. A calm fell over the lobby as each person stood rooted in place, mesmerized by what was happening as Devin listened to the sound of the shell.

He cupped his hand over Tera's, pressing the shell closer. Then Tera whispered, "Hi, Devin, remember me?"

Devin's face brightened. In a small voice, he said, "Hello, Motnees."

Chapter Forty-Seven

BALL LIGHTNING

Cotten left John at the Vatican Embassy so he could catch up on the latest Venatori intelligence briefings. It started to rain, and she heard distant thunder as she headed up Wisconsin Avenue and turned east on O Street in Georgetown. National Security Advisor Philip Miller had given her directions to his two-story townhouse, saying he had the proof she needed to confront Rizben Mace.

As she approached the Victorian home, she saw a black SUV parked in front. Miller had mentioned that there were two FBI agents on duty outside whenever he was home.

Cotten pulled into a curbside space and switched off the engine. The rain pounded harder now—the underbelly of the furious clouds swollen and menacing.

She got out and opened her umbrella. The passenger's side door of the agent's vehicle opened. Lindsay held up her hand. No need for them both to get soaked. The door closed again, and she stood by as the window came down a few inches.

"Ms. Stone, can I see your ID?" the agent asked as the downpour intensified. "Formality. Sorry, especially in this weather." His last words were buried in an ear-splitting crack of thunder.

Cotten pulled her press credentials from her inside coat pocket and passed them through the window.

The agent shone a flashlight on them and then out the window to Cotten's face. He returned the ID. "Try to stay dry. Dr. Miller is expecting you."

She ran along the front walk and up the entrance steps. At the door, she huddled beneath the portico and rang the bell.

A moment later, Mrs. Miller opened the door. "Ms. Stone. Good to see you again."

"Thanks," Cotten closed the umbrella and tried not to drip water on the hardwood floors. "You have a beautiful home."

"Thank you." She took Cotten's coat and hung it on a brass coat rack. "It was built in 1790. We've refurbished it from floor to ceiling and tried to maintain its heritage. It's been the home to three presidential cabinet members and two ambassadors over the years."

"Ms. Stone." Philip Miller came across the living room, his hand outstretched. "Nasty night out there."

"And getting worse." Cotten shook his hand. Another clap of thunder punctuated her statement. "Thanks for cooperating. I have to apologize again for accosting you and your wife on the sidewalks of Arlington."

"You were doing your job. And I'm grateful that you believed me." He gestured that she sit on one of two couches facing each other in the middle of the living room. Logs crackled and hissed in the fireplace a few feet away.

"Can I get you something warm to drink?" Mrs. Miller asked. "Coffee, tea?"

"Tea would be great."

"Philip?"

"Tea would be fine for me, too."

Cotten watched his wife disappear down a hall. Once she was gone, she said, "I know this is awkward for you because you work so closely with Secretary Mace. But I believe identifying the person who has been stalking my friend and her daughter is more important than you can imagine."

"Not awkward at all. It's time he paid his dues."

"Really? So you two don't get along."

"We behave in public. But I have good reason for my distaste. I made a bid for governor of Arkansas a number of years ago. Rizben backed my opponent with an incredible amount of funding and support. He wound up buying the candidate and the election as far as I'm concerned. And one of the biggest campaign issues was converting old military bases into private research centers. The argument was that it would create jobs and increase the tax base. All it really did was filter money back to Rizben, I'm sure. He was heavily invested in several of those research outfits that expressed interest in the plan. There were a lot of other ways those facilities could have been utilized for public good. There was plenty of name-calling and mudslinging. Consequently, there's still a lot of animosity between us. So, rather than me confronting Rizben, I'd prefer to turn over what I've found and let you do it through the media. I have no problem throwing him under the bus."

"Did he actually convert any of the old military installations into commercial projects?"

"One, maybe. The whole matter seemed to fade away after the election. I guess I had called too much attention to it, and it became a hot potato. Like I say, there is no love lost." He reached in his pocket and took out a thumb drive. "This will do the job."

"What is it?" Cotten asked.

"A collection of recordings of phone conversations from a wiretap— another reason it has to go through you. You do protect your sources?"

"Absolutely."

Miller waved the thumb drive. "This can never be connected back to me, but what I've got here is irrefutable proof that Rizben ordered the torching of the Jordan farm. What it doesn't explain is why."

"You don't have to worry about that. Figuring that out is my job, and I guarantee it will never be linked to you in any way. You have my word."

"Good. And there seems to be something else. I'm not sure what it's all about, maybe you'll figure that out, too. Let me ask you, does the word thodium mean anything to you?"

Cotten was about to say no when intense white light flooded through the windows as lightning struck. The explosive crack of thunder was instantaneous, telling Cotten the house was probably hit.

Miller got to his feet. "My God!"

Loud popping and sizzling caused them both to turn toward the fireplace. The blaze increased in brilliance as the fingers of flames leaped out into the room. Then a brilliant blue sphere, about the size of a baseball, emerged from the fire and floated a few feet above the hearth.

The globe sparked radial tentacles as it moved in a slow, random, zigzag. Behind it trailed a comet-like tail of white light.

Before either of them could react, the sphere shot from the fireplace and hit Miller in the forehead.

Miller screamed and clawed at his face, his hair on fire. Then he collapsed onto the floor.

Cotten grabbed a pillow from the couch and smothered the fire.

"Oh, my God," Mrs. Miller said. The tray of teacups and saucers slipped from her hands and crashed. "Philip. Philip." She rushed to his side.

Cotten knelt next to him and pressed her fingertips to Miller's neck, searching for a pulse in his carotid.

Nothing.

"Do something," Mrs. Miller screamed.

"Call 9-1-1," Cotten said. "And get the agents outside in here right away. Go!"

Cotten knelt beside Miller and started CPR. The odor of singed hair and burnt skin filled her nostrils as she leaned over him and pumped his chest.

Within seconds the first agent entered the room. "What the hell?" He had a gun in his hand but holstered it as he activated his radio and broadcast an alert for assistance.

"Step away from Dr. Miller," the second agent ordered Cotten. She ignored him and continued applying CPR.

"They're coming," Mrs. Miller shouted as she ran back into the room. "The ambulance is on the way."

"Ms. Stone," the agent said, "I need you to stand and step away."

Cotten got to her feet and moved back as the agent took over the CPR.

"What happened?" the other agent asked Mrs. Miller.

"I left my husband and Ms. Stone while I went to get them some tea. I heard a loud explosion. A second later, my husband screamed. When I rushed into the living room, Philip was lying on the floor and Ms. Stone was kneeling beside him."

Over the sound of the rain and thunder, Cotten heard the faint drone of a siren.

The agent looked at Cotten. "What happened to him?"

"We were talking when lightning must have struck the house. A bolt of lightning or an electrical discharge or something that looked like a glowing blue ball came into the house through the fireplace. It struck Dr. Miller in the head. He collapsed. His hair caught fire, and I put it out." She pointed to the blackened pillow on the floor.

There was a commotion at the front door as the EMTs entered and moved toward Miller's body. Cotten heard the static squawk of their radios and the crackle of plastic and paper as one paramedic opened his kit and peeled back the wrappings of needles and tubes while the other EMT cut Miller's shirt open.

She was sure they would do all they could to revive their patient, but in her gut, Cotten knew it was to no avail. This was more than a freak accident. This was another message directed at her. She was getting too close. *Back off.*

As she watched the medics work on Philip Miller, she noticed that his shoes were blown off and parts of his clothes burned. There was only a single red spot on his forehead. One button on Miller's shirt had melted into his chest.

Mrs. Miller stood beside them, sobbing, her hand over her mouth. The shock had to be so great that she wasn't even able to process what had happened, Cotten thought.

When the paramedic lifted Miller's hand to start an IV, she saw him quickly drop it.

"What the—" he said.

The flesh of Miller's right hand was fused to the melted thumb drive.

Chapter Forty-Eight

INDIGOS

Alan, Devin, Lindsay, and Tera stepped out onto the twentieth floor of CyberSys.

"That will be all," Alan said, leaving the guards behind.

The sleekness of the décor impressed Lindsay—all glass, aluminum, and mirror-finished stainless steel, and not a single fingerprint or smudge anywhere she could see.

Tera took Devin's hand as Alan led them to his private office.

A woman stood beside the desk looking at a computer screen. At their entry, she whipped around, seemingly startled. "Alan, I was just tidying up. I thought you were going to be out for a while."

"We were. But something came up. Kai, this is Lindsay Jordan and her daughter, Tera." He turned to Lindsay. "Kai Chiang is my personal assistant."

Kai leaned toward Alan and kissed him on the cheek as if she wanted to force a more elaborate introduction.

"Well, she's more than an assistant," Alan said. "Kai and I—"

"I'm pleased to meet you," Kai said. "We try not to be too obvious. Affairs in the workplace usually don't breed good morale."

Tera snuggled against her mother's side.

"Why don't we all sit down?" He motioned to the leather couches and matching oversized chairs.

Lindsay took one of the chairs, and Tera scooted in beside her. Kai and Alan occupied a couch while Devin plopped onto the floor at his father's feet.

"What's this all about?" Kai asked.

Alan stretched his arm along the rim of the couch behind Kai's shoulders. "Ms. Jordan says she has information regarding the kidnapping."

Tera squeezed her mother's hand.

"Really?" Kai glared at Lindsay. "You are aware that the case is closed—the kidnapper was identified?"

Lindsay nodded. "Yes, I saw that on TV, but I hope you will hear me out." Devin put the shell to his ear, looked across at Tera, and smiled.

Alan's delight in seeing the way his son responded to Tera was obvious.

Kai slid her hand onto Alan's knee and eyed Lindsay. "You understand that Mr. Olsen and his son have both been through quite an ordeal. We are trying to get back to normalcy and wouldn't want anything to interfere with that."

"No, of course not," Lindsay said.

Kai continued. "And Devin is a special child. We can't let him be exploited."

"Then you will be more open to what I am going to tell you. Like Devin, Tera is also special."

Kai leaned forward. "I don't think you understand." Her tone was condescending. She lowered the volume of her voice to almost a whisper as if that would keep Devin from hearing her. "Devin is an autistic savant."

"Indigo," Tera said.

"Shh," Lindsay whispered through her daughter's hair. "Remember what we talked about?"

"Indigo, Indigo, Indigo," Devin said.

Lindsay brushed Tera's bangs back. "Well, I wasn't going to start with that, but . . . have you ever heard of Indigo children?" she said to Alan.

Devin waved one hand beside his ear.

"I've done considerable research on my son's condition. And yes, one thing I've run across is the mention of a connection between some kids with autism and what they are calling Indigo children. Same thing with exceedingly gifted kids—and even some ADD and ADHD kids for that matter. So, yes, I've looked into that a little. I know they are given the name Indigo because of the supposed deep blue aura surrounding their bodies. And they are believed to have certain unexplained talents. But I have to confess that I dropped the ball and didn't pursue it much further—other than it inspiring me to choose the color for the CyberSys thunderbolt logo that is. I thought the whole concept was fascinating."

It's way more than fascinating, Lindsay thought. It's downright scary.

"And I certainly saw several characteristics in my son, but I think I just got sick of labels for Devin. To me, labeling is really the equivalent of name-calling, only on a socially acceptable level. I finally had enough. Devin is Devin."

"I agree," Lindsay said. She knew too well what it was like to protect a child from the rest of the world's misconceptions. The heartaches. "Maybe during that research you read about a recent wave of these— forgive the label—Indigo children being born. They believe there have always been Indigos, but not many. Then in the late 1970s, there was a major wave of births, but nothing compared to the Indigos being born since the year 2000. I believe they are really wise old souls who are here to lead us through terrible times. To prepare us for enlightenment, some say. These children have meta-gifts. Tera is an Indigo. I can't see their auras, but she can. When she saw Devin on the television, she recognized him as one of her own."

Kai rolled her eyes. "Alan, I think we should thank Ms. Jordan for her visit and—"

"No, please, Mr. Olsen. Let me finish. I promise you will be glad you listened."

Alan rested his forearms on his thighs and tapped his fingertips together. "Would you mind if Devin and Tera go to the playroom? It adjoins my office. I had it especially built for Devin. It's pretty much self-contained—bathroom, refrigerator, toys, games. There's no other way in or out other than through here. They'll be safe, and I'll feel more comfortable with our conversation."

Lindsay checked Tera's expression. "Okay with you, Ladybug?"

Tera nodded.

"Kai would you show the kids the playroom and maybe rustle up a snack for them?" Alan said.

From Kai's sour expression, Lindsay could tell that Alan's suggestion didn't sit well with his *special assistant*. But Kai agreed and led the children away.

"She's just trying to be protective," Alan said, nodding toward the closing door. "I am interested in what you have to say, and I don't mean to rush you, but I'm afraid I don't have much time."

"Thanks for your patience. I feel like I'm being a scatterbrain, but there's so much to tell."

Alan gestured for her to continue.

Lindsay took a deep breath. "Tera has unique gifts. She is an artist, a poet, and above all a spiritual child. All Indigos know who they are spiritually. I'm convinced they have some kind of heavenly connection. And I know how you must feel right now. I've been coming to terms with all this, bit by bit, for eight years."

"But this Indigo thing," Alan said. "Like I told you, I entertained it for a short time. But in the end, I realized that Devin is an autistic savant, no more, no less, and that's enough burden for him to bear."

"I don't know his specialty, but I understand that savants have immense gifts. He doesn't have to be a poet or an artist, or a virtuoso. Devin does have unusual talents, right?"

Alan stared at the floor. "Yes, if you mean his ability with numbers and dates. And he memorizes everything he reads." He looked up, seemingly pleased at his next thought. "Devin can read two pages at a time—one with his left eye, one with his right." His expression faded. "Ms. Jordan, you've given me plenty to think about, but I don't see what any of this has to do with Devin's kidnapping. So, why don't we call it a day."

Lindsay knew he was politely going to ask her to leave. It was hard to believe he had listened to her this long. She had to do something. She couldn't stop now.

Alan looked like he was about to stand. "I thank you for all your concern about my son, but—"

Lindsay didn't move. "I didn't want to come here." Her voice trembled with its rising volume. "But Tera was so insistent, so beside herself, I had to bring her. I'm convinced there is a link between Tera and Devin that will lead to uncovering more about Devin's kidnapping."

Alan shifted.

"I read there was never any ransom note. Did you ever pay anything to anybody?"

"No. But the authorities found a note. It hadn't been sent yet.

"Why would anyone kidnap a child for money and wait so long to make a ransom demand? It doesn't make sense. I think . . . Tera thinks there's another reason someone would want to kidnap your son."

Alan fidgeted, his face blanched, and she knew she had pricked a nerve. "All right, Ms. Jordan, what does your daughter think is the reason?"

"Tera said the kidnappers wanted to steal information your son had memorized—numbers he has in his head."

Chapter Forty-Nine

THE MOTIVE

Alan stared at Lindsay, his expression packed with shock. He seemed to be calculating if he should let her into his confidence. She could tell he was considering what she said about the motive for Devin's kidnapping.

"Your daughter has come up with an interesting theory."

He continued to stare at Lindsay, and she knew a debate raged in his head.

"Yes, there is another possibility," he said. "Your daughter is correct—Devin may have been kidnapped to obtain information. The numbers in his head."

"What kind of numbers?"

He rubbed his palms together. "My company, CyberSys, is on the verge of completing the world's first working quantum computer. It will revolutionize the speed of data processing and the power of encryption—the ramifications to global security and safety are enormous. But we're not the only ones trying to develop a quantum computer. There are a few others. As you can imagine, the race to be first to market is highly competitive. Obtaining confidential computer codes and information that might help someone beat us to the punch would be worth millions, perhaps billions of dollars."

"So, Devin could have been kidnapped to get a computer code?"

Alan nodded. "That's what made your daughter's observation startle me—that they want to steal something from Devin's memory. They wouldn't need me for that. Because of his extraordinary ability to memorize and recall copious amounts of information, Devin has everything they want right inside his head. I've tried to press Devin for details of what happened, but he's shut the door on the whole episode. The police think it was all about money—some white-collar criminal faked his own death then snatched Devin for ransom. The information my son carries around in his brain is worth more than any ransom.

"The police had no luck getting my son to reveal what happened, either. I was hoping it would come out little by little once Devin felt he was safely at home. But all he has told me is that while he was being held, he spent the time playing games. And yet, the authorities didn't find a computer at the kidnapper's cabin—not even a PlayStation or X-Box."

"That makes no sense," Lindsay said.

"I agree. The more I've thought about it, the more it isn't logical."

"Listen, I don't know much about computers or industrial espionage, but I do know that Tera and Devin are somehow tied together with what's going on. Mr. Olsen, Tera and I have been on the run. Someone is after my daughter. I think the reason Tera was so distressed and adamant about coming to see Devin is that she realizes they have the same enemy—what she calls the red people, the Rubies. I think there is more to this than we can figure out by ourselves. But I have a suggestion."

Alan leaned forward and rested his forearms on his legs. "I'm listening."

"If in your gut you think there's more to it than ransom money, then we need to do something. I have a friend who might be able to help. She's an investigative correspondent with years of experience. You have nothing to lose if I ask her to help. You might know her from television. Cotten Stone?"

"Sure," Alan said. "SNN. The Grail thing—I've followed her adventures with interest—gutsy lady."

"Right. If we can get her involved, maybe even ask her to come to Miami, I believe she can help unravel all this."

"I don't quite see her connection with Devin and Tera."

"She's an expert on solving mysteries that are out of the ordinary." Lindsay studied Alan's face as she waited for a response. "It would cost you nothing to talk to her."

He stretched back in deep thought. Finally, he rose, walked to his desk, and pressed a button on his phone.

"Yes, Mr. Olsen," a woman's voice came through the speaker.

"Call the Satellite News Network's offices in New York and see if you can get in touch with one of their correspondents. Her name is Cotten Stone. When you get her on the line, put her through."

"Will do, sir."

Alan sat in the desk chair and swiveled so he looked out the window. "It seems like a long shot, but I would do just about anything to find the son of a bitch who's responsible for taking my son."

"I don't blame you. There are many questions I need answered about Tera and the people who have been trying to track us down. I truly believe Cotten can help us both."

Kai came back into the room. "The kids are getting along fine. I made them sandwiches and cut up some strawberries. That okay with you, Ms. Jordan?"

"Perfect. Tera loves strawberries. And please, call me Lindsay."

Kai stood behind Alan's chair and massaged his shoulders. "Want to fill me in on what I missed?"

Alan stilled her hands with his before turning around. "Remember I told you I had this fear that Devin could have been kidnapped for the Destiny code?"

"Right, but—"

"Maybe he was."

Kai sighed as if she felt pity for Alan. "Oh, babe, don't torture your-self any more than you already have. There's no evidence that was the motive. We know who kidnapped Devin. Benjamin Ray. He was desper-ate for money and just didn't get the ransom note off before he had a heart attack. You shouldn't let someone stir you up over a theory that has no basis." She looked at Lindsay. "No offense, Ms. Jordan, but the police have already told us what happened. And Devin hasn't said it was anything else."

"I'm not sure," Alan said. "But I don't think we'll find out from Devin. I think we have to take action on our own."

"You . . . we have your son back," Kai said. "That's all that matters."

Alan turned his attention to Lindsay. "I think you and Tera should stay here for now. If the threat to your daughter is as real as you say, the security at CyberSys will keep you safe. There's a conference room down the hall. It has a couch with a foldout bed and a private bathroom. No four-star accommodation, but—"

"That would be wonderful," Lindsay said. "I don't know how we can ever—"

"Alan, she's a total stranger. Are you sure this is wise?"

Alan glanced toward the playroom. He could see Devin and Tera through the window sitting side-by-side, engrossed in watching cartoons on TV.

"Yes, I'm sure."

The phone on his desk buzzed.

"Mr. Olsen, I have Cotten Stone on the line."

Chapter Fifty

BAD NEWS

Lindsay stood at the CyberSys conference room window overlooking the Port of Miami. She had been up a few hours and tried to be as quiet as possible so Tera could sleep in. Now she heard a stirring and looked around to see her daughter sitting up on the foldout sofa bed. "Good morning, Ladybug. Did you sleep well?"

Tera rubbed he eyes with her knuckles. "This bed is lumpy."

"But we're thankful to Mr. Olsen for letting us stay here, safe and sound, aren't we?"

"I guess so."

Lindsay sat on the edge of the bed and wrapped her arms around her daughter. "I realize this is tough. You miss home. So do I." She stroked Tera's arms. "I know we'll be able to go back to Kentucky soon—I just know it. Mr. Olsen is going to help us. And you heard the great news. My friend Cotten is coming to see you. She'll help us, too."

Tera smiled at her mother. "My sister, Momma."

Lindsay studied Tera's eyes. There was no hint of fantasy only pure expression of what her daughter thought was fact.

"I don't like Kai," Tera whispered.

"Why not, sweetheart?"

"She's not nice to Devin."

"What do you mean?"

Tera shrugged. "I don't like her. She says mean things."

"Let's keep our feelings about Kai to ourselves. Okay?" She tickled Tera's ribs. "Are you ready for breakfast?"

A wide grin bloomed on Tera's face. "Yay, pancakes."

"I don't know about that, but Mr. Olsen said there's a fully stocked kitchen down the hall. Let's get you dressed and go check it out."

Tera hopped from the bed and scampered to her bag on the floor. She pulled out a pair of jeans and a bright orange T-shirt then darted off for the bathroom.

Lindsay watched her daughter disappear behind the door. How had all this happened? She and Tera were plain Kentucky farm folks. Nothing special, and yet they were submerged in an ocean of madness. People with ruby-red glowing auras that only Tera could see were trying to harm them. Lindsay had no proof any of it was true. Some things were best left unsaid. Indigos and Rubies were enough. Alan Olsen would never believe that her daughter chose her parents before she was born or that Tera knew Devin in Heaven. And this whole thing about Cotten being Tera's twin sister. In her heart, Lindsay believed it all. But in her mind, in her intellect, she struggled. And so would Alan.

It was a miracle he had given them the time of day, much less a safe place to stay. He must want to do whatever it takes to find who had kidnapped Devin.

Besides Tera and Devin being Indigos, what was the big link between them? Lindsay prayed they would find the answer so she and her daughter could go home and have a normal life. That's all she wanted.

That's all she ever wanted.

Lindsay heard a soft knock at the door, and she opened it.

"Good morning," Alan said. "I hope you guys are hungry." He held a large takeout food bag in each hand.

"Mr. Olsen, you really didn't have to do that. We'd have found something in the office kitchen."

"God only knows what's in there." Alan smiled, holding up the bags. "I've brought fresh fruit, bacon, eggs, bagels, even waffles and pancakes."

"Pancakes!" Tera squealed as she ran across the room and wrapped her arms around him.

"I take it that's what she wants."

"Her favorite." Lindsay tried to ease her daughter's bear hug on Alan.

"Then she'll love these. They're from Devin's favorite restaurant a few blocks away." He cocked his thumb toward the hall. "Let's head for the kitchen and eat before everything gets cold."

"Is Devin here?" Tera asked.

"He's waiting for you."

Tera sprinted off ahead of them.

"I can't thank you enough, Mr. Olsen," Lindsay said.

As they followed in Tera's wake, Alan said, "First of all, it's Alan, not Mr. Olsen. And second, you already have thanked me. You know, Tera is all Devin has talked about since we left you guys last night. He is the calmest, most coherent, most . . . normal I've ever seen him. I don't know what it is about your daughter, but she has a profound effect on my son. And for that, I'm eternally grateful."

Lindsay took one of the bags from Alan. "Tera thinks the world of him, too."

"Okay then," Alan said as they entered the kitchen. "Who wants pancakes?"

***

Kai stood with her arms crossed, staring out Alan's office window. Lindsay sat on the couch in front of his desk and leafed through a copy of Newsweek.

Her daughter and Devin were in the playroom watching TV.

It was almost noon, and Alan had passed the last thirty minutes in silence reviewing a stack of financial statements. His phone rang. When he pushed the button, a woman's voice came through the speaker. "Mr. Olsen, Cotten Stone and Cardinal Tyler are here."

"Show them in." Alan glanced at Lindsay. "This should make you feel better."

Lindsay closed her eyes, relieved. "I know Cotten can help us. I'm sure of it."

Alan peered into the playroom. The television was on, but Tera and Devin ignored it, choosing instead to draw on sheets of chart paper that Alan had taken off the easel in the conference room. "It's so amazing to see how the two of them connect."

"Tera desperately needed a friend," Lindsay said. "They are good for each other."

"I agree."

Kai turned from the window as the office door opened. Lindsay thought she noted harshness in the woman's expression. Perhaps it was the glare from the window that caused Kai to narrow her eyes and tighten her face.

Lindsay stood as Cotten and John came into the office. She smiled at the sight of her old friend. Moving to her, she opened her arms. "Cotten, thank you so much for coming."

"Lindsay." Cotten hugged her. "It's been too long." She pulled back at arm's length and nodded toward John. "This is a dear friend of mine, Cardinal John Tyler. He's here to help."

"Thank you both so much. I don't know what I'd do…"

"We want to get to the bottom of all this as much as you do," John said.

Cotten touched Lindsay's hand. "And, Lindsay, I'm so sorry about Neil. I know it's been hard on you both. And now with all this craziness. I wish I could have gotten to you sooner."

"But you're here now." Lindsay hugged her again. "That's all that matters."

They broke their embrace and Lindsay said, "Cotten, I'd like you and Cardinal Tyler to meet Alan Olsen, president of CyberSys."

Alan was already moving toward them. He shook Cotten's hand. "I'm a big fan of yours, by the way." Then he turned his attention to John. "Your Eminence. It's a pleasure."

"Thank you for taking care of my friend and her daughter," Cotten said.

"My pleasure."

"And this is Kai Chiang," Lindsay said. "Mr. Olsen's . . . personal assistant."

"It's okay, Lindsay," Kai said. "Alan is my significant other," she announced, but didn't bother to leave her spot by the window.

Alan addressed John. "Cardinal Tyler, it's an honor to meet you. I still remember following the amazing Grail Conspiracy story in the news. That must have been such an adventure."

"Kept us on our toes." He acknowledged Kai with a nod. "Nice to meet you both."

"Why don't we all make ourselves comfortable?" Alan gestured toward the couches.

Cotten and John sat with Lindsay while Alan waited for Kai to join him on the opposite couch.

As she sat, Kai said, "Ms. Stone, your friend insisted that you come here to help her solve the mystery of the connection between her daughter and Alan's son. Alan and Devin have been through a hard time, and we—"

Alan patted Kai's leg. "We've been under quite a bit of stress lately, so please forgive Kai. She wants us to get through this as quickly as possible and move on with our lives."

"Alan, you don't have to apologize for me." Kai placed her hand on his.

"I understand your concerns," Cotten said. "And I thank you both for helping Lindsay and Tera. Unfortunately, I don't believe we will get to the root of what is going on quickly enough." Cotten took in a deep breath. "Lindsay and Tera are in danger. It's not imagined. Not only are they being hunted, but those who are doing the hunting are extremely dangerous people."

Kai leaned back into the couch with a huff.

Cotten turned to Lindsay. "I went to Loretto to find you, but you were already gone. When I visited your farm, it revived a lot of fond memories. I took time to wander around. I saw Tera's paintings, drawings, read her poems. It's clear that your daughter has special gifts, not just talent." Cotten swallowed then said, "Lindsay… I'm sorry to be the bearer of bad news. I hate to tell you. It's so awful. Everything is gone. Someone set fire to your home and burned it to the ground. The house, the barn, the big oak, all of Tera's beautiful work, destroyed."

"Oh, no." The color in Lindsay's cheeks faded. She hid her face in her hands. "No, no, no. That's all we had." Her voice sounded pinched from holding back tears.

"Who would have done that?" Alan asked.

"While I was in Kentucky," Cotten said, "my cell phone was stolen. That's the reason I didn't get your messages, Lindsay. The person who stole it used my cell to call Cardinal Tyler and threaten my life. The message was for me to back off my search for you. They also said that burning down your farm was a warning of worse things to come."

"Sounds like a teenage prank," Kai said.

"It wasn't a prank," John said. He gave a hard look at Kai like he couldn't believe what she had said. "Kids don't burn down houses as a *prank*." He paused then looked at Alan. "We were able to track Cotten's phone to Washington, D.C."

"Alan, this is just plain nuts," Kai said. "I don't see what this has to do with Devin or the kidnapping."

Cotten glanced from Kai to Alan. She was fighting a losing battle with Kai. It would be better to direct everything to Alan. "My phone was tracked to someone in the White House."

Alan sat up straight. "Are you serious? That's unbelievable. Do you know who?"

"Yes," John said.

"Yesterday evening," Cotten said, "I met with Dr. Philip Miller, the National Security Advisor. He was about to give me a thumb drive with recordings of phone conversations that would prove beyond a doubt who stole my phone, who ordered Lindsay's farm destroyed, who threatened my life, and who is trying to find and kill Lindsay and Tera."

"You have the drive?" Kai asked, her voice rising in pitch.

"No," John said. "Dr. Miller was killed in a freak accident as he was about to hand over the evidence to Cotten. The drive was destroyed."

Kai exhaled. "There you are, Alan. Just another bit of conjecture, guesswork, rumors. I think we've heard enough."

"Dr. Miller had already disclosed to me the identity of the person responsible," Cotten said.

"Who is it, Ms. Stone?" Alan asked.

"The Secretary of Homeland Security, Rizben Mace."

The hush that descended on the room was suddenly interrupted by a piercing scream coming from the playroom.

Lindsay sprang to her feet. "It's Tera!"

Alan raced right behind Lindsay across the office into the playroom. Devin sat on the floor shaking his hands beside his head and rocking. Lindsay rushed to Tera and swept her daughter into her arms. "Baby, what is it? What's wrong?"

Chapter Fifty-One

RED ALERT

Tera stopped screaming and pointed to the TV screen. "He's red! Momma. He's one of the Ruby people."

Everyone focused on the image of a man speaking at what appeared to be a news conference. Across the top of the image was the banner, *The Tragic Death of Dr. Philip Miller*. Underneath the speaker was the graphic text title, *Rizben Mace, Secretary of Homeland Security*.

"My God," Alan said. "She's pointing to Secretary Mace. And she says he's—"

"Red. A Ruby," John said. He turned to Cotten. "That goes along with Miller's suspicions connecting Mace to the theft of your phone."

Unlike the others, Cotten was not looking at the television. Her eyes were transfixed on Tera. The others were talking, but to Cotten their voices were background noise like wind through distant trees. Nor could she see anything other than Tera as cascades of lights swirled about and blinded her to everything else. She felt as if she gazed through a tunnel of dazzling white light with Tera in the center.

"Cotten?" John said. "Are you okay?"

Lindsay had her arms wrapped around her daughter. She let go as the child met Cotten's gaze. A wide smile grew on Tera's face. "Hello," Tera said in a soft voice.

"Hi," Cotten said. An avalanche of emotion rolled over her. "Motnees." Cotten went to her knees.

Tera touched Cotten's tear-streaked face. "I knew you would come. I told Momma you would."

Cotten enfolded the girl in her arms. She recalled childhood memories of Motnees appearing in her room at night. They would talk for hours about the things of life that Cotten now realized were, at the time, beyond her years.

She held Tera at arm's length. "The time is near, isn't it?" she said in a soft voice.

Tera nodded. "Devin is blue, like me—Indigo. But the bad people are red—Rubies."

At that instant, Cotten understood the danger, the urgency, and the risk. The final conflict was about to happen if she couldn't stop it. Only one force could win. Good or evil. Indigos or Rubies.

***

After the scene in the playroom, everyone, including Tera and Devin, returned to Alan's office.

"So what is a Ruby?" Alan asked when the group was seated.

"Before I explain, let me give you some background," Cotten said. "I was recently in Moscow. You may have heard about the presidential assassination attempt on the news."

"It was a brave thing you did," Alan said.

"Thank you. It was just before I was to leave for home that I received an urgent call from Lindsay. She told me that Tera was in danger—that someone was coming to take her daughter from her."

Tera nodded as she sat beside her mother. "Rubies."

Lindsay hugged her. "Hush, sweetie."

"It's all right, Lindsay. In reality, Tera may know more about this than anyone." She looked at Alan. "You mentioned when you called me that you don't believe your son was kidnapped for ransom. You said it may have been industrial espionage—that Devin had memorized vital computer code for your Destiny project and the kidnappers needed to have him recreate it for them. Is that right?"

"Yes," Alan said. "It makes more sense than the ransom theory."

"Then, we need to find a connection," Cotten said. "And we think it's what Tera calls Rubies."

"This is ridiculous," Kai said. "There is no connection. This is a total waste of time."

"Please, Kai," Alan said. "If you're right, then we'll all be out of here by lunch." His eyes turned back to Cotten. "You believe that Rizben Mace is a—"

"Mace, Mace, Rizben Mace," Devin said, one hand jiggling chest high. Alan spoke to his son. "Devin, let the adults—"

Devin looked up at the ceiling. "Forever, Kai. Love, Kai."

"What's he talking about?" Kai said. "Alan, can't you shut him up?"

Devin juddered his hands on each side of his head. "Return path. Kai at Cybermailserv. Received from mxm-0-one dot corp to rmace at dhs dot gov."

Kai stood and stepped away, her face flushed.

In a monotone, Devin continued, "Rizben, I can't take it anymore. I need you, I need you, I need you. Forever, Kai."

"What is he saying?" Cotten asked.

"E-mail. Devin's repeating e-mail he's read," Alan said. His eyes settled on Kai as he appeared to understand.

"This is bullshit," Kai said. "I can't believe—"

"Return path," Devin said. "Rizben Mace at dhs dot gov. Received from zzp-0-six dot corp to kaic at cybermailserv dot com. Tor working on the little bastard. Hades project almost complete, but the element is unstable. Found a way to fake the kidnapping. It won't be long now. I need you, too. RM."

Devin stopped rocking and his hands dropped to his lap. Like every-one else in the room his eyes were trained on Kai.

Chapter Fifty-Two

THE TRUTH

"He's making this shit up, Alan," Kai said. "He doesn't know what he's talking about." Kai inched away from Devin.

For a moment, Alan seemed speechless. This guy, this Rizben Mace, was Kai's lover? And the Hades Project had to be a quantum computer that Mace was building. Kai knew who had kidnapped Devin all along. She was a part of it. "You're right," Alan said. "My son doesn't know what he's talking about. He's reciting something he's seen, like any of the thousands of texts he's read. But this time it's your e-mail, Kai. Devin can't make things up. He doesn't know how."

"Fucking little retard," Kai said. "Snooping around where he doesn't belong. He gives me the creeps."

Alan moved within inches of her, backing her against the wall. His jaw clenched and the tendons in his neck stood out. "All along, you've been feeding Rizben Mace inside information about my company and our product. But you couldn't give him the Destiny code because you didn't know how to get access to it. So you allowed Devin to be taken from me." He balled his fists at his sides. "Jesus Christ, Kai, who are you? I loved you. I trusted you. And all this time—" Alan shoved his fingers through his hair as he looked around at everyone in the room. "Fuck." He shot his gaze back at Kai. "Fuck you!"

After a long silence, Lindsay said, "Why don't I take the kids to the playroom?" She gathered Devin and Tera and led them away, closing the door behind them.

Kai tossed back her jet black hair and smoothed her red, silk brocade dress about her hips. "All right. It's true. But it's nothing personal, Alan.

I'm not in love with Rizben Mace. That was just to get him off. It was something I knew he wanted to believe." She raised an eyebrow at Alan. "I don't love him or anyone else. It's a job. That's all. After this one, there will be another. As they say, every woman has her price."

"Funny you should say that," Alan said, "because I don't think you calculated the price you are going to pay. I'll make certain you're arrested for conspiring to kidnap my son and for industrial espionage. The Destiny code is worth millions, and my son is priceless. You'll have a tough time working your next job from inside a federal prison. I'll do whatever it takes to put you away for life."

"And what proof do you have?" Kai asked. "The word of your little carnival freak reciting some e-mail that's long been deleted? The cops already told you who kidnapped Devin and why. I'll walk away from this free and clear."

Alan stabbed his finger toward Kai. "You'll deal with the FBI first. You can count on that. Deleted emails are easily recovered."

Cotten and John stood. Alan turned to them. "I'm sorry you had to see this. I apologize." He looked back to Kai. "You're a disgrace. You disgust me."

"You don't have a clue who you are working for, do you, Kai?" Cotten said.

"I'm freelance. I work for myself."

Cotten laughed. "Wow, you are in denial."

Kai's almond black eyes flashed. "What are you talking about? Tor is a friend of mine. He recruited me to work for Rizben Mace."

"You've been duped by the best," John said. "Mace is a big fish in an even bigger ocean of brimstone."

"What are you talking about?" Alan said.

"Before you call the FBI, ask yourself what is really going on," Cotten said.

Alan glared at Kai. "I think I already know, but why don't you tell me, anyway."

Cotten continued. "It's obvious that you've been betrayed. Kai risked your son's life. She helped steal the secrets to your Destiny computer. That much we can surmise. Correct?"

Alan crossed his arms and nodded. "What are you getting at?"

"Rather than asking why Kai did it, which is obvious, ask yourself why Rizben Mace, the Secretary of Homeland Security, wants the operating system code to your quantum computer."

"Maybe he's got an investment in our competition."

"And who is your competition?" Cotten asked.

Alan appeared to consider the question. "Because the technology is still in its infancy, most of our competitors are research facilities and universities."

"Do you think a research facility or university would be a likely candidate to kidnap your son and plant Kai in your organization to steal your secrets?"

"Well . . ." Alan said.

Cotten tilted her head. "If it's not research facilities and universities, then who else could it be? And for what purpose?"

"I assumed that it would be the competition. Or could even be the Chinese."

"What if it were terrorists? Powerful terrorists." John said.

"I guess it could be," Alan answered. "But there would have to be a lot of capital and talent. It's a possibility. But I think that information would be leaked or evident. It's a very small community of groups trying to build a quantum computer. Although many are trying, I believe we're way out front in actually developing one. And our specific progress is only known in a small circle inside CyberSys. Me, Max Wolf, and . . ."

Alan looked at Kai.

Kai raised both hands. "You're way off. I don't work for fucking terrorists. For God's sake, I'm fifth-generation American. I love this country. It's my home. And I'm sure Rizben doesn't have anything to do with terrorists. He told me he reports to an old guy who wants this quantum computer so he can sell it—for profit. Millions and millions. They're not terrorists. It's all about the money."

She really doesn't have any idea, Cotten thought. And the *old guy* Rizben reports to—Cotten knew who that was. How was she going to lead Alan to this conclusion without him thinking she was deranged?

"We know the lynchpin is Rizben Mace," Cotten said. "If he's not your competition, or a terrorist, or working for another government trying to steal your Destiny computer, then who is he? Who does he work for?"

"I don't know," Alan said.

Cotten glanced around the room. "Think about it, Mr. Olsen. Tera already answered that question."

Chapter Fifty-Three

NEGOTIATION

Cotten realized she was stepping into risky territory. But it had to be done.

"Mr. Olsen, you said you were a fan of mine. I assume that means you've followed my career?"

Alan bore an inquisitive expression. "Yes."

"Then you are familiar with the kind of reporting I've been involved in. I'm going to ask you to suspend disbelief and hear me out. I know how it will sound to you, but bear with me."

Alan raised both brows and spoke in a cautious drawn-out style. "O-kaaaay."

"If you remember the Grail Conspiracy story, you will recall that someone was attempting to take the DNA from the Holy Grail and clone Christ—a creation of the Anti-Christ in a blasphemous Second Coming. And then several years ago, there was a rash of unexplained suicides around the world. But there are those who suspect they were caused by demonic possessions."

"Yes. I remember both very well."

"I'm convinced that we are up against the same group that orchestrated both those events—the same group Tera calls Rubies, and she has identified Mace as a Ruby. He's not just some industrial thief. He's not doing it for money as Kai thinks. He kidnapped Devin to gain the technology to build this Hades Project mentioned in the e-mail. He tried to kill Tera for one reason—because she can identify him and members of the group he works with."

"You're asking me to take big leaps here with all this Ruby talk. I understand the Indigo stuff. I've done the research because I know my son, but now you're talking about something else altogether."

"You're right, it will be a huge leap," Cotten said. "But whether you take the leap or not doesn't change the fact that both groups exist. The Indigos are being brought into this world for a purpose—to do the good work of God. The Rubies are here for just the opposite reason."

"I'm sorry, Ms. Stone, but I'm not a religious man. I don't know if I can make the giant leap you're asking.

"All right," John said. "We would be remiss if we didn't tell you what we think but you don't have to buy into everything. All you need to do is understand that Rizben Mace is building a quantum computer to be used for a terrible purpose. Will you give us that much?"

Alan nodded. "For now."

Cotten turned to Kai. "You know she holds the answers. And she's a working girl."

Alan stared at Kai as if experiencing a revelation. "Maybe you can help me make the leap Ms. Stone wants. What's your price, Kai?"

"Always negotiable," Kai said with a shallow smile and wicked glint in her eye.

"Not really," Alan said. "I can call the FBI, or as Cotten suggests, you can cooperate."

"If I tell you what I know, I want guarantees."

"Like what?" Alan asked.

"When this is over I want to walk away. But I have expensive tastes. You know that. My lifestyle would demand a great deal of compensation." With a flick of her hand, she flipped her hair over her right shoulder and dropped into one of the large, leather chairs. She crossed her legs, and the hem of her dress rode up mid-thigh.

Alan worked his jaw, the muscles distending and relaxing. "Perhaps it could be arranged. But it will be a one-shot deal, Kai. When you are out of my life, if you try to come back, it will be with an FBI escort."

Kai rolled her eyes and gave a quick chuckle. "Fair enough."

"All right, then," Cotten said. "Let's go back over one of those e-mails that Devin told us about. I have some questions. Do you mind, Mr. Olsen?"

"Call me Alan. And no, I don't mind."

"Hades Project. What is that?"

Kai re-crossed her legs. "It's what Rizben calls a plan he has for the computer."

"Details," Alan said.

"I don't know any—only that he and Tor had spent a lot of time mapping out a plan."

"That's another question I had," said Cotten. "Who is Tor?"

"He's the computer geek—the guy who designed the Hades Plan and the computer. Rizben doesn't know that much about computers. He relies on Tor. Tor's the one who tried to get the Destiny code from Devin—and, like I told you a minute ago, Tor recruited me." She blinked slowly at Alan, almost flirtatiously. "My mission was to establish a relationship with you. At first, we thought I could get the Destiny code, but that didn't work out, so all I did was relay updates on your progress and any other scraps of information I came across."

"You told them all about Devin, didn't you?" Alan said.

Kai nodded nonchalantly. "And when you were taking Devin to the football game. It was a big break for Rizben. He had tried to find a way to get to Devin, but that wasn't an easy task. The ballgame fit the bill— crowds, confusion, and no Code Adam. We knew Devin would fall for a chance to try a new video game."

"Damn you." Alan's expression looked as if he had a bad taste in his mouth.

"You're paying for the truth," Kai said. "You let me know when you don't want to hear it." She smiled, only one side of her mouth turned up and one brow arched.

"Where is this Tor?" Cotten asked.

"He's at the Hades facility."

"Where is that?" Alan said.

"No clue. All I know is that it's in some remote location."

"You don't know much," Cotten said. "I think Alan is overpaying you."

"I have a question," Alan said. "There was something in the email about an element not working. What element was he talking about?"

"Some weird shit they needed for the computer," Kai said. "They had a small amount, but it was unreliable, didn't work all the time. Sodium. Podium. Something like—"

Alan's head shot up.

"Thodium?" Cotten said.

"Yeah, that's it," Kai said.

Alan turned to Cotten. "How do you know about thodium?"

"Miller asked me if the word thodium meant anything to me."

Alan had already crossed the room and punched the button on his phone. "Get Max Wolf up here."

Chapter Fifty-Four

CUBITS OR QUBITS

"This Mace guy has a source of thodium," Alan told Max after he had explained what had led up to this moment.

"Could be he's found a way to create more than a few atoms at a time, but I doubt it," Max said.

"You want to know where he got the thodium?" Kai said. "Heavens, Alan, for the price you'll be paying me, all you had to do was ask."

"Spit it out, Kai," Alan said. "If you've got information, give it. Can you do that?"

"I have to admit, it is entertaining to see all the gyrations. But all right." She pressed her forefingers together and pointed them at Alan. "I don't think you'll believe me, though."

"Try me," Alan said.

"Rizben has a collection of archaeological artifacts. He's a collector. Anyway, from what he told me, he had a fragment of Noah's Ark. How he got it from the Baghdad Museum into his collection is a long story, and it doesn't really matter, so I won't go into that . . . unless you want me to take the time."

Cotten could see that Kai's over-politeness was grating on Alan. She stepped in. "No, we don't need all the background."

Kai sank back in the cushions. "Rizben said the Ark was built from lumber that came from some tree mentioned in the Bible—in Genesis—you know the one?"

"The Tree of Knowledge or the Tree of Life?" John said.

"The second one," Kai said. "The Tree of Life. And this particular wood secreted a sap, or resin I think he called it. After a long time that resin crystallizes into the stuff he needs for the computer—thodium. He extracted the thodium from splinters of Noah's Ark. I thought it was pretty wild, actually. Tree of Life. Fucking Noah's Ark." Kai glanced at Alan. "You never were any good at hiding your feelings. I can tell from your face you don't believe me."

"You're right. I don't."

"Maybe she's telling the truth," John said. "In one translation of the Bible, God tells Noah to build the Ark out of gopher wood. In another translation, God says to use resin wood."

The door to the playroom opened and Lindsay came out carrying a sheet of chart paper against her chest, the blank side showing.

"I found this in the playroom from when the kids were drawing earlier. I don't know, but I think it might be important."

"What is it?" Cotten said.

"Tera said she drew this as Devin described it to her. She says it's a sketch of the man who was holding Devin."

"Turn it around," Alan said.

Lindsay flipped the paper around so everyone could see the image. "It's certainly not Ben Ray," Cotten said.

"No, that's Tor," Kai said. "Wow, she's an amazing little artist."

Alan didn't acknowledge Kai's remark. "Thanks, for showing us the sketch, Lindsay." He sounded disappointed. "It is important, but we've already identified—"

John got to his feet. "Wait a minute." He walked closer to the sketch of the young goateed man in glasses and T-shirt. He touched the image of the shirt. "Look at this. It says *Cubits or Qubits, they all add up*."

"What does it mean?" Cotten asked.

John turned around. "Isn't qubits, spelled with a Q not a C, a computer term?"

Max said, "It's short for a quantum bit, a unit of quantum information stored in a quantum computer."

Alan's face grew curious. "Qubits and cubits is an interesting play on words."

John said, "Looks like Kai is being honest about where Mace got the thodium. It's too much of a coincidence for this guy, Tor, to be wearing a T-shirt that says cubits or qubits. The shirt suggests there's a connection between the two. Cubits, spelled with a C, is an ancient measurement of length. God gave Noah the dimensions of the Ark in cubits—three hundred cubits long, by fifty cubits wide, by thirty cubits high."

"What did you say?" Max's eyes blinked. "Can you repeat that?"

"Three hundred cubits, by fifty cubits, by thirty cubits."

Max thrust his arms in the air. "Holy shit!"

Chapter Fifty-Five

THE LEAP

"What is it, Max?" John said.

Max had both hands on top of his head in amazement. "Those measurements, the dimensions of the Ark, are the same as the dimensions of the thodium crystal we intend to use in the Destiny computer—three hundred atoms by fifty atoms by thirty. Each one of those atoms holds a qubit of information. Destiny will hold four hundred fifty-thousand qubits."

Alan's face grew solemn, and he stared blankly.

"You all right, Alan?" Cotten asked.

"Yeah, yeah, I'm fine." Alan met John's gaze. "You told me I didn't have to buy into everything . . . and I didn't. But now . . . I don't know. There's just too much for me to ignore. I don't like it. I've always considered myself grounded in certainty—scientific facts. But we just made that leap from science into something else. Something foreign to me."

John put his hand on Alan's shoulder. "The perceived gap between science and religion is not as wide as it seems once you are willing to accept it. Trust me, Alan. I've seen other people with the same doubts more times than I can count. It always takes a little time. No need to rush it."

"It's not a matter of rushing anything. I just feel like I've been blind-sided. When I got up this morning, I never expected anything like this." He ran his hand over his face. "Where can we get a piece of Noah's Ark?"

"Kai said Mace got it from the Baghdad Museum," John said. "That's obviously out. Who knows where any of the artifacts from the Ark are now—the museum was ransacked right after the invasion. And you know what's funny? When those pieces of the Ark were first discovered, there was very little news about it. I think that, mostly, no one believed it. It was regarded as a hoax by a majority of the scientific world. Like the Ossuary of James. I recall that only months before the Iraq War, there were tests being scheduled to authenticate the fragments—date them and things like that. Then the museum was wrecked, so nothing ever came about."

"Do you think there might be remains of the Ark somewhere?" Cotten asked. "Could we track them down?"

"Forget it," Kai said. "Rizben likes to tell the tale that he bought his fragments at a museum auction, but in reality, he's the mastermind behind the ransacking. He has all the pieces of the Ark that were in the museum."

"Dead end," Max said.

"The only way to stop Mace and his Hades Project is to beat him to the punch," Alan said. "It will take another quantum computer. Destiny."

"Isn't there any other source of thodium?" Cotten asked.

Max shook his head. "We haven't been able to find one."

John said, "Lumber from the Ark would have been quite valuable after the Flood waters receded. They would need it for building, for fire, tools, many uses. There might be some structure, some item still in existence. Or maybe there were other objects made from the Tree."

"How would we find out?" Cotten asked. "Where would we even start? Does it say anything about other items in Genesis?"

"No," John said. "We won't find the answer in the Bible this time. But there are other sources."

"Like the Dead Sea Scrolls?" Alan said.

"You're close," John said. "There is a church called St. Mary of Zion that houses thousands of ancient Gnostic texts, scrolls, codices, and gospels. What we might be looking for is what's called the Book of Emzara. Many years ago, I remember reading it was among the documents in the treasury church of Saint Mary of Zion. You don't hear much about the church's depository other than the suspicion that the Ark of the Covenant is hidden there. A lot of people believe that's where it is. There's no real proof."

"Like Raiders of the Lost Ark?" Kai said.

John smiled at her. "Exactly."

"So who is Emzara?" Cotten asked.

"Noah's wife."

"And where's the church?" Max asked.

John pointed out Alan's office window toward the east. "Axum, Ethiopia."

Chapter Fifty-Six

AXUM

The twin turboprops roared when the Ethiopian Airlines DHC-6 swung around for its approach to the small airfield in Axum. Cotten and John occupied the first two of the six passenger seats. The flight from the capital city of Addis Ababa had been turbulent because of a bad weather front that swept in earlier from the Red Sea.

The late afternoon light cast long shadows as Cotten stared down at the countryside surrounding the old city. Jagged peaks formed from the remnants of ancient volcanoes dotted the highland landscape while a few dirt roads stretched across parched farmland.

Cotten was not comfortable flying on any airplane, much less one so small. She gripped the armrests and glanced at John across the narrow aisle. "I hate landing."

The tires bit into the dusty landing strip, and the plane vibrated as the pilot applied the brakes and reversed the engines. Soon, the plane slowed enough to turn and taxi toward the small terminal.

Once the aircraft was parked and the engines wound down, the passengers were allowed to disembark. Cotten and John clutched small carryalls as they made their way across the open field to the terminal and on through the building to the gravel parking lot.

A short, potbellied black man came toward them. He wore a threadbare three-piece suit, a New York Yankees baseball cap, and sandals. With a heavy accent, he said, "Your Eminence, it is my extreme honor to greet a prince of the Roman Church." He grasped John's hand, dropped to one knee, and held it to his forehead.

John blessed the man with the sign of the cross.

The man rose and spoke in English though his phrasing gave away that English was not his native tongue. "We welcome your presence. I am Berhanu, your guide." He shook John's hand and then Cotten's. "And it is also the huge pleasure to meet famous person like you." He looked back to John. "Many funds were wired ahead to pay my services for you and also your rooms at the African Hotel. How long are you to stay?"

"Just tonight," John said. "We leave on the return flight to the capital tomorrow morning."

Berhanu pointed to a vintage Land Rover parked a few yards away. Its color was a combination of faded orange and lime green among patches of rust and Bondo. Cracks spider-webbed from a bullet hole in the side window.

"Someone use your car for target practice?" Cotten asked as they approached it.

"Oh, no. They trying to *kill* me." Berhanu laughed as he held the side door open for her. "Lucky they were not so good shooters. War is always close in Ethiopia."

Cotten got in the back seat while John joined Berhanu in the front, and they drove from the airfield toward town.

The ride was noisy, and Cotten had to lean forward to be heard. "Did they tell you why we are in Axum?"

"Yes," Berhanu said. "You wish that to visit the holy church of the St. Mary of Zion." He crossed himself.

"Right," John said. "An arrangement has been made for us to meet with the guardian monk."

"And I am your person who translates all that he speaks."

"Can we go there now, Berhanu?" Cotten asked. "I know it's late in the day, but we are anxious to speak with him."

"I am driver for you. If you wish straight away, then I take you."

Cotten watched as they passed small shops and open food markets that lined the dirt roads. The thick dust, like the poverty, was everywhere. Young boys swarmed the car with outstretched hands, trailing behind the Land Rover, begging for handouts or a few birr. The buildings were old and in disrepair—she saw only dirt roads and ill-kept paths connecting the neighborhoods. Piles of trash and garbage dotted the landscape. She felt something close to guilt or shame for having money in her pocket and the lifestyle she enjoyed with her job at SNN.

"Berhanu, do you live here in Axum?" Cotten asked.

"Yes. I was birthed here and am the worker for the Ministry of Culture. My job is to keep watch out with an open eye for the treasures of Axum." He turned the Land Rover onto a potholed road and motioned to the right. "What you see there is all that remains of the palace of the Queen of Sheba, King Solomon's wife."

A hundred yards down the side of a sloping hill, Cotten made out the remnants of low walls that formed the ruins of an ancient building.

About a mile farther along the bumpy road, Berhanu said, "And there is the destination for which you are arriving." He motioned to a spacious walled compound on their left. It contained two churches, the larger one appeared old, and the smaller a much more recent design with a domed roof and a bell tower in the shape of an obelisk.

"Which is St. Mary of Zion?" Cotten asked.

"Both," Berhanu said. "The ancient church dates to the seventeenth century. It was the building for which the great Emperor Fasilidas made."

"And the new one?" John said.

"The treasury church became built about thirty-five years previous from today."

"Is it true that the Ark of the Covenant is kept inside?" Cotten asked.

"Quite, yes."

"And have you seen it?" John asked.

"No, no." He crossed himself again and glanced up at the inside roof of the Land Rover as if seeking forgiveness for even thinking himself worthy. "The guardian monk is the all who sees what is inside the treasury church. He alone can look upon the blessed Ark."

"Have you met the monk?" John asked.

"The guardian monk lives in seclusion. He received his calling before my birth, so he is never seen by my eyes."

Berhanu pulled the Land Rover up to the front gate of the church of St. Mary of Zion. "And now we arrived."

Cotten got out and looked at the older of the two churches. It reminded her of a castle with its tall, grand turrets and imposing battlements ringing the tops of the walls.

Cotten, John, and the interpreter moved through the gate. They passed through the large double-latticed doors and entered the old building. Within its dimly lit interior, Cotten saw murals covering almost all the walls and ceiling including one that depicted the life of Mary. Another series illustrated the Crucifixion and Resurrection. There seemed to be a perpetual veil of candle and incense smoke that created a milky, soft glow to everything. From the far recesses of the church beyond the altar came the sound of the scrape of feet on stone. A figure appeared.

The stooped man leaned on a prayer staff as he shuffled toward them. He was bearded and old and dressed in a long white robe that billowed about his feet as he moved. When he stood before them, from a toothless mouth he spoke at length in Tigrigna, the local language.

His voice reminded Cotten of an un-oiled door hinge. When he finished, Cotten and John turned in unison to Berhanu.

Berhanu kept his eyes cast downward in the presence of the holy man while he conversed briefly with the monk. Then he looked to Cotten

272

and John. "He asked who you are, and I told him you are the visitors he agreed to see. He says he has pleasure in meeting you and has wishes to serve you."

"Tell him we are pleased as well," Cotten said. Berhanu again looked at the floor as he translated.

Introductions complete, the monk extended his hand to John. Then he turned to Cotten and did the same. As she grasped it, Cotten smelled the faint but unmistakable scent of frankincense. "It is an honor."

The guardian monk stiffened. His eyes met hers, and although they were clouded and sunken with age, he focused intently.

As a trace of a smile crossed his lips, Cotten felt uneasiness rush through her, and tried to release his hand.

He kept his grip firm.

The monk spoke barely above a whisper before he let go of her hand. John glanced at Berhanu.

Cotten's mouth dropped open.

The guide shrugged, his jaw agape. "I am sorry, but I did not understand." He looked perplexed and frustrated. "His speaking is foreign to my ears."

Cotten stared at the monk in amazement. He had spoken in Enochian, the language of Heaven, the tongue of the angels—a language she understood, which meant he understood who she was—her legacy and her destiny.

And his words filled her with wonder.

Chapter Fifty-Seven

BEYOND THE VEIL

"What did he say?" John asked. They stood in the back of the sanctuary of St. Mary of Zion church.

"That he knew my father." Cotten was still dazed from having the monk speak to her in Enochian. "That my father is pleased I have come here, and there are things inside I should see."

"That's impossible," John whispered. "How would he have known your father?"

Cotten shrugged. "I don't know—"

The guardian monk mumbled to Berhanu as he opened a door leading out through a walled garden to the smaller treasury church.

They followed, but Berhanu held up his hand to John. "I'm afraid we can go not beyond this door. The holy monk speaks that it is forbidden. Only Miss Stone may proceed into the treasury church."

John turned to meet Cotten's gaze. "You don't have to go alone if you're uncomfortable. Let's just tell him what we need—give him a list."

"I want to go. After what he said, I'm compelled."

"Are you sure?" John touched her arm.

She closed her eyes and relished his touch for a moment. "Yes. Maybe I'll learn something about my father—if nothing else, that he's finally at peace."

The guardian monk spoke again to Cotten. John gave her a questioning look.

"He said he will show me the Book of Emzara—that it will reveal all we seek."

"I don't feel good about this."

"I need to do it," Cotten said. "Let me go get what we came for and be done with it."

With obvious reluctance, John stepped back. "I'll be waiting right here."

As she followed the monk through the church door, she glanced over her shoulder at John before the door closed with a sense of finality.

The treasury church was a short walk along a path through a thick stand of trees. Twilight already embraced the countryside. The heavens were now cloudless, and all things about her basked in pale moonlight, the glow from the town, and the African star-filled sky. The building loomed before her, a boxy stone structure about fifty-feet square surrounded by a tall brick wall topped with iron fencing.

The monk unlocked a barred metal gate and led Cotten a few yards farther to the treasury entrance—an imposing wooden door on which was painted a portrait of St. Mary surrounded by saints and angels, St. Joseph, and the infant, Jesus. He inserted a key into the lock and pulled the massive door open.

As Cotten followed him, she was struck by the intense fragrance of candle smoke and incense. Around the perimeter of the large room hung hundreds of candle lanterns suspended from heavy wood beams by chains of varying lengths—each flame encased inside red glass lenses. The room glowed with a shimmering ruby red light that constantly moved like sunbeams through water.

Shelves lined the walls that reminded Cotten of what her mother called pigeonholes and cubbies. Each differed in size and held books, scrolls, piles of paper and parchment, and other small objects. There were thousands.

In the middle of the room stood a marble altar on which sat a collection of what appeared to be hundreds of antique objects—crowns, crosses, daggers, ancient books bound in thick leather and encrusted with jewels, and many more items Cotten could not identify through the smoky haze.

As she stood mesmerized by the uniqueness of her surroundings, a breeze brushed past her, causing her to wonder where it came from in the closed building. In the distance, through the mist, Cotten saw a thin veil of gauze-like cloth hanging from ceiling to floor—the breeze had moved it just enough for her to distinguish it from the smoke.

In English, the guardian monk said, "Do you wish to go beyond the veil and cast your eyes upon the Ark of the Covenant?"

Stunned, Cotten spun around. "You speak English?"

"I speak many languages."

A chill enveloped her. A shudder moved through her like the first tremors of an earthquake. Maybe coming alone was a bad decision. Lightheaded, Cotten braced herself against a wood bookcase. Her sight narrowed like looking through a tunnel. Darkness squeezed in and blurred her peripheral vision.

"Something wrong?" The monk's form became less distinct as he drifted in and out of the smoke.

She pressed her fingertips to her temples. "No. I'm fine." A buzzing sound filled her ears, and the violent thump of her heart pumped against her sternum.

"I asked if you wish to look upon the Holy Ark."

"No." She fought to keep her equilibrium. "I'm here regarding a different Ark—Noah's Ark. And the Book of his wife, Emzara. I need to see . . ."

She fought to focus her thoughts. *Keep talking. Keep your mind on task.* "We have to search the Book of Emzara for any reference to objects that could have been forged or shaped from the Tree of Life. I need to know if there is a manifest."

She saw a twisted smile on his face. When he spoke, the sound came to her ears as an echo.

"Since you do not desire to look upon the Holy Ark, it is all the more reason you must. For within it lies your destiny. Let it reveal the secrets of your father, Furmiel."

Mindlessly, remarkably lacking any self-will, Cotten followed him until they stood before the thin cloth veil—a translucent barrier that obscured what she guessed was the Holy of Holies, the Ark of the Covenant.

Cotten noticed light coming from the other side. More candles, intensely red, lit the chamber behind the sheer material.

Using the tip of his prayer staff, the monk separated a seam in the veil. Holding it open, he motioned for Cotten to proceed.

Like the main sanctuary, this one also had dozens of hanging candle lanterns, their ruby light glittering. In the middle of the chamber, a long canopy of silky gauze hung from the ceiling and flared at the bottom. The monk moved to the canopy and slipped his hand into a space in the material. With apparent reverence, he pulled back one side of the canopy and exposed a golden chest resting upon a low marble stand.

Cotten gasped as her eyes filled with the reflection of the flickering candlelight. It was as if the object had trapped the stars. The golden sides were embossed with the image of a spreading tree, and atop the chest were two kneeling cherubs. They faced each other, and their outstretched wingtips met in the center. The air thickened, and her breathing became labored. Beads of sweat formed and dribbled down her back and between her breasts—her legs wobbled.

"Come forward. Bear witness to the wonder."

Cotten stepped within inches of the golden chest. She extended her hand and held it over the relic. Its energy flowed through her. Like the faint tingle of electricity, it stimulated her skin.

The monk grasped the hinged top of the Ark and swung open the lid with its shimmering cherubs. Like the outside, the interior was lined with gold. Cotten leaned over and gazed inside. What she saw made her reel backward, and she realized in that instant she had made a terrible mistake.

Chapter Fifty-Eight

ASHES

When Cotten gazed into the Ark of the Covenant, she did not see the expected tablets of the Ten Commandments. Instead, she stared into the eternal fires of Hell.

The sickening odor of sulfur replaced the aromatic incense, and a blast of blistering wind slammed her onto the floor. Like a magician's flash paper, the silky gauze canopy that enclosed the Ark erupted into flames. The ashes of the fabric floated through the air like black leaves from a diseased tree.

Screams of tormented souls filled the church, a sound that resembled the scrape and grind of giant metal machines colliding. Cotten pressed her palms to her ears to block out the piercing noise. Above her, the ruby candle lanterns spun in wide arcs and blazed like exploding stars.

As if she glared into a blast furnace, the glow from the Ark intensified until the priceless chest melted into a molten mass.

Cotten realized that the guardian monk had transformed. Standing over her was a gray-haired man—old, but not stooped or bearded or toothless. The wrinkles in his face were not folds of weary flesh, but rather chiseled lines, and his eyes raged with fire deep within the dark irises.

He was dressed in a suit of raven feathers. In his hand he held a book—its cover and bindings ancient and worn like an old leather glove, its pages ready to crumble into tiny pieces and rain down. "Is this what you seek?"

His words cut through the screams and cries coming from the depths of the Ark. She tried to focus on the book, but the maddening effect of the spinning candle lanterns made her dizzy.

"The Book of Emzara." He extended it to her.

Like fighting a raging river current, she tried with all her strength to take the book. As her fingertips touched its surface, the book ignited just as the gauze canopy had done—a momentary flash before it vaporized. She watched its ashes drift away and knew the source of the answers she sought had just vanished forever.

"Go home, daughter of Furmiel. Your task has ended—you are too late, and too weak."

As quickly as the tumult began, it was over. The vision of the Old Man faded as he became part of the smoke-filled room.

Cotten lay breathless on the church floor, the heat receded, the voices of the damned died away, and the frantic motion of the lanterns stilled. She rose to her knees then stood on shaky legs—the odor of incineration everywhere.

In the middle of the floor, the remains of the Ark of the Covenant had become a pool of smelted gold. As she stumbled away from the Holy of Holies, she saw that piles of ashes filled the thousands of pigeonholes. Upon the altar, the ancient relics were nothing but unrecognizable heaps of cremation. A thick pall of gray haze settled over the interior of the church while Cotten made her way to the entrance. She pulled on the heavy door then stumbled into the clear African night. Her lungs took in a deep, clean breath. The stench, bitter taste, and terrible cries dissolved.

She looked up through a cloud of confusion and blurry eyes—a man rushed toward her, and she fell into the arms of John Tyler.

***

Cotten looked into John's face. "Where am I?" She lay on a bed in a sparsely furnished room—the only light was a lamp on a bedside table.

"A room at the African Hotel." He sat on the side of her bed. "You passed out. Berhanu and I brought you here. I wanted to take you to a medical clinic, but he said the closest one is across the border in Asmara, about seventy miles away."

Cotten sat up and dropped her legs over the side of the bed. She felt despondence wash over her. "The church, the Ark of the Covenant, all those priceless objects and documents, all burned to ash."

John gave her a confused look. "Burned?" He shook his head. "What are you talking about?"

Chapter Fifty-Nine

THE ARCHIVES

"Cotten, nothing burned." John wiped her face with a cool, damp cloth. "This should make you feel better."

"Where is the guardian monk?" She took the cloth.

"At the monastery, I assume. He followed you out of the church and said you were overcome by the smoke of the candles. He suggested we take you some place to rest."

Cotten recalled the transformation of the monk, him taunting her with the Book of Emzara, and warning to go home. She put her face in the cool cloth. He hadn't been the guardian monk at all—the man who led her into the treasury church was evil incarnate, her mortal enemy, the Son of the Dawn—Lucifer. He had lured her inside to terrorize her with a dramatic display of his power and to let her know he had the secrets to the Book of Emzara, and that she never would—that she could never defeat him. She also understood what he had meant when he said he knew her father, Furmiel, the Angel of the Eleventh Hour. He referred to knowing her father before he had repented eons ago when Furmiel and Lucifer were both a part of the legion of the Fallen Angels. Lucifer abhorred Furmiel—the only Fallen Angel ever to beg for God's forgiveness. Most of all, Lucifer hated Cotten—the living reminder of Furmiel's betrayal.

"If this is all of my needs for this tonight, I will be gone home to my family," Berhnau said.

It was the first time Cotten had noticed the guide sitting in a nearby chair.

Berhanu glanced at his watch. "Will there be more of my services?"

"No, nothing else," John said.

Berhanu bowed, and John walked him to the door. The guide stepped into the hall, but then turned, his palms together like he was praying. "I hope with sincerity that Cotten Stone will feel much fine and have a pleasant trip back to America."

"Thank you, Berhanu." John blessed him. "We wish you and your family well."

He closed the door and returned to Cotten's bedside. "I'm sorry you had to go through this for no reason."

Cotten stared at him.

"The monk told us that as he retrieved the Book of Emzara from a pile of ancient scrolls, it literally disintegrated to dust in his hands. He said he offered to search through other books in the church library, but that's when you became dizzy and wanted to leave."

Cotten slowly shook her head.

"He said when you first entered the church, you asked to see the Ark of the Covenant, but he had to refuse. No one is allowed to see it but the guardian monk. He told us you demanded to see it."

"I did see it. He showed it to me." She whispered, "I witnessed it melt and burn…" Where to begin? she thought. But she knew where to start.

From the moment she had looked into the eyes of the Beast.

***

They sat in the waiting area of the Bole International Airport in Addis Ababa, Ethiopia. Their British Airlines flight to Rome was about to board.

"Then it's obvious that the Book of Emzara is extremely important to the Fallen Ones," John said. "We can assume that an item made from the

Tree is noted in that book, either in narrative or on a manifest. The big questions are—do any of those objects still exist, and if so, what and where?"

"And they already have the book," Cotten said, "which means they have a head start on finding what might be the only source of thodium left in the world."

She still experienced the effects from the incident the night before—unsteady and lethargic, even after a restful sleep in the African Hotel. A native breakfast of *injeera*, a baked flatbread similar to pizza, covered with local meats and cheese, helped her regain her energy before she and John flew back to the Ethiopian capital.

"You're right," John said. "Why else would the Fallen stage such an elaborate illusion?"

"Even if we identify a possible object from Noah's Ark, what are the chances that it's still around after five thousand years?" She scrubbed her forehead with the heel of her hand—a dull headache had persisted through the night and refused to go away. The faint odor of sulfur still lingered in her nostrils even though she had taken a long, steamy shower. "Not to mention that we'll never find another copy of the Emzara text."

"Our chances are better than you might expect. I'm convinced that a copy survives somewhere. I've got the Venatori research division looking in two places—the Coptic Museum in Cairo where the Nag Hammadi Library is housed and also in the Secret Archives of the Vatican where they should find transcripts that originated from the First Council of Nicaea. In both cases, early Christian Gnostic texts had references to Noah and Emzara. Maybe we'll get lucky."

"I've heard the term, Gnostic," Cotten said, "but I don't know what that means." She watched a group of tourists wander by, their conversation washed in a heavy French accent.

"Gnostics were religious groups that existed in the first couple of centuries AD. The Gnostic Gospels are ancient texts that contain details on the life of Christ not included in the New Testament—texts such as the Gospels of Mary Magdalene, Philip, Sophia, Thomas, and others. But they also include transcripts from the writings of the Old Testament including a prediction of the Great Deluge. There are a few partial documents that refer to Emzara. Some are only fragments, but at this point, it may be all we've got."

John's cell phone rang, and he pulled it from his belt clip. Looking at the caller ID, he said, "It's the Archives prefect." He listened intently for a moment before ending the call. With a smile, he turned to Cotten and winked. "You must be living right."

***

The black S550 Mercedes slipped through the Porta Sant'Anna entrance to Vatican City. It sped past the Vatican Bank and the Apostolic Palace. Turning right, it pulled up in front of a gated courtyard about fifty feet beyond the Vatican Library. The driver and front-seat passenger, both Venatori agents, got out and held open the rear doors. Two members of the Swiss Guard stood beside the gate and saluted as John motioned Cotten into the courtyard. A dozen paces beyond was the nondescript, easily overlooked entrance to the Secret Archives.

Inside, Cotten was surprised to see what resembled a hotel check-in desk staffed by two young men.

In a thick Italian accent, one of the men said, "Your Eminence Cardinal Tyler, welcome. It is always a pleasure to have you visit us." He turned to Cotten. "Ms. Stone, it is an honor to meet the person who recovered for all mankind, the Cup of Christ." Then he stepped around the desk and shook both their hands. "This way, please. They are waiting for you."

He led them through the ground-floor library and *sola di studio* where a handful of scholars worked.

"They limit the number of researchers allowed in here to about two hundred a year," John said to Cotten. "And the approval process to get in can take an eternity as well. If you're permitted to do archives research, you must stay seated in this room and request what you need from the assistants. Everything is brought to you."

Cotten saw two rows of antique desks, each one about six feet long.

"The electrical outlets at the desks are fairly new after an outcry to use laptops," John said. "Wireless will take a miracle."

Leaving the studio of the scholars, they headed for a tiny European-style elevator, the kind that barely holds three people at a time. As they stepped inside, Cotten felt it bounce when the cables stretched.

"Below us is what they refer to as the Bunker," John said. "It's the manuscript depository where the bulk of the archives are housed. But we're headed up to the *piani nobili*, the rooms that contained the original secret archives. The Borghese Pope Paul the Fifth established the archives in 1610. He had a somewhat inflated ego and decided to have his name chiseled dead center over the main entrance to Saint Peter's Basilica."

Cotten shook her head in incredulity. Above all else, the popes were mere mortals, she thought.

They got off the elevator and headed into a long, narrow room with lofty ceilings covered with colorful murals of celebrated papal events. An enormous portrait dominated one wall.

"Speak of the devil." John chuckled and pointed to the painting. "Paul the Fifth, ego and all."

A series of *armadi*—wooden closets—lined the room. Cotten saw two priests in black cassocks standing beside one—the door agape. All the other closets were closed and padlocked. In front of the open closet stood a table covered with yellowed parchments.

As Cotten and John approached, one of the priests said, "Your Eminence, we have located the records of the First Council of Nicaea."

"And you've found a transcript of the Book of Emzara?" John asked.

"We have, Eminence," the second priest said.

"Is there a list of items carried on the Ark?" Cotten said.

"Yes," the first priest said.

Cotten's pulse quickened with excitement. Perhaps they were not chasing a lost cause after all.

"And," the priest added, "we have come across something extraordinarily puzzling, and much, much more."

Chapter Sixty

GHOST OF GALILEO

Cotten stood in the Meridian Room, the uppermost chamber of the Torre Dei Venti, the Tower of the Winds. Constructed high above the Vatican's Secret Archives, the room had remained unchanged since the sixteenth century. She stared at frescoes by Nicolo Circignani that depicted events in the life of Christ and Saint Paul. Her heart beat quicker knowing she stood in the same spot where Galileo had argued with church curia that the Earth revolved around the sun and not vice versa. But more importantly, she pondered the riddle found in the Book of Emzara.

She heard footsteps and turned to see John coming up the circular set of metal steps. He held a small stack of papers.

"Standing in this place is such a rush," she said as he approached.

"It does tend to humble you."

"So what have you found?"

"I ran the Greek and Latin translations by three of our best linguistic scholars. They all came to the same conclusions."

"Which are?"

"There is one curious item in Emzara's list of what was brought aboard Noah's Ark. One amazing revelation on what the Ark was constructed from, and for you and me, the answer to a nagging question."

"Read it to me."

John looked at the papers for a moment. "Emzara overhears God talking to her husband. She writes, 'And God said to Noah, You are righteous and holy. And God said, preserve that which is righteous.

Protect all that is created from the seed of Adam and the blood of the Tree of Life. For I will make a covenant with you and your sons. I will set my bow in the clouds as a sign of my covenant. I will never again destroy by water that which man has made. Not from the clouds but from the seed of Adam will come the thunderbolt. And it will be there on the day when my vengeance will once again destroy that which violates my land. And God said, Fear not, for they will know that I am the Lord Thy God, and I will show them the sign.'"

"What is the thunderbolt?"

"Not sure." John shuffled through the pages. "The actual inventory—the manifest if you will—is very close to the list in Genesis. Seven pairs of all the clean animals and two pair each of the unclean."

"Clean? Unclean?"

"Probably indicated the animals they were allowed to eat or not eat." He glanced at the notes again. "Emzara also mentions they gathered together clothing, food, seeds, grain, bedding, nails, a couple of oxen carts, farm tools, and finally the mysterious reference to the thunderbolt, something made by Tubal Cain from the blood of the Tree of Life—an item that has stumped everyone."

"Then whatever the thunderbolt is, it's got to be the object we're looking for. Right?"

"That's the best guess. It's the only item on her list that mentions who made it—Tubal Cain, the great, great, grandson of Adam. He was a blacksmith, and his specialty was weapons. Thunderbolt must refer to a weapon forged by Tubal Cain from the hardened sap of the Tree of Life."

"So what's the revelation?"

"That the Ark was constructed from the actual Tree that grew east of the Garden. This confirms what Kai confessed was the source of the thodium being used in the Hades Project—crystallized resin from the

Ark. Genesis says God commanded Noah to construct the Ark from resin wood. So far, no one has ever positively identified what resin wood is. This nails it."

"And there's the reference to the signs God would leave us. They've been there all along—the signature thunderbolt on all of Tera's artwork. Even the CyberSys logo. How could we have missed those obvious connections?"

"How many times have I told you the answer to everything is right in the Bible?"

"Even the qubits and cubits conversion—the dimensions of the Ark and the exact dimensions of the storage qubits needed for the quantum computers. Maybe I should start listening to you more often," she said with a smile.

John spread his hands in an "I told you so" gesture.

"If the thunderbolt is a weapon—" Cotten heard a commotion coming from the base of the spiraling metal steps. She turned as murmuring voices were followed by the muffled sound of footfalls on the metal.

A man came up the steps. At first, Cotten saw his snowy hair, thick and wavy. Then the pale face with the wire-rimmed glasses, the white cassock, the gold chain with the crucifix hanging from his neck—the famous red shoes.

"I'm grateful there are few stairs in the Vatican like those," he said in a slightly winded German accent. "Perhaps that's why I don't make the trip up here too often."

"Your Holiness," John said. He dropped to one knee and kissed the ring on the outstretched hand of the pontiff.

The pope motioned for him to rise. "John, I have been told by reliable sources that you and Ms. Stone are hoping the ghost of Galileo will help you solve your five-thousand-year-old mystery."

Cotten stepped forward. "Galileo's ghost hasn't granted us an audience, Your Holiness, but it is an honor to meet you." She took his hand in both of hers.

"Ms. Stone, the honor is all mine. In this very building, perhaps no more than a few hundred paces from where we stand, rests the single most important religious relic of the past two thousand years—the Cup of Christ, the Holy Grail. And it is here solely because of you. Not only did you recover it—twice, I might add—and present it to the Church, but you did so after stopping what would have been a great and terrible tragedy."

The pope stood back and stared up with a look of wonder at the ceiling of the Meridian Room. "Do you see the mural of Christ calming the sea?"

Cotten and John gazed in the direction he indicated.

"Look in the top right-hand corner, in the middle of the portrait of the elderly gentleman puffing his cheeks. There is a small opening approximately the side of a coin." The pontiff then pointed to the marble floor of the Meridian Room where the signs of the zodiac were etched and a meridian line cut down the middle. "Each March twenty-first, the sun shines through that tiny hole and strikes the vernal equinox line here on the floor. The first official Vatican astronomer, a brilliant priest named Ignazio Danti, designed it in the 1500s." He gestured to the symbols at his feet. "I have stood on this spot and witnessed it. Quite moving." The pope smiled at them both. "Now you want to know what is the meaning of the reference to thunderbolt in the Book of Emzara?"

"Your Holiness," Cotten said, "it is imperative we find the object known as the thunderbolt."

"We are afraid that if we don't find it first, it will fall into the hands of the Nephilim," John said. "And from what we have learned, they plan to use it to bring about global chaos."

The pope silenced them with an upturned palm. "Like the others, I, too, was confounded by the thunderbolt in the Book of Emzara. And so I did what I do whenever I seek understanding. I handed over my question to God and trusted He would answer. And so He has." He fixed his eyes on Cotten. "Part of the answer came to me by remembering who you are and what you have done. Ms. Stone, the Cup of Christ once held the blood of Jesus Christ collected at the Crucifixion. Correct?"

Cotten nodded.

He looked to John. "What caused the blood to flow from Our Savior into the Cup?"

"A Roman centurion pierced Christ's side with a lance," John said, appearing to think out each word as he spoke. "According to the Scriptures, out poured a mixture of blood and water."

The pope gripped the cross that hung at his chest and set his eyes on Cotten's. "You have come full circle, Cotten Stone. What you seek is within your grasp."

Chapter Sixty-One

THE LEGEND

Cotten watched out the window of the Gulfstream G150 as it streaked across the amethyst evening sky on a course over the Adriatic Sea from Rome to Vienna. The Vatican City crest sparkled on the jet's gleaming white skin. She was tired but could not sleep. Though she had long accepted her destiny in this world, it still weighed heavily, especially when everything always seemed to spiral back to who she was—the daughter of a Fallen Angel, the product of a pact between her repentant father and God.

She heard the pope's words again in her head. "The revelation given to me about the thunderbolt began with my recollection of who you are." He went on to tell her that Noah carried the Spear forged by Tubal Cain onto the Ark, and it was the same weapon that was later used to pierce the side of Christ. Blood flowed from the wound, and His blood filled the Cup. The pope reminded Cotten that she had held the Cup in her hands, and now she searched for the object that caused it to fill with the blood of Jesus Christ—thereby coming full circle in her quest. His exact words still rang in her mind. "The thunderbolt you seek is the Holy Lance, known to the world as the Spear of Destiny."

Cotten turned away from the darkening sky. She and John sat in leather seats, a narrow aisle separating them. In front of John was a curly maple-top desk on which rested a thick red folder, its cover inscribed with the words: For the Eyes of the Director. Beneath the inscription was the seal of the Venatori—a round emblem showing a raging lion and a longsword with the motto: *Umbrae Manium, Arma Dei*—Shadows of

Ghosts, Armor of God. The folder contained John's daily security briefing.

At the other end of the short desk, in a seat facing them, was Carlo Zanini, a thirty-five-year-old Italian priest who had joined the Venatori to work in their research division as an expert on medieval mythology and Old Testament history.

Under a tousled mop of thick black hair, Zanini stared at an open laptop screen through thick, horn-rimmed glasses. He scrolled down a series of data files and chose one with the click of the mouse. Once it opened, he said, "The Spear has an amazing history, just as His Holiness told you. The Book of Emzara refers to it as Thunderbolt and claims it was forged from the blood of the Tree of Life by Tubal Cain, a black-smith and seventh generation grandson of Adam. No doubt the blood refers to the hardened sap from the Tree. As we've already learned from Emzara's text, God instructed Noah to carry the Thunderbolt aboard the Ark to be preserved and protected for use at some future time. It is the only article, other than the actual Ark, that we know was made from the Tree—the vessel was constructed from timbers cut from the Tree." Zanini opened another document as he pushed the heavy glasses up his noble Roman nose.

"The next time it shows up is at the Crucifixion?" Cotten asked as she made a note on a yellow legal pad.

"Actually, no," Zanini said. "We found a reference in the Nag Ham-madi Library scrolls in Cairo that mentioned Joshua holding up the Thunderbolt Spear as he signaled his soldiers to shout a 'great shout' which brought down the walls of Jericho. Also, in the Cairo library our researchers found a text stating that the Thunderbolt Spear was hurled at young David by King Saul in a fit of jealousy.

"The Spear wound up in the possession of Pompey who later gave it to Julius Caesar. Caesar presented the Thunderbolt Spear to a Roman commander in recognition of years of devoted service. That commander was the grandfather of a soldier named Gaius Cassius. Many years later, in the hands of the grandson, the true legend of the Thunderbolt Spear began."

Zanini silently read off the laptop's LCD for a moment, then said, "On April fifth in 33 AD, Annas, the advisor to the Sanhedrin, and Caiaphas, the Jewish High Priest, conspired to have Jesus crucified and his body mutilated to prove to the masses that he was not the Messiah but only a mortal man and a heretic. It was on a Friday, and the Sabbath began at sundown.

"Jewish law decreed that no man should be executed on the Sabbath. As the day wore on, and Jesus hadn't died, Annas and Caiaphas panicked since time was running out. They wanted to make sure Christ didn't expire after sunset, so they petitioned Pontius Pilate to let them send their own temple guard out to Golgotha—the Place of the Skull—and make sure Jesus and the other two men crucified that day died before sundown. The Roman soldiers on duty turned their backs in disgust at the brutality of the temple guards as they clubbed and crushed the skulls and limbs of the two thieves, Gestas and Dismas.

"Now, remember the grandson, Gaisus Cassius? This was years later, and he was the senior Roman officer on duty that day. He saw that Jesus had expired, and decided that rather than let the Jews disfigure the body, he would confirm Jesus was already dead, thus avoiding the mutilation.

"Gaisus was a veteran warrior, but he was getting old and his eyesight failing. He carried Caesar's gift to his grandfather with him at all times. So with the lance in hand, he rode his horse up to the cross on which Jesus hung and thrust it into Christ's right side between the fourth and fifth ribs. This was a Roman battlefield practice that when they wanted to prove that a wounded enemy was truly dead, they pierced him with a spear or sword. The logic was that blood would not flow from a dead body. To everyone's surprise, out flowed blood and water from Christ's wound. As the blood ran down the shaft of the Spear, Gaisus got some in his eyes. In that instant, his failing sight was completely restored. Thus we have the first evidence of the Spear's power."

"I thought the Roman Centurion was called Longinus?" John said.

Zanini nodded. "That's correct, Eminence. After he had his sight restored, he became known throughout the region as Longinus the Spearman. Soon after that, he left the military and converted to Christianity, spending the rest of his life preaching the teachings of Christ until he was martyred in Cappadocia in the first century. We know him today as Saint Longinus. Immortalized by Lorenzo Bernini, in Saint Peter's Basilica there is a bronze statue of Longinus holding the Spear."

"Okay," Cotten said. "But how did the Spear wind up in a display case in the Hapsburg Museum in Vienna?" She stood, took an aluminum carafe of coffee from its holder and refreshed John's and Zanini's cups before topping off her own.

Zanini said, "Legend states that 'Whosoever possesses the Holy Lance and understands the powers it serves, holds in his hand the destiny of the world.' The next time we hear of it, the Holy Lance is in the possession of the illegitimate son of a Roman general and an innkeeper's daughter. The boy grew up to be one of the most powerful historical figures of all time, the Roman Emperor Constantine the Great. With the Spear in hand, he declared himself to be the 'thirteenth Apostle' and proclaimed Christianity as the official religion of the Holy Roman Empire. As emperor, he established Constantinople, today's Istanbul.

"In 443, Attila the Hun laid siege to the city and said he would spare Constantinople in return for two things from then Emperor Theodosius—six thousand pounds of gold, and the Holy Lance. Theodosius paid. Nine years later, Attila reached the gates of Rome but had to withdraw because famine and disease ravaged the city. The legend says that when the Roman officers surrendered the city, Attila threw the Holy Lance at their feet in disgust and left.

"The next owner became the second giant historical figure to possess the Spear of Longinus."

"Charlemagne," John said.

Zanini nodded. "In the course of changing the face of the world, it was said that the Holy Lance never left his side."

The phone on John's armrest chirped. "Yes?" A few seconds later, he hung up. "The pilot says we're forty-five minutes out of Vienna International Airport."

Cotten sank back into the thick leather. "So far, this has been fascinating."

"We haven't even gotten to the best part," the Italian priest said. "In 1424 Sigismund of Luxembourg sold the Lance to the town council of Nuremberg. It stayed on display there until 1806 when Napoleon came looking for it. German authorities smuggled it to Austria just ahead of the French troops so Emperor Bonaparte could not have it.

"The Holy Lance sat in a display case inside the Hapsburg Museum for years until along came the third historical figure to possess it—Adolf Hitler. His fascination with it probably began from his love of Richard Wagner's opera, Parsifal. The Spear played a major role in the work."

"Now we're into an area where I've done intense research," John said. "Hitler annexed Austria, then ordered his SS troops to seize the Holy Lance, correct?"

"Yes, Eminence. Under Hitler's orders, the relic was transported on a heavily guarded express train to Nuremberg where he could have access to it whenever he wanted. It was kept in a fortified bunker beneath Saint Katherine's church. The vault was built in secret and at a huge expense to protect the relic from Allied bombs. Hitler hoped to rebuild the Holy

Roman Empire with himself as supreme Emperor, and he believed he needed the Lance to do so.

"And in an ironic twist, on the afternoon of April 30, 1945, the Holy Lance was discovered and fell into the hands of American forces almost at the exact moment that Adolf Hitler committed suicide."

"Here's what I don't understand," Cotten said. "If the Lance is so powerful, why is it that some of its owners succeeded at using it while others, like Hitler, failed?"

"Just a theory," John said, "but I believe success or failure is determined by what's in the heart of the person who possesses it."

The three seemed to ponder John's statement for a moment. Then Zanini said, "Here's another strange twist. While Adolf Hitler waited for so many years between his first sight of the Lance and the day he finally possessed it, Heinrich Himmler, Reichsfuhrer of the SS, was so captivated by it that he had a replica made in 1935—three years before his fuhrer marched into Austria."

"What happened to the replica?" Cotten asked.

Zanini shrugged. "No one knows for sure."

"So after the American forces captured the Holy Lance, its new owner was Harry Truman?" John asked.

"Technically," Zanini said. "Although he never actually touched it, while he had control over it, he introduced the world to the most destructive power in history—the atomic bomb."

"When was the Lance returned to Vienna?" Cotten asked.

"There was a bit of a debate about that between the U.S. and the Soviets. It seems that Stalin wanted to claim it after the Red Army raised their flag on the roof of the Reichstag in Berlin. But, in the end, Truman and Stalin agreed to let a U.S and Soviet delegation deliver the relic to the Austrian government, who then gave it back to the museum. That's where it's been ever since."

The phone in John's armrest chirped again. "Yes." He listened for a moment. After the call was over, he turned to Cotten then back to Zanini. "That was the Vatican ambassador to Austria. The director of the Hapsburg Museum has agreed to the direct request from the Holy Father and will allow us to take the Spear from Vienna and transport it to CyberSys headquarters in Miami. Alan Olsen and our friends are scheduled to land about an hour behind us."

Cotten sighed out loud. "Once we have the Spear of Destiny, the threat of the Hades Project could be over in a matter of days."

Chapter Sixty-Two

THE COLLECTION

The curator of the Kunsthistorisches Museum, which housed the enormous Hapsburg Dynasty art and antiquities collection, waited near the display case containing the Holy Lance. It was dark already. He glanced at his watch. 7:56.

Nearby stood two museum guards holding assault rifles and wearing body armor. Two more guards waited in an armored truck parked outside the museum, ready to transport the precious cargo to a restricted hangar at the Vienna Schwechat International Airport. There it would be loaded aboard a private jet and flown directly to Miami.

For the third time, the curator adjusted the position of a rolling cart on which rested a silver Anvil Iron flight case the size of a large attaché. Also on the cart was a black Kevlar outer sleeve that would fit snuggly over the case once the relic was securely inside. The Anvil Iron's lid lay open—the interior filled with thick foam padding. A precise cutout in the shape of the Lance head awaited the treasured relic.

The curator would not remove the Holy Lance from the display until Cardinal Tyler and Cotten Stone arrived to witness the event. Once packed and ready for transport, there would then be numerous papers and forms to sign and exchange, starting with a guarantee from the Holy See that the Vatican's insurance would cover loss or damage in the amount of $20 million.

There was a letter of authenticity from the museum stating that the ancient artifact, referred to as the Holy Lance, was the same object presented to the Hapsburg Collection on January 4, 1946, by U.S. Army

General Mark Clark, who did so at the direct order of Supreme Allied Commander Dwight D. Eisenhower.

Another document specified the dimensions and location of the tiny sample to be extracted by CyberSys from the Lance's surface—in a place hidden beneath the gold and silver outer sheaths. That way, it would not be visible to any museum visitors after the relic was returned to its home in Vienna.

The curator looked at his watch again. 7:59 p.m. That's when he heard the sound of a galloping horse.

***

"The official name is the Kunsthistorisches Museum," Zanini said from the front passenger seat of the Mercedes as he spoke over his shoulder to Cotten and John. "That means art history museum. But everyone refers to it as the Hapsburg Museum because it contains the royal family's collection spanning centuries." He turned to the driver, a young Austrian Venatori agent. "If you look up the word 'opulence' in the dictionary, you'll probably see the name Hapsburg in the definition."

The driver gave Zanini a courteous nod as he steered the performance sedan past the Karlsplatz Plaza near the center of Vienna, a few blocks from their destination.

"Are you sure we aren't going to run into any snags or red tape problems?" Cotten asked Zanini.

"No, all is set," Zanini said. "Just a few forms to sign—pure formalities. The security firm supplying the armored car is already there and ready to go. I have been in contact with the crew of the CyberSys corporate jet. All flight plans and government documentation are filed and cleared. They are fueled and ready. Mr. Olsen, his son, and Max Wolf, his director of engineering, are there. Lindsay Jordan and her daughter are with them, relaxing onboard and anxiously awaiting our arrival with the relic. I'm told they all had a pleasant flight over from the U.S. We should be at the private hangar and airborne within an hour of leaving the museum. The Vatican embassy resolved all Customs and Immigration formalities in advance."

"Good work," John said. He turned to Cotten. "We're almost there."

"I know there was hesitancy about allowing Lindsay and Tera to come along," Cotten said, "but think about it from her point of view. I wouldn't want to sit by like a bystander in some corporate conference room when I knew someone was out to harm my daughter. I'd have insisted to be right here as things were happening, too."

"It didn't take much persuading," John said. "I think Alan understood."

***

The curator spun around at the sound of horse hooves cracking like gunshots on the marble floor. The two guards snapped in the same direction. The three men stared with open-mouthed shock as what appeared to be an armor-clad Greek warrior, sword in hand, charged across the gallery on the back of a giant gray steed.

Even from a distance, the curator saw that the warrior's teeth were clenched and his eyes aflame. The warhorse's breathing resounded throughout the museum like an accelerating steam locomotive. The warrior raised his muscular arm, his weapon ready for the kill. With a gasp, the curator realized his identity—the Greek cavalryman depicted on the Greco-Hellenistic frieze from the Ephesus section of the museum.

"What is this?" the curator muttered, dropping back against the wall. In a nightmarish manner beyond his comprehension, the two-thousand-year-old stone carving had come to life. He was witnessing a third century BC warrior from the epic battle between the Galatians and the Greeks barreling down on him. As real as his own skin, he saw the horseman's flesh glistening with sweat. This was no illusion, and the warrior looked hell-bent on killing him.

The sound of automatic weapons filled the gallery as the two guards opened fire on the charging warrior. But the bullets ricocheted off the surface of the soldier and his mount—their forms seeming as impenetrable as the stone from which the frieze was carved.

From his right came a shriek so piercing and feral it could have come from a wildcat. A woman rushed toward him, her hair a squirming and slithering mass of snakes. Rubens' Medusa.

Another female rushed across the floor at the curator—blue tunic, bare breasts, bronze war helmet—Minerva.

The walls sprang alive with Roman soldiers, Greek warriors, gods and goddesses, emperors, kings, pouncing tigers, clawing bears—all with burning eyes, screaming mouths, and flashing teeth.

The Greek warrior on his battle steed swung his sword and sliced off the head of a guard with the ease of a gardener snipping a rose from its stem. The second guard dropped to the floor, his body riddled with arrows that rained from the same executioners' bows that ended the life of Saint Sebastian in Mantegna's masterpiece—their shafts piercing the guard's body armor as if it were paper.

The curator screamed when Medusa's coiling knot of snakes struck his face and neck. As he went down, the metallic flashes of daggers and swords, the meaty odor of blood, and the sound of flesh ripping and bones crunching saturated his senses.

With his cheek flat on the cold marble floor, the dying curator's eyes took in what remained of the guards—heaps of tendons and entrails, pools of blood spreading across the marble like spilled red ink.

Then, from out of nowhere, the face of an elderly gentleman stared down at him.

The curator's eyes fluttered as the Old Man went to stand over the case containing the Holy Lance. The curator tried to speak, but only a thin wheeze gurgled in his throat.

He saw the Old Man open the display and grasp the Holy Lance.

The echo of the Old Man's retreating footfalls faded as the curator drew his final, shallow breath. His last vision was of the army of antiquities melting back into their canvases and carvings.

Chapter Sixty-Three

CRIME SCENE

A police car, blue lights flashing, raced past the Mercedes. Cotten saw the emblem of the Bundespolize on the side and the word Polizei on the back.

"Federal police," the Austrian Venatori agent said as he stared in the rearview mirror. "Here come more." A second and third car raced by.

Cotten glanced at John. "I've got a really bad feeling about this."

"I know, I know," he said.

"Federal police?" she said. "They're not rushing to a traffic accident or other routine crime."

As the agent steered their car into the wide park-like area between the Naturhistorisches Museum and the Kunsthistorisches Museum, Cotten realized it already contained many emergency vehicles. The classical statues and sculptured hedges in front of the majestic buildings were awash in red and blue. A group of men in military gear gathered near a large black van parked at the front entrance of the art museum. Probably the Austrian equivalent of a SWAT team, Cotten assumed. A couple of news trucks also pulled up—one bore the SNN logo on the side.

The Venatori agent brought the car to a stop and got out. "Wait here," he said before walking toward the police perimeter. He spoke at length to one of the officers. Soon, he led what appeared to be a high-ranking officer back toward the Mercedes.

Cotten, John, and Zanini gathered in front of the car.

"Your Eminence," the agent said. "This is Oberkommissar Heinz Gruber. He is in charge of the emergency response team. Oberkommissar, this is His Eminence, Cardinal John Tyler, director of the Venatori."

"A pleasure," Gruber said in fairly good English.

After shaking Gruber's hand, John turned to Cotten. "Oberkommissar, may I present Cotten Stone, Senior Investigative Correspondent for the Satellite News Network. And this is Father Carlo Zanini, Vatican historian and advisor to the Venatori."

Gruber said to John, "I understand you were coming here tonight to meet with the museum curator to take possession of a valuable religious artifact?"

"That's correct."

Gruber looked at each one of them. Then he said, "The Holy Lance, correct?"

"Yes," Cotten said. His question shot a pang through her, colder than the freezing Vienna night. Even without hearing the details, she knew they were too late. Just as in Axum, the Fallen had arrived before them.

"I must inform you that the artifact is missing," Gruber said. "Not only has it been stolen, but whoever took it is responsible for the vicious murders of the curator and two security guards."

The news made Cotten feel sick. "What happened?"

Gruber gave her a grave expression. "What was done here tonight was heinous. These are the most brutal and savage murders I have seen in my twenty years in the National Police Force. The scene is too grisly to attempt to describe." He shook his head. "I am close to being physically ill at recalling what I just saw inside the museum."

Cotten turned away from Gruber, not wanting him to see the tears of frustration in her eyes. The battle was never-ending.

John nodded at Gruber. "Have a copy of the official report sent to my attention."

"By all means, Your Eminence."

"In the meantime, if there is anything I can do to help with the investigation, please contact me through the Vatican embassy."

"Short of telling me who did this horrific act of brutality," Gruber said, "I cannot think of anything." He extended his hand and shook John's. "I will be in touch if I have any questions." After a courteous bow, he turned and walked briskly toward the cluster of police cars and gathering media vehicles.

Cotten left the agent and Zanini by the car and pulled John aside. A few paces away, she said, "We know who did this. But if we tell the Austrian authorities, they'll have us locked up in the loony bin."

"Worst case scenario is that the Fallen have a portable version of the computer like Max Wolf's, which means they could be slicing the thodium sample out of the Lance right now."

She glanced over at the SNN remote truck. "Max said miniaturizing the computer down to a portable size was a big deal—that even the major research universities hadn't accomplished it yet—only CyberSys. What if the Fallen still have to get the relic to their Hades facility? If that's the case, there may still be time to stop them or find out the location. We need to put roadblocks in their way."

"What have you got in mind?" John asked.

"Let me have your phone."

John handed it to her.

Cotten tapped in a number. A moment later, she said, "This is Cotten Stone. I'm calling from Vienna, Austria and I need to speak to Ted Casselman."

Chapter Sixty-Four

THE REPORT

The President of the Russian Federation stood in his bathrobe and channel surfed. He had just stepped out of the shower and wanted to catch the news on a few of his favorite English-speaking stations before breakfast. As he towel-dried his hair with his left hand, he used the other to click the remote—his arm still in a sling from the bullet wound. He paused a moment on the BBC World News. Next, he went to the Satellite News Network's headline news channel. He liked the SNN early morning female anchors because they were young, blonde, and always showed more cleavage than their Russian counterparts.

When he saw his favorite SNN newscaster, he gave a smile of approval. Appearing to be in her mid-twenties, she was saying, ". . . brutal and bizarre incident took place in Vienna last night and has made headlines across Europe this morning. It seems a religious object dating back to the Crucifixion of Christ was stolen from the famed Kunsthistorisches Museum, home of the Hapsburg Dynasty art collection. The robbers left behind no evidence of how they gained access to the building, but during the robbery, the curator and two museum guards were viciously attacked and killed. With details from the scene, we go to SNN Senior Investigative Correspondent Cotten Stone in Vienna."

The image switched from the blonde to a shot of Cotten with a microphone in hand standing in front of the museum. The early morning light of dawn silhouetted the building behind her. A mass of police vehicles still cluttered the grounds.

"Just after the museum closed last evening," Cotten said, "a robbery took place that claimed the lives of three men—the museum curator and two guards. Police found their bodies after responding to a call that reported automatic weapon fire heard coming from inside the building."

The video switched from Cotten to panning shots of the interior of the museum—ornate, decorative, and opulent.

"The police SWAT team swarmed the museum but found that the robbers had made a quick exit, leaving behind no clues. What the authorities discovered were the mutilated bodies of the three men. Unconfirmed reports describe a scene of extremely violent attacks in which at least one man was decapitated and another shot with more than fifty arrows. We learned that the curator might have died from multiple venomous snake bites to the head and neck."

The video changed to a close-up of a police officer. Beneath his image was the inserted text: *Oberkommissar (Chief Commissioner) Heinz Gruber, Austrian National Police.*

"It was without a doubt the bloodiest murder scene I've witnessed in my years as a law enforcement officer."

"Do you have any leads to the identity of the killers, Oberkommissar?"

"None whatsoever." He shook his head in disgust then turned as if being called away. "Excuse me."

The image returned to the establishing shot of Cotten in front of the building. "So what was stolen? What was so valuable to warrant such vicious killings? An ancient relic known as the Holy Lance was the only object determined to be missing so far."

A file shot of the Lance taken from an SNN historical documentary series filled the screen. The camera slowly moved from the tip of the spearhead down its length as Cotten said, "The Holy Lance, also known as the Spear of Destiny, is attributed to being the object used to pierce the side of Jesus Christ as he hung on the Cross over two thousand years ago. Among the powerful historical figures that once possessed the Holy

Lance were Constantine, Charlemagne, and Adolf Hitler. The legend of the Lance is that whoever possesses it holds in his hand the destiny of the world.

"One theory is that it might be sought after in the highly competitive race to develop the first functioning quantum computer—a device that could render all security and encryption codes around the world useless. Some historians theorize that the Lance is made from an extremely rare element called thodium, the material needed for storage of data in a quantum computer. If this is true, then the stakes are extraordinarily high, and the Holy Lance might just be one of the most valuable objects in existence today—certainly for the handful of facilities developing the latest computing technology.

"My sources tell me that inspections at all borders throughout Europe are being stepped up to help intercept and recover the artifact before it reaches its final destination.

"The Austrian National Police are forming a task force to track down the missing artifact and locate the person or persons responsible for the deaths of these three men. They've assured me they will stop at nothing to solve this heinous crime. For now, this is Cotten Stone, SNN, Vienna."

The blonde anchor said, "Thanks, Cotten. Stay tuned to SNN for the latest developments in the theft of the Holy Lance, or you can visit us online for up-to-the-minute news."

The president pushed the mute button on the remote before walking to his bedside table. He picked up the phone receiver and waited until his personal secretary answered. In Russian, he said, "Call the Satellite News Network's Moscow office. Tell them I need to speak with Cotten Stone immediately."

Chapter Sixty-Five

ANOMALY

The Satellite News Network anchor looked into the camera and read from the teleprompter. "The Time and Frequency Division of The National Institute of Standards and Technology reported today that a strange, never-before-seen anomaly occurred at midnight, Greenwich Mean Time, last night. For a few seconds, the atomic clock—the one maintained by the NIST and used to synchronize all the computers, GPS, and satellite systems in the world shifted the current date into the future by exactly six hundred and sixty-six years. Before any action could be taken to correct the time shift, the system appeared to fix itself as the atomic clock jumped back to the accurate time."

The video showed an exterior shot of the NIST facility in Boulder, Colorado. A woman identified as an NIST spokesperson said, "Our engineers are working to identify the cause of the strange time-shift anomaly. So far, we believe it was just a glitch in a new version of software recently installed. We want to assure everyone that the problem is under full investigation, and at this time we have no reason to believe it will occur again or affect any systems that rely on us for proper time synchronization."

The image switched back to the anchor. "Thousands of extremely critical systems rely on the atomic clock for synchronization, including those used by air traffic controllers, global positioning systems, military protocols, and others. An error in the atomic clock could have serious global consequences if not corrected immediately—everything from cell phones to atomic reactors to ICBM launch coordinates. Some organizations are suggesting that the time shift of six hundred and sixty-six years, or the number six-six-six, has biblical or satanic overtones. Are they right? I guess we'll have to wait and see. And coming up next, the latest sports scores."

***

Cotten stood in the main cabin of the CyberSys corporate jet and stared at the TV monitor. They had reached cruising altitude on their flight from Vienna back to Miami. "Was anyone else watching just now?"

Alan and John were deep in conversation. Lindsay sat next to Tera as she and Devin played a board game. Max Wolf was engrossed in a project on his laptop.

Everyone glanced at Cotten. "What did you see?" John asked.

"A report on an anomaly in the atomic clock?"

"What's the atomic clock?" asked Lindsay.

Max looked up from his computer. "Among other things atomic clocks are the basis of the GPS or global positioning system. Each of the GPS satellites has an on-board atomic clock. They all synchronize with each other and the main clock at NIST to make sure everyone is marching to the same beat, so to speak."

"So what's wrong, Cotten?" Lindsay asked.

Cotten turned to face the group. "The report said something strange occurred last night. For a few seconds, the NIST clock shifted six hundred and sixty-six years into the future."

Max ran his palm over the crown of his thick brown hair. "Did they say what caused it?"

"Possibly a software glitch."

"Well, that could be, I suppose." Max went back to his laptop.

"Six-six-six," John said. He got up and walked toward Cotten. "Interesting choice of numbers."

"Why do you say that?" Alan asked as he followed behind.

"Six-six-six—the mark of the beast," John said. "In the book of Revelation—the Apocalypse—it says, 'Here is wisdom. Let him that hath understanding count the number of the beast—for it is the number of a man—and his number is six hundred and sixty-six.'"

"I remember that from the movie, *The Omen*," Lindsay said. "It was on the boy's head."

"Right," Cotten said. "It might be nothing more than a coincidence, but now that we know about the Hades Project from Kai, this could have something to do with it. Max, you told us in Miami that it would take a global event to trigger the launch of the computer virus. Could this be it?"

Max shrugged. "Maybe. The launch could be done with an unusual event that everyone assumes would never happen, like an outrageous time shift. All clocks, including the atomic clock, are set to GPS time. To alter the clocks would mean that someone who works on the inside would first have to drop a virus on the government server and alter the system. Every day, millions of computers call home by synchronizing to the atomic clock. If a computer had the Hades worm buried on it, when it saw the date change, it might be the launch event.

"No one believes that the government's main servers can be altered. So the momentary time shift in the atomic clock would be considered just a wild anomaly. But like I said, it would have to be executed by someone working inside."

"How hard would it be for the Secretary of Homeland Security to plant someone inside a government facility?" Cotten asked.

The realization seemed to hit everyone at once. "Not very hard," Alan said.

John said, "Let's say Mace did manage to plant someone inside NIST, and they were able to infect the system. And let's say the time-shift anomaly was the trigger mechanism for the millions of computers infected with the worm. What do you think would happen next?"

Max said, "If it were me doing it, I would have the virus fool or eliminate the redundancy checks on the system." He thought for a moment. "Or even better, fool the humans at the controls—like an air traffic controller—into thinking there's a problem when in fact everything is fine. The operator would react to what he sees as a critical issue and make a correction. In reality, his correction actually creates a real problem."

"Like what?" Cotten said.

"Let's say he thinks a commercial airliner is a thousand feet higher than it really is," Alan said. "There's a good chance that when the plane attempts to land, it would plow right into the ground."

"Or some guy at a nuclear reactor sees a sudden and significant drop in core temperature," Max said, "and overcompensates. Next thing you know, he's shooting fuel rods on a direct course to China, and the property value around the reactor drops for a few thousand years."

"But wouldn't there be backup checks?" John said. "Safety procedures in place?"

"Sure," Max said. "But since they are all seeing the same fake problem, they all confirm that the correction is appropriate. Then when real problems start popping up, everyone overcompensates again. The house of cards starts coming down."

"How about communications?" Alan said.

"They would be highly disrupted," Max said. "Once an operator is fooled into correcting a non-existent problem in the GPS system, the subsequent effects will not only stop time, but stop most cell phone and RF communications. Almost every cell phone switching site utilizes GPS signals for instant conversation hand-off and decryption between sites."

"So if you have an emergency, you can't call anyone to report it?" Cotten said.

"Exactly," Max said. "If it were me, once I caused enough havoc, the very last thing I'd do is target the power grids. The electric company sees a huge jump in line usage and starts rolling brownouts, which create blackouts. No electricity, no traffic signals, no emergency vehicles getting through. Can't call the police or fire department. Can't call anyone. No money from dead ATMs, no natural gas or water flowing. Traffic comes to a standstill with no signal lights. Even if a gas station has a backup generator, it would be next to impossible to drive there with the chaos and gridlock on the roads. Everyone becomes an isolated individual fearing for his life."

"How quickly could this happen?" Lindsay asked, her arms around Tera in a tight hug.

Max shrugged. "Days, maybe hours. Depends on how fast the human operators react to the fictitious problems and start causing tragic corrections."

"What about the military?" Cotten asked.

"Christ," Max said. "I didn't even think about that. There's the Global Information Grid, part of the Defense Information Systems Agency Network. Reliance on the GIG is so critical that if it were to be taken down, it would send military operations into the Stone Age. Cross network infrastructure would be compromised, and the Hades worm could gain access to the Cheyenne Mountain Operations Center and the North American Air Defense, not to mention their counterparts in other countries. The military systems are triggered to display launch preparations from Russian and Chinese nuclear missile silos. To take this to the highest level, if fake launches were displayed, and there was no way to communicate for confirmation, the U.S. Nuclear Security Council would have no choice but to authorize a nuclear response."

"I think we get why the name Hades was chosen," John said. "We're potentially facing a global threat with catastrophic implications."

"Hell on Earth," Cotten said.

"And it may already have been triggered," Max said.

"With the possibility that we have only hours to stop it," Cotten said.

The intercom phone rang, and Alan picked it up. He listened for a moment before holding it out to Cotten. "You have a call."

"Who knows I'm here?" she said, reaching to take the handset from Alan.

He handed her the phone. "Apparently the Kremlin. It's the president of Russia."

Chapter Sixty-Six

CONFERENCE CALL

"Hello, Mr. President," Cotten said. "This is such a pleasant surprise."
She eased into a nearby seat. "How is your arm healing?" Cotten listened
for a moment. "That's great news. Yes, my wounds have healed up fine.
Thank you for asking."

John and Alan had taken their seats as everyone on the corporate jet
stopped what they were doing to watch Cotten.

"To what do I owe the honor of this call, sir?" She listened for several moments, then said, "Actually, I'm onboard a private jet. We took off
from Vienna about twenty minutes ago and are in route to London to
refuel and then on to the U.S." She glanced around the cabin as if taking
a head count. "Yes, Cardinal Tyler is with me, along with Alan Olsen,
the president of CyberSys, and his director of engineering, Max Wolf. A
few other friends and family are with us."

Again, Cotten listened before replying, "Mr. President, with your
permission, I would like to place you on speakerphone. Would that be
acceptable?"

Cotten gestured to Alan who took the phone, pushed the conference
button, and placed the receiver back on the communications console.

"Mr. President, you're now on speaker," Cotten said.

The heavily accented voice of the President of the Russian Federation filled the cabin. "What I was saying was that the brutal murders
committed during the theft of the Holy Lance seemed out of proportion.
And I was asking Ms. Stone why she thought these men died such a
violent death for something that is admittedly valuable, but not as
priceless as other items in the collection."

"We're not entirely sure, Mr. President," Cotten said. "But we have some theories."

"After all," the president said, "the crown jewels of the Hapsburg Empire are there, along with works of some of the greatest artists of the past thousand years. If I were the thief, I certainly would have taken them before the Spear." He laughed. "No offense, Your Eminence," he said. "I know how precious the Holy Lance is to the Church."

"None taken, Mr. President," John said.

"I watched your news reports, Ms. Stone. Now I want to hear the details on which you base your theories."

Cotten shrugged.

"Go for it," John whispered.

"Mr. President, our theories are based as much on scientific fact as they are on legend. The Holy Lance has a history traceable back to the Garden of Eden. We think it was forged by the third-generation great grandson of Adam—a blacksmith named Tubal Cain. He produced the Lance from the hardened, crystallized sap of the Tree of Life, and Noah used lumber from the same tree to construct the Ark. We have found ancient writings that show that God commanded Noah to carry the Lance aboard the Ark because it would be used in a future event. We think that future event is about to happen. We believe the Lance contains a rare material now known as thodium. It's needed for storing data in a fully functional quantum computer—a critical element in the final development of the computer.

"The reason we think the Lance was stolen is that there is a group building a quantum computer they call the Hades Project, and will use it to break the security framework of the world's resources. Their goal is to bring down governments, militaries, financial institutions, power grids, and international communications. The result will be chaos, anarchy, global war, and maybe the end of civilization."

Cotten took a deep breath, wondering if what she had just said sounded as incredulous and ridiculous as she thought it might.

Seconds drifted by—ten, twenty, thirty. Finally, she said, "Mr. President?"

Silence.

Cotten was about to ask Alan if he thought they had lost the connection when the Russian president said, "I am still here."

"Mr. President, I hope you don't think—"

"Cardinal Tyler," the president said, "do you believe everything Cotten Stone has told me?"

"Yes, Mr. President. Not only do I trust her instincts, but I have been a part of this since it first came to light. And I think if we don't stop the Hades Project, the outcome could be even worse than she described."

There was the sound of paper rustling.

"Mr. Olsen," the Russian said. "I am looking at your dossier as we speak. As an expert in the field of . . . encryption and advanced, high-speed data processing, do you believe what Ms. Stone has just told me?"

"Mr. President, I do. After meeting with Cotten and Cardinal Tyler, and based on the recent events in Washington concerning the death of National Security Advisor Philip Miller, I have no hesitation in believing her."

There was another long silence with the additional sound of pages of paper being turned.

"Mr. Wolf, the same question, please," the president said.

"I believe we're on the verge of a global event that could bring down all order and security as we know it."

The president could be heard conversing in Russian with someone. Then he said, "Ms. Stone, as you Americans say, there is good news and bad. But in this instance, I have bad news, good news, and really good news." He seemed to smile through the phone at his cleverness.

"Please, share it with us," John said. "We could use good news right now."

"The good news is that in the process of you saving this old Russian's life, you stood within a few inches of the Holy Lance."

Cotten could not understand what he meant as she racked her memory of the night in the tunnel dodging bullets.

"And the really good news?" John asked.

"The object stolen from the museum in Vienna is a worthless fake."

There was a collective gasp in the jet's passenger cabin. "Are you positive, sir?" Cotten asked.

"Yes. No doubt. The stolen object is a replica produced by an overzealous Heinrich Himmler in 1935. The Reichsführer of the SS was obsessed with the occult. While impatiently waiting for Hitler to invade Austria and take possession of the Holy Lance, he had a replica made. The man was insane in so many ways—this should come as no big surprise."

"How did the replica get into the museum?" John asked.

"The switch took place at the orders of Joseph Stalin when the Allies returned the Lance to the Hapsburg Museum at the end of the war."

"Is this common knowledge?" Cotten said.

"No," the president said. "It's one of those little secrets, what's the American word—tidbits—that gets passed to each Russian president. The tsar's escape tunnel is another tidbit. Somewhat like that third secret of Fatima that each new pope gets to learn, Your Eminence."

"I understand, Mr. President," John said.

"You said I stood within inches of the Holy Lance when I was in Moscow. You're telling me the authentic Lance is there somewhere in the maze of underground passageways?"

"Actually, no. Stalin considered the Holy Lance his prized possession and kept it hidden away for almost eight years. Then in a private ceremony held in 1953, he honored Vladimir Lenin by placing the Holy Lance inside the sarcophagus under Lenin's body. That same night, after dinner with Nikita Khrushchev and a few other party members, he collapsed in his bedroom and died. While you and I were in Lenin's Tomb, you passed within inches of the relic."

"And it's still there?" Cotten asked.

"Yes." He paused and spoke Russian to someone with him. "Mr. Olsen? I assume that you are prepared to counteract this so-called Hades Project threat by using your own technology?"

"Yes, sir. We have a miniaturized version of our Destiny quantum computer onboard along with the mechanical apparatus necessary to extract a sample of thodium. All we need is the Lance. Once the system is up and running, we can go online, find and hack into the Hades machine, and shut it down."

"Then I would recommend you alter your flight plan immediately. I will arrange for your plane to be given priority clearance through Russian airspace. Once you have landed in Moscow, you will be flown by military helicopter to the Kremlin. We will get you your thodium sample, Mr. Olsen, and we will wait with anxious anticipation as you rid the world of this Hades threat. Is that acceptable?"

"More than acceptable, Mr. President," Alan said.

"Are there any other questions?" the Russian asked.

Cotten spoke up. "You told us you also had bad news."

"You're right, Ms. Stone. Do you remember the Chechen rebels who tried to assassinate me?"

"How could I forget?"

"The bad news is, they were not Chechen, and they were not trying to kill me. They were trying to kill you."

Chapter Sixty-Seven

THE BEGINNING

"Cotten, wake up," John said, shaking her arm. "We've got a problem." She had dozed off soon after Alan informed his flight crew of their new destination—Sheremetyevo International Airport outside Moscow. He told everyone the flight would take about five and a half hours. Overcome from so much flying time and the fatigue from the last few weeks, Cotten had settled into one of the seats and fallen asleep. Now she shook her head and tried to clear the dark place she had gone in her dreams.

"What is it?" she asked.

"The pilot says there have been numerous plane hijackings reported across Europe, and the ATC centers are diverting traffic to alternative destinations."

"Hijackings?" She stared up at him in confusion. "Who's hijacking what?" She peered out the window but saw only darkness. "Do you think this has anything to do with the Hades threat?"

"Not sure. Maybe. It could be these aren't true hijackings, even though planes are squawking hijack codes. It could be part of the Hades chaos that Max predicted."

Cotten stood and glanced around the cabin. Lindsay, Tera, and Devin were all asleep. Max was at his usual place at a table up front, working with his laptop. She noticed that while she slept, he had brought out a few other computer cases—a great deal of electronics hardware was scattered around the cabin on tables and in seats.

"What do we do?" she asked.

"Because we've been given a presidential priority clearance, we may be able to proceed according to our revised flight plan," John said. "But the pilot says there's a lot of confusion and disruption in communications. My guess is this may be the beginning of what we expected."

"If it is, it sure didn't take them long," Cotten said. "Come on, I've got a question for Max." She walked to the front of the cabin, John following, and waited for the director of engineering to look up from his work.

"Cotten, how was your nap?" he asked.

"Sporadic. Max, something's been bothering me since we had the conference call with the Russian president. If the object that was taken in Vienna was a replica, and not made from thodium, how are they going to proceed with the Hades Project? If this is the start of their assault, how are they carrying if off?"

"Good question," Max said. "My guess is, they have another sample of thodium. After all, we have simulated thodium in particle accelerators, but only a few atoms at a time. Or what they've got could be damaged. If their sample was indeed from the Ark, think of how long it was exposed to the elements of nature. It could have degraded. We don't know enough about thodium to predict the long-term effects. Objects that date back that far are subject to all kinds of external forces. Or maybe it's not really thodium, but something with similar characteristics that we haven't thought of. Even if they have degraded thodium, it's enough to get their project launched." He scratched his head. "Still, they did go to a lot of trouble to steal the Holy Lance from the museum, thinking it was the real thing."

"Wait a minute," Cotten said. "If they've already started the attack, that means they don't *need* the Spear. But they do need to keep us from getting it. If Alan has a better quality sample and can finish the Destiny computer, then they can be stopped. Their project was already underway when they stole the Lance. It's a good, solid sample, and they don't want us to get our hands on it."

323

Max smiled a wicked grin. "Someone's in for a big surprise when they discover Himmler's replica is probably nothing but a piece of iron."

Cotten turned to John. "That presents a bigger problem."

"Which is?" he said.

"When they discover the Lance is a replica, they'll become desperate. They've started this thing, and they won't back down. By now, they know we've changed course and are headed for Moscow. It's only a matter of time before they figure out why. We have to get to Red Square first."

Chapter Sixty-Eight

MIDAIR COLLISION

Cotten looked out the window of the CyberSys jet into the night. "Where are we?"

"Over Belarus I think," Alan said. "The capital city is Minsk—it should be off our left wing. We're roughly four hundred miles out of Moscow."

"I think I see the city lights," Cotten said. "I'm also seeing what looks like fires." She grew nervous. "A couple of big ones."

Alan went to a control panel and dimmed the interior cabin lights. Everyone found a window.

"You're right, Cotten," Lindsay said. "Some are pretty big."

"Is our navigation system working?" John asked Alan.

"Our instruments are working fine, but our pilot told me we can't synchronize or communicate with anything outside the plane. There's no contact with Russian air traffic control. After our conference call with the president, I warned the guys up front this might happen. They'll get us to Moscow, but where we land is the big question."

"I see lights from two aircraft in the distance," John said. "Looks like passenger jets. It's hard to tell in the dark."

"Where?" Alan asked.

John pointed.

"Oh, Jesus," Alan said.

Lindsay gasped.

Cotten backed away from the window, her hand to her mouth. She saw the planes collide and burst into fireballs. Wreckage streamed down like misguided fireworks—chunks of burning debris leaving swirling tentacles of smoke as they dropped into the darkness.

"What is it, Momma?" Tera rushed to her mother's side. Lindsay took her daughter into her arms. "Everything's okay."

Cotten scanned the disturbingly quiet cabin. Everyone had slipped into a seat and stared unfocused at some distant spot. Over the muffled sounds of the aircraft, she heard the soft grunts of Devin rocking.

John crossed himself. "God help us."

Chapter Sixty-Nine

MiG-29

"There's another plane!" Tera called.

"Where, sweetheart?" Lindsay said.

Tera had her nose to the window.

Cotten saw the girl's breath pluming on the glass.

"A military jet," John said.

Cotten stared into the dark Russian sky at the jet fighter, so close she could see the glow from the instrument panel on the front of the pilot's faceplate.

"It's a MiG-29," Max said. "My cousin built a model kit of one not long ago. I think NATO calls them Fulcrums."

The cockpit door opened, and the CyberSys co-pilot emerged. "Mr. Olsen, the Russian pilot wants us to follow him."

"How did you communicate?" Alan asked.

"Most RF is down, but there are still a few radio frequencies that are hot. The fighter pilot held up a small whiteboard with a frequency written on it. When he lit it with a flashlight, we knew where to find him."

"Where is the Russian pilot going to take us?" Alan said.

"All three of Moscow's international airports are shut down," the co-pilot said. "He wants us to go to Zhukovsky Airfield near a town called Ramenskoye. The airfield is used by the Gromov Flight Research Institute—a training and testing facility."

"Know what that means?" said Max. "Some infrastructure and communications are still in place. Cotten is right about them not wanting us to get the Spear in our hands. The Hades computer is unstable. If we can get the Spear, Destiny can stop them."

"I pray we can," Alan said. He looked to the co-pilot. "Thank you. Do whatever it takes to get us on the ground safely."

As the co-pilot returned to the cockpit, Cotten said, "Where is this airfield?"

Max called up the info on Google Earth. "About forty-six kilometers from Moscow."

"Look, Momma, that plane is going in front of us," Tera said.

Cotten saw the MiG-29 accelerate and disappear beyond the nose of the CyberSys jet. She turned to Max. "What do you need to do to get ready before we land? Is there anything we can do to help?"

"No. I have prepared all the gear for transport." Max pointed to two suitcase-size containers sitting on a table across the aisle. "One is the portable Destiny computer processor and interface, and the other is the spectral hole burner."

"You're going to burn holes in things?" Tera said, standing nearby. She smiled with wide-eyed wonder.

"In a way," Max said. "Once we get the Holy Lance, we'll be storing one or two qubits of information per atom in the crystallized thodium that it's made from. Then we'll address the individual atoms by tuning the laser frequency—"

"Max, please," Alan said, holding up his hand. "A simple yes would have done just fine."

"Sorry." Max looked at Tera. "Yes." Then he went back to typing data into his laptop.

Cotten stared at the data on Max's computer. "If we're forty-six kilometers from Moscow—that's about twenty-six and a half miles."

"I see a lot more fires," Lindsay said from a window seat.

"They picked a perfect name for what they're doing," Cotten said.

"Tor said it." The voice came from Devin, who had hardly spoken since they left Vienna.

The group turned in his direction as Alan said, "Said what, Devin? Tor said what?"

"Welcome to Hades."

***

Cotten heard the sound of the jet engines changing pitch. The plane's nose angled as the aircraft banked to the left. The fasten seat belts light came on, and a chime sounded in the cabin.

"We're on final approach," Alan said, hanging up the intercom phone to the cockpit. "Get situated and belt yourselves in. This may not be a normal landing."

"What do you mean?" Lindsay asked.

"Don't worry," Alan said then sat in a seat next to Devin. "We just don't know what the conditions are on the ground yet."

"I see the runway," Cotten said. She watched the dark countryside slowly move toward the plane as they descended. The glow from Moscow city lights dotted the horizon. There were also a handful of fires. "What do you think is causing the fires?"

"Could be anything," Max answered. "Gas leaks, vehicular collisions, electrical fires."

"They are going to create hell on earth," Cotten whispered.

From out of the blackness of the night, the MiG-29 appeared alongside. It quickly distanced itself to give the private jet room to land. As Cotten gripped the ends of the armrests, she saw the runway lights pass underneath. The corporate jet seemed to float weightlessly for a moment, then it descended, and the tires bit into the concrete. It bounced once then with a roar, the pilot slowed the plane using the jets and applied the brakes. It continued down the long runway until a complex of buildings appeared on the left. Several military and emergency vehicles lined the runway, and they drove beside the jet until it taxied off the main runway.

"Everybody okay?" Alan asked, glancing around the cabin as the engines wound down.

The cockpit door opened, and the pilot emerged, the co-pilot right behind him. The pilot said, "Mr. Olsen, the Russians want us all off the plane right now."

"But I was planning on leaving Devin and Tera here with Lindsay and you," Alan said.

"Sorry, sir. There's a helicopter waiting to transport all of us to Moscow."

"All right." Alan motioned to the table with Max's cases. "Give Max a hand with his stuff." He looked around the cabin. "Grab only what's essential."

The pilot unlatched the side door and swung it open. A ground crew was already rolling a set of steps up to the side of the plane.

When Cotten peered out the window, she saw soldiers gathering at the base of the stairs. She and John moved forward behind Lindsay and Tera. "Why do they want us all in Moscow?" she asked the pilot as she got to the door.

"They told us there's growing disorder in the city and the government felt we would be safer remaining together," he said. "If we got separated, they were concerned that we might not find each other again."

The group assembled at the bottom of the steps. In English, a Russian officer said, "Follow me."

A few hundred yards away, a large military helicopter sat with its rotors spinning, its turboshaft engines hissing. The side door stood open with two soldiers beside the aircraft ready to help the passengers onboard.

They heaved the children up first, followed by Lindsay and Cotten. John and Alan boarded next—Max stood by, directing the hoisting of the delicate computer cases into the cabin.

Quickly, they were seated and strapped in. Then Cotten heard the turbines spin up and transform from a whine down. The rotors accelerated until the helicopter vibrated then became airborne.

"You're about to come full circle," Cotten whispered as she stared into the darkness.

Chapter Seventy

AMBUSH

The Mil Mi-17 Russian turboshaft helicopter swooped in over the Moscow River from the southeast. Seated inside, Cotten saw the onion domes of St. Basil's Cathedral slip beneath the aircraft, followed by sprawling Red Square. At 150 mph, the trip from the airfield had taken only seven minutes, but it had been unnerving.

The night was lit by the glow of city lights, but she also saw sporadic fires, a few city-block-sized blazes, and what appeared to be the crash site of a huge airplane—small explosions were still bursting around it. Emergency vehicles clogged the streets and trapped the mass of traffic to a standstill. As the news of the chaos spread, Cotten figured thousands must be trying to leave the city.

Along with the CyberSys group, sixteen armed Russian soldiers were inside the cabin of the military helicopter since they left the Gromov Flight Research Institute.

It settled onto the great expanse of cobblestones outside the walls of the Kremlin. The door slid open, and the soldiers were the first out. The last two turned and assisted Cotten, John, and Max, and helped with the two Destiny computer cases.

The officer in command turned to Cotten. "I am Captain Markov. We have received word that an international situation has developed and is escalating. The president cannot meet with you but has ordered that we take you and Cardinal Tyler to retrieve the artifact. We will split up with half my men escorting Mr. Wolf and his gear to a secure crisis room inside the Kremlin. There he can set up his computer and prepare for when we deliver the object. Any questions?"

Cotten hesitated a second before she gave the okay to Markov. Then she turned to Alan who was about to step down from inside the helicopter. "There's no reason for you to go with us, Alan. Stay with Lindsay and the children in case they have to evacuate you. We'll retrieve the Spear. Once Max has everything up and running, and it's safe, we'll have them bring everyone inside."

Alan looked at Max.

"She's right, boss," Max said. "Stay with your son."

Alan glanced back at Devin, then at Lindsay and Tera. "Fine." He stepped back into the cabin of the helicopter, its blades rotating slowly overhead. "Good luck."

"Okay," Markov said. "Follow me."

They had landed near the State Historical Museum on the north end of Red Square, a few hundred yards from Lenin's Tomb. The boxy mausoleum had been built on the outside wall of the Kremlin. As everyone came around the nose of the helicopter and were about to split into two groups, Cotten noticed a large formation of what appeared to be soldiers amassed outside the mausoleum. Unlike the green military uniforms of the Russian Federation Army soldiers escorting her, these men were dressed in black, similar to the rebels who had attacked her and the president in the tsar's tunnel. Cotten also noticed an odd visual distortion, like waves of heat rising off a highway in the summer sun. The black soldiers seemed to drift in and out of focus as the waves undulated.

Once everyone cleared the aircraft and were walking across the open space of Red Square, the black soldiers opened fire with automatic weapons. Their guns were silenced, so the muzzle flashes appeared like hundreds of tiny sparks in the night.

A few of Captain Markov's men dropped onto the cobblestones.

Markov yelled, "Get back to the helicopter—run!"

John grabbed Cotten's arm as they retreated to the protection of the aircraft.

She heard bullets strike the street and the metal skin of the chopper. As the Russians gathered behind the protection of the aircraft and started returning fire, Cotten, John, and Max ran to the open side door.

"What's going on?" Lindsay called. "Who is shooting at us?"

"Stay down!" Cotten yelled.

"We've got to get out of here!" Alan shouted.

The turbines spun up, and the rotors increased speed. The pilot called out. His words needed no translation. He had to take off to save his aircraft. And they must jump back on board quickly.

"We can't leave without the Lance," Cotten yelled over the sound of the gunfire and the screaming turbines.

"What choice do we have?" John said. "They've got the entrance to the Tomb blocked."

Cotten went to the rear of the aircraft and peered around it. The St. Nicholas Tower gate entrance to the Kremlin was only two hundred feet away. "We've got to make it to the gate," she called to Captain Markov while pointing toward the Kremlin wall.

Markov nodded that he understood and relayed the order to his men. He motioned for two soldiers to bring the computer cases and follow him—the rest would give cover fire while he and the Americans raced across the short distance to the gate. He made eye contact with Cotten. "Okay, we are ready."

"Thank you," Cotten said.

"What are you doing?" Max said. "We need to get out of here. The helicopter is leaving."

"We can't leave," Cotten said. "If we do, they win and there will be no place for us to go. This is it. And unless you give me a crash course in running that Destiny device, we need you with us."

The helicopter rumbled, and the downdraft from its blades made it nearly impossible to hear. He yelled to Cotten, "What the hell. Lead the way."

As the Mil Mi-17 rose off the cobblestones with the force of a hurricane, Cotten thought she heard Lindsay scream for them to come back. But the words got lost in the sound of the loud rotor chop.

Markov's men opened fire on the black figures blocking the Tomb while he led the small group toward the tower gate entrance.

"How are we going to get into the Tomb?" John yelled to Cotten once they passed under the majestic tower into the safety of the Kremlin walls.

Never slowing, she called over her shoulder, "Ivan the Terrible's praying seat."

***

Tor stared at the monitor that displayed the operating system interface to the Hades quantum computer. Things were holding together amazingly well, even with the degraded thodium. He held the Holy Lance replica in his hand and figured he'd hang it on the wall of his bedroom. That's about all it was worth.

Mace hadn't warned him about the Son of the Dawn delivering it personally. That was something he never wanted to experience again. Out of all the Ruby ceremonies and rituals Tor had attended, the Son of the Dawn had been a distant figure. Few Ruby children or Nephilim adults ever approached him.

And yet, he came to Tor, showing up out of nowhere like an apparition. He'd been deep into his work when heard that distinctive voice come from behind. It scared the shit out of Tor. Because he had spent so many days and nights in the old military facility alone, at the sound of another voice, he almost came out of his skin.

And then when he had to give the Son of the Dawn the bad news—that the Lance was a fake—he thought he might shit himself. The only redeeming part was when Tor was told it was not his fault.

He felt sorry for Mace. Rizben would take the brunt of the punishment. He'd already heard the news headlines. *The Secretary of Homeland Security resigns citing personal reasons.* In a way, Mace had it coming, Tor thought. The guy was cocky, self-centered, and basically an asshole. And being a Fallen Angel, the worst that could happen was he would be sent to some shit-hole assignment. Served him right for acting like a prick.

Tor even regretted turning Mace on to Kai. She was a bitch but the most amazing woman he'd ever met. A free spirit and a free agent. He wondered what she was doing now that Mace was out of the picture.

He glanced back at the monitor. Not bad for a piece-of-shit sample of thodium. It was still holding together—barely.

That's when the intrusion alarms went off.

Chapter Seventy-One

VLADIMIR

Once inside the Kremlin walls, Markov asked Cotten, "Where do you want me to take you?" They moved briskly along the sidewalk in front of the Arsenal building.

"Cardinal Tyler and I must get into Assumption Cathedral. Mr. Wolf and his electronics gear can go on to your crisis center."

At the corner of the two-story Arsenal, Markov stopped and relayed the orders to the two men who carried the computer cases. He pointed to the right. "Mr. Wolf, follow these men to the Grand Kremlin Palace." Then Markov led Cotten and John to the left, passing in front of the State Kremlin Palace and on to the churches surrounding Cathedral Square.

They ran past the front of the Church of the Twelve Apostles then turned right and headed for the entrance to the Assumption Cathedral. Half way up the steps to the southern portal, Cotten looked at the huge paintings of the two archangels guarding each side of the door. "We could sure use their help."

Markov nodded in agreement.

The iron mesh gates stood open, but the great wood and metal double doors were closed and locked. Captain Markov pulled on the handles, but there was no give from the three-hundred-year-old entry. "We will have to get someone to come and unlock the church," he said to Cotten.

"Captain, there's no time. Please get us inside, even if it means you have to break down the doors."

Markov stared at her as if she had asked him to urinate on the Russian Federation flag.

"Captain," John said. "You mentioned there was some sort of escalating international situation going on. I can assure you whatever it is will be mild compared to what's in store for us all if Ms. Stone does not gain access to this church. Captain Markov, I am a cardinal in the Roman Catholic Church and director of the Vatican's equivalent of your Federal Security Service—your old KGB. Please believe me when I tell you that what is happening tonight all over the globe is the beginning of a tragic series of events that could culminate in a possible—"

"Captain Markov, shoot the locks!" Cotten demanded.

The soldier stared at her for a moment before he turned toward the entrance of Assumption Cathedral and pulled back the bolt on his automatic assault rifle. A second later, he fired a burst of rounds into the lock of the four-inch-thick wood doors—splinters and shards of metal flew everywhere. Without hesitancy, he kicked in the door. The wood crunched and split. Markov looked over his shoulder and said, "This way."

All of them rushed into the cavernous cathedral. Memories of the rebel attack overwhelmed Cotten. Only a handful of lights were on, giving her the same feeling of eerie, otherworldliness that surrounded her that fateful night such a short time ago. As they ran across the marble floor, her eyes lingered briefly on the spot where her crew had fallen, murdered. Even in the dim light, the damage to the artwork that ringed the columns was evident.

Markov stopped. "Now where?"

Cotten pointed to the structure that housed Ivan the Terrible's praying seat.

"Let's go," he said and hurried across the floor of the cathedral to the miniature building.

Cotten motioned to the narrow space behind it and the wall. She squeezed through and opened the gate that led inside. Dark stains on the floor marked where the murdered PSS agent died. The Tsar's chair had been returned to its original position. Cotten pushed it aside, exposing the trapdoor. She lifted it. "Through here."

"Wait," Markov said. "I'll go first in case anyone is waiting to ambush us again."

Cotten watched him drop into the hole. John went next. Just before it was her turn, she stopped and listened. She swore she heard the faintest of footsteps. If the black soldiers were coming, this was not the place to stand and fight. From here on there was only one way out. As she turned to climb down, she thought she saw two small figures dash through the dark shadows.

"There's a light switch on the wall next to the platform," Cotten called to Markov as she closed the trapdoor above her.

A second later, the bulb flicked on. "Keep going to the bottom. Follow the tunnel and always bear to the left."

As they approached the end of the first light string, the group stopped. "There's another light switch on the wall," Cotten said. But before Markov could turn it on, she heard the slight thump of the trapdoor close again. "We're being followed." She gestured to Markov to switch on the next set of lights.

The passage widened just as Cotten remembered. They moved past the openings to many tunnels and drainage pipes, most appearing as if they had not been disturbed for hundreds of years.

Ahead was the set of stone stairs that angled up the wall and led to the storeroom entrance. She made her way in front of Markov. It opened with a groan. "Come on." She found the storeroom light switch. Across the room, she grabbed the handle of the door on the opposite wall and pushed it open into the dark marble hallway.

"We are very close to the entrance where the rebels were shooting at us," Markov said. "Come behind me." With his gun at the ready, he led Cotten and John down the hall and into the main chamber of the Tomb.

As Cotten remembered, it was coal black and softly lit. In the center sat the long, glass-enclosed sarcophagus. Only this time, there was a major difference.

It was empty.

Chapter Seventy-Two

IMPOSTER

Cotten's heart sank as she stared at the place where Lenin's body had lain. The side of the glass enclosure was open and rested on the top of the structure.

"Where is...? Markov stood rooted at the sight of the empty sarcophagus.

"I don't believe this," Cotten said. She moved to the enclosure and extended her hand inside, running it along the satin-like material where the body of Vladimir Lenin had been in repose since 1924. There was no Holy Lance. Only the small, white pillow remained—a slight indention marked where Lenin's head rested.

"Is this what you seek?"

They turned at the sound of the voice.

"Dear God," Markov whispered, taking a step backward. He looked spellbound by the sight of the man who stood in the corner of the mausoleum.

John's mouth dropped open, his eyes wide in disbelief.

For a moment, Cotten thought her heart had stopped. The air became hot and suffocating. She doubted her own senses as she watched the man walk toward her, the Spear of Destiny held to his chest.

The man was almost bald, and his eyes were small and dark. He donned a mustache and goatee. His suit was black, his shirt white with a dark tie. And he spoke with a thick Russian accent. She knew who it was.

The mausoleum remained so hushed that Cotten could hear the blood rushing in her ears.

Then Markov whispered, "Comrade Lenin? Is it really you?"

"It's an illusion, captain," Cotten said. To John, she said, "He is the Beast. Remember Axum?"

At the sound of her voice, John seemed to shake off the shock.

"He took the form of the guardian monk before, and now he tries to trick us again."

"You are observant, priest," the Lenin imposter said, his body surrounded by a pale ruby aura. "I can take any form that suits me."

The air in the Tomb became sweltering. "Give me the Holy Lance," Cotten said.

"Did you not learn your lesson, daughter of Furmiel? I told you in the treasury church to go home. Why didn't you take my advice and save yourself so much disappointment?"

"Give her the relic," John said. "We have come face-to-face before. You lost that time, and you will lose here, too. You can't win against God. I will exorcise you as I did before."

Lenin held up his hand. "Do not speak again, priest. Your God is not my god." He tauntingly extended the Spear of Destiny. "Whoever possesses this Holy Lance and understands the powers it serves, holds in his hand the destiny of the world." The figure held it high. "Now I am the power it serves. I will determine the destiny of the world." He took a step toward Cotten. "Daughter of Furmiel, you have failed."

"No," John said. He made the sign of the cross and lifted the gold crucifix he wore around his neck. "In the name of Jesus Christ, our Lord. Behold the Cross of the Lord, flee bands of enemies. May Thy mercy descend upon—"

"We cast you out." The voice came from the hall leading from the storeroom and tunnel.

Cotten and John turned to see two figures emerge. Their bodies were clothed in cloud-like white robes giving off an indigo blue radiance that filled the room. Cotten remembered the painting of the two archangels guarding the southern portal entrance to the cathedral. Could these be the same figures?

One came forward to stand before the apparition of Lenin, and quoted from Isaiah. "How you have fallen from heaven, O Lucifer, morning star, son of the dawn." The archangel stretched forth his hand and took the Spear of Destiny. "Begone from this place, you and your vile black army. For God has cast you into the abyss."

The apparition of Lenin staggered.

As the archangel took hold of the Spear, the form of Vladimir Lenin collapsed onto the floor. It became rigid and waxen like Cotten remembered when first seeing it. She looked at the angel. "Who are you?"

The archangel gave the Spear to Cotten. "Be not afraid, daughter of Furmiel, for *destiny* lies in your hands." The archangel turned and rejoined her companion. Then the light surged in brilliance, causing Cotten, John, and Markov to cover their faces.

When Cotten opened her eyes, the two angels were gone. Her heart raced inside her sweat-drenched body. She stared at the Spear of Destiny gripped in her hand. The relic made her palm tingle as she looked at John.

"Are you all right?" she asked.

Before he could answer, voices came from the hall, calling her name. Cotten could not believe what she saw. Tera and Devin ran toward her. She bent and took them in her arms. Tears streamed down her face.

Right behind them were Alan and Lindsay, along with six Russian soldiers. All were winded.

"How did you...?" Cotten asked.

"Tera and Devin jumped from the helicopter just as it took off," Lindsay said. "You were already running toward the gate. So we jumped out, too."

"We tried to get the pilot to come back," Alan said. "But he was in the air, and there were bullets flying everywhere."

"The children followed you as if they knew exactly where to go," Lindsay said. "What happened here?" She glared at the body of Lenin on the floor.

Cotten smiled while she hugged Tera and Devin, feeling as if they were two angels in her arms. She stood and handed the Holy Lance to Alan. "Go stop this madness." She shifted her gaze to Markov. "Captain, please take him to Mr. Wolf."

She looked at John and spoke softly as she wrapped her arms around him. "Do you think the children—were they the ones?"

"Maybe they have revealed to us who they really are," he whispered through her hair.

"Then maybe this battle is over at last."

Chapter Seventy-Three

FINISHED

The chill was what Mace noticed first. Sure, it was fall in D.C., but this cold, freezing air that stung his nostrils and burned in his lungs was not because of the season. It was a cold that smoldered like heat—an unnatural, aberrant phenomenon that could only mean one thing.

He stuffed his hands in his pockets and wheezed out a cough as he turned the corner. The early season ice storm that encapsulated the nation's capital suspended in time and motion even the smallest twig within a glistening, clear cast. The ice crystals on the sidewalk crunched beneath his shoes. Now, at dusk, the city mystically twinkled in radiant prisms as the last vestiges of the sun bounced off the shards of ice.

Mace paused at the granite lion that appeared locked inside its own hoarfrost tomb. The statue and its twin posed silently as they guarded the building's entrance. Mace took the three levels of steps one at a time, safeguarding his balance on the slippery surface. The building was closed as was everything since the Hades Project got into full swing. He slid his key inside the lock, and the heavy wooden door whined open.

Inside he glanced at the elevator but decided against it. The power could go off at any minute. Wouldn't that be a hell of a note, to be stuck in the goddamn elevator? The Old Man would never listen to such an excuse.

Mace gripped the brass banister and stared up at the winding stairs. Seven flights to the enclosed courtyard seemed eternally distant. He rewrapped his neck with the black wool muffler and started up. The steps creaked beneath his feet as he climbed.

By the fourth flight, he could hear his every breath wheeze on the outflow. It seemed colder in here than outside—the fucking heat was off, and by his own goddamn doing. He found humor in that, and a spontaneous laugh rasped from his chest.

On the seventh-floor landing, Mace waited to catch his ragged breath. The bastard knew he would have to climb all seven flights, and that's why he demanded they meet here. It would have been just as easy to meet in the comfort of Mace's living room. Tea by the fire. But this wasn't going to be a pleasant meeting, and he knew it would be freezing in the courtyard.

Mace's footsteps echoed as he approached the door to the courtyard. Opening it, a gust of cold wind burst through. His eyes stung and watered. He sniffed up the congestion that dripped from his nose.

"You are on time, Pursan," the Old Man said from the center of the courtyard. The crescent moon cast skeleton shadows of the leafless trees across the stone floor.

"Did you think I would be late? Have I ever been?"

The wind whipped through the Old Man's ashen hair and blew it back, but came in the opposite direction at Mace, and threads of his hair thrashed against his face. He used a gloved hand to push it back to no avail.

"You know why I have summoned you, Pursan?" The powerful voice rumbled across the space between them. He paused and smiled. "Of course you do."

Mace's fingertips were numb, even with the protection of the gloves, and his nose and cheeks stung.

"It is over. You have failed me. A sad disappointment. I gave you such power, such position. But you were not appreciative, nor heedful. You were once a favored general in my legion. What has become of you?" He turned his back on Mace and seemed to be absorbed by the night. "What should I do, Pursan? What do you suggest?"

"I will make it up to you," Mace choked out.

The Old Man looked back, his face illuminated by the faint light—stony, pale, and chiseled—eyes that penetrated. "You cannot make it up to me."

"Please. I have served you well, with only this single stumble. We can regroup, build stronger weapons. The Hades Project was just the first idea. The next one will—"

"Stop. Can you not see even a second into the future? We have been tricked from the beginning. As I suspected, the young girl is a soldier of God. She is Furmiel's other twin daughter, and one day will lead God's army against us. That is her heritage. She was sent in disguise so we might not identify her. Now, she stands at Cotten Stone's side."

"How was I to know?"

"Because I gave you that responsibility, Pursan. You were to stop her. Must I tend to every minute detail? It is so exhausting. That is why I depended on you." He glanced down at the circle and pentagram carved into the stone floor of the courtyard. "And the other child, the boy—he, too, has our enemy's blessing. He will lead the army with the girl. Together they will rise to power. In time, they will command the Indigo army and wage war on the Rubies. That is their destiny. Ironic, isn't it, that the CyberSys quantum computer is called Destiny?"

Numbness crept up Mace's legs. "All I ask is just one more chance."

The Old Man raised his hand, and a blast of icy air roared through the courtyard. "I am finished with you."

Chapter Seventy-Four

THE OAK

The grind of the backhoe's metal gears was stiff competition for conversation.

Lindsay stood with Alan where her house had once been while they watched Devin and Tera pilfer a pile of building materials for items they could use to build their fort.

"They don't seem fazed at all by everything they went through," Lindsay said.

"No, they don't. That's the beauty of being a kid," Alan said.

"Lucky for them they can't imagine what the world would be like today if Max hadn't been able to get the Destiny computer up and running and start shutting down the Hades worm. I believe we'd have been thrown back to the Dark Ages if he hadn't. The kids wouldn't be searching for scraps to build a fort, they'd be scrounging for survival."

"Worse than that. We'd all be killing each other."

"I gotta say, it was so gracious of the Russians to return the Holy Lance to the Vienna museum. The presentation by the Russian president with Cotten and John standing beside him was amazing."

"Now that it's the real thing, I'll bet they put the relic under much tighter security this time around."

Lindsay gestured toward Devin and Tera. "Look at them. They are such innocents, yet they've touched billions of lives."

Alan smiled. "Speaking of innocent, I guess poor Ben Ray's name has been redeemed. In the end, his family has something good to hang on to. He sacrificed his life for Devin's. Little by little Devin is revealing everything that happened—it's a bit disjointed—but I'm putting the pieces together. I have to remember to listen to my son and fill in the blanks for him. I almost missed the radio station numbers he kept repeating. And that was what helped the FBI zero in on the location of the Hades facility. Between Max doing his thing and them storming the facility in Arkansas, we are waking up today on a safer planet."

Alan grinned as Tera tossed Devin a piece of particleboard. "I didn't know little girls were into building forts."

"Cotten and I had one," Lindsay said. "Actually, it was more of a tree house. It was in the big oak that used to be right over there." She pointed to a charred trunk. "Such a magnificent tree. What a shame."

"I wish we could bring everything you had back to the way it was before the fire, but under the circumstances, all we can do is leave something behind—a memorial."

"What you are doing for us is very special."

"It gives me great pleasure," Alan said. "There should be something here in memory of what happened. Once this horse rescue and rehab is complete, it will carry on your name—Jordan Oaks Horse Center."

"I'm happy to give up the land for such a wonderful cause, but it's hard. This is where I grew up. Sometimes I feel so lost, Alan. Thank God you're here or else I would have nowhere to turn."

"I know you hate to leave here. Roots run deep. It has to be painful. But you and Tera, Devin and I, have to go underground. If our kids are easy to locate, the Rubies will hunt them down and hurt them. I'll find a place—I've got the money and resources to take us out of sight. I understand that you don't like to accept handouts, but you have to realize this is not a handout. This is a necessity if we're going to survive."

Lindsay bowed her head in thought. "Okay, I guess it won't be so hard. I don't have many friends and neither does Tera. We can start anew, anywhere in the world, I suppose. Living in a hut in Sumatra is better than being afraid Tera is going to be hurt."

"Good," Alan said.

"That brings Kai to mind. What do you suppose she is doing now in her new life?"

"You mean who is she fleecing next?"

"You couldn't see because you were on the phone, but I watched her when you were speaking to security. When she heard you tell them to escort her out of the building, I thought fire would shoot out of her ears."

"She'll get over it."

The sound of a diesel engine coming up the drive made them turn. A huge flatbed trailer threw clouds of dust and ash into the air. "What is this?" Lindsay said.

"Something to mark the spot where your farm once stood. A living reminder of what happened here after you and Tera are gone."

Lindsay's hand went to her mouth when she saw the truck's payload.

Chained to the deck was a huge sprawling granddaddy oak.

Chapter Seventy-Five

ME, TOO

The sky looked polished, spit-shined blue, not even a tiny puff of a cloud. The sun shone through the car window and along with the heater kept it toasty inside, considerably different from the 23 degrees outside. Cotten had one hand on the steering wheel and the other on the console where John's hand was wrapped around hers.

"I wish we'd had time to look at Christmas lights," she said as she drove into the Louisville International Airport parking garage.

"Guess it wasn't high on our list."

"No. Still, it seems we never have time to just catch up. Time alone. I know I should be grateful you had business in New York and were able to fly out here for a couple of days to bring in the New Year, and it meant a lot to Lindsay and Tera."

"I'm glad I came, too. I'd like a little time together—even better than looking at holiday lights." John glanced at his watch. "Unfortunately, there are only a few moments left before I have to check in."

"I don't want you to go," Cotten blurted, twisting in the seat so she faced him. She heard the slight crack in her voice and was certain he heard it, too.

"I'll miss you, as I always do," he said. "You're a special lady."

Cotten hung her head and wiped a tear from her cheek. "I promised I wouldn't do this. I'm sorry." She fumbled for her purse, took out a tissue, and dabbed her nose. "Okay. Glad I got that over with and out of the way."

He smiled. "You don't always have to be a tough cookie."

"You know what I think?"

"No, what?"

"Timing is everything."

"What do you mean?"

"What if we'd met years ago before you decided to do the priest thing?"

John smoothed her hair back. "But we didn't, and we can't change that."

"I know." Her voice was shallow, and it quaked.

"We are lucky people, you and I. Blessed, really, that we did meet."

"Why does this have to be so damn hard?" She felt the tears again. "You bring out the worst in me. Nobody likes a girl on a crying jag. And it makes my mascara run. I must be a real sight."

John laughed then held her face with both his hands. "You're beautiful. Even when you cry."

Cotten stared into his deep blue eyes, the bluest she had ever known. "I didn't mean it. You don't bring out the worst in me. You're the best thing that ever happened to me." She glanced at the clock on the instrument panel and heaved out a loud sigh. "You better get going or you'll miss your flight. I'd walk you in, but I'd make a fool of myself blubbering away as you disappear down the concourse." She said it almost whimsically then hesitated before she spoke again. This time her voice was strangled and serious. "I just can't watch you walk away."

"It's okay." He opened the door. "Pop the trunk for me." Cotten pressed the button and heard the lock spring. She got out and walked to the back of the car and watched him take out his bags.

"John," she said.

He folded his garment bag over his arm and looked up at her. She knew her mouth was open, ready to speak, but she didn't dare say the words.

John put down the bag, draping it over his suitcase, then folded her in his arms.

"Me, too, Cotten Stone. Me, too."

About the Author's

As a native Floridian, **Lynn Sholes** was intrigued by the prehistoric people of Florida which birthed the seed ideas of her first six novels while writing as Lynn Armistead McKee. Now writing as Lynn Sholes, she has teamed up with Joe Moore writing international bestselling thrillers. Lynn has presented numerous fiction writing workshops and has been a writing trainer and coach for schools in Broward and Citrus County, Florida. She now writes full-time from her home in the Sunshine State.

Joe Moore is a former marketing and communications executive and two-time EMMY® winner with 25 years' experience in the television postproduction industry. He has written articles for national and international trade magazines covering the field of professional sound recording and video. As a freelance writer, he reviewed fiction for the South Florida Sun-Sentinel, the Florida Times-Union, and the Tampa Tribune. Joe is president emeritus of the International Thriller Writers. He writes full time from his home on the banks of the Blackwater River near Pensacola, FL.

Coming Soon!

THE 731 LEGACY
A COTTEN STONE MYSTERY
BOOK 4
BY
LYNN SHOLES AND JOE MOORE

The 731 Legacy, Book Four, in the Cotten Stone series. It devastated the earth thousands of years ago. Its remnants are scattered across the human genome waiting to be reassembled into a deadly viral killer. Now a new generation of suicide bombers will use the virus to kill with something as innocent as a cough. Everyone is a target. No one can survive. Only one person can stop the heinous plot and its mastermind . . .

**For more information
visit:** www.SpeakingVolumes.us

On Sale!

COTTEN STONE MYSTERIES

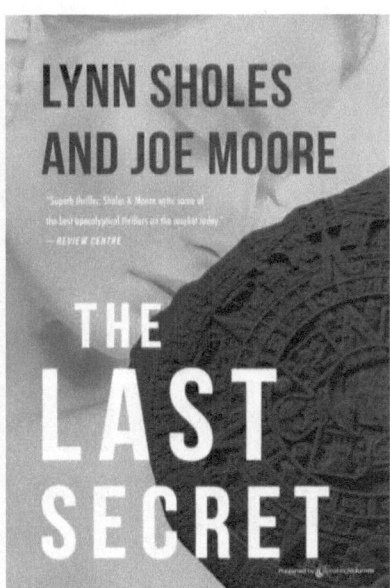

The Grail Conspiracy: "This page-turner is bound to show up on Da Vinci Code read-alike lists at public libraries across the country."

—*Library Journal*

"Fascinating and breathless, *THE LAST SECRET* will leave you glued to your chair. Sholes and Moore are true storytellers, with unerring eyes and the souls of artists. You'll love this one!"

—Gayle Lynds,
New York Times bestselling author of *The Last Spymaster*

**For more information
visit:** www.SpeakingVolumes.us

On Sale!

MICAH T. DANK'S
INTO THE RABBIT HOLE SERIES
BOOKS 1 - 6

For more information
visit: www.SpeakingVolumes.us

Sign up for free and bargain books

Join the Speaking Volumes mailing list

Text

ILOVEBOOKS

to 22828 to get started.

Message and data rates may apply.

www.ingramcontent.com/pod-product-compliance
Lightning Source LLC
Chambersburg PA
CBHW030810260626
47169CB00001B/273